Fixing to be Mine

LYRA PARISH

VALENTINE

Texas

Fixing to be Mine
Valentine Texas, #5

Editor: Jovana Shirley
Unforeseen Editing
unforeseenediting.com

Proofreader: Marla Esposito
proofingstyle.com

Cover Design: Bookinit! Designs
bookinitdesigns.com

MEET THE VALENTINES

Beckett Valentine
Kinsley Valentine
Harrison Valentine
Remington Valentine
Colt Valentine
Fenix Valentine
Emmett Valentine
London Valentine
Sterling Valentine
Vera Valentine

in order from oldest to youngest

**Each book in the Valentine Texas Series
is a stand-alone with rom-com vibes and
a Happily Ever After.**

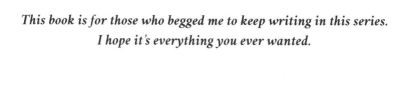

This book is for those who begged me to keep writing in this series.
I hope it's everything you ever wanted.

YOU KNEW WHAT YOU WANTED AND BOY, YOU GOT HER

—TAYLOR SWIFT
SO HIGH SCHOOL

CHAPTER ONE

SUNNY

The wedding gown is perfect. It was designed by one of the most elite fashion companies of this century—Bellamore. It's one of a kind, hand-stitched, and it was custom-made for me two months ago. The silk molds to my body like it was made to remember me, and every inch of it whispers elegance and exclusivity against my curves. I'm stepping into the next chapter of my beautiful, perfect, charmed life. But right now, I can't help but feel like a dressed-up prop that's pinned down. I'm just trying to breathe.

The bridal suite smells like roses, expensive perfume, and hair spray. The energy is odd. My therapist would say it's excitement, but it feels like anxiety. The whispers about the two powerful families coming together are not helping my nerves. Let me be clear: I don't have cold feet.

Stylists circle me like bees, adjusting curls and dabbing my makeup. My mother is chatting with two of her best friends in that well-practiced tone. My best friend, Cora, is filming behind-the-scenes videos to create a montage of memories while my other bestie, Jade, complains about her peep-toe designer heels.

"Has anyone seen Skye?" I ask, searching around the room for my sister.

Everyone shakes their heads. I keep my expression neutral because I've learned I'm asked fewer questions when I don't give reactions. From boardrooms to black-tie galas, I know how to command a room. I've had media training since I was ten, interviews since I was sixteen, and my parents have controlled my image longer than I've had control of my heart. That happens when you're in line to become CEO of your family's highly successful company.

Today is supposed to be the happiest day of my life. It's one I've dreamed of since I was a little girl, my fairy tale moment. I'm *finally* marrying the man I love after four years of being together. Donovan has always understood the weight I carry and never asked me to set it down. He held my hand when the press got too loud, when the world spun too fast, when the sun shone too damn bright.

I found safety with him, and for a woman like me, softness in a man is rare to find. It still doesn't make sense that I'm nervous.

We're both marrying into two different empires. Into legacies that were formed before we ever existed, that are full of scrutiny. He's never seemed intimidated by the success I've had. If anything, him by my side is like armor.

A quiet panic has been circling my chest for the last twenty minutes. It's emotion that comes before something big and life-changing happens. It's too loud in the room, and I need to step away from the chaos and clear my mind. I need a breath to center myself before I become a wife.

No one notices as I slip out of the room. I'm careful not to step on my veil as it trails behind me. My heels click against the marble floor. There's a room at the end of the hall, and I push the door open and move inside, but I immediately know I'm not alone.

Through the thin wall, I hear a familiar laugh that's followed by his voice. It's laced with amusement, which only confuses me more. My stomach hollows as the skin at the back of my neck prickles. Instinctively, I brace myself for impact.

I move toward the sound, unsure what I'm even looking for. There's another door, slightly cracked, light spilling through the narrow seam. That's when I hear her whisper his name—*Donovan.* She says my fiancé's name desperately, the man I'm supposed to marry in less than an hour. I don't need to push the door open; the crack is wide enough to see my little sister and my fiancé.

My world shatters.

His lips are on her neck, and her laughter follows. Donovan whispers back to her in the same tone that told me he loved me yesterday. The same one that proposed and promised me forever. Her dress is hiked up over her thighs, and his hand is dipping inside her panties. They're pressed together like they've done this a hundred times before, like this isn't the first time, but a pattern I somehow never noticed.

They're giggling and kissing like they're in love. They're treating this day like it's a joke, like I'm the joke.

I don't gasp or run or fling the door wide like a woman in a soap opera. I don't need to see more than I already have. I've gotten enough confirmation.

I step back, the fabric of my gown brushing against the doorframe as I leave. I'm done. I'm done performing and pretending. I move down the hallway that feels like a trail to my personal hell. Every step echoes like a countdown to an ending, not a wedding.

I enter the bridal suite, and it takes all of two seconds for the noise to catch me. Cameras. Champagne. People who believe I'm moments away from the best day of my life congratulate me. I've never been so fucking pissed. I look around, feeling numb from head to toe. My mother says something, but I can't take it, so I

3

leave everything behind. The last thing I want to do is draw attention to my escape.

"Okay, make sure you're back in ten minutes," she calls to me, then returns to her conversation with her friends.

I move toward the front exit, and people on the sidewalk stare at me.

"Look, she's a princess," one little girl says to me as I strut past her.

I try to smile, but it feels forced.

A valet stops me when I walk up to the vintage Camaro convertible that has a *Just Married* sign attached to the back. "Ma'am, excuse me."

"Yes?" I ask, tearing the sign off the back and throwing it on the ground.

I pop open the trunk, rip the veil from my head, and throw it inside. I slam it shut, wondering if a part of me always knew they were sleeping together. I thought they were friendly and was happy they got along so well. It's all beginning to make sense.

I stop and turn to the valet. "Give me the key."

He opens his mouth, and I speak up and interrupt him. "Look, I saw my fiancé fooling around with my little sister forty-five minutes before we were supposed to get married. I need to get out of here right now. *Please.*"

"You're going to get me fired," he says.

"They won't. I can guarantee it," I tell him.

He sighs, reaches inside his pocket, then gives me the key ring that's attached to a mini disco ball.

"Thank you," I whisper, my jaw clenched tight.

"You're really scary," he says.

"I know," I tell him, sliding into the driver's seat.

I turn the key and shift the car into first gear, not looking back as I peel off. I drive across the city like I'm not wearing a wedding gown that cost a quarter of a million dollars, like there's not a ceremony unraveling behind me in real time.

I pull into the private side of the bank I've used since I was eighteen—not the main entrance, the back one for high-net-worth clients who don't want to be seen.

When I walk inside, I don't ask to speak with a teller. The manager appears, smiling, until he registers what I'm wearing and the hard expression on my face.

"I need to withdraw fifty thousand in cash," I explain.

He doesn't blink, but I see the flicker in his throat when he swallows. "Of course. Any particular denominations?"

"Small enough to fit in a bag. Large enough not to be a pain in the ass."

"Absolutely. No problem," he says.

It takes less than ten minutes because they know who I am. They don't question the timing, the dress, or the fact that my diamond-studded heels were meant for vows, not bank offices. I sign the slip and take the leather bag he provided that's packed with stacks of cash. A security officer escorts me back to my car.

There is no hesitation as I crank the engine and drive away. I have fifty grand that says I can disappear however the hell I want for however long I need.

Today, I was supposed to walk down the aisle, but instead, I'm walking away. I might have lost myself, but it's time I remember who I am.

The bag of money sits heavy on the passenger seat, seat belt looped lazily across it.

I haven't cried. I don't feel like I can. My whole body is locked in something that's colder than sadness and heavier than grief. I feel stupid and humiliated, but above all, I'm angry.

I believed in him. I believed in *us*.

Donovan said the right things at the right times. He knew how to look at me when the cameras were on and when they weren't. That's what hurts the most. That it wasn't only betrayal; it was a performance, and I stupidly fell for it. His actions were nothing more than a long game that I didn't even know I was playing.

And my little sister. My maid of honor. I don't let myself linger on that part yet. Not when I'm still wearing the makeup she picked out and the pearl earrings my mother insisted matched hers.

The highway eventually opens wide, and I press the gas harder than I need to. The lines blur, lights stretching across my vision like ribbons I'll never reach the end of. The silence is too much, but I keep driving, jaw locked tight, eyes focused on the road.

Somewhere past the third highway merge, long after the city lights fell behind me and the roads turned flat and empty, I remember something one of my friend's wives said at a dinner party a few months ago. It was a conversation that happens once the champagne kicks in, when honest opinions start slipping through.

"If I ever needed to disappear," Lexi said, her red lips turned up into a smile, "I'd go back home to Valentine, Texas. It's a town people drive to when they don't want to be found. It's charming. Friendly. In the middle of nowhere. It's the type of place people go to get lost."

At the time, I laughed because I never thought I'd need to disappear. Well, until now.

Four hours later, I pull off at a gas station that's barely lit. It has a single pump and a flickering *Open* sign that looks like it's been dying since the '90s. I park, pull some slacks and a cute crop top from my duffel bag that was supposed to go with me on our honeymoon, then step inside a one-person restroom. I wiggle out of the dress, realizing I have no shoes other than the heels on my feet.

I grab a coffee and then type my destination into the GPS that was installed in the heavily restored vintage car.

My next destination? Valentine, Texas.

A small dot appears on the screen that's across the other side of the map.

It's thirty-one hours away and south of nowhere, and I decide

I'll take my time driving there. I tap the route and let the voice guide me back onto the highway.

I've got a full tank of gas, fifty thousand in cash, no phone, zero responsibilities, and absolutely nothing left to lose.

Right now, I need to get lost, and I hope I'll be able to find myself again. I'm not sure who I even am anymore.

But one thing is for certain: love doesn't exist.

CHAPTER TWO

COLT

It's just past eight, and already, I've got that feeling in my chest, like my day's about to turn into something I didn't plan for. It bubbles under the surface. After scarfing down a hearty breakfast at the diner on Main, I swing by my twin sister, Remi's, place. Now that she and the love of her life, Dr. Cash Johnson, are renting one of my properties in town, I don't feel bad about dropping in unannounced, even if it pesters them. That's how it is around here.

In a family of ten, it's easy to get drowned out, but not when you're a twin. Remi and I have always found each other in the chaos. Not to mention, the attention was always on us because our parents loved to dress us the same.

I take the porch steps two at a time, grinning as I catch sight of them through the window. They're chatting in the kitchen like they don't have a care in the world. With a smile planted on my face, I knock on the door.

When Remi opens it, I'm already wearing a cocky smile. "Good morning, sunshine. Did you have fun last night?"

She gives me a look like I'm three cups of coffee too

enthusiastic. My sister is still in her pajamas, bare feet, and I doubt she's taken her first sip of caffeine yet.

"Are you gonna invite me in?" I ask, giving her the full once-over.

"No," she deadpans.

Before the knob can catch, I move my boot forward and hold the door open. "I'm coming in. Sorry to bother the newlyweds, but Mom told me to tell you that dinner is on Thursday."

Her expression twists into disbelief. "You came here to tell me that?" she asks, even though she already knows.

The truth is, I've missed her company.

"Yep, and to share with you that I think I might've figured out what happened with Fenix," I say, wandering toward the kitchen, where her husband, Cash, is standing.

He gives me a head nod like me being here is normal. It is.

"Seriously?" Remi crosses her arms, tilting her head.

The two of us have made it our mission to understand what happened to Fenix. If someone hurt her, I will fuck them up. No one messes with our little sisters.

Fenix is almost six years younger than us. Her ditching her full-ride scholarship, quitting the equestrian team cold, then showing up on our parents' porch with nothing but a packed car and silence has been a mystery. She recently finished her degree online and is living at home with our parents and my youngest sister, Vera. None of us know why she left college, and every time I ask, she shuts me down. I want to know she's okay.

"Yeah, it had to do with—"

A sharp knock cuts me off, and the three of us glance toward the front door.

Someone presses their face against the frosted glass, but it's too cloudy to see clearly.

"Answer it," I say, grabbing myself a mug like I live there too.

Cash smirks, not saying much. He's not a morning person

9

though, so it doesn't surprise me that he's quiet. She opens the door, and suddenly, the air changes.

A woman stands on the porch—dark-haired, green-eyed, and so completely out of place that it feels like the universe is playing a trick on me. I can't hear what they're saying, but she's got this way of holding herself like she's built from stone.

"Oh, um ... one second," Remi says, then pivots and shoots me a glare I know all too well. "A gorgeous woman is searching for you."

I laugh, skeptical. "I'm not falling for that."

"I'm serious," she insists.

Cash raises his brows at me like, *Good luck, buddy.*

"I'm telling the truth." Remi sighs and turns back to the doorway. "Would you like to come in?"

The woman steps inside, a little taller than Remi, with a cute nose that upturns at the end and lips that beg to be stared at. When her sparkling eyes meet mine, the whole room shifts. The air completely evaporates, and gravity tugs at us a little harder.

"Now, who are you searching for?" Remi asks, giving me a cocky-as-fuck *told you so* expression.

The woman's gaze locks on me. "Are you Colt Valentine?" Her voice is soft, smooth, and, holy hell, something about her sends a jolt straight through me.

The coffee mug slips from my fingers, crashing to the floor like the second half of a thought I never finished.

"Darlin', I'll be anyone you want me to be."

Remi's brows furrow as she mouths, *Be cool*, like I'm not already unraveling.

Cash chuckles low, quietly cleaning up the pieces of my broken mug while I step past him, drawn to her like a magnet. She's even prettier up close—with brown hair with a dash of red; green eyes, sharp enough to cut clean through a man; and lips I can already imagine tasting. She chews on the bottom one like she's nervous, but her eyes? They don't flinch.

"How can I help you?" I ask, voice controlled.

She lifts her hand, holding a folded sheet of paper. "I saw you had a listing for this house online. I'm searching for a place."

I glance at Remi, then back at her. Damn timing. "Sorry, I rented it to my sister and her hubby. Happened last week."

Her shoulders drop a little. Disappointment flashes in her eyes.

"Oh, do you have anything else? The lady at the grocery store said you had several properties."

I shake my head, the truth landing heavier than I thought it would. She looks away first, breaking the tension between us, but it still lingers like static. I wasn't ready to meet her.

"Okay. Sorry to bother you."

She gives a polite smile and turns, walking out the door like she didn't gut-punch me with her presence. The screen door snaps closed behind her, and I'm frozen in place.

"What are you doing? Go get her number," Remi urges. "She might still be in town after we move out of here in November."

It snaps me into motion. "Oh fuck, right."

I rush through the front door and off the porch, spotting her already opening the door to a vintage black Camaro convertible— mid-'90s and well-kept, like it should be on display somewhere. It has a mountain of dust caked on it and looks like it's seen much better days.

"Damn, nice car."

She slides in without looking at me, turns the key. The engine rumbles like it's angry.

"Wait," I say, stepping closer.

She rolls down the window, and I lean against her door, trying not to look desperate.

"Give me your number."

She eyes me like she's trying to decide if I'm worth the trouble. I fucking am.

"If something becomes available, I'll call you," I add.

She grabs the flyer that came from the grocery store bulletin board and pulls a pen from the middle console, uncapping it with her teeth. The sight does something stupid to my insides. She scribbles her name and number on it. Our eyes meet again as she hands it over.

I glance down at her name.

"*Sunny*," I mutter, letting a grin spread.

"Bye, Colt Valentine," she says, like she's not afraid of a darn thing.

"I don't believe in goodbyes, darlin'."

"Southerners," she mutters and rolls the window up, giving me a cocky smile before backing out of the driveway.

Dust kicks up and leaves something heavy in her wake. I stand there, arms crossed, grinning like a fool in love.

From behind me, the front door creaks open.

"Ahem," my sister grumbles. "Are you okay?"

"I think I just met my wife," I tell her, still watching the road with my hand held over my heart.

"You're ridiculous."

"You might eat them words when I marry that woman," I say, returning to the porch with a pep to my step.

Remi stands tall like a security guard, arms crossed, eyes narrowed—classic twin-sister mode. She's got that stubborn Valentine woman stance locked and loaded, and I already know I'm not winning whatever argument is about to start.

"Oh, so I'm not invited back inside to finish my coffee?"

"Nah," she says, shaking her head like I've officially lost my mind.

I stare at her for a beat, then glance back at the empty stretch of road Sunny disappeared down. There's a hitch in my chest I don't know what to do with.

"You have the haunted house you've been renovating. Let her stay there."

"I live there," I tell her, like she doesn't already know that.

She blinks. "Maybe it's time you got a roommate. Company would be good for you."

I raise a brow. "That's ridiculous. Who in their right mind would want to stay there?"

"You." She shrugs casually. "You're such a chicken. She didn't seem like she was that into you anyway. And I know for a fact that she won't find anything else in Valentine 'cause I've looked. Now, you need to run along. I'm gonna have a quiet breakfast with my hubby. If you don't mind."

I glance behind her, at the life she's building that somehow came together like it was meant to. For half a second, I wonder if I'll ever have that too.

"Fine. Don't be late for dinner on Thursday," I mutter, stepping off the porch, keys spinning around my finger like I've still got control of this situation.

"Text her," she calls out, slamming the door before I can shoot back a word.

As I walk to my truck, I stare at the paper still in my grasp.

Sunny.

Even her handwriting is pretty. My fingers curl around the flyer like it might burn me if I'm not careful. I shove it in the glove box and then continue to the grocery store to grab food for the week. As I push the buggy down each aisle, my boots shuffle across the floor, and I think about running into her again. The thought of her has me so damn distracted that I don't even remember checking out.

Once I'm home, I kill the engine and sit for a second in the quiet.

The two-story farmhouse stares back at me. It looks worn down, chipped, and tired, but I see what it's gonna be. It was built in the 1800s and has a wraparound porch and sits on ten acres of land that feels like peace, no matter the time of day. She was abandoned back in '95, but her bones are solid. These walls hold stories, and it's my only project right now.

The work that I need to put into making her perfect doesn't scare me. If anything, it's my own personal challenge. It's a task half the town doesn't believe is possible. Basically, I've got a lotta shit to prove. She might look like a dump now, but one day, it will be the best-looking thang in a two-hundred-mile radius.

One of my best qualities is that I can see potential in things.

I step onto the porch, the boards creaking, as the plastic grocery bags dig into my wrists and hands. Mid-morning sunlight hits the old wood, catching on every nail I've reset and every rotten board I've replaced. Things are changing around here, but not fast enough for my liking.

Once inside, I walk down the wide hallway toward the large kitchen that overlooks the old barn I recently rebuilt. I catch a glance of my horses grazing and smile as I set the bags down on the breakfast nook. It takes me no time to put the groceries away.

After a deep breath, I grab the whiskey bottle from the cabinet. I know it's nearly ten in the morning, but a few sips never hurt the creative process. I crank up the old country playlist I keep cued up for long workdays. I scan my to-do list scribbled across the whiteboard on my fridge. It's my own personal roadmap, and I take it one task at a time, only wishing I had an extra set of hands to help.

My eyes scan down it.

1.Sheetrock: living room, hallway, dining room, library

2.Baseboards

3.Paint

Considering it's only Sunday, I might be able to finish the living room and hallway before the rodeo comes to town. I still haven't decided if I'm going or not though.

I'm not on a specific schedule, but I'm racing against time to finish remodeling before the first cold front rolls through.

There are a few livable rooms—the kitchen, one bathroom,

part of the living room, and the primary bedroom downstairs. The rest is still bones and echoes for now.

I glance around, thinking about Sunny. She had that same unfinished look, like something was cracked wide open and she was trying to hold herself together. Beautiful but strong, even while breaking.

I wonder if I called her right now and made the offer, would she take me up on it? There was something sizzling between us. I felt it, and by the look on her face, she did too.

The paper she wrote her number on is still in my truck, but I don't go get it. I've learned over the years not to force stuff. If it's meant to be, things happen.

The rest of the day passes in rhythm—measure twice, cut once, repeat. I've got the living room insulated by the time I hear the rumble of a truck barreling down the driveway. Clouds of dust kick up, country music blaring louder with each second they move closer. Only one person announces themselves like that— Emmett.

I step out onto the porch as the truck comes to a stop. He kills the engine and climbs out with broad shoulders, messy hair, wearing a shit-eating grin. My little brother is stacked with muscles.

"Howdy!" he hollers as he walks up the porch, looking at the house like it's gonna bite him. "This place still gives me the fucking creeps."

When we were growing up, ghost stories swarmed around, and this abandoned property was the center of a lot of hazing back in the day. Most folks avoid it, saying it's cursed, and, hell, maybe it is, but it doesn't bother me. When I'm here, I feel at peace, safe. I see what it'll be one day, not what it's always been.

"Good," I tell him, patting him on the back. "Appreciate your help with this."

The Sheetrock is stacked against the wall, waiting to be hung. I could manage it solo, but having an extra pair of hands makes it safer, especially with the high ceilings.

Emmett grabs a pair of gloves without me asking, and we quickly get to work. He grumbles under his breath the whole time. That's the thing about Emmett: he may give me shit, but he always shows up. He's dependable and caring, even if he's an asshole.

It takes us close to two hours, but the living room is finished. When we take a step back to look over our work, I smile. My brother looks around.

"Wow, you've gotten a lot of shit done since the last time I was here," he says. "Gonna be nice when it's finished."

"I can't wait," I tell him. "Want a shot of whiskey?"

"Nah. Gonna go home and take a shower, then head to Boot Scooting."

It's the local bar in town that has pool tables and dancing; it's one of the hangouts for forty and under, and it's always busy, especially on the weekends.

"Of course," I tell him, moving to the kitchen and grabbing the bottle anyway. It's where I left it this morning before I got started.

He follows behind me.

"Kitchen looks nice as fuck," he says. "Impressed."

I lean against the counter, taking a swig, and feel the soreness in my muscles from the work I completed today. "Thanks. And thanks for your help. Tomorrow, I'll start in the hallways, then make my way into the dining room, and then the library. First floor is almost done. Two weeks, max."

He grins, and his phone buzzes in his pocket. He pulls it out and looks at the screen, immediately declining the call.

My brows lift curiously.

He straightens his stance. "Anyway, gotta go. Let me know if you need more help tomorrow. Be happy to stop by after work." He heads toward the door, and I follow behind him. "Oh, don't forget dinner plans on Thursday."

"Thanks. I'll text ya if I need help," I say, appreciating the extra set of hands more than he'll ever know.

"You goin' to the rodeo this weekend?" I ask.

"Yep," he tells me, and I watch that grin spread across his face like he's already thinking about whoever's waiting for him.

"With more than one person?"

"Hopefully," he says, climbing into his truck.

Classic Emmett. Known playboy. Refuses to commit. And I've got a good guess which heart he's currently messing with. Only problem, she ain't innocent either.

I stand on the porch, whiskey in hand, watching my brother's taillights disappear down the long dirt road. He turns onto the highway, and his lights fade away.

For a while, we were roommates. Two bachelors living on oven pizza and bad habits. But the second I laid eyes on this place, I knew I needed it. Not just for a project, but to build something more permanent.

The moon hangs low in the sky, swollen and golden, like it's been watching me. I lean against the porch railing, letting the whiskey burn down my throat as I enjoy the view.

I walk inside, knowing I've put hours into these walls, patched scars into strength. It's where I'm dropping roots, preparing a life for my future wife and kids. The vision is so vivid that I can't help but smile. I can't fucking wait to fall in love again.

CHAPTER THREE

SUNNY

My anxiety crept in somewhere near the gas station with the taxidermy bobcat and a road called Snakebite Ridge. When I walk up the front steps of the bed-and-breakfast, I'm barely holding it together. The place is picture-perfect—fresh paint, blooming flowers, and a front porch that looks like it's hosted its fair share of good conversations and glasses of sweet tea. It feels gentle, even if I don't.

I knock because it feels more respectful. A moment later, the door opens, and the woman from yesterday stands there. Colt's sister. Her dark brown hair is pulled up, and she's wearing a soft T-shirt with some kind of faded logo over her heart. Her expression shifts the moment she sees me. Not surprised, but more curious.

"If we keep runnin' into one another, you're not gonna be a stranger anymore," she tells me, stepping aside and allowing me in.

This is the second day I've knocked on a random door, and she's opened it.

"Oh, hi," I say. "Do you work here?"

She nods. "Yep. I don't know if we've officially met. I'm Remi Johnson. Was Valentine until recently."

"Very nice to meet you," I say, looking around this gorgeous place.

She continues the conversation. "My older brother, Beckett, and his wife, Summer, own Horseshoe Creek Ranch. I help run the bed-and-breakfast. What can I help ya with?"

"So, the motel in downtown Valentine that I was staying at the past few days doesn't have any availability for the next two weeks. The woman gave me this address to see if, by some miracle, you had any rooms open. I made a few phone calls, and every motel, hotel, and Airbnb within a hundred miles is fully booked."

Remi looks out at the pasture; the sun has already dipped below the horizon, and it will be dark soon.

"We don't have anything tonight, but let me check the rest of the week to see if anyone has canceled. Follow me." Remi leads me to the counter, where a computer is set up. "The rodeo's coming to town. It starts this weekend and runs for two weeks. People started booking rooms last year."

My timing is shit—that's what I've realized.

"I didn't know. I left the city on a whim, stupidly believing Valentine was a place to get lost."

"Oh, it usually is," she confirms, studying me. Her blue eyes are sharper than her tone. Remi isn't judging me, but she's assessing me like she's already seen a dozen women trying to outrun their lives. I think she's deciding whether I'm worth the risk or not.

The room smells like warm vanilla and fresh laundry. There's a little basket on the desk of sweet peppermints that melt in your mouth, and a wooden key rack mounted on the wall. It feels lived in, but taken care of, like someone who remembers birthdays and still writes thank-you notes runs the place.

"Gah. I'm booked too," she says, tapping her fingers against the counter.

"Thank you for checking." I nod, even though disappointment is already squeezing my chest.

I'm not sure what I thought would happen, but I had hope. Maybe this is a sign I need to get my ass back to the city. If I don't find anything by tomorrow night, I'm leaving town.

She pulls out a notepad and scribbles something on the paper before ripping it off and handing it to me. At the top is the logo for the bed-and-breakfast, a cute horseshoe with a sans serif font.

"Try this address," she says.

I glance down at it.

"Where does this lead me?"

She grins. "To Colt's. He lives ten miles that way in a house he's rebuilding. He wouldn't offer you to stay with him because it still needs a lot of work. But if you show up and tell him you have nowhere else to go, he'll figure it out. He's a helper with a big heart. Being around him might be good for you."

I stare at the paper for a second too long.

"Why are you helping me?" I ask.

Remi shrugs like it's obvious. "That's what Valentines do. And there's something about you I admire. A fighting spirit."

I give her a smile, understanding what she means. "Thank you."

Remi walks me to the door. "If something comes available, I'll let you know, okay?"

"Thanks again," I tell her, walking down the steps toward my car.

I'm not sure what to expect when I show up at Colt's like a stray, but I know I've run out of options. And for the first time in a long time, that doesn't scare me half as much as it should.

I plug the address into my GPS, and it says I'm fifteen minutes away.

I take the long, dark road away from the B and B, and all I can think is, *This is how women disappear.*

All it takes is one bad decision, a dirt road, and an address written on paper.

My eyes stay on the side of the road, and I pass deer grazing, which doesn't make me feel great. If one jumps out in front of my car, this thing is totaled. Would I survive the impact?

I haven't seen another vehicle in ten minutes, which feels less like peace and more like I'm auditioning to be the main character of a true crime podcast episode. This feels like a massive, dusty, potentially life-threatening mistake. Being here, in the middle of nowhere, reminds me of how I tend to make decisions based on emotion.

I guess some things don't change, but I don't have regrets. While New York feels like a million miles away, I can't return yet. I can't face Donovan or Skye. I'm sure they're consoling each other.

I ease the Camaro onto the dirt path like I might fall into the pits of hell. I'm currently one pothole away from losing a tire and the last shred of my patience I have left. There are no street signs, no lights, only a mailbox leaning at a forty-five-degree angle, like it's halfway through a nervous breakdown.

Me too, mailbox.

My anxiety doesn't loosen when I check the burner phone I bought in Missouri for emergency situations. I have two percent left and was stupid and didn't purchase a phone charger for my car.

What if he's not home? I guess I'll sleep in the back seat.

As I travel down the road, feeling more isolated than I should, a little voice tells me I should turn around before I get in too deep with this man. Yesterday, I felt the instant attraction sizzling between us. Right now, I should do a hundred things, but mostly, I shouldn't be following directions given to me by a woman I met yesterday.

Remi—with her brown hair, sharp blue eyes, and a voice like she doesn't take shit from anyone—saw right through me. The first time I met her, she was polite and invited me inside. It wasn't something I would've done. Then I saw him standing there like every bad decision I needed to make.

Colt Valentine.

My heart does that flutter thing I haven't felt in years. *Fuck.*

I glance at the rearview mirror, and there isn't a single set of headlights for miles. It's isolation that city dwellers like me aren't used to, and it's unnerving. I keep driving down the dirt road toward the man who looks like he belongs in a whiskey ad and has no business smiling that confidently or calling me darlin' in that thick Southern drawl.

I'm thirty-four, bruised from a life I thought I'd figured out. He's, what, in his mid-twenties? Is he even old enough to drink? He's built like sin, and he smiles like life's still generous. That detail hit me the moment he looked at me. He's too laid-back, too confident. *Young.*

The trees surround the road like they're whispering to each other, and then it opens to nothingness. In the distance, I can see a porch light glowing, but nothing else. I roll my window down halfway to make sure the world still exists out here. It smells like cedar, dust, and something familiar I can't quite name. It's something I haven't had in a long time—freedom.

"This feels right," I say to no one, grabbing the steering wheel a little tighter, wishing I knew what this pull was, tugging me forward.

It's so dark; I can see stars like I've never witnessed before, and a part of me wants to pull over, get out, and look up.

When I'm close to the house, it doesn't give me that warm, welcome feeling that the B and B did. Still, it dares me like a challenge with a slanted roofline and chipped paint, standing strong, like it's got something to prove. Charm might have lived here before, but it packed up long ago and left when hope did.

The wraparound porch is partially lit, casting long shadows across the yard, and I'm not sure if I'm supposed to feel invited or warned. I cut the engine, and the silence swallows everything. There's no city hum. No traffic or sirens or voices. Only the rapid pounding of my heart and a cricket or three.

I don't move as I stare out the windshield. This house is big and broken and braver than it should be, but it's still standing, kind of like me.

Looking over at the passenger seat, I glance at the paper with the B and B logo at the top. The ink's smudged where I pressed too hard, folding it earlier. There's a tiny, ridiculous smiley face at the end of the address.

Remi's overly optimistic, or maybe she knows something I don't. This could be a reckless decision, but one that I need.

The breeze shifts through the open window, carrying the scent of freshly cut wood and something male, like salt and smoke and earth, and then I see him.

He's sitting shirtless on the porch swing with one hand resting on a whiskey bottle. The other is stretched out along the back of the swing, like he's waiting for someone to join him. He's silhouetted against the glow of the porch light, golden and lean, like he was cut out of stone. It's almost like he's part of the house, like he's always been waiting right there for me to arrive.

He's staring out into the dark like he's lost in it, like nothing out there matters. And then, without warning, his eyes find mine. There's a subtle flick of his gaze, but it pulls at me. Something shifts between us, and I can't unfeel it once it settles.

He doesn't stand or wave. He watches me from the swing like I'm a ghost or a stray dog or something else entirely. His expression doesn't give much away, but his jaw tics, and that's enough.

I inhale and hold it, then shove open the door before I change my mind.

The gravel crunches under my boots as I step out into the spotlight. I'm suddenly hyperaware of the sweat at the base of my neck and the way my shirt clings to my skin. My hair's a mess, and my makeup's a memory.

I should say something, like *hi* or *remember me* or *please pretend not to notice I'm falling apart*, but I don't. Instead, I stand with my feet on the gravel as he watches me.

I glance at the porch swing, noticing how the old wood frame hardly sways from his weight. Something about the way he grips the bottle of whiskey makes me wonder if he's spent the whole evening right here, completely comfortable in his skin.

I can't relate because every part of me is stretched too tight. One more wrong word, one more closed door, and I might snap. I need a break from life.

"You lost, darlin'?" His voice is low and lazy, but it hits like a full-body jolt.

I don't answer right away. Mostly because I don't know how to respond. And also because my pride is somewhere under the driver's seat, curled in the fetal position.

What am I even doing here?

I've known this man for two days, and now I'm standing on his land like I've lost my mind. I'm emotionally bankrupt, running on granola bars and spite, and this—this man is half reclined on a porch swing like a temptation. I don't know whether to turn around and run or fall apart right here.

"I'm not sure yet." My words are drier than I meant them to be. "You tell me." I swallow hard and square my shoulders.

It's not a greeting, but it's enough. I walk up the steps to get closer to him before I change my mind.

The porch groans under my boots like the wood is judging me. Upon closer inspection of him, I realize how muscular he is, how broad his shoulders are, and how absolutely no part of this was a good idea.

Still, I keep going, studying the tattoo on his chest. It's a cattle brand—his family brand, if I had to guess. He doesn't move, just tracks my every step like he's trying to understand what the fuck I'm doing here. But also, I'm asking myself the same question.

I stop a few feet away from him.

"Hot damn, Sunny," he says, smirking. "You're not the person I planned to see tonight."

"Remi gave me your address," I say, trying to sound like I do this sort of thing often.

He raises one brow, gaze sweeping over me from head to toe, like he's reading the fine print. "Did she?"

He's being too flirty without even trying.

"I stopped by to book a room at the bed-and-breakfast."

He takes a swig of whiskey. "They're booked up. The whole town is until after Labor Day."

"I learned that the hard way." I cross my arms even though I know it makes me look defensive. "She said you were too stubborn to offer your house, but not mean enough to say no."

It's the gist, and it earns me the twitch of a smile.

The porch swing creaks as he leans back, stretching one long leg out, like this is all very casual, like I'm not a stranger.

"Reckon that sounds about right." His gaze slides over me like he's making up his mind about me. His eyes narrow, perfect mouth curved upward, showing that billion-dollar smile. "Truth be told, a woman like you deserves better than what I've got to offer. You seem like a girl who likes the finer things in life, not a half-renovated house."

There's no edge in his words, just a quiet truth he seems to believe. And somehow, it's worse than if he'd told me to leave.

I let out a breath, placing my arms at my sides. "Right now, my choice is sleeping in the back seat of my car at the rest area down the road. If I can't find somewhere soon, I'm leaving town."

A flicker of a smile pulls at the corner of his mouth. It's not much, but it's enough to soften the moment. He stands, and the space between us tightens.

He's taller than I remember. All shoulders and shadows, with a quiet heat that radiates off him, like he's built to burn steady, but not fast.

My throat goes dry, and I don't recall a time when a man ever made me feel like this, but I hold my ground.

He is too young.

He doesn't move closer, but he watches me for another second before tipping his chin toward the door.

"I'll give you an official tour," he says, voice low. "You should see it first, then decide if the back seat of your car is better. Come on."

He leads me inside, and I pause at the doorway.

The place is rough, but there are some walls. Tools are neatly organized on a makeshift table with wood horses. A ladder leans against the wall like it's had a long day. But there's intention everywhere I look. Sheetrock, wood, and trim are stacked in different areas with care. The screws are set flush in the wall, and everything seems to be waiting. Even him.

This house isn't a wreck; it's a project—or rather, a beautiful home in progress.

He watches me like he expects me to turn around and run, but I don't.

"Kitchen's through there," he says, nodding to the left. "Bathroom's done, and the primary bedroom is too. The rest is still under construction, but it's livable."

He walks ahead, pointing out what spaces will be when they're finished. His voice stays even, almost proud, like this isn't weird for him—like it's totally normal to give a late-night house tour to a woman who showed up with more baggage than sense.

I trail behind him, taking in the details. I love the high ceilings, old floors that creak in the best way. He takes me to the kitchen, and I look out the gigantic bay window that shows the stars. In the back is a barn.

"I've been fixing it up for a while now," he says. "Bought it with the plan to raise my family here."

My heart drops. "Oh, I'm so sorry. I didn't ask if your wife would be okay with this."

A chuckle escapes him. "No wife. No fiancée. No girlfriend. I'm preparing for my future."

The way he says it—it's not only about the house. It's about roots and intention. About *building* something and being prepared for a future he wants. It's so respectable that it steals my breath away.

"It should be finished by next summer," he says to me in the hallway.

He's still carrying the whiskey in his hand, and I can't help but admire the way his muscles stack across his back.

He turns around, catching me.

"You don't have to decide now. But if it's a yes, you can have my room."

I should say *thank you* or ask a dozen questions. Instead, I stand there, staring at him, trying to figure out if this internal buzz that happens when I'm around him is real.

I don't answer, not because I don't want to stay—I do. God, I do. But wanting something or feeling a connection with someone doesn't make it safe. In my world, accepting anything without question always comes with a cost. I can't help but wonder what it says about me that I'd accept a stranger's help because he's the first person who doesn't demand anything in return. He's offering me a lifeline—or at least a temporary roof until I can make my next move.

I glance around again at the exposed beams and unfinished walls. The rawness of it shifts something inside of me. This house is unfinished, imperfect, but somehow, it's what I need right now.

"I don't want to overstep," I say quietly, my voice threading through the stillness. "I know this wasn't part of your plan. I can be gone in the morning."

"Do you want to leave?" he asks. "Valentine, I mean."

My lips part. "Not really. I like it here, and I desperately need a place to heal my heart. Valentine sounded like a good town to do that. I want to be able to breathe for a minute without having to explain myself while I contemplate my future."

Colt doesn't shift. Just watches me with that calm, unreadable expression of his. "You can stay as long as you need. I'm not going anywhere, and neither is this house."

I keep my gaze focused on a knot in the hardwood floor. My throat tightens before I admit, "You don't know me."

"And?" He shrugs. "We might be strangers now, but not for long."

There's a flicker of something in his eyes. He doesn't ask questions I'm not ready to answer. He waits, giving me space with my asking.

I take a breath and reach into my back pocket, pulling out the folded cash I've been carrying since the gas station earlier. I haven't touched my accounts since I left because the second I do, someone will know where I am. And right now, I need to be lost.

"I can offer this for the night," I say, holding out several hundred. "And I have plenty more."

He glances at the money, then back at me. His jaw tightens. "Keep it."

I hesitate. "You don't even know how much it is."

"Don't matter. It could be ten thousand dollars. I don't need it."

I let my hand fall back to my side. "So, you'd let me stay here for free?"

"Nah. You can earn your keep," he says, nodding toward the living room. "I could really use an extra set of hands. If I had help, I might be able to finish this house before next summer. That's my only goal. I have plenty of money."

I raise an eyebrow.

"You want me to help?" Laughter falls from my lips, and I look down at my hands. Thankfully, I removed the manicure set I had that screamed *bride-to-be*.

His expression doesn't change. "Unless you're above manual labor."

I glance down at my boots. They're worn, the laces frayed, and the soles uneven. "I'm in borrowed boots. Nothing is beneath me right now, but I have zero experience. I'd hate to be a shitty partner."

"Don't worry, darlin'. I'll teach ya to do things the way I like," he says, and heat rushes through me.

I try to calm myself, glancing back at the vintage boots a woman at the motel gave me. I had shown up in a pair of heels that were better suited for a corner office than a gravel parking lot. I almost twisted my ankle.

Colt licks his lips, and I wonder what that whiskey tastes like on his tongue. "Are you in?"

The attraction is undeniable, and I know I should walk out of this house, get in that car, and never return to Valentine again. But something won't allow me to do that.

"I can already see the answer on your face." He smirks like a decision has been made.

It has though, and we both know that I'm not walking away from whatever this is.

Weirdly, I'm relieved. Not because it's easy, but because for the first time in days, I'm standing still and breathing evenly. I feel like I'm choosing something that chose me first, and that I'm meant to be here. It scares the fuck out of me, but I can't ignore that feeling.

"I'm in," I echo, and I immediately feel the shift beneath my feet, like my entire world is changing.

When that cute-as-fuck smirk spreads across his lips, I think he feels it too.

"Music to my ears. Welcome home, babe."

I can't help the smile that takes over.

CHAPTER FOUR

COLT

She says she's in, and for a second, I forget how to breathe. Not because she said yes, but because of how she said it, like it was the only possible answer. It wasn't a surrender or a decision made from desperation, but rather a personal challenge. Her voice carried grit, like someone who'd been clinging to the edge too long and finally found a branch.

Sunny steps forward, and she's so damn close that I can smell her shampoo. I glance down into her green eyes, and before I can say anything, she reaches for the whiskey that's still grasped in my hand. She doesn't ask, doesn't pause, but wraps her fingers around the neck of the bottle, lifts it to her plump lips, and takes a long, unbothered drink.

The sharp oak and fire always hit the hardest at first, but she takes it like a champ without wincing. This brand of whiskey burns its way down and stays in your belly awhile. She gulps it down like she wants it to hurt, or she needs it to hush whatever's screaming inside that pretty little head of hers. The way she grabbed that bottle said what she wouldn't. I don't know her, but I know she's not fine, even if she's still standing.

It was easy for her to reach for something that wasn't hers, and it makes me want to give her everything she's ever wanted.

The hallway is silent, except for the faint creak of the old floor beneath her boots and the distant hum of the fridge in the kitchen. I can't stop watching her or admiring how pretty she is as she takes a breath, then goes in for round two. She drinks like something inside her is unraveling, and the liquid fire will keep it together.

When she hands the bottle back, our fingers brush together for a second too long.

Fuck. It's almost too much.

I'm suddenly aware of how close we're standing. The heat of her clings to my skin like the summer sun. She's suddenly everywhere all at once as her eyes slide down to my lips and my chest. For once, I'm glad I didn't bother putting a shirt back on when I got out of the shower. She looks back up at me with those sparkling green eyes, and I take a step away from her before I do something stupid, like slide my lips across hers. It's so fucking tempting as the electricity swarms between us.

A blush hits her cheeks, and she tucks her bottom lip into her mouth, like she wants the same thing.

"I think I needed that drink," she tells me, the smoky whiskey already on her breath.

Whatever's got her running is braided with pride because she's not in distress from what I can tell. I think that's what gets me most about her. It's obvious this woman isn't looking for someone to rescue her. Nah, I think she's more than capable of saving herself, which is why she's here. But I do believe she's trying to land somewhere without falling apart.

"Did someone hurt you?" I ask. My voice is soft, but my jaw clenches tight.

"Not physically. I'll live. I'm pissed," she says, nostrils flaring, and I immediately know she's dealing with heartbreak.

I push the bottle back toward her. "Pissed I can deal with. Glad I'm not going to have to track a motherfucker down."

Her brows pop upward. "You would?"

"Without a doubt," I tell her.

"You're something else." She chuckles and takes another swig before letting out a hot breath.

I can't believe this woman, who's been on my mind for two days, is standing in my hallway, drinking my whiskey.

"Apologies. I've had too much to drink tonight," I tell her. "Right now, I'm wondering if this is really happening."

She reaches forward and pokes my stomach. "Yep. It's real."

"This is a very unexpected turn of events," I mutter.

"I agree," she says.

I clear my throat, trying to shake whatever the hell that was. I'm under her spell.

"This way," I say, nodding toward my bedroom.

She follows, her boots scuffing over the worn wood. I walk a few steps ahead, but I can feel her behind me, probably eye-fucking me again. The thought makes me more aware of my breathing and the way I carry myself.

The house is halfway decent, depending on the room. Now that she's here, I wish I'd cleaned up more or finished painting the trim. Hell, I wish I had a finished house that would impress her. I don't know what to do with that thought. I stop at the last door on the right and push it open. The hinges groan in protest.

"This is the only fully finished area in the house other than the kitchen. Sheets are clean, and the bathroom is right across the hall."

She steps inside, her eyes scanning the simple space. There are no frills. Just a solid bed, a dresser, a full-length mirror, and a window that looks out over the barn with a sheer curtain because I like to wake up to the sunrise. I cleared my tools and work gear out earlier this week, and it still smells like fresh paint.

I lean against the doorframe, arms crossed, as I watch her. "If you need more towels, there are extras in the linen closet. Water's hot, but you've gotta let it run for a minute, or it will burn the fuck outta you. And this is country livin', so sometimes, you've gotta hold the toilet handle down a little longer than you'd think."

I notice a flicker of something behind her eyes, like a smile she's not quite ready to share. Sunny steps farther inside and sets her hand lightly on the footboard, like she's bracing herself more than leaning. Her hand trails along the edge of the wood like she's memorizing it. Her eyes skim across the dresser, the small window, the lamp on the nightstand.

She turns to face me. "Where will you sleep?" The question isn't sharp or demanding.

"The couch. I've slept there plenty of times before."

Her expression is unreadable, but her shoulders aren't as stiff as they were when she walked in.

"That's not fair," she says after a second. "I'll take the couch."

"Absolutely not." I let out a soft breath, more amused than anything. "Life isn't fair. Besides, the couch is comfortable."

She raises an eyebrow, like she's not sure if I'm lying.

"I'm not just sayin' that. It's better than most of the places I crashed in my early twenties," I add, shrugging.

Her brow lifts. "What? Like last year?"

A low rumble releases from me—unexpected and rough, like I forgot I had laughter left. "I'm in my late twenties, thank you very fuckin' much."

She chuckles.

I glance toward the front of the house, then back at her. "You got bags in your car? I can grab 'em for you."

Her posture straightens a little too fast. It's not panic, but it's a reaction that makes a man instinctively take a step back. Her fingers twitch. Her throat works around a breath she doesn't take.

"I've got it," she says quickly. "I can get them. You've already done enough."

It comes out too practiced, like she's used to fixing discomfort before it shows. She acts like accepting help feels more dangerous than doing it alone.

"You have a body stuffed in your trunk or something?"

She playfully rolls her eyes. "Not that I know of."

"Listen, I'm a fixer, babe. Doin' things for others and listening are my love language, so if you're staying for a while, which you are, you're gonna have to start gettin' used to that."

"Thank you. However, I find it very hard to accept anything from people without an exchange. It's not a behavior I'm accustomed to. Truthfully, my trunk is a mess, and I'd prefer to grab my shit myself."

"Okay, I can respect an independent woman," I tell her.

"Thank you."

For some reason, I want to reach for her, but I don't. It's too soon for that, so I nod instead. "I'll keep the porch light on for ya. Take your time. Door stays unlocked."

"Unlocked?" she questions, almost alarmed. "Isn't that dangerous?"

"In the middle of nowhere?" I look at her like she's grown a third head. "Trust me, sweetheart. No one in their right mind would turn down this road in the middle of the night. Except you."

"You're damn right about that." She exhales, and her shoulders ease further.

"I'm real glad you're here," I tell her. "Haven't been able to get you off my mind since we met."

She chews on her lip and glances away from me, which only makes me smile. I'm under her skin, and, fuck, she's buried under mine too.

"Do you always act like this?"

"I'm not afraid to say what I mean. So, if that's what you're referring to, yeah. This is it. I'm no bullshit."

"I like that," she offers.

"Good." It feels like time freezes between us. "Well, if ya need anything, I'll be in the living room, tryin' to sleep off the quarter bottle of whiskey I drank this evening."

"Sweet dreams," she says.

"Ah, currently livin' the dream, babe. Don't wake me," I offer with a smirk, backing out of the doorway. I give her a final glance, but I don't let it linger as I pull the door behind me. I leave it cracked, not because she asked, but because I know what it's like to need a door left open and how it feels when it's closed.

The smile that fills my face as I move to the living room feels permanent, and I'm so glad I finished putting the walls up the past two days.

I look at the couch, and it honestly isn't bad. Hell, I've slept on it dozens of times after long days in the barn or late nights, watching old Westerns. I sit on it with a grunt, lean forward, elbows on my knees, and glance toward the hallway. Tonight, the cushions feel stiffer, like they are jealous and know they weren't my first choice. At this angle, I have the perfect view of the door to my room.

I run a hand over my jaw, realizing I need to clean up this scruff, and I wonder if she's still drinking my whiskey. The bottle isn't full, but it's not empty either. It's like everything else in this house—halfway to something better when I get around to finishing it.

Sunny caught me off guard tonight. Not by randomly showing up because that happens all the time around here—family dropping by unannounced, townsfolk who can't mind their business if you paid 'em. But her arrival was different, it was full of intent, like she couldn't stay away from me either, like there was some invisible lasso pulling us together.

I don't know her, not really. Not yet. But my name on her lips hit like something personal, like she was searching for me with purpose. I've been thinking about her since the moment our eyes met.

I ease deeper into the worn cushions, and they creak beneath me as I lie back, pulling the quilt off the back. The whiskey starts to hit hard, and the buzz takes over. I look past the fireplace I haven't finished, toward the hallway, where a thin slice of light continues to spill from the bedroom I gave away tonight. I close my eyes, hoping sleep takes me under because thoughts of her swirl in my head.

I didn't let her stay just because I was a good man. Something about her told me she needed this place more than I did.

The house is quiet now, like the calm before the storm. This woman doesn't owe me her story, but I want to be part of it. In a way, I already am.

She thinks I gave her shelter. Turns out, I opened the door and walked straight into the storm, and the scariest part is, some reckless piece of me doesn't want to run. Nah, I want to ride this out with her and see what happens.

CHAPTER FIVE

SUNNY

I sit on the edge of his bed, one hand resting on the mattress, pressed into the quilt, and the other holding the bottle of whiskey. I drank too much, too fast, and my head is spinning, or maybe that's the aftereffects of being around Colt.

The room smells like wood, fresh paint, and him. It's warm in here, but that might be me. The ceiling fan hums, pushing the air around, but my body is still on fire. The heat feels like it's coming from the inside out.

My hair is pulled into the same knot I twisted it into when I drove to Alpine this morning, searching for somewhere to stay. It feels too tight, so I remove it and shake my hair out, releasing the tension from my scalp. I should lie down or take a shower. I should do something, but I sit here, breathing in a space that doesn't belong to me.

I think I'm shocked, which isn't something that happens often. When I woke up this morning, the last location I thought I'd land was at Colt Valentine's unfinished house. A laugh escapes me, and I shake my head, thinking I might be losing it.

As if in response to my thoughts, the house groans, like it has a mind of its own. It's so quiet that my ears ring, and I'm not used to stillness like this. In the city, peace always feels borrowed, but here, it feels like it might last an eternity.

Nine days have passed since I left Manhattan with no more fucks to give. I took my time driving across the United States, stopping at every roadside attraction that interested me, hoping to clear my mind. I went shopping and bought new clothes and peeled off the engagement ring in a random parking lot.

No one is searching for me; I checked, using my new phone. Due to my background and extensive media training, I know my family is currently in crisis mode, sweating and probably wondering why I left. I didn't have cold feet and had been sure of my decision. I wanted to marry Donovan. Every person in my life knew that.

Donovan and Skye know what they did, but I'm willing to bet my inheritance that they're pretending to be worried while fucking around. I'm not sure what I'll say when I face them again. No amount of lying or gaslighting me will ever make me forget what I witnessed with my own fucking eyes. That image has haunted me, given me night sweats, and woken me from a dead sleep more times than I'd like to admit.

I gave my sister everything. I dedicated most of my life to making sure she was safe and had someone watching out for her. And this is what she did to me?

I push the thoughts away, swigging back several more gulps of whiskey, wanting it to erase my memory. At least for tonight.

I think about the woman who runs the motel in town—Kathy, *with a K*, who had silver hair and wore tie-dye shirts every day. She gave me the boots and told me they were made for walking, then acted like she knew what had happened.

My thoughts are suffocating and overwhelming, so I stand with stiff legs that are slow to cooperate. The denim clings behind my sweaty knees as I walk across the room. I pull the bedroom door open and quietly step into the hallway.

The house is dim as darkness presses in from all sides. The

sound of the fridge humming cuts through the silence as I tiptoe toward the living room. When I see him on the couch, I pause.

Colt has a muscular arm tucked behind his head, the other resting low across his stomach. He must be carved from stone because he's solid like a statue. He's all angles and heat, built like someone who uses his body, not poses with it. Men like him don't exist in New York.

It's something about the way he exists in this space—with his bare skin, work-worn muscles, and the faint line of a tan on his hips. Memorizing him like this feels too intimate for a man I recently met.

His face is relaxed, and my eyes slide over the scruff on his chin, over his perfect lips, and high cheekbones. I should focus somewhere else, but I can't. It almost feels impossible as I watch him breathe, trying to remind myself that I'm not here for that. Even if he's attractive, sexy, flirty, and kind, I can't get lost with this man, but I want to.

With every ounce of strength I have left, I pull my drunken gaze away from him and ease open the front door.

I slip into the late summer night, and the air hits me like a wall. The breeze sticks to my skin and doesn't let go. Behind me, the screen door creaks closed, and I let out the breath I was holding since I saw him sitting on that porch swing. I don't know what I expected when I escaped to Texas, but it wasn't Colt Valentine.

Gravel presses under my boots as I step off the porch. The Camaro sits under the porch light's reach, coated in a film of dust from too many small towns and in-between gas stations. Seeing how filthy it is brings a spark of joy to my life. Donovan would lose his shit if he saw it now.

Good.

He should be glad I didn't shift it into neutral and push it off a cliff before I came to Texas.

I open the trunk, and my duffel bag is right where I left it, along with a suitcase full of new clothes I bought. My gorgeous wedding dress is crumpled and stuffed inside without care. The satin heels, studded in diamonds, are thrown on top. The dress waits for me like a reminder of how trust, love, and family mean nothing.

My stomach turns, and a rolling nausea rises like it's trying to crawl up my throat.

That was the costume I was wearing when the curtain was pulled back on my life. I still remember the sound of the zipper when I yanked it down and how I ripped the fabric, trying to wiggle out of it. The silk felt like it was burning into my skin as I dragged it off in a blind, shaking rush in a random gas station. I didn't fold or hang it. I balled it up, threw it into the trunk, and slammed it shut, like that could erase everything. Seeing the expensive, custom dress now feels like a punch. The mess of white silk and beading is like a ghost, haunting me, and I stare at it like it might sit up and scream my secrets into the silence.

"Fuck you," I whisper, pulling my luggage from the trunk, then pressing my palm flat against the cool metal of the car. The snap echoes into the darkness.

I turn around, looking up at the big open sky, seeing a sea of stars above. I've never seen so many at once, twinkling just for me. A star glitters across the sky, and I close my eyes to make a wish, then head inside.

I pull open the screen door, careful with the creaking hinges, and slip back inside. This time, I don't focus on the couch. I can't let this sexy Southern man with his sexy accent distract me.

With all my strength, I lift the wheels off the hardwood floor as I move down the hallway, so it doesn't wake Colt. It weirdly feels like I've done this a million times before. I gently push open the bedroom door. Nothing has changed. The same soft hum of the fan nudges the arm around the space, but it feels different, comfortable. I open my suitcase and dig through the clothes I brought for this escape.

I'm unsure if I'm running from or toward something, but it feels like I've finally arrived.

AT SOME POINT, I must've fallen asleep after staring at the ceiling.

Sunlight spills through the window in long golden rays. I blink hard; sleep still clings to me, but I haven't felt more rested. It's the first good night of sleep I've had since I left the city. I suck in a deep breath, wishing the elephant on my chest would leave.

I smell it first, and then I hear the sizzling of bacon, followed by the clinking of a pan and whistling. I swing my legs over the side of the bed and stand, slow and stiff, like I'm stepping into a different world. The hem of the T-shirt I borrowed from his dresser brushes against my upper thighs.

I move down the hallway that opens into the large kitchen. I pause, my eyes sliding down his back, and I swallow hard at the muscles I nearly reached out and touched last night. Men like him should be illegal.

When he reaches for plates, I see he's wearing black-framed glasses. His hair is damp, curling at the ends. He smells like soap and cedar, clean and grounded and unfairly good. He doesn't see me right away, giving me a few seconds to watch him move comfortably in his space. His biceps flex as he reaches for the salt.

"Wow," I whisper, not realizing the word fell out of my mouth.

He glances at me over his shoulder. "Mornin'. How'd you sleep?"

It nearly unravels me when I see him so comfortably domestic.

"Great, actually." I move into the kitchen, closer to him, and have to keep myself from floating. "You cook?"

He shrugs. "I eat. Seemed like a logical skill to learn."

It makes me laugh, something not many can do.

"Want some coffee?" he asks, nodding toward the maker on the counter. "Mugs are in the cabinet above the pot," he tells me.

I graciously move forward and take his offer.

"Creamer in the fridge."

"Thank you," I say, pouring it into the mug. I immediately blow on it. "No cream. I like my coffee black."

"Oh, so it's like that?" he asks, his eyes lingering on my mouth.

"I guess it is," I say.

"You know what they say about women who drink their coffee black." He sets a paper towel on top of the plate and places bacon onto it.

"I don't actually." I take a sip, realizing how strong he made it.

"Means you're trouble," he says. "Will give a man a run for his money."

"Or a run for the hills," I mutter.

He chuckles, and I like the sound of it.

"How do ya like your eggs?"

I take another sip of coffee. "I'm not picky. Surprise me."

His brow lifts. I have to force my eyes away from him as he cracks eggs into the pan like it's second nature. I drift toward the table, sliding into the nearest chair and pulling my knees up beneath the T-shirt. The table's old, worn smooth at the corners, with a thin crack running across the top, like it's survived reconciliations and everything in between.

"Do you always do this?" I ask, watching the way he moves around without missing a beat.

"Cook?" he asks.

"Wake up with the sun and cook breakfast for strangers?"

His mouth twitches. "Only the ones who haven't eaten a hot meal in over a day."

"That's not an answer," I say.

"That's not denial." He flips the eggs, and a minute later, he's sliding food in front of me with a fork. Seconds later, he's delivering toast, butter, and grape jelly. "The answer is yes. I start my days early. I have a whole house to renovate. No time to be lazy."

"You have a work ethic. I like that."

He looks like Clark fucking Kent, and I try my best not to stare.

"I think the longer you stay here, you'll discover a lot more things about me that you like," he says.

"Confident too," I add as he makes his plate and joins me.

I pick up some bacon and take a bite. It's crispy and smoky and exactly how I like it. "This is incredible."

"I know," he says. "Had you said it sucked, I'd have kicked you out."

Laughter rolls out of me. "No, you wouldn't have."

He shoots me a wink. "I'd have considered it."

This easygoing conversation knocks something loose in my heart, something that's been held together by deflection and distance. I look away first.

"I appreciate all of this, but you don't have to be nice to me," I tell him.

He doesn't rush to reply, and I brace for the awkwardness to thicken, but it doesn't. He sits before me like it's the most natural thing in the world.

"I'm Southern," he says, like that fact explains everything. And somehow, it does. "It's what we do."

"So, if anyone rolls up to your house and asks for a place to stay, your answer is yes, because you're Southern?" I question.

"Not exactly. I'm intrigued by you," he admits. "I plan on figurin' out why."

I swallow hard. His admission makes my breath catch. "I don't think I've ever met anyone quite like you, which is saying a lot."

"Love to hear it, darlin'," he tells me with a smirk, drinking his coffee. "You won't ever meet anyone like me again."

I take a bite of eggs, which are warm and salted perfectly. The bacon is crisp without being dry. The toast is golden at the edges, and I smear enough butter on it for it to taste like comfort. It's not fancy, but somehow, it's perfect.

He doesn't fill the silence as he eats. He stays calm and collected, like there's nothing strange about any of this, like I don't intimidate him. Maybe if he knew who I was, that would be different, or it wouldn't.

I chew slower than usual, trying not to devour it. After a few bites, I glance up and catch him watching me with a lazy grin, like he's figuring me out, like I'm a puzzle.

He's curious, but a little cautious.

"What are you thinking?" I ask directly.

His eyes drift from my face to the hem of the oversized shirt resting high on my thigh, then back up to meet my gaze again.

"Thinkin' about how my shirt looks good on you," he says. It's a truth he doesn't need to dress up.

I freeze for half a second, my fork halfway to my mouth, then force a small smile. "Sorry. I grabbed my suitcase and realized my pajamas were in my duffel bag in the car."

"Don't mind. Whatever I have here that you need, it's yours. Sharing is caring," he says.

Suddenly, I don't know what to do with how hot my skin feels beneath this fabric.

"I mean that," he offers. "You're my guest of honor."

His words are simple, but they land heavy.

"Thank you," I say, and we finish eating.

We steal glances across the table. I can't deny the electricity humming under the surface, and I probably shouldn't like having his attention as much as I do. When he glances at me wearing his T-shirt, I can't help but wonder what else of his might look good on me.

CHAPTER SIX

COLT

"Thanks for everything," she says, setting her fork on top of her empty plate.

She didn't leave a single crumb behind, and, hell, I love to see it.

"You're welcome," I say, meaning every word.

I noticed how she took her time with each bite, like it had been a while since someone had fed her a home-cooked meal. That alone is enough to make me want to prepare breakfast for her from now on.

The old, mismatched chair lets out a familiar creak as she stands, but it's the absence of her across from me that hits louder. She picks up her plate like she's still finding her footing in this place.

"You can leave it in the sink. I'll take care of it when I'm done."

"Sure. I'm gonna change clothes," she says over her shoulder. "Anything specific I need to wear to be your handy-helper today?"

I smirk—can't help it. Handy-helper. I like the way that sounds. "Something comfortable, but not too loose. Something you're not afraid to sweat in or get paint on."

She grins. "Perfect. Meet you in ten."

And then she's gone, disappearing down the hallway like she's on a mission. There's a new energy to her—lighter, sharper, like she's ready to throw herself into work if it means keeping her mind from going too quiet. I know that feeling better than I probably should, which is why I think her helping me may help her.

I've got five rental properties scattered across this county and a garage full of tools. I've always used work to push through the thoughts I couldn't sit still with. Every house I've worked on has some memory packed into the drywall and floorboards. The only difference with this old house is, it's got a beautiful woman in it.

Once I finish the last bite of my toast, I rinse both plates, letting the motion settle me. She wore my shirt like it belonged to her and sat at my table like it was always her seat. And for some reason I can't explain, it felt right. Too right.

I slide the dishes into the washer and wipe my hands on a towel. Then I grab my coffee and head down the hall toward the living room. The floors creak under my boots like they're just as uncertain about where this thing with her is heading.

I've got at least a dozen things I could knock off my to-do list, but today, my focus is drywall. I want to get the hallway done. It's a simple task. Or at least it was, until I hear footsteps behind me.

She doesn't announce herself and enters like she's done it every morning of her life. Hair twisted up in that messy, loose knot, pink tank top hugging her curves, legs bare, and blue jean cutoffs that should be illegal this early in the day.

"Reporting for duty," she says, meeting my eyes with that look that says she's not afraid of a challenge.

I hand her the tape measure. "Hold this."

She grabs the end, and I stretch it to the edge of the hallway closet, watching the numbers roll out between us.

"Eighteen feet," I call out, then double-check my reading to be sure. "That's four and a half panels, plus two and a half. So, seven."

I walk the tape back to her, our fingers brushing as I take it from her hand.

"You ever worked with drywall?" I ask, more curious than anything.

She lets out a low laugh and steps closer. "Hate to admit that this is a first for me."

Her eyes flick down to my mouth before they climb their way back up.

"Mmm." I offer her a soft smile. "Guess I've got a few things to teach you."

She's sizing me up, and I swear the air between us gets warmer. We make our way to the front room, where I keep my tools and supplies tucked out of the way. I flip a full sheet of drywall onto the sawhorses, and she watches me like she's trying not to get caught. With her arms crossed, she tugs her lips upward, like she's holding back a grin she doesn't want me to see.

"All right," I say, slapping the panel once with my palm. "You're very distracting."

She raises a brow. "Speak for yourself."

God help me.

"Come closer," I say, grabbing the T-square and lining it up along the edge as she moves beside me. I can feel the warmth of her skin radiating from her. "First rule of drywall. Straight lines only. One cut. Mess it up, and you've wasted time, patience, and a perfectly good sheet."

Her arm brushes mine. "So, you're saying, precision is sexy."

"Confidence is too." I pass her the pencil, letting my fingers trail against hers. "Mark it at twenty-four inches. We're cutting a two-foot strip."

She stays planted beside me for a breath too long. Sunny is close enough to scramble every useful thought in my head as she leans in and draws the line. Her scent clouding my focus.

"Like this?" she asks.

"Mm-hmm."

I move in behind her, reaching around to hand her the utility knife. Her fingers wrap around the handle as I press the T-square firmly in place.

"Keep the blade tight against the square," I say, lowering my voice. "Only cut the paper. Keep it straight. Go slow."

"Got it," she says, though her voice has lost a little of its edge. It's softer now and a little breathy.

She leans in to make the cut, and I watch every second. Her shoulder brushes my chest, and she doesn't move away.

With one clean pass, the paper splits with ease.

"You're a natural," I offer.

She straightens, holding my gaze a beat too long before passing the knife back. I score the opposite side and snap the panel. It breaks clean.

"Wow, that's a good cut," she says, sounding impressed.

I dust off my hands and nod toward the stack. "We'll carry four of those to the hallway. Then this one."

I hand her the two-foot strip, letting our hands meet in the middle. She takes it without hesitation.

"This is fun," she says.

"Ah, you say that now."

Working beside her like this is dangerous. I came into this thinking I'd teach her a few things. Turns out, I'm the one getting schooled.

We knock out hanging the wall in the hallway in an hour. Her focus is steady, her pace sharp. We move in sync without needing to talk much and roll straight through to finish in the living room. Three hours in, I set the drill down and roll my shoulders. We're making great time. We continue into the dining room and the library.

"Let's take a water break," I tell her, leading us into the kitchen. I add ice to two glasses and get filtered water from the door of the fridge. We drink it down. "I can't believe how much we got done."

"I know. I'm having fun though. Thank you for allowing me to help."

"Happy you're here. Truly. Now, you ready to get your hands dirty?" I ask.

Sunny finishes her water, sets the glass in the sink, and then follows behind me. "I thought I already did."

"Not even close," I say, grabbing the joint compound and popping the lid off with the end of a putty knife. "You haven't even seen dirty yet."

"Yeah?" She raises a brow like that's a challenge. "Will you show me?"

"Oh, darlin'," I say, scooping out a thick glob and slapping it on the seam. "Promise me you'll try to keep it on the wall."

"I think I can manage."

She grins and takes the second putty knife I offer her.

"Okay," I say, motioning toward the seam. "Feather it out. Press hard in the middle, ease up at the sides. Don't overthink it."

"I never overthink anything," she says, straight-faced.

I snort. "Right. And I'm a ballerina."

"A cowboy ballerina," she mutters, scooping a bit too much compound and slapping it onto the wall. It plops thick, but she smooths it out, biting her lip as she works.

Damn, if that doesn't make me forget what I'm doing, I don't know what else will.

"Pretty good," I say.

She glances over at me. "You sound surprised."

"Nah. I'm impressed." I narrow my eyes. "You sure you're not a secret house flipper?"

Right as I reach to guide her hand, her knife jerks sideways and sends a blob of mud flying, landing square on my cock.

"Oh my God," she gasps, glancing down at my putty-covered crotch.

"You did that on purpose," I say, looking down at the splatter.

She lifts her hand. "No! I swear!"

I shift my gaze to her. "Ya sure about that? They say look where you want to aim."

She creates space between us, laughing. "It was an accident!"

I dip my knife into the bucket, giving her a look.

"No," she says, eyes wide. "Don't you dare."

"I told you this gets messy."

"Colt."

"Sorry, darlin'. You brought this on yourself. What's fair is fair."

She squeals and dodges, but I swipe a line of compound across her arm before she gets away. She stares at it, eyes narrowing, then lifts her chin like she's about to charge.

She lunges toward me, bright laughter spilling from her. I catch her by the waist before she gets too far. My grip locks firm as I spin her around, pinning her gently against the unfinished wall. Her hands land on my shoulders, and she's breathing harder now.

There's compound on her cheek, dust smudged across her tank top, and when I glance down into her pretty green eyes, I forget about the drywall, the house, or that we're strangers.

"You look good, covered in my mess," I say before I can stop myself.

Her breath hitches, but her hands don't fall away. The laughter fades enough for the tension to take its place. I don't pull back as her lips part. I don't think I can.

"I bet you say that to all your handy-helpers," she whispers.

"Only the ones I don't want to let go of."

We let the electricity buzz; the moment stretching between us. It's full of desire and excitement, the mutual attraction almost too much to handle.

She chews on her bottom lip, almost as if she's daring me to kiss her, but I take a step away, creating much-needed space. I don't want to rush whatever this is.

"We should probably finish up here, then call it a day. We can start painting tomorrow."

"Good idea," she says, and I notice the chill bumps creeping across her arms.

I crank the country music, and we work for several more hours until every screw and seam are covered. Afterward, Sunny sweeps stray dust into piles as I put away tools. She hums under her breath as she bends down for the dustpan, her ass cheeks showing.

I catch myself staring and force my eyes away, needing to be a gentleman. When she rises, she stretches, arms lifting overhead until her shirt shifts and reveals the bare slope of her waist. My eyes drag over that exposed inch of skin like it might answer every question I didn't mean to ask. She's doing this on purpose, to tempt me, and I'd be a fucking liar if I said it wasn't working.

There's drywall dust in her hair, a streak of spackle on her forearm, and she manages to look like every good decision I haven't made yet.

"If you keep it up, you might become my permanent handy-helper."

Or my wife. But that part I keep to myself.

"This is day one. You won't be saying that for long," she says. "No one keeps me forever."

I shoot her a smile. "Give me a chance."

She arches a brow. Her eyes are warmer, even a little dangerous. "You're relentless."

"You're right," I tell her.

Once everything is picked up, my eyes scan over what we accomplished, and I'm proud.

She watches me for a long beat, her eyes dancing with mischief as I zero in on her.

"I can't believe we finished so much."

"We're a good team," I say, grinning. "Have to warn ya though. You're gonna feel every moment of working with me tomorrow."

She chews on that bottom lip again, and I take a step forward, gently grabbing her chin.

"Please, stop doing that."

"What?" She looks up at me.

"Biting on your lip like that. Drives me fuckin' wild," I mutter. And, damn, I want to kiss her more than I want my next breath.

"It's a habit when I'm nervous."

"I make you nervous?" I whisper.

"Yes, because I feel like I already know you and shouldn't," she admits.

That hits deep in my heart, and I take a step back. Not because I want to, but because I need to, before I rush this and fuck up any chance I might have. My hands flex at my sides like they're still reaching for her.

"I understand what you mean."

She doesn't seem surprised. It's mutual.

"Yeah?" she asks, louder than a whisper.

"Yeah," I confirm, my voice rougher than it was a second ago. It's not something I can deny.

"I don't know how to do this," she says.

"Do what?" I ask.

"Be single," she admits.

"You just have to *be*," I mutter. "That's it. Nothing else."

For a beat, neither of us moves as the current between us hums.

She clears her throat, breaks the gaze, but not like she's retreating, more like she's gaining control.

"I could use a shot of something hard," she says, but there's grit under her tone.

"Got plenty in the kitchen," I offer.

She hesitates for half a second before she turns. And, God, the way her hips sway when she walks away is like a dare.

"Will you join me?"

"Fuck yes," I mutter under my breath, hands braced on my hips.

I watch her go, every cell in my body trailing after her like I've already made up my mind. I don't know how long she'll stay, but I'll take every damn second of getting to know her better.

I join her in the kitchen and pull bottles out of the cabinet. Her fingertips tap the tequila bottle like she's sizing it up.

"Is that a worm?" she asks, holding it up with a raised brow.

"It's how you know it's legit," I say, grabbing two shot glasses and filling them full.

We pick them up, and she lifts hers without hesitation. "To learning new things."

"To meeting the right people," I add.

She taps her glass to mine. "All of the above."

We knock them back, and it burns more than I remembered. She doesn't blink, just refills both glasses with a practiced flick of her wrist.

"One's never enough," she says, and there's something in her voice that's playful.

I follow her lead, but she doesn't have to ask twice.

"Can I ask you something?" She lifts her second shot.

"You can ask me anything, anytime," I say, leaning into the counter like I want her closer—because I do.

"How old are you?"

That makes me smile. "Twenty-eight."

Her lips twitch like she's holding something back. "That explains a lot."

"Does it?"

Her teeth catch her bottom lip, and it takes everything in me not to reach for her.

"Yeah. The cooking. The muscles. The confidence. All classic signs of a man in his late twenties with too much charm and not enough fear."

"You're not wrong."

Her eyes drag over me, and there is no hesitation or hiding it this time. "You're too young."

"For you?" I ask, even though I already know.

She flushes but doesn't look away.

I step a little closer. Not enough to crowd her, but enough to let her feel it. "I'm old enough to teach you a thing or two."

"You're too much to handle."

I feel her breath catch before I hear it. She doesn't move back or blink.

"Then find less," I say, shooting her a wink, and we down that shot of tequila.

"Oh, trust me, I have." The words land sharp, like a knife in wood. Her eyes flick away for the first time since we started drinking. "Shitty exes."

"I figured. I have a few of those myself," I say, gentler now, but I don't press.

She doesn't need to explain, unless she wants to. I don't give a shit about her past relationships.

She grabs the bottle like she's ready to steer it somewhere lighter.

"How old are you?" I ask.

"Thirty-four," she says.

I let out a low chuckle and shake my head.

"What?" she asks.

"You're worried about six years?" I lean in. "You acted like you were my mother's age and I was a toddler."

She blinks. "I don't date anyone who doesn't have a three or above in their age."

"Who said *anything* about dating?" I ask, wearing the smirk I know drives her a little wild.

"I, uh ..." Her throat tightens.

She takes a swig straight from the bottle like it's a life preserver.

"Rules are made to be broken," I tell her.

She takes another shot, and if I'm counting correctly, that's four.

"You tryin' to get shit-faced, darlin'?"

"Maybe," she whispers, staring at my lips. "I should probably take a shower."

"Go ahead. You earned it. Also, we have unlimited hot water."

"We," she repeats.

"It's our place until you leave," I tell her.

Her eyes stay on mine for a moment too long, like she's working up the nerve to say something she's not ready to let out. But in the end, she stays quiet. I can see the alcohol making its way through her system, her eyes somewhat glassy.

"Thank you for everything," she says. "You don't know how much I needed this."

"I think I do." I take another shot. "Have a nice shower."

Sunny walks away, her silhouette vanishing down the hall like a decision I can't chase.

I stay rooted in place, like if I move, I'll lose the thread of what passed between us. We built something today. It might not look like much to anyone else, but to me, it was real.

A moment later, I hear the shower turn on. The stream runs steady, and even though I can't see her, I can feel her presence everywhere—the echo of her laugh, the press of her hand still faint on my chest. My thoughts start pulling in directions they shouldn't, all heat and bare skin and closeness I promised myself I'd take slowly if I found it again.

I try not to imagine her under the water with steam curling around her sexy body. I try—oh, God knows I try—but fail. Before I get wrapped in the fantasy of her, I hear a moan.

It's soft and quiet, and it lands like a match in dry hay.

I drag my hand across my jaw and try to focus on anything else, but it's no use.

She's not just in my house anymore; she's under my skin, and nothing about it feels wrong. I only hope we survive each other.

I'm not searching for a fling. I want forever.

CHAPTER SEVEN

SUNNY

The second the bathroom door clicks shut, I brace both hands on the vanity and stare at my reflection like it might tell me what the hell I'm doing. My skin's flushed, my pulse won't settle, and my body is vibrating from everything that's happened between us. The tequila swims through my blood, making me give no fucks. Inhibitions being down around him is bad.

Colt didn't kiss me, but I'm still wrecked because I wanted him to.

I try to pretend this is another shower in another place with nothing on my mind, but all I can see is him and the way he looked at me today. I'll never forget how his voice dropped when he told me I looked good, covered in his mess. He caught my chin, his gaze locked on my lips, and told me I didn't know what I was doing to him. That damn drawl, combined with those baby-blue eyes, is deadly.

It would've been easier if he *had* kissed me. At least then I'd have something to explain why I'm this undone. Then I'd know if there is a real spark between us.

My whole body sings from our chemistry. It's electrifying. A simple look has me coming undone.

I tilt my head back and let the water pour over my face, over my neck, down between my breasts, and over the tight pull in my belly that hasn't let up since he pressed me against that wall. The moment I close my eyes, I see him, T-shirt clinging to his chest, sweat dripping down his neck, fingers smeared with drywall compound and temptation. Those black glasses framed his face perfectly, giving him that nerdy but sexy vibe.

The water cascades down my body like liquid fire, each droplet a searing reminder of the tequila coursing through my veins. Four shots deep, and I'm fucking buzzing, my skin hypersensitive, my mind lost in a whirlwind of Colt.

Colt. Colt. Colt.

His name is a mantra, a prayer, and a curse. He's only twenty-eight, six years younger than me, but fuck if he doesn't make me feel like a teenager again. Three days of knowing him is all it's taken. Three fucking days, and I'm already imagining his hands on me, his mouth on me, his cock—Jesus Christ, his cock—pounding into me like he owns me.

The thought has my breath catching in my throat.

I imagine what would've happened if I'd kissed him or if I hadn't stopped my hands from slipping under the hem of his shirt. My hips already shift forward, and I brace one hand on the tiles, the other sliding down my stomach, tracing the path I wish his hands would take.

I touch myself, fingers carefully gliding over my clit, the water making it easier to pretend it's his voice in my ear or his big, strong, calloused hand between my thighs.

I bite my bottom lip to keep quiet, but a soft moan still slips out. Thankfully, it's swallowed by the rush of water. A gasp escapes me as my fingers find my clit, already swollen, already begging for attention. I circle it slowly at first, teasing myself, but, fuck, I can't help it—I'm too desperate, too needy. My fingers dive into my pussy, two at once, and I moan so loud that I'm afraid he'll hear me.

I shove my fist into my mouth to stifle the sound, biting down on my knuckles as I finger-fuck myself harder, faster. My hips buck against my hand, and I imagine it's him. Colt. His thick, veiny cock stretching me open, filling me up, making me scream. I can almost feel his hands gripping my hips, his breath hot on my neck as he catapults me into oblivion. My fingers curl inside me, hitting that sweet spot that makes my knees weak, and I whimper.

"Colt," I whisper, his name slipping out like he's my secret.

My knees wobble, and my back arches as my hand works faster. He's on my mind and in my head as I imagine that sexy smirk and his eyes I want to drown in. I tilt my head back, my mouth parting as my fingers work over my pussy. My body's never felt so hot from something as innocent as banter or flirting. His Southern sex appeal nearly has me unraveling.

My clit throbs under my touch, and I rub it quicker, my fingers a blur as I chase the orgasm that's been building since the moment I met him. My ex—that cheating bastard—couldn't get me off, but Colt? Colt ruins me with one look.

The rhythm builds faster than I expected, like my body's been waiting all day for permission, and I give in to the fantasy of him. The thought of him hearing me, of him walking in and seeing me like this—naked, wet, fucking myself raw with his name on my lips—sends me over the edge.

My body convulses as I come, my pussy clenching around my fingers, my thighs trembling. I slide down the shower wall, my legs giving out as the pleasure rips through me like a fucking earthquake. I'm utterly wrecked as I think about how he looks at me like he's already decided our future.

My chest heaves as the water washes over me, but it's not enough to cool the fire he's lit inside me. I'm in too deep, too fast, and I'm fucking scared. I haven't been single for four years, and I don't know how to act.

I close my eyes and take it all in—the guilt, the longing, the fear that this thing with him is already too big to handle.

I want him. God, I *need* him.

Once I grab an ounce of control, I get out, wrap a towel around my body, and step into the cooler air outside the shower. Steam swirls around me like it knows what I did. My legs still feel unsteady, like my body hasn't caught up with what happened. I grip the edge of the counter and take a breath, trying to calm my pulse.

My reflection stares back at me through the fogged-up mirror —flushed cheeks, parted lips, damp hair curling at the ends.

I look like I've been fucked. I wrap the towel tighter around my body, like I can hold myself together with it.

God, what am I doing?

I'm a thirty-four-year-old runaway bride with a chip on her shoulder and a suitcase full of regret. And I got myself off in a stranger's shower because he had smiled at me and had manners.

Pathetic.

I grab my toothbrush as if it might transport me back to reality, but my body still surges with need. Doesn't help that his deep voice still echoes in my head. I close my eyes and hope he didn't hear me when I moaned his name with my hand between my thighs like he already belongs there.

I open the door to the bathroom and look down the hallway to see if he's on the couch. He's not. I quickly cross to his bedroom, and when I walk inside, I drop the towel. Only then do I realize he's standing at the dresser, shirtless, in gray sweatpants.

Colt turns, and his mouth falls open, then he immediately shifts his back toward me.

"Oh my God," I mutter.

I stop breathing altogether as I freeze in place. Not because I'm embarrassed, but because my whole body goes molten in an instant. Heat floods every inch of me, and it's not only from the shock of being seen. It's him.

I pick up the towel and try to quickly wrap it around my body. "I'm sorry! I didn't know you were in here!"

His back is rigid, one hand braced flat against the dresser. I can see the flex in his arm and how his breath is uneven. He's trying *so* hard not to turn around.

I stand there, dripping, towel snug, my body still wet from the shower and flushed from a release I can't explain.

His voice comes out strained. "I didn't see anything."

"Bullshit. You saw everything," I say, my voice a challenge. "Don't lie."

"Okay." He doesn't deny it this time, and he doesn't move. "I didn't mean to. I needed to change clothes."

My pulse pounds in my ears as I move toward the bed, grabbing his shirt that I took off this morning. I slide the shirt over my head because I can feel him even without looking. The tension in the air is alive. The hem falls against my thighs, fabric clinging to every curve of my breasts, my nipples hard. I don't bother with panties. There's no use pretending I have anything left to hide.

"I'm decent," I say, and he turns, giving me a look that could burn the whole goddamn house down.

His eyes drag over me, and the only way to describe it is hungry. "I'm sorry."

"Don't apologize," I tell him, my voice too breathless to pass for casual.

He takes one step forward, and it's enough to tilt the room. Or that's the tequila.

"Sunny," he says, my name a warning.

I take a step too. Then we're five feet apart, four, and soon, we're standing in the middle of the room like gravity pulled us there without permission. His gaze drops to my mouth.

I feel him before he touches me.

Every muscle is tuned to the moment he closes the distance. And then, like he's giving me every chance to stop him, he lifts his hand and drags his fingers across the edge of my jaw, down the slope of my neck, stopping above the curve of my breast.

I stop breathing.

"I heard you say my name," he says.

My heart stutters, but his gaze doesn't drop.

I take his hand and press it against the center of my chest, right where my heart is pounding like it wants out of my body. "Do you feel that?"

"Yes," he says.

"I'm scared shitless," I admit.

Colt smiles. "Don't be. Live in the moment."

He places his hands on my shoulders, and I have to get a grip. Colt's blue eyes are unreadable, but I can see the muscle in his jaw twitching, like he's trying to rein something in.

My throat tightens.

"That shouldn't have happened," I mutter, moving past him before I do something I might regret, like kiss him. The loss of his closeness is instant.

I can feel his eyes on me as I lift my suitcase onto the bed, but I avoid his gaze.

"What shouldn't have happened?" he asks carefully.

I grab a pair of panties and slide them on as he watches.

"I didn't mean for you to hear that." I suck in a breath. "I got carried away. The tequila. With everything."

Silence stretches, but he doesn't let me sit in it long.

"That wasn't tequila, and you know it." His voice is unapologetic.

I look up at him.

"You said my name," he repeats. "Say it every damn time. You want to fall apart with me on your tongue? You do it."

My chest tightens, heart thudding against my ribs, like it's trying to warn me away from this perfect man.

"Colt," I say, louder than a breath.

"Don't deny yourself the things you want, especially not me," he adds.

I blink a few times, tucking my emotions behind my ten-foot wall, and straighten my back. "I can't have you."

He smirks. "Why?"

"This conversation is ridiculous." I stare at him.

"We both know where this is headin'. Gotta be honest though, I do have some rules if we move forward."

He takes a step toward me and places his hand on my hip. "Forward with what, exactly?"

"This. I know you feel it too," he says.

I open my mouth to speak, but lose the ability.

"Tell me your rules," I finally say.

"No strings attached. I want you to live your life without thinking you need to uproot your entire life to be with me."

My brows furrow. "You act like I'm going to fall in love with you."

"You will. And you know you will. That's why you're so hesitant." His brow cocks up as he watches me. "But you also want me out of your system."

"Seriously?" I want to deny it, but I can't. That would be a lie, and I've already told enough of those since I left New York. I add a scoff at the end for good measure.

"Deny it if it's not true," he simply says.

I look at him—really look at him. He easily sees straight through me.

"I recently got out of a very serious four-year relationship. The last thing I need to do is have—"

"Fun. I agree," he says. "Especially considering what will happen if this line is crossed. That's why you have to make that decision. Not me."

My mouth falls open. "You're so confident and cocky about this."

"No, I'm just direct. Something you're not used to handling from me," he says. "You don't intimidate me."

I scoff, but it turns into laughter. "I do intimidate fragile men. I can't deny that. But trust me when I say, I'm not going to fall in love with you."

"*Okay.*" He says it so casually; it shouldn't make my breath catch, but it does. "Before we move forward with this, I have a question for ya."

"Yes?"

"If you met the perfect partner, would you want to have kids?" he asks.

I stare at him, trying to figure out why he's asking me this. "The perfect partner doesn't exist."

"Darlin', you're wrong about that. Now, come on. Quit stallin'. Your answer determines everything. You have to be truthful," he says, moving away from me. He pulls his dresser drawer open, slides out a shirt, then tugs it over his body.

I cross my arms tighter over my chest, trying to build some armor between us, but it's useless. He already heard me come undone. He heard me say his name like a prayer I didn't mean to whisper.

"If the perfect man existed, then yes," I say, blinking up at him. "Well? Did I pass or fail?"

"Right answer. I can't cross a line with anyone who doesn't eventually want to have a family." He grins, and it's cocky, but it holds a promise.

"I understand. But if I met the perfect man and he didn't want children, I'd make that sacrifice for true love," I tell him.

"You're perfect," he tells me, and I know he means it. "The perfect person for you wouldn't ask you to sacrifice anything."

My cheeks go crimson.

He steps closer, not touching me, but close enough to make it clear he could. I breathe him in. Colt is steady and dangerous in all the right ways.

"I can't fall in love. It would only complicate my life."

"Then don't." His expression doesn't falter. "All I'm askin' is for you to stop running from something that could be real good for you, even if it's only temporary. No expectations."

"Okay," I whisper and pause for a few seconds. "But what if I want there to be expectations at some point?"

He chews on the inside of his cheek, grinning. "That's easy. You stay."

I stare at him and wonder how he believes I'm the perfect one when he says things like that with such ease and confidence.

"And what if you want me to go?"

His eyes soften around the edges. "I don't and won't."

"How can you be so positive?"

"Because when you know, you know."

CHAPTER EIGHT

COLT

I can't sleep. Not after the way she said my name. Not after how she looked at me in my shirt like she wasn't sure whether to kiss me or run. I gave her space, watched her pull away with her arms crossed like a barrier, her breath tight in her chest.

After her shower, I cooked steaks and potatoes, we ate, and then we went our separate ways.

I lie on the couch, staring at the ceiling, listening to the sounds the house makes. The floorboards groan like they know better, and the air conditioner hums low when it kicks on. And the silence that follows the day we had together? It presses in on me.

As I'm drifting, I hear something, and it's enough to make me sit up straight on the couch. It's followed by another broken sound, the kind that doesn't belong in a dream, unless it's the bad kind.

I'm standing before my brain catches up to my body. The floor's cool under my feet as I step into the hallway. The walls in here are freshly hung with smooth seams ready for paint. I follow the sound and hesitate outside of the bedroom with one hand lifted. Then I hear her again. It's soft and choked, words that are desperate and too close to a cry.

I don't knock; I open the door, careful not to startle her. Moonlight filters through the creamy curtains, casting a glow across the tangled sheets she's twisted in. Her limbs are tight, chest rising in uneven bursts, like she's running in her sleep.

"No," she mumbles, head shaking. "Skye. Why? Why?"

My heart stutters.

"Hey," I say softly, moving to her side. "It's a dream. You're okay."

She jerks once, shoulders tense, but she doesn't wake.

I sit on the edge of the bed, placing a hand on her arm, and her skin is clammy.

"Sunny, hey." I brush her hair from her face and try again. "You're safe."

She startles hard this time, sits up, gasping like she's been underwater. Her eyes are wide, wild, like she doesn't recognize where she is.

"It's me," I offer. "Colt Valentine. You're in my house, remember?"

She blinks at me like she's still sorting the dream from reality. Her chest rises and falls in sharp, ragged waves.

"Breathe," I say, holding her gaze. "Breathe with me, all right?"

A beat passes, and another follows it. Finally, her shoulders drop an inch, and she swallows hard.

"I'm sorry," she whispers, voice raw. "I didn't mean to wake you."

"Don't apologize. I wasn't asleep." I shift closer.

She lets out a hollow laugh, then rubs her eyes.

I want to pull her into my arms and ask her what the hell she dreamed about that tore through her like this, but I don't. I sit there, close enough that she knows I'm not leaving.

"It was a nightmare," she whispers, and her voice cracks.

"I figured," I say, watching her through the dim light, noticing her hair's stuck to her cheek and her hands are still clenched like she's bracing for something that already happened.

My jaw tightens, but I stay still.

She speaks so quietly that I almost don't hear it. "No one's ever really loved me, Colt. Not without needing something in return. Every person who has ever said they loved me has hurt me the worst."

That's the moment that undoes me.

I move without thinking, pulling her into my chest. Her body hesitates for half a heartbeat, then sinks into mine like we were built to hold one another. My hand finds her back, and I hug her tight. Her breathing is ragged at first, then calmer. Each inhale is like a piece of her is coming back.

"I don't know what happened to you," I mutter. "But I'm so fucking sorry it did."

She doesn't speak. Doesn't have to. She stays in my arms, and if she'll let me, I'll show her what it feels like to be loved for being who she is.

The silence surrounds us, and I eventually pull away.

"Will you stay with me?" she asks.

My chest tightens at how easy it is to say yes.

"If that's what you want," I whisper. "I'm not going anywhere."

"Please," she says, trying to adjust the blankets that are in a heap.

I shift my body enough to lie back, one arm tucked behind her, the other across her waist. She moves closer to me like it's the only place she's ever meant to be, her breath evening out. She doesn't ask for anything else as she snuggles into me like I'm the only thing holding her together. Maybe I am. I keep her steady in my arms, the blanket over us both, careful not to let the moment slip.

I lie there, memorizing the way it sounds when she lets her guard down.

If she asked me to stay like this forever, I would, and I don't know what the hell that means yet.

But I want to find out.

THE LIGHT'S different when I wake up. It's soft and golden, slipping in through the sheer curtains like it knows not to wake her too harshly. The house is quiet, except for the faint rustle of sheets as I shift my arm beneath her. She's still here, but so am I.

Her hair's a mess, her cheek pressed to my chest, and I swear she fits like she was carved to be next to me. I keep still, not wanting to break whatever spell this is. I don't even know what time it is, and I don't care. Holding her sets my soul alive.

She stirs a little, her breath shifting against my skin, and then she freezes as she peels herself off me.

I keep my eyes closed, trying my best not to start smiling. She shifts carefully, trying not to wake me as she slips out of bed. The sheet slides off her legs, and I open one eye in time to see her walking toward the hallway, still in my shirt. Bare legs. Messy hair. Absolutely beautiful.

The morning light catches her at the right angle, and it's all I can do not to groan like a man who's about to be ruined by a woman he doesn't know.

When she's gone, I lie there, soaking it in. Then I swing my legs off the bed and scrub a hand over my face, wondering when the hell I started liking this feeling. This whole her-being-here thing isn't just comfortable; it's *right*.

I move through the kitchen, letting the rhythm of it settle my thoughts. The coffee maker gurgles, filling the room with that rich aroma that always reminds me of home. I grab her the pale blue mug she reached for yesterday and set it gently beside mine.

There's a comfort in the ritual. Mornings have always been mine, but today, it feels like it belongs to us.

I lean against the counter, arms crossed, watching the sun stretch long across the floor. It pours in from the backyard, cutting through the windows in wide gold streaks. Dust particles dance in it, and I'm wildly aware of her closing presence.

She walks in, revealing enough of her thighs to make my chest tighten. Her hair's loose around her shoulders, soft and wild, like the dream she left behind. And her skin glows in that sunlight, like she stepped out of a damn painting.

I don't move. I watch her as she stretches one arm over her head like she got quality sleep.

"Well, hey there," she says, voice husky with sleep and something else that curls low in my gut.

"You always look like that when you wake up?" I ask, tilting my head.

"Like what?" She smirks.

"Like a damn dream."

She laughs—really laughs—and I want to bottle it up and keep it forever.

"Careful, cowboy. It's too early to be flirting."

"Oh, darlin'," I say, pouring her some coffee and sliding the mug toward her, "it's never too early for that."

She takes the mug, fingers brushing mine. "Thanks. For this. And for last night."

I nod once, the weight of it still lingering in my chest. "You okay?"

She nods, wrapping both hands around the mug like it's keeping her steady. "More than okay."

"How'd you sleep?"

She smiles into her cup. "Perfect once you joined me."

"Yeah?"

"Better than I ever have," she says. "Like my whole body finally shut off. It was rest I desperately needed." Her voice softens on the last word.

"Good," I tell her. "Happy to hear it."

Her eyes meet mine, unguarded and bright. "I swear it's you."

And damn if that doesn't undo something in me.

"I do have a question for you, and you can absolutely not answer it," I say.

We stand there for a beat; her sipping coffee; me drinking her in.

"Okay," she replies.

"Who is Skye?"

Her body tenses, and she lets out a sigh. "My little sister."

"Oh. You kept saying her name," I offer. "Is she ... alive?"

This makes her chuckle. "Yes, but I very much want to hurt her right now."

"Ah," I say, understanding.

Then she sets the mug down and leans in a little, quickly changing the subject. "So, what's on our to-do list today? I have to earn my keep since you won't let me pay you."

My grin spreads. "Your company is more than enough. It's been lonely doing this shit by myself."

"Even if I don't have the proper skills?"

She bites her bottom lip, and I can feel the heat building under the lightness of our conversation. The slow burn between us is warming back up like it never cooled.

"Damn right," I admit.

She turns toward the window, her silhouette outlined in sunlight, and I don't know what I ever did to deserve waking up to this view of her.

"I'll be right back, okay?" I say, moving past her.

Sunny watches me disappear down the hallway. I move into my bedroom, and in the closet, next to my box of journals, I grab the extra one I bought a few months ago. It's leather, hardcover, with a heart-shaped brass lock on the side. I didn't know why I was drawn to that specific one, but it called out to me, and now I know why.

I move back to the kitchen and step toward her. "Close your eyes."

"I don't like surprises," she admits.

"Oh, well. Now, hold your hand out," I tell her, and when she does, I put it in her palm. "You can look."

Her pretty eyes trace over the cover, and then she flips through the blank pages. "What's this?"

"A gift. You don't have to write anything down. But when my head's too full, sometimes, it helps. You write it, close the cover, lock it up, and you don't have to carry it with you anymore. It's a safe place for your thoughts," I add, tapping the little lock. "No one reads it but you. No pressure. Figured it'd help."

She stares at it like it's too nice to touch. "It's beautiful. Thank you."

It's not just the words; it's how I handed her something with no strings attached. "I can see the weight you're carrying. I want to help however I can."

Her lips part. "I think this is the nicest thing anyone has ever done for me."

And that's the moment I realize she doesn't need a place to stay. She needs a place to *be*.

I walk back to the counter as she slides the journal closer, running her fingers along the spine, like she's thinking about all the things she'd write.

And when it starts to feel like the beginning of something, I hear a knock at the front door.

Sunny's brows lift.

"Expecting someone?" she asks.

"Nope," I say. "Are you?"

This makes her laugh. I don't know who's on the other side, but I've got a feeling that the moment I open it, this perfect morning we've shared is about to get complicated.

CHAPTER NINE

SUNNY

T he knock hasn't finished echoing before something shifts in Colt's posture. He's not tense, just overly aware, like he recognizes the cadence of whoever it is.

"That your secret girlfriend?" I offer.

"Darlin', you're the only woman in my life right now," he says, and I swear his drawl thickens.

I swallow hard, my eyes trailing over his muscles. He looks good—barefoot, messy hair, coffee in hand, smirking at me like I'm the best damn thing ever to enter his kitchen. Maybe I am. I find that hard to believe though.

"Might be one of my brothers or sisters stoppin' by on the way to town. Happens regularly," he tells me, breaking me out of my daze.

Another knock follows, but this time it's louder and more impatient. Whoever it is, they're impatient as fuck.

"Well, shit. Guess I'd better go get that," he mutters, setting his mug on the counter. "I'll be right back."

He heads for the front door, and my body feels like it's on fire. I suck in a deep breath, glancing at the journal he gave me. It's such a sweet thing to do, and it shows that he has emotional intelligence—something my ex certainly lacked.

A moment later, the door creaks open, and the sound pulls me from my thoughts.

"Colty," a high-pitched voice says. It's syrupy sweet and Southern, and I wonder if it's one of his sisters. "Heard you were livin' out here in this big, haunted house. I never understood your obsession with it."

"What're ya doin' here?" Colt's voice drops, and I hear the edge in his tone. Because of that, I know it's not family.

The silence drags on, and I imagine him staring at her, waiting.

"Are ya gonna invite me in? Give me the grand tour before you fix it up?" she purrs.

I roll my eyes, and jealousy washes over me. Who the hell shows up unannounced and nearly demands a red carpet?

"No, I'm not," he says flatly. There's no hesitation, and he leaves no room for misinterpretation.

Whoever it is, they aren't welcome here.

Curiosity drags me down the hallway toward him, and I catch a sliver of her through the cracked-open door. She's beautiful, tall, tan, and perfectly highlighted. If I had to guess, it's one of his exes.

I don't hesitate as I wrap my arms around Colt's waist from behind, like I've done it a hundred times, like this moment belongs to us. He doesn't flinch when I touch him. Instead, he turns his body and curls his hand around my hip, pulling me closer to him, like it's second nature. I'd be lying if I said being in his arms didn't feel as good as him holding me as I fell asleep.

Colt's shirt hangs loose on my frame, and it feels like armor disguised as cotton. She looks at me like his name is written in cursive across my skin. It's enough to make her tense, but it doesn't bother me. Thanks to my background, I'm not intimidated by anyone, man or woman.

"Oh, hi," I say, sweet as sin, turning back to Colt. "Had I known we were having company this morning, I'd have put on some pants."

Her eyes drop to my bare, tanned legs, linger on the shirt, then flick back to Colt. He holds me tighter, his strong hand and fingertips pressing into me. I imagine them roaming my body and force myself to pay attention. He's too damn distracting without even trying.

"Please excuse my manners. I'm Sunny, Colt's *girlfriend*. And you are?"

I see her heart rate increase, and her lip quivers. She doesn't like me being here.

"Tessa," she says, and I hold out my hand to shake hers. She glances down at it, then back at me. "I'm the love of Colt's life."

My smile doesn't budge. "Really? You said Teresa?"

"*Tessa*," she spits out.

I tilt my head curiously. "That's so strange. He's never once mentioned you, *Tessa*."

I know it stings, but she needs a reality check.

"How long has it been since you two broke up? Recently?"

Exes aren't a conversation we've had, and it's not one I want to discuss.

"Nearly three years," Colt answers.

Her brows pull tight, and her perfect lips move into a straight line. Colt's arm settles more comfortably around me, and I think he enjoys watching her squirm.

"I'd like to speak to Colt in private." Her voice is clipped but too demanding for my liking.

"Don't think so," he says. "If you've got something to say, you can say it in front of my girlfriend."

Girlfriend. The word lingers, and I like how he said it, like it was true without a doubt.

His smirk follows, and for a moment, it's just the two of us with our eyes locked and hearts beating steadily.

She clears her throat. "You didn't tell me you were seeing someone."

"He doesn't owe you that," I say gently, tone soft but firm. "Colt has moved on. It's been three years. You should as well."

Her eyes move back to me, and if looks could kill, I'd be dead. "How long have you known each other?" she questions.

"Long enough to know this feels right," I say lightly, resting my head against Colt's shoulder.

Colt lets out a low laugh, shaking his head like I'm trouble.

She scoffs. "You're really something, aren't ya?"

I glance up at Colt, giving him a wink. "That's what he keeps telling me."

He coughs—a laugh this time—and his fingers skim the edge of my shoulder, a soft, lingering touch. Goose bumps trail over my arms, and I like the way he makes me feel. I shouldn't though. He's too young. I've got too much baggage. He lives in Texas. I live in New York. I don't believe in love, and I know he does. We're on opposite sides of the coin, and that's what scares me the most.

"He used to worship me too … a lot."

"That's enough," Colt says. "What do you want?"

"Well," she says, still looking at me like I'm a little green man from outer space, "I thought I'd stop by and say hello. I wanted to catch up for a minute and invite you to join me at the rodeo this weekend."

I don't know this woman, but something about her sets a version of me loose that I haven't seen since I left the city. The bold, confident part of me that doesn't apologize for knowing her worth.

"You've said hello, and I'm not available. Not anymore," he tells her, staying planted in the doorway like a human blockade. One arm is still wrapped around me, and the other is resting casually on the frame like he has no intention of moving.

"You should still join me. As friends." Tessa shifts her weight onto one heel, her glossy pink lips curving like this is a misunderstanding she's about to correct.

"The answer is no." Colt's voice stays calm, but there's no warmth in it.

Her smile is pulled too tight, too controlled, but I know she disapproves of his answer. "Right. Of course."

She straightens, smoothing her hand over her already-perfect golden hair. Her brown eyes fall back on me with more edge this time, like she's trying to pick me apart, one messy strand of hair at a time.

"We don't really like out-of-towners round here," she says to me, and it comes out like a warning.

"You're not gonna threaten her. It's time for you to go," he says, still polite, but now there's no mistaking the annoyance beneath the manners.

The air ripples around us, and it's clear he's done with her and this conversation.

She doesn't respond right away. She drags her gaze over him like she's memorizing something she used to own.

"I really thought a woman staying here was a stupid rumor," she says.

Ahh, there it is. She didn't come here to reconnect. She wanted confirmation.

"I hope you got the answers you were looking for. It was nice meeting you, Tessa," I say, smiling politely, holding Colt a little tighter, like I can protect him from her. There's no bite in my tone, but there's enough sugar to make her teeth ache.

Colt gives my shoulder a gentle squeeze. It's enough to say he's got this, and that I don't need to finish anything.

Tessa forces a smile. "Lookin' real good, Colty. Call me if things don't work out with your tourist."

And like that, Colt steps back and slams the door shut. He gives her no apology or hesitation, just the clean, satisfying sound of a boundary being locked into place. The second it's closed, I let out a breath I didn't realize I had been holding.

His hand still rests on my waist. "I'm real fuckin' sorry about that."

"Don't apologize for her rudeness. It's not your fault," I say, my body reeling from his electric touch. I might burn alive.

We're so damn close as I gaze up at him. Tall, broad shoulders, perfect face. This man could model blue jeans for a living if he wanted.

His eyes are warm and locked on me in a soft way that I don't quite know how to handle.

"You have no idea what you've done," he says, amused.

I arch a brow. "Should I be worried?"

"Depends." He tucks a strand of hair behind my ear, laughing under his breath. "By sunset, the whole town's gonna think I'm in a serious relationship with an out-of-towner. Can you handle that?"

I have the urge to kiss him, to see if I experience the same sparks as I do with his hand gripped around my waist. I swallow hard, my breath growing ragged. "You don't know what I can handle."

"I have an idea." He lifts my chin with his other hand, and we're locked in a moment of time together. "Honestly, I didn't think I'd be dealing with a girlfriend rumor this week."

"I'm sorry about that," I whisper.

"Don't be. Just get ready to play the part."

I blink out of my haze. "Excuse me?"

"You started it, and now the games have begun."

"No, no, no. I was trying to piss her off. Make her realize what she'd lost. I didn't volunteer myself to be your fake girlfriend," I say as he guides me toward the kitchen.

"Sorry. That's not how things work around here," he says. "You confirmed a rumor. It's an avalanche now."

He makes me want things I haven't wanted in a long time, things I didn't know could exist.

I return to my seat at the table in the kitchen. Colt pours us fresh cups of coffee as I stare out the bay window. In the back pasture, I see a large yellow barn and two horses grazing.

"Do you ride?"

He grins, glancing out the window. "Yeah. I'm surprised you didn't assume. You know, with all the Texan jokes floating around. Most think we take our horses to school."

I snicker. "Did you?"

"We sometimes did," he admits, handing me a fresh cup.

There's a long pause.

"So, Tessa … she's very pretty," I offer because it's true.

"So are rattlesnakes," he replies without missing a beat. "They'll still kill you."

That earns a full-on laugh from me, and I notice how his eyes soften at the sound. It does something to me, and I'm suddenly aware of how natural it feels, being with him.

"Are blondes your type?" I ask, halfway teasing, but I genuinely want to know.

"Smart and confident is my type," he says. "Wanting to know if you're my type?"

My mouth parts, but I can't answer. It's too direct. He's right, it's not something I'm used to experiencing with men.

"You are," he confirms. "Sassy little brunettes drive me fucking crazy."

"When I leave, will you be running back to her now that she seems interested again?" As soon as the words are out, I wince. "Sorry. That's none of my business. You don't have to answer that."

He stares at me, like he's trying to figure me out. "And what if the answer was yes?"

My stomach tightens. I don't like the idea of him carrying any emotions for her, especially not when he's looking at me with so much adoration in his eyes that I can't unsee it.

"Wait, is that jealousy?" he asks, but I have a feeling he already knows the answer.

"Maybe." I shrug. "But she's not the one standing in your kitchen, wearing your shirt, now, is she? Or the one sleeping in your bed."

His brow lifts. "You're a tiger."

"If you only knew."

"Actually, after that little show you put on this morning, I think I've got a pretty good idea. Now, how about some breakfast? I'm in the mood for some corned beef hash," he says, and I know a subject change when I hear one.

"What's that?"

"A Southern delicacy," he says, grabbing a cast iron skillet from the cabinet and a carton of eggs from the fridge. "I'll make you some. If you hate it, I'll cook something else."

I watch him work, taking in the way he moves like this space is his kingdom—barefoot, half-dressed, ridiculously attractive. My fingers drift to the cover of the journal he gave me. My thumb traces the edge of it.

He looks back at me. "Go ahead. I know you want to ask me a million questions right about now. I can handle it."

I hesitate, but he's right. I do have a lot of questions. "Was she really the love of your life?"

"At one point, I would've said yes, but I now realize our relationship was built on lies, so I don't feel like it counts," he says as the pan sizzles. "We dated for three years, and I thought I'd marry her. Luckily, I figured out she was dishonest before she had the chance to ruin my life. Some things you can't ever come back from, no matter how pretty you are. Once my trust is broken, it's never the same."

"I understand that." Guilt washes over me because I've said certain things to protect myself.

He turns back to the skillet. "I don't have feelings for her and would never ever, ever get back together with her. I told myself I wouldn't date again unless certain criteria were met."

Now my curiosity is piqued. "Like?"

"I have to feel the spark. You know that underlying current that drives you insane?"

I nod, knowing what he's referring to. "The one that puts you in a complete choke hold?"

"That's the one," he admits, his voice rough and sexy. "There has to be a mutual attraction. No one-sided bullshit. I can't do that again. Sex drives must match. I'm not looking for a fling when I want forever."

My brows lift. "And what's your number one nonnegotiable?"

"If I'm in a relationship with someone, I don't do guessing games. I need someone emotionally available. I don't need polished or perfect. I want something real, someone I can spend forever with. What about you?"

"I want the same things," I whisper. "I need freedom to say what I mean without being gaslit, guilted, or minimized for it. I need a partner who can commit."

He smirks. "Sounds like I'm your man."

"Oh, you'd better stop," I tell him.

"I've learned that some men are highly intimidated by strong women. Not me. I'm secure and encourage boss bitches."

I take a sip of coffee, and the warmth spreads through me. "There are times I feel like I'm too much and other times when I'm not enough. It's a very hard place to be in," I admit for the first time in my life.

"I think you're perfect the way you are," he says.

"You don't have to say that."

He moves toward me. I stand in front of him, and he places his hands on my shoulders, staring into my eyes.

"Be yourself while you're here. Your true self. The one you hide from everyone else."

His thumb brushes against my lower lip, and I'm lost in the morning haze with him.

"What are you doing to me?" I ask, scared I'll lose myself in his spell.

"It's you, not me," he says with a grin, then focuses on the sizzling skillet.

I let out a ragged breath and return to my seat, glancing at the journal. I could fill it full of everything in my head right now.

Colt cracks an egg and drops it in the hot pan.

"My little brother Emmett is a playboy, but he's not a fool. Tessa kept making moves on him when I wasn't around. So, Emmett, being Emmett, set her up. Told her to meet him in a hotel in Alpine, wearing some lingerie he had bought for her. Only it wasn't Emmett who walked into the room that night." He shakes his head. "You should've seen the look on her face."

My breath catches as I realize the betrayal and understand how horrible it feels.

"He never fucked her. But he could have. It would've wrecked my relationship with my brother. She only cared about herself," he adds quietly. "That's unforgivable behavior. Our entire relationship would've had that stain on it. She tried to twist the narrative, but I no longer believed a word she fed me. To think I almost married her."

His words hang in the air like Texas heat.

"I'm glad you didn't," I say.

"Me too," Colt says, flipping the egg. "Had I married Tessa, I wouldn't have met you. My girlfriend."

"Girlfriend. Kinda like the way you say it."

"Yeah?" He rubs a hand over his jaw and grabs a spatula. "Keep it up, and engagement rumors will be next."

I'm like a teenager with their first crush. How is that even possible?

"I didn't mean to start anything. Small-town rumors are outside of my wheelhouse," I say. Even though I've dealt with rumors about myself on a national scale, this still has me more nervous.

Colt leaning against the counter short-circuits my nervous system. "Could've fooled me. You wrapped your arm around me like you owned me."

"It's called improvising," I explain.

"Yeah?" He glances back. "You gave her all the proof she needed. And something tells me you're not the type to stir up drama unless it serves a purpose."

"Only when it's strategically beneficial. Which is why I've decided I'll only be here until next weekend."

His smile fades before I even finish the sentence.

"That's less than two weeks. Why?"

"I need to go home and settle some things."

There's a pause, but he doesn't push.

"And where's home?" Colt asks.

I hesitate—not because I'm hiding, but because saying it aloud makes it real. "New York City."

His eyebrows lift. "City girl. I knew it."

I smile at him as he processes that piece of information like he's trying to figure out what it means.

"And what happens when you return to NYC?" he asks.

"I confront the ones who hurt me," I say honestly.

The thought of confronting Donovan and Skye makes me physically ill.

"Your sister?" he asks.

"She's on the list."

"Speaking your truths to those who hurt you is needed so you can get closure. It doesn't matter if they accept what you have to say or not. If you ever want to talk, I'm a real good listener, and I'm a vault. Nothing will ever be repeated, I promise," he says, pulling two plates from the cabinet.

"Thank you." I glance down at the journal. "I hope writing it helps."

"I hope so too. I've kept a journal since I was a teenager. Not because I wanted to, but it's how I earned my allowance. My mama told me if I wrote in my journal every day, she'd give me one hundred dollars every single month, so I kept up with it for years. Earned several thousand."

I smile. "I already love her."

Colt grabs his coffee. "I think my mama would love you too. She appreciates a fighting spirit."

Before I can reply, his phone starts ringing from the living room—he must have left it there last night before he joined me.

"And so it begins." He sighs as he walks away.

I sip my coffee, trying not to think too hard about what he's shared.

"This is Colt," he says.

There's a beat of silence as he heads back toward the kitchen, and his voice gets louder.

"My girlfriend? Yeah. Dinner tonight? Shit, I almost forgot."

My eyes snap up, and I whisper, "What the hell?"

He winks at me like he's enjoying this a little too much as the food sizzles in the pan. It smells delicious.

"Yeah, it was gonna be a surprise," he says into the phone, grinning, and I can hear a woman talking. "She'll be there. Remi told you about her? Yeah. Mm-hmm. Gorgeous. Prettiest woman I've ever seen."

Another pause, then a low chuckle. I realize I'm blushing.

"All right, Kins. Tell Mama I want apple pie with Bluebell. I don't care if you do a love reading, but I don't want to hear about it. Okay. *Okay.* Bye. You hang up first! Bye!"

He listens to her for another minute, then ends the call. He sets his phone on the counter like my actions didn't change the trajectory of my time here.

"And who was that?" I ask.

"My older sister, Kinsley. She works for the newspaper and hears all the local drama. Apparently, I was the talk of the diner this morning. Someone was asking whose Camaro was parked outside my house. Kathy, the lady who works at the motel in town, told them it was a woman from New York City. Did you know we'd met on the internet and you're moving to Valentine to be with me?" he asks, totally unbothered. "Probably where Tessa heard it from."

"That's what's spreading around?" I blink at him.

"Yep," he says, laughing. "Ridiculous. By Sunday, I'm sure they'll move to us being engaged."

"Oh God, and you told your sister I'm joining you for dinner?"

"You threw your arm around me this morning and called yourself my girlfriend. What's a man supposed to do?"

I gasp. "I don't know. Deny it?"

"Not my style," he says, stepping closer. "I'm following your lead."

The air shifts. Silence stretches between us.

My body says yes. My heart flinches. My head says run.

"I, um ..."

"Cat got your tongue?" he asks. "It's ten days. What's the worst that could happen?"

My heart kicks up. "Faking out your ex is one thing. Pretending for your family? That's a whole other level."

"Don't act," he says. "Be yourself."

"You're too confident about this."

"Says the woman who stormed into my life like she had been made for it." His voice is wrapped in that drawl I'm starting to crave. "It will be an adventure."

I exhale, but I'm smiling now. He's right; I won't be here for very long.

Colt brushes past me to grab something from the pantry, and I love the way he smells like mountain air.

"Don't you think we should set some ground rules?" I ask after seeing goose bumps form on my skin. I try to rub them away.

"My only rule is to be yourself," he says with a box of pancake mix in his hands. He pulls a waffle maker from a cabinet. "The rest will figure itself out. It always does."

I roll my eyes. "This could be a disaster."

"Disaster?" He winks. "Nah. It'll be a moment. Trust the process."

He mixes batter like he doesn't have a worry in the world.

"Okay, but I have rules too," I say, narrowing my eyes.

"Gimme 'em."

As soon as the batter hits the hot waffle press, the room fills with the scent of sugary sweetness.

"But know that the second you say no touching or no flirting, I'm gonna have to do those things."

My brows furrow. "You can't be serious."

"I'm a Valentine, babe," he says, grinning. "We're rule breakers. That's why it's safer not to have any."

I sigh. "Okay, so what about PDA? That's a line we shouldn't fake."

"You're right. Hand-holding is innocent enough. That'll get the point across at the rodeo."

"The rodeo!" I repeat. "I didn't agree to that."

He shrugs like it's obvious. "Okay, but how else am I supposed to introduce my girl to the whole town at once?"

I stare at him. He called me his girl, and I like it.

"I cannot fall in love with you, Colt Valentine," I say, mostly to myself.

"Then don't kiss me. That's when the curse kicks in."

I look at him like he's out of his mind.

"The curse?"

"Yeah, it's a Valentine thing. I have a way of gettin' under women's skin and stayin' there for a long damn time, and all it takes is one kiss. Why do you think Tessa showed up today? I've not been with anyone since her, and she's threatened that I might be moving on."

"Are you?" I ask.

"Darlin', I think you hold the answer to that question, not me."

He grins, and I hate what it does to me.

"I can't answer that."

"One day, you will," he encourages.

As I sit in his kitchen and he makes me breakfast, this begins to feel like the start of something unraveling.

A week and a half of hand-holding, rodeos, family dinners, and pretending I'm not attracted to the most irresistible man who's too young for me will be fine ... said no runaway bride ever. But even so, moving forward with him feels like everything I need in my life right now.

CHAPTER TEN

COLT

The second I finish getting dressed, I regret every life choice that led me to invite a woman I hardly know to my family dinner. It's a big deal, even if we're only friends. An unspoken rule that's always been followed is to only bring someone to dinner if they mean something. My brothers have only invited women they were serious about.

Tonight is a statement.

They'll see the truth in my eyes, especially Remi. She always reads me better than any of them. Twin life, I suppose.

I hear something fall in the bathroom, and I move into the hallway. She continues humming a soft tune, so it must have been nothing.

For the past hour, Sunny's been holed up in the bathroom, like she's soothing herself before walking into a lion's den full of Texans who love nothing more than being nosy. I'm already praying they don't bombard her with questions. But I know they probably will.

I think what scares me the most is that I want them to like her as much as I do. If they don't, it will be confirmation that there is no future for us. My family is everything, and I need a woman who fits into my life.

I rub a hand over the back of my neck and try to remind myself that I'm thinking too far ahead. This is a temporary two-week situation that'll end in time to ruin me.

I lean against the hallway wall and wait. She's been quiet for over a minute, and that worries me more than the humming.

Eventually, I move to the bathroom door and lightly knock twice. "You alive in there, darlin'?"

"Partially," she calls back, voice muffled but teasing. "Your bathroom lighting is offensive. I'm scared I look like a clown."

I smirk despite myself. "Didn't realize. I'll upgrade it for you. I'm sure you look great."

The door opens a crack, and I meet her green eyes, which sparkle like gemstones, then roam down to her red lips. She bites the corner, and I force myself to take a step away before I cross a line that we're not ready to tumble over.

Sunny's wearing a cute sundress that's a soft sage green. It hits mid-thigh and clings to her in a way that makes me forget how words work. Her dark hair is down in loose waves, and for the first time, I notice she's wearing earrings—diamonds that flash every time she moves.

She tilts her head and smiles. "You're staring."

"Yep," I say because I've given up pretending. "You're dazzling."

She gives me a once-over, her eyes trailing up to my cowboy hat. "You clean up nice too, cowboy."

I'm wearing a plaid pearl-buttoned shirt and dark jeans, along with my nice boots. The belt buckle isn't obnoxious, but it's there. This is my usual Thursday best. Mama doesn't care if we show up looking like we rolled with pigs because she'd rather us come messy than miss a gathering.

"Who am I meeting tonight? Can you give me a quick run-down?" she asks sweetly as I follow her into the bedroom.

I lean against the wall as she sits on the bed and puts on some strappy heels.

"Okay, so take a deep breath first."

"Um, not sure I like the sound of that," she says, glancing up at me.

"Hope you're good at remembering people." I grin. "There's my older brother, Beckett. He'll be the one checking you out like a parole officer. His wife, Summer, is sweet and owns the bed-and-breakfast over at Horseshoe Creek Ranch. She'll probably ask you to stay forever. She and Beckett used to hate each other, but now they're inseparable. Also, Summer is Kinsley's best friend."

Sunny laughs. "That's a cute love story."

"It wasn't cute when they were trying to rip out each other's jugular.

"Then we have Kinsley, my oldest sister. She's real woo-woo—charges her crystals during a full moon, and she might try to read your palm if you get too close. Her partner is Hayden Shaw, and his family owns Main Street Books. He's got the best book recs in town. A nice guy who treats my sister right. They were high school sweethearts, and then they broke up. A couple of years ago, he moved back to Valentine to be with Kinsley."

"Oh. Now you're spilling tea."

I shoot her a wink. "You won't forget them because of it. Now, Remi's my twin, who you already met. Cash, the guy at her place when you waltzed in, searching for yours truly, is her husband. They got married a few weeks ago. He's the only equine vet around town. The clinic is on Horseshoe Creek Ranch. You might've seen it when you stopped by."

She nods. "Actually, I don't remember. I was in a weird place mentally. Is that all?"

I chuckle. "Nah. There's Harrison, the jokester of the family, and his partner, Grace. They've been besties since they were kids. Inseparable. Oh, Harrison and Beckett are business partners and work together.

"Now, those are all my older siblings. Remi and I are basically the middle kids."

"Ahh," she says. "I'm the oldest in my family. It's not fun."

"That explains it," I say, crossing my arms over my chest.

"What?" she asks, standing. The shoes give her several more inches in height. She walks toward me.

"You have big-sister energy. It's a good thing," I tell her. "Oh, there are more."

"More?" Her voice rises an octave. "I honestly don't know how your mother handled so many kids."

"Sometimes, I don't either." I laugh. "Now, the youngsters. We have Fenix. She's one hell of a barrel racer, but she doesn't ride anymore. No one knows why. Only lots of speculation. There's Emmett, who I already told you about. He's a playboy flirt who works on my parents' cattle ranch. No matter what any woman tells you in public, she is not his girlfriend, trust me."

"Damn," she says, like she's making mental notes.

"It's a lot. Sorry. Up next is London. She's the talented one, but somewhat of a wild card. Has balls of steel and dreams of being famous one day."

"Wow, really? Tell me more about her," she says.

"Well, she's been playing guitar and singing since she was a little kid. Mom recognized it very early, and we all did. She was in lessons, won all the local and state talent shows, but has never had her moment. Instead of giving up, she decided she'd start booking her own gigs because nothing will stop her," I explain. "One day, she'll meet the right person, and her entire trajectory will change."

"You're right. When does she play next?"

"Funny you should ask, this weekend at the rodeo."

She grins and chews on the corner of her lip, knowing what that does to me.

"Wrapping it up, there's Sterling, my youngest brother, who's training to be a farrier. Then Vera, who's the baby. She recently graduated high school and works at the nursery. She's got a heart bigger than Texas and could probably revive a cactus.

"And I think that's everyone."

Sunny blinks a few times as I lead her down the hallway. "I'm suddenly overwhelmed, and the night hasn't started yet."

Before I twist the knob for the front door, I glance over and see the bouquet of flowers I picked up from town earlier. "Shit," I mutter, breaking the growing tension I was basking in. It's been a long time since anyone's presence has made me feel so damn alive.

For a while, I thought I might never feel this flame with anyone again. I return to her in the entryway. The late evening sunlight glistens through the crystal glass of the door and casts a kaleidoscope of reflections around. The moment almost feels magical.

"These are Mama's favorites. I'd like you to give them to her."

She takes them carefully, her fingers brushing mine. The spark is undeniable.

"We should be honest," she says. The guilt in her voice is evident.

"We will." I hold her gaze. "However, it won't matter what status we give because after they see how we interact, they'll assume we're together even if we deny it until we're blue in the face."

She tries not to smile but fails. "Seriously?"

"It's the way you look at me, babe. Why do you think Tessa believed it?"

Her perfect, kissable lips part.

My phone buzzes with a timer. It's my alarm to leave, so we're not late. We step outside, and I lock up, making sure the porch light is on for us when we return. As we move down the porch, I want to grab her hand, but I opt for opening the truck door for her instead. She slides inside, and then I move behind the steering wheel.

"Time to meet the people who are gonna interrogate you over a home-cooked meal. And if we're late, there'll be a small army of dishes waiting with our names on 'em," I say as I crank the engine.

We take the long road that leads straight to my parents' ranch. The sun hangs low in the mountains, causing everything to glow a golden hue. It's one of my favorite parts of the day.

By the time we pull up to the Valentine family house, the sun's even lower, the porch light is glowing, and I already know we're one of the last to arrive. I try to figure out who's missing.

I can hear their laughter before we even get out of the truck. Somewhere between Kinsley's sharp cackle and London's dramatic storytelling voice lies Harrison's voice, agitating them both. There's music coming from the open windows, something twangy and upbeat, and the smell of grilled corn hits me square in the chest.

"Wow," Sunny murmurs, eyes wide as she takes it in. "This is where you grew up?"

"Yep, this is it," I tell her.

"You're so lucky," she says. "This is like … a sitcom."

"Yeah. It's called *Meet the Valentines*, and the show starts now. Come on, darlin'. We don't want to be doin' those dishes, trust me."

She smiles but looks nervous.

Headlights swing into the gravel driveway behind us, and it's a jacked-up black truck.

"Shit. It's Emmett," I mutter. "We gotta hurry."

Sunny glances at me. "Right now?"

"Yep, unless you love washing dishes," I say as I hop out of the driver's side and come around to her door. "Can you run in those shoes?"

"Um," she hesitates.

Before she can answer, I grip her by the waist and lift her off the seat.

"Colt!" she yelps, laughing as I haul her up and over my shoulder like a sack of flour in a sundress.

"I can't afford you busting your ass," I say, already sprinting for the porch.

"Seriously!" Her laughter spills into the warm night air, and damn if it doesn't light me up from the inside.

I set Sunny down at the top of the porch, gently, both hands on her waist. Her hair's a little messy from the sprint, and she's laughing, cheeks flushed and glowing in the porch light.

We're close. Too close. Her hands are still on my chest. Mine are still on her hips. She looks up at me, breathing a little fast, lips parted. And for a second, everything else fades out.

I could kiss her right now. I *want* to. God, I want to.

"Damn it," Emmett yells in the distance. "You cheated! Unfair advantages! Long legs, dirty tactics, and apparently no shame!"

"I warned her about you," I holler back at him.

"About little ole me?" Emmett acts offended, but he stops running, giving up. "You look up *Southern gentleman* in the dictionary, and you'll see a picture of my beautiful face."

Remi cracks open the door. "Y'all comin' in or gonna keep flirting on the porch all night?"

"We'll be right there," I tell my sister, glancing down at Sunny, and I'm still holding her close.

Something dangerous flickers in her eyes, so I let my hands fall away and step back, clearing my throat.

"Let's go, darlin'. Time to introduce you to the Valentine army."

The house is buzzing with voices while laughter rolls from the dining room and the faint sound of a Willie Nelson song drifts in from the kitchen speakers. The air smells like comfort with the scent of butter and warm bread.

We stand inside the entryway, the bouquet still tight in her hand. Her eyes sweep over the space, taking in the old wood floors, the gallery wall of mismatched frames, and the way nothing here is curated. It's lived in, full of love, and loud.

She doesn't move, and her shoulders stay a little too high.

I reach for her hand. "You okay?"

She nods, but it's small. Her gaze lingers on a crooked photo of all of us in the front yard when I was about thirteen, my arm in a sling, and Emmett grinning like he caused it. I had fallen off a horse after it spooked.

"This is what going home is supposed to feel like," she says.

"Yeah," I admit, studying her.

She doesn't say anything for a beat. "I don't think I've ever felt anything like this."

I glance at her, my eyes scanning over the dress, the earrings, and the pinkness blooming on her cheeks. I notice the weight she carries and how her edges go sharp when she's trying not to show anything real.

"I'm so damn happy you're here with me," I say.

Her eyes meet mine, and something I can't name shifts between us. It's like a live wire is being pulled tight. She doesn't look away. Neither do I.

The door behind us swings open, and Emmett glares at me, then lifts a brow at Sunny. "Don't I get a proper introduction?"

I roll my eyes.

Sunny grins at him. "I'm immune to flirting."

He bursts into laughter. "I like you."

From the other room, a chair scrapes across the floor, followed by London yelling that dinner's ready.

The moment breaks apart, and I lead her into the dining room.

We step inside, and the chatter stops. Focus is on us.

Beckett looks up from slicing the brisket.

"Everyone, this is Sunny," I say.

I go around the table, pointing out everyone, and they smile, saying hello. Once introductions are done, Sunny hands the bouquet to Mama like she rehearsed it, smiling enough to be polite. Mama melts immediately, holding the flowers like they're a promise.

"Thank you, honey. This was very sweet," she says, giving her a hug, and I swear I feel Sunny exhale beside me.

My dad shakes her hand and introduces himself politely.

We take the last two open seats—side by side, of course—and the second we sit down, a dozen conversations fire off at once.

Kinsley is recounting a dramatic tarot reading she did earlier that day, then fills us in on some town gossip. Emmett is already halfway into a story about being chased by a rooster this morning. Fenix is arguing with London over the best George Strait album. Vera is chatting with Harrison as Sterling passes around a bowl of mashed potatoes like it's a sacred ritual. Remi watches us, not saying much, along with Beckett.

Beckett eyes us over his fork. "When's the wedding?"

"Don't start," I shoot back.

Summer leans in. "We're glad you brought someone. You never have."

"Y'all sure he didn't hire her?" Emmett grins at Sunny. "I mean, she's beautiful and smart. It's suspicious she's with you."

Sunny doesn't miss a beat. "I'm not for sale."

Laughter rolls through the table, and my hand brushes hers beneath it. She doesn't pull away, and I don't move either.

The conversation shifts again. Vera talks about a flower order mix-up at the nursery, and London talks about her gig at the rodeo. With so many of us at dinner, there is never enough time to completely catch up.

"You're coming, right?" London glances around the table.

"We'll be there," Sunny says. "I'm looking forward to it."

"Thank you," my sister replies, beaming. "I expect you all to be there."

"I'm tryin' to figure out how you ended up with my brother," Harrison says, and Grace elbows him hard in his side.

Sunny tilts her head and gives Harrison a look like she takes no shit. "Colt is charming. Caring. Funny. Why not?"

"See," I say, smirking.

It's all in good fun until Remi tilts her head, eyes narrowing.

"So ... is this serious?" she asks, but I have a feeling my sister already knows the reality.

The table goes quiet, but Sunny doesn't react to the attention. It slides off her shoulders like she's been in the hot seat before. This woman is confident, unbothered, and I find that so sexy.

Sunny doesn't flinch. "I don't know what this is. I'm hesitant to give titles to anything."

Mama lifts a brow like she's impressed. "Smart woman."

I shift in my seat and give Sunny's hand a little squeeze under the table. She squeezes back once.

Once we've cleared our plates, Mama passes out pie and peach cobbler like we won the lottery. Sunny chats with Kinsley and Summer, and I can't help but watch her as she laughs.

"Yeah, I heard Tessa was still trying to convince folks she was Colt's soulmate today in town. You know, some girls peak in high school. She's one of them. Never liked her," Kinsley adds.

"How about we talk about something else?" I ask. "Unless you want me to start talkin' about your exes."

Hayden chuckles as Kinsley rolls her eyes.

After we eat dessert and chat about the weather this week, the table starts to clear in waves. Emmett tries to disappear before the dishes are picked up, which earns him a sharp elbow from Remi and a death glare from Mama.

As Sunny chats with Vera and Fenix, I pick up empty plates and carry them to the kitchen. Beckett catches me at the sink.

"You look calm for someone who's in over his head," he says, leaning one hip against the counter like he's got all night to get to his point.

I shoot him a look.

He smirks. "You're not as smooth as you think."

I wipe my hands. "You done?"

"Not quite." He nods toward the dining room. "She's got anchor energy. The kind that roots people before they even realize it. How old is she?"

"Thirty-four," I tell him. "Does it matter?"

"No. She seems like she has her shit together, unlike everyone else you've ever been with. Are you ready for commitment?"

I follow his gaze, catch a glimpse of Sunny as she smiles and easily holds a conversation without me needing to be by her side.

"She's temporary, Beckett," I say, though the words feel like gravel in my mouth.

"Sure. Make sure *you* remember that when she leaves because from where I'm standin', it looks like she's already got her hooks in and you're not trying to stop that from happenin'."

Before I can reply, he's gone, like he didn't walk up and punch me with a paragraph.

I glance back at Sunny, still seated, still looking like she belongs here in a way that makes my chest tighten.

I remind myself again that this is temporary. Even if I don't want it to be.

Emmett moves into the kitchen, cursing under his breath. "Wanna help?"

"Did you help me last time?" I pat him on the back with a laugh. "That's your answer."

He groans, and I leave the kitchen. Sounds of plates clank together, along with running water. When I move back to Sunny, I can see overwhelm in her eyes. I lean in, brushing my hand lightly against her back.

"Come on," I say under my breath. "You look like you could use some air."

She glances at me like she's surprised that I even noticed. Everyone else moves into the living room or the kitchen to help Emmett.

I guide Sunny out through the front door, holding it open as she steps onto the porch. The warm night air greets us, heavy with the scent of honeysuckle and the soft chirp of crickets. The house glows behind us, but out here, it's quieter.

I motion toward the porch swing. "Sit with me for a minute."

She does, tucking one leg beneath her. Her dress shifts with the movement as she settles in, and it looks like she's still deciding whether she belongs here.

I sit close beside her and let the quiet settle between us.

"You okay?" I ask, keeping my voice low in case any of my family members are eavesdropping.

She exhales and then nods. "Yes. Makes me realize how families are supposed to act."

"Your family doesn't get together?" I ask.

"They do, but no one wants to be there. I'd say it's like we're a bunch of strangers in a room, but after that friendly, welcoming experience, I'm not sure I can use that analogy again." She looks over at me, and something like gratitude flickers in her eyes. "You noticed I needed a breather."

"It was easy," I tell her. "I'd been watching you all night."

She huffs out a quiet laugh. "You're intense with your truth bombs."

"Maybe," I say, leaning back against the swing. "But it's not bullshit, which I'm sure you appreciate."

She lets the words hang between us and leans in a little closer.

"I don't remember the last time someone made sure I was okay."

"You deserve better than that," I tell her.

She turns toward me, and the way she glows in the warm porch light nearly knocks the breath out of me. Her hair is loose again, a little windblown. Her lipstick has worn off. She looks soft and a little raw.

"You're so fucking pretty."

I stretch one arm along the back of the swing, not quite touching her. She leans into the space like she's comfortable.

"I forgot what this felt like," she says.

"What?" I ask.

"Belonging. Even if it's for a night."

"You didn't just belong," I say. "You fit."

Her eyes meet mine, and I know I said too much, but I don't take it back.

We stay like this, with our shoulders touching, for several long seconds.

She tilts her head, studying me. "You're not what I expected."

"Good." I smile.

She brushes a piece of hair behind her ear, and the movement is small, but it unravels me.

I want to kiss her. I almost do. Instead, I lean away from her, against the armrest beside me, needing contact with something solid to keep myself grounded.

She glances away, her voice soft as she says, "We're fucked, aren't we?"

"Yep. We sure are," I say with a smile, appreciating the confirmation that we're on the same page.

Sunny laughs, scooting closer to me, not letting me escape her. I wrap my arm around her shoulders, and she leans her head against me, and that's how we stay for a long while.

We're two people caught between something neither of us can name.

CHAPTER ELEVEN

SUNNY

By the time we get back to the house, my body is tired, but my brain won't settle.

Dinner was beautiful. So many people talked over each other and somehow still listened. It was the type of chaos that filled an empty part of me. I felt like I belonged with them.

Colt's family is big, unfiltered, and kind. Every single one of them treated me like I was a gift. Summer offered to pack us leftovers. Kinsley asked if I wanted my palm read. Vera slipped a flower into my hand and complimented my dress.

Remi pulled me aside in the kitchen and said, "He's never brought anyone to dinner before. You should know that."

I'm still holding on to those words, but I don't want to admit how good it felt to be chosen.

This town is the opposite of everything I ran from. I'm not used to quiet nights, crickets, unlocked doors, or people who wave when they drive by. I don't have to dodge camera flashes or fake my way through small talk about hedge fund mergers or strategic branding partnerships. Valentine is a small town where people build lives, not résumés.

My face hurts from smiling so much. I move to the bedroom, still wearing the sundress, and sit on the edge of the bed.

The room is quiet and safe, but my curiosity gets the best of me.

I reach for my phone on the nightstand, even though I know I shouldn't.

No one's texted me—not that I expected them to, since no one has this number. I open the browser and type my name into the search bar. The headlines come fast and merciless.

Heiress Disappears Before Lavish NYC Wedding

Sources Say It Was Cold Feet

Tech Mogul Donovan Left Alone at Altar

PR Powerhouse Vanishes Without a Trace

THERE ARE PHOTOS TOO.

Donovan is standing in front of the venue with his bow tie, holding a glass of champagne like he's trying to appear composed and worried. In another one, he's sitting on the venue steps with his head in his hands, surrounded by security. The angles are too perfect, too staged. I know a planted narrative when I see one.

There's even a shot of my clothes in the bridal suite. The cute pink pantsuit I wore to the venue before I changed into the dress is hanging on the door. A caption underneath it reads: *No dress. No bride. No warning.*

I lock the screen and set the phone down with a little more force than necessary. My pulse increases, and my jaw clenches tight. That familiar tension curls around my heart like a snake.

I know that PR crisis language. I used it to bury stories worse than this.

But this time, I'm the story, and Donovan is acting like a victim.

And whoever fed them these quotes wants me to stay gone so they can rewrite it all.

Skye.

I inhale, then exhale through my nose, trying to calm myself down before it spirals out of control. My sister not only took my fiancé, but now she's working against me.

Colt walks in, running a hand through his hair, but he looks exhausted. He glances at me but doesn't push. He heads to the dresser to pull out a T-shirt.

I speak up before I can second-guess it. "Will you sleep in here again? From now on."

He pauses, then looks at me with a crooked smile. "Whatever will make you happy."

"You say that like you care," I say.

"I do," he admits, kicking off his boots. "I want the best for you."

A part of me knows that's true.

"You deserve someone who can love you like you need," I tell him. "I don't believe in love anymore."

He smiles. "You will."

"You're so confident." I remove my earrings and set them on the bedside table.

"My older brother always told me that when I met the woman I was supposed to be with, I'd know," he says, sounding too casual as he smiles.

"What does that feel like?" I ask, needing confirmation if this is what's swirling inside of me. It's never sizzled like this with anyone else, but right now, I don't trust myself or my emotions. I've been through too much shit, too fast.

He unbuttons his shirt, and I can't peel my eyes away from him.

"You tell me." He smiles. "I know you feel this too."

My breath hitches. "You're so direct."

"I don't have time to waste, darlin'. You're leaving in thirteen days. I plan to make each one count," he admits, sliding his belt from his jeans.

Colt moves to his dresser and pulls out a pair of black pajama pants.

I pull my gaze away from him.

"Please choose your favorite side," I add, trying to change the subject. "Or the whole bed. I don't care ..." I tug at a loose thread on the hem of my dress. "I sleep better when you're close. You calm everything down in me."

He glances at me like he can hear every single word I'm not saying.

"Welp, now that I know I calm you down, I might sleep in the middle."

The weight in my chest loosens enough to give me some relief.

He gets dressed for bed, and I steal glances at him, knowing I shouldn't.

When he turns around, he tosses me another shirt. "This one is soft."

I unfold the burgundy shirt and see his name written on the chest. On the back is the cattle brand he has tattooed on his chest. "Mmm. Trying to claim me with your family brand?"

This earns me a deep chuckle.

"Eventually," he says. "I need some water. I'm suddenly parched. Would you like a glass?"

"No thanks," I say.

He leaves the room, giving me privacy to change into his shirt. I glance at myself, wearing his name over my breast in the full-length oval mirror that's beside his dresser. When I turn, I look at the room and imagine beautiful artwork hanging above the bed, a plush rug under my feet, and a few tall lamps. The furniture is beautiful, all handmade. I wouldn't change a thing, only make small additions.

He walks in, catching me staring. "Imagining our future?" he asks.

I playfully roll my eyes, but the truth is, I was. I crawl under the covers and turn on the bedside lamp. "You're not used to chasing someone, are you?"

"No," he admits. "I've never had to work for it. Truthfully? I love it."

He climbs into bed and gives me space without feeling too distant. We lie there in the dark, not touching, not talking. Just breathing in the same rhythm.

"Good night," he says.

I move closer to him, and he wraps me in his arms. For the first time since I left New York, I don't want to run anymore. But based on the headlines, my past might catch up to me.

THE SUNLIGHT FILTERS IN, and I blink against it, finding myself already smiling, even before I open my eyes fully.

Colt is still asleep. One arm is tossed behind his head on the pillow, the other resting across his stomach. The sheet is low on his hips, and the sight of him, bare-chested, stubbled, almost makes me forget this is only temporary.

Almost.

I slide out of bed carefully and pad barefoot into the kitchen. He joins me a few minutes later, wearing a worn gray T-shirt and jeans, like sin disguised as simplicity. His hair is still sleep-ruffled, and he smells like soap and cedar and everything tempting. He's not wearing his glasses today.

"Morning," he says, grabbing a mug from the cabinet.

I nod, already sipping from mine. "How do you look that good without trying?"

He grins. "It's a burden. Always has been."

"Not for me," I mutter. "More like a treat."

He's too smug and too hot and far too comfortable in this house, in this kitchen, with me standing so close.

"You ready to run into town with me?" he asks, sipping his coffee.

"Do I have a choice?"

"Nope. It'll be good for ya," he offers. "Change of scenery."

After I'm dressed, I follow him out to the truck. The morning air is already warming up. It's a comfortable heat that wraps around you rather than beating you down. It smells like fresh grass and something sweet, like flowers.

Colt tosses a few bags into the bed of the truck before circling to open the passenger door for me. It's unnecessary and charming, which describes him far too well.

Once we're on the road, he drives with the windows down and one hand on the wheel, the other in the breeze. Every time he turns the wheel, his forearm flexes enough to make me forget what day it is. He hums along to a country song playing low on the radio, drumming his fingers against the steering wheel in a rhythm that feels carefree. I steal a glance at him when he smiles, and something about it lands too deep in my heart, too fast. He looks like a man who's never had to second-guess whether he belongs somewhere.

The wind lifts strands of my hair across my cheek, and I close my eyes for a second, letting the sunlight kiss my skin. It's warm, and I feel alive. This is the closest thing I've ever had to true freedom.

It will eventually come to an end, and I try to remind myself of that. But sitting here, in his truck, in this tiny town, with nowhere to be and everything to feel—it makes me want to believe things could be different. That could be true if I were someone different. But I'm not.

We head down Main Street, and he pulls the truck into the gravel road of the feed store.

Colt's practically a local celebrity in boots and a ball cap, speaking to every third person we pass. Before we even make it inside, an older gentleman stops him to chat about his house.

"The rumor is that old place is haunted. You think it is?"

"No, sir," Colt tells him with a chuckle. "Only thing hauntin' those walls are me and my music."

"Tell your daddy I said hello," the guy says with a wave. He gives me a nod, then heads to his truck.

Colt opens the door for me, and we walk inside.

Everyone knows him by name. But today, they look at me too. Not in a judgmental way or with surprise, but rather curiosity—like they've already heard the story of me and they're now seeing how it plays out in real time.

The woman behind the counter glances at our hands like she expects them to be linked. I keep mine at my side, but the air between us feels warmer than it should. I can read it on every person's face—they all believe we're a couple.

"Need to get some feed for the horses. Few bales of alfalfa too. Have 'em load it for me, please," he says, glancing at me. "Would you like anything? A Coke? Candy?"

"No, thank you," I tell him as he pays.

He places his hand on the small of my back as he leads me through the store and back outside. A few teenagers are already placing the items he purchased in the bed of the truck. Colt slips them a few dollars, then opens my door.

"Ready for stop number two?" he asks.

I nod, but my voice is caught somewhere in my throat as we pull into the parking lot of the local nursery.

The moment we step onto the gravel path, I smell earth and blooming things and sun-warmed stone. Vera isn't working today, but every flowerpot we pass feels like something she put together. Lavender, creeping thyme, and wild roses stretch toward the sky.

Colt crouches to inspect a flat of basil, running a hand over the leaves, like he's making sure they're strong enough to be chosen. I stand beside him, arms crossed, watching the muscles in his back shift beneath his T-shirt when he moves.

He glances up, catches me staring, and grins. "You're not even pretending not to stare."

"Don't need to," I admit, folding my arms tighter to keep from reaching for him.

He straightens, brushing a bit of dirt from his palms. "Pick something out for the herb garden I'm planting."

I wander a little, trailing my fingers along the edge of a glazed pot until I find what I'm searching for. I hold it up.

"This one," I say. "Cilantro. If you plant tomatoes and onions, then we can have salsa."

"Love that idea." Colt reaches for my hand without thinking. It's instinctive, smooth, like he's done it a thousand times before. His palm is warm against mine, his fingers wrapping around like a promise I didn't ask for.

"You're really committed to the bit," I say as we head back to the truck, but I don't let go of him.

His thumb brushes over the top of my hand. "As long as you're convinced, that's all that matters to me," he says, shooting me a side-glance.

I shake my head but find myself smiling. *Flirt.*

By the time we reach the grocery store, the heat has crept higher, baking off the pavement and making everything sizzle. We take our time inside, picking up things we probably don't need. I chuckle in the aisle when he pushes the cart alongside me.

As we check out, he grabs two bottles of cream soda from the small fridge and puts them on the belt. "You gotta try this."

I do.

I take it without speaking, and we move to the checkout together, hand in hand, like it's second nature.

The woman ringing us up doesn't blink. "You two going to the rodeo this weekend?"

I open my mouth to respond, but Colt beats me to it.

"We wouldn't miss it."

He doesn't look at me when he says it, but I can see the smile tugging at his mouth.

Outside, the sun presses hot against my skin as we climb into the truck. I sink into the passenger seat, the cilantro and basil plants resting in my lap, the cream soda cold in my hand.

Colt starts the engine and lets his arm fall across the back of my seat as he backs out.

"You're quiet," he says.

"I'm thinking," I reply.

I turn toward the window, watching the town roll by. It's all dusty roads, shop windows, and hanging baskets overflowing with petunias. Locals wave, and Colt returns it. I can't help but smile when I see a dog napping in front of the bakery.

He nods once. "About what?"

"About how this place feels like home."

Colt doesn't say anything. His hand squeezes mine, but I don't pull away. I just smile.

CHAPTER TWELVE

COLT

Another day of working beside Sunny. One less day I'll get to spend with her before she leaves.

I've hand-sanded this same damn section of baseboard three times. Partly because I want it smooth so it's easier to paint, but mostly because I can't stop glancing at her.

Sunny's crouched on the floor at the other end of the hallway, barefoot, covered in specks of white paint. She's wearing a sports bra and the shortest pair of cutoffs I've ever seen. Her hair's piled on top of her head in a messy knot, and she's humming along to the playlist she created on my phone. And right now, I am not okay.

The house is warm today; the air conditioner seems to be struggling. So, we opened the windows, along with the front and back door, so a draft would blow through. Box fans are running, but sweat still clings to the back of my neck. Even so, this Texas heat ain't nothing compared to her.

She's on her knees, bent forward slightly, while she smooths a bead of caulk across the baseboards like she's done it a hundred times. My girl is a natural at renovations, and she strives for perfection.

She's completely unbothered by the fact that I'm hanging on by a thread over here. I shift my grip on the sandpaper and try not to steal a peek again, but I fail miserably.

This time, she glances over, catches me staring, and lifts an eyebrow like she's half amused.

"You okay, cowboy?"

I blink. "Yeah. Just checking your ... *lines.*"

Curves.

She stands and stretches her arms overhead, spine arching just enough to make me forget what words are. I see her flat stomach and her cute little belly button.

Must. Stop. Staring.

"You've gone quiet on me," she says, reaching to grab more painter's tape. "Makes a girl wonder if she's doing something wrong."

"Nothing's wrong," I mutter. "You're just extremely distracting."

She grins like she's satisfied. "Not my fault."

"Oh, please. It's definitely your fault."

"It's a burden," she says, batting her eyes at me.

It's the words I told her a few mornings ago when she couldn't stop staring at me. The attraction swirling between us is explosive and undeniable.

I go back to sanding more baseboards with a little more focus than necessary, hoping like hell she can't see the effect she's having on me. But judging by the smirk she's wearing, she knows, and she's enjoying it. We work like that for a while—me sanding then hanging, her caulking and painting. It should feel like a task, but it doesn't. It feels like teamwork, and we're building something together, even if neither of us knows what that is.

When she passes behind me, her shoulder brushes mine.

She doesn't move away fast, but neither do I.

Eventually, she returns to where she was working. Sunlight streams across her thighs, and I glance away before I do something stupid, like drop to my knees, place my palms on her cheeks, and kiss her.

I never expected the hand-holding, family dinners, or small-town smoke and mirrors. I didn't expect to memorize the curve of her back while she helped to paint my hallway, or to have her enjoy this place like it was more than just a detour.

She's going to ruin me if I'm not careful. Truth is, I'm okay with it.

We take a break in the late afternoon when the sun has turned mean and the hallway smells like paint and pinewood and whatever magic lives in her shampoo. I grab two bottles of water from the fridge. Sunny's already sitting on the floor, her back against the wall, legs stretched out in front of her, which are speckled with dried paint.

I hand her one.

"Are you always this intense?" she asks.

I sit down across from her, wiping sweat from my brow with the back of my hand. "Only around pretty girls."

She smiles as she takes a long sip, the water bottle pressed against her lower lip. My eyes flick there for half a second too long. She doesn't miss it.

"Is this where I apologize for the shorts?" she teases.

"No," I say, my voice rougher than I meant it to be. "This is where I try not to ask you to wear them every day."

She laughs, light and easy, but when she leans her head back against the wall, the expression on her face shifts into something quieter. "This is the most I've smiled in months," she says. "It feels good."

I nod. "Looks good too."

She glances around the room, eyes landing on the unfinished trim, the paint rollers, and the boxes of screws that are lying around. We sit in the stillness for a few moments. The hum of the fans and the chirp of cicadas outside fill the space where words don't need to be.

"I never thought I'd enjoy building something that wasn't mine."

I follow her gaze. "It could be yours."

She blinks. "What?"

"I'm taking wife applications." I rest my arm on my bent knee, watching her. The mood grows serious. "This house was never only about finishing a project. I'm fixing it up for a future I wasn't sure I'd ever have. One I only imagined was possible," I admit.

She doesn't speak, only watches me like I'm saying something that wasn't supposed to be said out loud, but I don't care.

I glance away, my voice a little quieter now. "I told myself that if I built a strong foundation and became the best version of myself possible, the right woman would show up." I feel as if I've said too much, gotten too deep, so I add, "And if she didn't ... at least I'd have a damn good porch to sit on, alone.

"No one else in my life can see what this house will be one day. Just you."

The sunlight shifts through the open door, casting long golden lines across the floor. It lands on her knees, then across her collarbone, lighting her up like a promise.

She lifts her water but doesn't drink from it. Her eyes are still on me.

"I see it," she says. "The hardwood floors, high ceilings, large windows, and open space." She smiles like she's imagining it. "It will be beautiful."

"It already is," I say, not taking my eyes from her.

For a minute, neither of us moves.

I clear my throat. "We should pick up our mess, then get ready to go. Kinsley said she's gonna drop off some clothes for ya," I explain as I pick up the paint trays and brushes.

"Great. I'm excited to attend my first rodeo," she says.

"Lookin' forward to it," I tell her.

Sunny disappears down the hall to take a shower, and I wipe

down the counters and try not to think too hard about her being just one door away, wet and naked.

I fail miserably.

As I finish cleaning up, sweeping the hallway, I hear a car pull up. A moment later, the screen door creaks open, and there's a light knock.

"Coming!" I call out, leaning the broom against the wall.

"Delivery service, Southern edition," she singsongs. "I expect a tip!"

I meet her at the door. She's in cutoff overalls, flip-flops, and sunglasses that are way too big for her face. In her hand is a huge canvas bag that's been packed with enthusiasm rather than logic because clothes are hanging out of the top.

"You said one outfit. This is your closet," I say, taking it from her.

"Options are important." She winks, then props a hand on her hip. "I'm waiting for my thank-you."

"Thank you," I tell her. "Thanks for saving the day."

"Where is she?" Kinsley glances past me.

"In the shower," I explain.

Kinsley raises her eyebrows. "And you're standing here, talking to me, instead of joining her?"

"Jesus, Kins."

"What?" she says, laughing. "I'm just saying, if someone I was mutually attracted to was showering under my roof, I wouldn't be standing around talking to you."

"It's not ..." I pause because I don't know how to finish that sentence anymore. "It's not like that."

Kinsley narrows her eyes like she's reading the truth straight off my face. "You're adorable and in denial."

"I'm not. Want to come in?" I ask.

"Thought you'd never ask." My sister steps inside, amazed. She doesn't stop smiling as she enters the living room. "I pulled your tarot last night."

"I said I didn't want to know." I groan, hoping Sunny can't hear this ridiculous conversation.

"Come on. Don't be a sourpuss. Appease me."

I cross my arms over my chest. "Fine."

She steps in front of me, glowing. "The Tower. Total upheaval. You built your whole life one way, and then something—or someone—knocks it flat. Present card? The Moon. Confusion, hidden feelings, resisting what's obvious. Basically, you're lying to yourself, and it's not even subtle." She holds out her hand like this is case in point. "And your future position?" She pauses dramatically. "The Ace of Cups. A new emotional beginning. Big, romantic energy. Like *life-altering love* kind of stuff."

She grabs my arms and shakes me with excitement. "I'm so happy for you right now! Ahh!"

"None of that means anything. You know that, right?" I lift my brow.

She pokes her finger into my chest. "You'll eat those words, little brother. The cards don't lie."

The water turns off, and Kinsley waggles her brows at me.

"Thanks for the clothes."

"Anytime," she says over her shoulder. "Tell Sunny the sparkly boots are from Summer. She said no girlfriend of yours is showing up to the rodeo in ballerina flats.

"You've done a damn good job in here. Can't wait to see it finished."

"Me too. Thanks, sis," I say, and she gives me a hug before pulling away.

I walk her out, standing on the porch as she moves to her truck. "Now, how about you marry her? Give me some nieces and nephews?"

"Maybe I will," I say under my breath as my sister drives off.

She gives me two quick honks, and then she's out of sight.

As soon as I return inside, the bathroom door creaks open, and Sunny steps into the hallway.

A fluffy towel is wrapped around her body, and another one is twisted on her head. She's barefoot, glowing, and not aware she's about to ruin me. Or maybe she is.

Her eyes land on the bag in my hand.

"Did she deliver a closet?" she asks, like this is the most normal interaction we've ever had.

"That's what I said." I try not to sound like my brain just stopped functioning. "Kinsley said the sparkly boots are from Summer."

I walk over to her, carefully keeping my eyes on her face and not on the fact that her collarbone is still damp and the towel is dangerously low on her chest.

"Thanks. I honestly don't deserve any of this," she says, reaching for the bag.

Her fingers graze mine, and that's all it takes for heat to crawl down the back of my neck.

"Of course you do, darlin'. You deserve it all."

She holds the bag against her hip and gives me that gorgeous smile of hers. "Don't go anywhere."

I blink. "What?"

"I need your help," she says, backing toward the door. "I want to seem like I belong at this rodeo, and if anyone can help me pass, it's you. Being a cowboy is your wheelhouse."

I stare at her. "You want me to pick out your clothes?"

"Yep," she says, amused. "Help me play the part."

She disappears into the bedroom with a laugh and the bag of clothes swinging at her side, leaving me standing in the hallway like I've been punched in the chest.

I press my hands to my hips and shake my head. This woman is going to be the end of me. And the worst part is, I don't even mind.

Without a word, I step inside with her, and I can't help but notice how naturally gorgeous she is. My brain short-circuits.

She's wrapped in a single white towel, her bare legs and

shoulders still dewy from the shower. Her hair's damp and already curling at the ends. She smells like soap and something vaguely citrus. Carefully, she empties the big bag on the bed, sending different-colored fabrics spilling everywhere. On top are the sparkly silver boots.

"Okay," she says, hands on her hips. "Make me a rodeo princess."

I notice the curve of her collarbone, how the towel clings just above her chest, the line of her thigh when she shifts her weight to one leg. I've never had the urge to kiss someone more in my life.

She glances back at me. "You with me, cowboy?"

Barely.

"Yeah," I say, clearing my throat, stepping closer to the bed.

I force myself to focus on the pile in front of me.

"Darlin', you'd better be glad I grew up with so many sisters."

"I am," she says as I spread all the shirts and shorts on the bed.

There are crop tops, tank tops, and short-sleeved checkered-pattern shirts in different colors.

"Let's start with this." I grab a blouse with a ruffle and hand it to her, then grab a pair of dark-washed cutoffs. "With these shorts. It's a good outfit. Honest."

She takes them from me, fingers brushing against mine. "Honest," she repeats. "Is that cowboy code for *tight?*"

"It's cowboy code for *you're gonna kill me, along with every other man who's there tonight.*"

She laughs, then picks up the cutoffs. "Just my size."

My throat goes dry.

She tosses them onto the bed. "Hmm, there's only one thing missing."

"What's that?" I ask.

"A cowboy hat."

I cross my arms over my chest and tilt my head at her. "You know what they say. Wear the hat and ..."

Her brows lift. "And what?"

Words disappear.

I excuse myself and walk into the closet, grabbing one of my cowboy hats. When I return, I place it on her head. "Wear the hat, ride the cowboy."

That lip finds its way between her teeth. I turn her around to face the full-length mirror. She adjusts the brim as she checks her reflection. This woman is wrapped in a towel, wearing my hat, and smiling like she knows *exactly* what she's doing to me.

I drag a hand down my face. "You're dangerous."

She turns, wide-eyed and innocent. "Me?"

"*You.*"

She takes a step closer to me. Not much, but it's enough for me to notice.

"Good," she says. "I like keeping you on your toes."

I want to press her back against that dresser, pull her face into my hands, and kiss her like I've been thinking about doing since the first time she smiled at me like that. But instead, I clear my throat and step away. Boundaries cannot be crossed.

"You've got fifteen minutes," I tell her. "If you're not ready by the time I'm done showerin', I'm comin' to finish the job myself."

She smirks. "Promise?"

With a chuckle, I move into the hallway to give her privacy. She's going to be the death of me, and I'm starting to think I'd let her.

I take the fastest shower I can manage, letting the cold water run longer than necessary to help cool me off. It doesn't help as much as I'd like. My pulse is still racing. My mind's still back in the bedroom, stuck on the image of her skin wrapped in that towel, wearing a smile that feels like it was reserved just for me.

When I step out, my hair is still dripping, and I've got a towel slung low on my hips.

I walk into my bedroom, and she's sitting cross-legged in the middle of the bed like she belongs there. One hand is flipping through the pages of the leather journal I gave her, and the other is twirling a pen between her fingers. She freezes when she sees me.

I smirk, knowing two can play this game. Her gaze starts at my face, travels down past my tattoo, and lingers a little too long on my stomach before landing squarely on my cock.

"Something wrong, darlin'?" I ask, my voice calm, enjoying this more than I should.

She opens her mouth to speak, but nothing comes out.

I cross the room to my dresser and pull out a clean pair of jeans. I know she's still watching me because I catch her in the mirror. I let the towel fall and make no effort to hide myself as I pull on some boxers and Wranglers.

I hear her suck in a sharp breath behind me.

I smile to myself as I button and zip my jeans. "You sure you're too damn old for this?"

Her silence tells me she's trying to form a comeback, but can't quite find one.

I turn toward her, still shirtless, noticing how she's ogling me. "That's what I thought."

She shakes her head and laughs, flustered, but trying not to show it. She closes the journal a little too quickly.

"I think I liked you better when you were shy," she says.

"I was never shy. Just respectful," I reply, putting on an undershirt, then moving to my walk-in closet. "Had to see if you could handle it."

"Guess I passed?"

I dip my head out of the closet. "Ya did. Now I'm gonna make sure I'm not the only one losing my mind in this house. You tease me. I'mma tease you back."

She scoffs. "Is that a threat?"

I grab a black Western shirt with pearl buttons and slide it on over my shoulders, then grab my nice pair of boots. I move to the bed, sitting beside her as I put them on. "That's a damn promise."

We're close—too close—and her smile softens as she stares at me. Sunny moves her journal onto the nightstand and swings her legs over the bed.

"Ready to go show off?" I ask.

"I suppose," she says.

She stands—boots already on, shirt on, cutoffs barely legal, and that damn hat tilted so effortlessly. I adjust her shirt, pushing the sleeves down her shoulders.

"Should be worn like this," I tell her, noticing goose bumps trail across her arms when I touch her.

The golden light from the window cuts across her bare shoulders and legs, and for a second, I forget we're not strangers.

I take a step back just to get a full view, like I need distance to survive it.

"Damn," I say because it's the only thing that makes it out of my mouth. "You're a cowboy princess."

She grins, tilting the brim of the hat. "Yeah?"

"You're dressed like you belong," I confess.

She walks toward me with lethal confidence.

"Well," she says, stopping just shy of my chest, "that was kind of the point."

I stare at her lips for a beat too long. "Behave."

"No promises," she offers as she brushes past me.

Every part of me wants to reach for her. Touch her. Say something that means more than it's supposed to. But instead, I grab my keys and follow her out the door, trying to pretend she isn't exactly what I've been waiting for my entire life.

CHAPTER THIRTEEN

SUNNY

T he fairground lights come into view long before we pull into the lot. Rows of trucks line the dirt road. The air is thick with dust and the kind of excitement that can't be faked. A steady thump of country music hums through the evening heat, layered with laughter and the occasional cheer from the arena. In the distance, there's a Ferris wheel and a few carnival rides.

Colt drives with one hand on the wheel, the other resting casually on the console between us. His fingers tap out a rhythm like he's at ease, but I can feel the energy rolling off him. It's focused, a little wired, or maybe that's only me. I try to keep my breathing even.

This isn't the first time I've gone somewhere where all eyes will be on me, but I'm nervous. I want to fit in here.

Colt kills the engine, and we sit still. I'm suddenly hyperaware of everything. The cutoffs clinging to my legs. The weight of his hat on my head. Nerves flutter beneath the surface of my skin. I've stood in front of thousands of people before, but this is different. I care if this town likes me.

His eyes move from my neck to my waist to my thighs, like he's memorizing something. Or maybe warning himself not to.

"Are ya ready?" he asks with a lazy smile.

"Are you?" I counter.

He grins wider, and it's easy, cocky, and unfairly hot. "I was born ready, darlin', especially for this."

Colt hops out of the truck and walks around the front to open my door. He's wearing a black Stetson, and it suits him. I step out into the buzz of the small-town energy. The rodeo grounds are packed with trucks lined up like dominoes. Horse trailers are parked on the other side. The air smells like kettle corn and fried food with the faint scent of hay. Kids run wild with gigantic sticks of bright blue cotton candy while speakers blast country music. In the distance, an announcer speaks, followed by cheers from the crowd.

"This is unreal," I whisper.

It's like we're walking onto a Hollywood set, and the two of us are the main characters.

"I'd agree with that," he says.

Our hands brush together, and then Colt catches mine, interlocking our fingers like they belong there. I feel that electric shift again. It's the same one I experienced the moment our eyes met in Remi's kitchen when he dropped that mug and it shattered across the floor.

As we enter the fairgrounds, laughter and gossip are already in motion. Sweat gathers at the back of my neck, and I don't think I've ever felt this way in my entire damn life. Colt greets everyone we pass by name, even the little kids, offering howdies and head nods. The small talk he makes is smooth and polite. He's incredibly charming, and I find a man with manners very sexy. But I remind myself that the bar I have set for men is in hell. It's why I don't trust myself or my decisions right now.

Colt glances over at me, and his perfect lips tug at the corner of his mouth. "Lookin' real good, darlin'."

My cheeks heat, and I almost forget the role I'm supposed to be playing to fool the town. "Do you think they're buying it?" I lean in and ask him.

He leans over and whispers in my ear, "No doubt 'cause I almost am."

His hot breath and lips so close to the softness of my neck makes me lose my fucking mind.

"Stop flirting," I tell him as my heart pitter-patters a little harder.

If he doesn't stop, I might do something I shouldn't, like trip the wire between our boundaries. He's walked the fine line but hasn't crossed it.

I'm not convinced he will, and I don't know if I can.

It's a dangerous place to be while the clock counts down. Part of me doesn't want to leave with regret because what if Colt Valentine is the best damn thing that's ever happened to me?

We walk hand in hand, past a small crowd near the food trucks and deeper into the heart of it all. The scents of charcoal and cattle settle in my lungs, and the excitement of the crowd watching mutton bustin' washes over me. Kids hang on to the back of sheep as they bolt out of the gate super fast.

Colt covers his mouth and yells, "Keep holdin' on."

A few seconds later, the little girl rolls off onto the ground.

"Do they raise you to do that?"

Colt licks his lips, meeting my eyes. "Yep."

He glances away, and I'm so damn thankful for it.

I cannot fall in love with this man. I cannot.

With an easy stride and cowboy confidence, he pulls me away so we can continue the tour around the arena and vendor area. I like seeing him in his element, but he's never too far from me. Our bodies constantly touch, and neither of us pulls away, even though it drives me wild.

"Thirsty?" he finally asks, looking up at a six-foot lemon on top of a booth.

"Oh, you have *no* idea," I mutter, waggling my brows at him.

"I got something that will quench your thirst," he adds, shooting me a wink as he steps up to the booth.

I snicker beside him as he orders us two of the biggest hand-squeezed lemonades possible. A minute later, we're holding lemon-shaped cups. I take a sip, hoping this cools the heat bubbling inside me. It's sweet and refreshing, like Colt.

"The last public event I was at was with Tessa," he says. "Everyone thought I'd get back with her."

"Oh," I say, twirling the straw around in my big cup. "Being here is a bigger deal than I thought."

"Apparently. Too many people in my business." He takes a long drink before scanning the crowd.

"You're proving them wrong," I tell him. "Good job. You should be proud. That shit is hard to do, not everyone can. It's sending a clear message."

"Which is?" he says.

"You're moving on. Congrats."

He reaches for my hand and threads his fingers through mine. "And what about you?"

Families, couples, friends in boots and jeans and cowboy hats steal glances at us as we pass them. Thankfully, I understand how to act in the spotlight.

I breathe in a little deeper, not knowing how to respond. "I'm not going backward."

Music spills from the speakers strung across the arena, where they're doing barrel racing. Light beams down overhead. This place is alive and packed. The two of us take a seat on the bleachers and watch.

"Fenix has the record."

I draw circles on his palm. "She doesn't ride anymore—like, at all?"

"No." He lets out a long sigh. "I heard rumors that she quit college and riding because of someone else."

"Who?" I ask, wanting to know more.

"I was told a broken heart can destroy a person," he explains. "She doesn't talk to anyone about it. Still hasn't started riding again. Beckett and Harrison have begged her to give lessons at their barn. Sponsors call her every damn week."

The crowd perks up as the announcer's voice cuts through the summer haze, interrupting our conversation.

"All right, folks, keep your eyes on the chute. Up next, riding out of West Texas with more championship buckles than I can count, Jace Tucker."

The name means nothing to me, but the crowd goes wild. I scan around and realize it's nothing but women. This man has a fan club.

Colt's posture shifts beside me—shoulders back, arms crossed over his chest. "Well, I'll be damned."

I squint toward the gate as the rider appears—tall, lean, and confident in that quiet way that makes a woman look twice. He adjusts the brim of his hat, loops the rope once around his hand, and settles into the saddle like he was born there.

The calf bolts from the chute. Everything after that happens too fast for me to track. Jace leans low, the rope spinning above him once, twice, and then he lets it fly. It lands clean around the calf's neck, and before I even blink, he's off the horse and on the ground, tying it in three quick motions around its legs like it's second nature.

The whole thing takes seconds. Maybe less.

The crowd roars.

Colt lets out a slow clap. "Still has it. Of course he does."

"Who is he?" I ask, watching as Jace tips his hat toward the stands and heads for the rail with unhurried ease.

"Jace Tucker," Colt says. "Used to live here. Was best friends with Emmett. Raised hell, won everything, and then he packed up and went pro. One of the best ropers in the circuit."

"He's good," I admit, still watching him.

Colt glances at me sideways. "Don't get any ideas, darlin'."

I smirk. "Relax. He's not my type. Way too young. Under twenty-five is a hell no."

"Yeah?" Colt raises an eyebrow.

"Also, too much swagger. Don't want to be with a man who craves attention or has a fan club," I say, even though I can't quite stop watching the way Jace moves, confident, like a man who takes what he wants.

Colt grunts. "Mm-hmm. That swagger's about to cause some trouble."

I glance across the arena; I catch someone else watching Jace.

Fenix.

Her jaw's tight, and her arms are crossed over her chest. And whatever she's thinking—whatever that look means—I get the feeling I just watched a fuse light itself. She's livid.

Colt tilts his head as he watches them. His brows furrow.

"What?" I ask.

"If I find out Jace is the reason Fenix stopped riding," he says, more to himself than anything else, "I'll fucking kill him."

I squeeze his thigh and pull him out of whatever big-brother spiral he's in.

He wraps his arm around me. "We should probably head to the stage. London plays at nine. We miss it, and she'll never forgive us."

"Let's not be late."

We scoot out of the bleachers and wander past food trucks, where people are gathering near a stage.

String lights blink on above us, and London strums her guitar. It's a song that's easy, one meant to draw people onto the grass in front of the stage.

"Wow, she's incredible," I say, recognizing talent immediately.

"Yeah. I'm proud of her," he says. "She's been working hard. Wants to make a career out of it. Now that she's twenty-one, she's been booking more gigs."

We move closer, and London spots us. She shoots me a wink as she continues her song.

"Would you like to dance?" Colt asks.

"I don't dance," I say.

He holds his hand out to me. "Come on. Because you don't know how?"

"I know how," I admit, taking his grasp as he pulls me close to him. I giggle. "I have two left feet. I suck at it."

"Maybe you had sucky partners?"

His arm slips around my waist, and my body reacts before I can tell it not to.

"Or I'm the common denominator," I say.

He spins me around and dips me.

"Doubt it," he mutters, nearly stealing my ability to speak.

We reach the dance area, where couples are already swaying under the string lights. Colt pulls me closer, and I settle into him, my heart thudding against his chest. We sway together, and I think this is something I could get used to. The grass beneath our boots is soft, the lights warm above us, and the rest of the world fades away.

We're so damn close, and I feel his breath on my temple. I inhale him, and he smells like cedar and clean soap and the kind of safety I don't let myself want. I lift my chin enough to meet his gaze, and he's looking at me like I'm already his. Like I always have been. And suddenly, I can't remember what part of this was supposed to be pretend.

I want to kiss him.

I want to feel his lips brush across mine, but I don't close the space. I don't ask for more. It's not a line I can cross with him, not when I know my time here is slipping away. Instead, I keep moving, caught in a slow circle under glowing lights, pretending my hands aren't trembling and my heart isn't halfway to his already.

"This is right," he confesses, and I can hear the smile in his voice as he holds me a little tighter.

His words hit harder than I expect. I pull back enough to meet his soft summer-sky-blue eyes, full of adoration.

"I'm glad I'm in Valentine," I tell him.

The song ends, and he spins me gently, dipping me on the final note.

"Would you like some Valentine in you?" he asks.

I laugh—loud and full and completely unfiltered—as the lights flicker above us and the crowd claps for London. It's too much and not enough all at once.

"Hilarious."

With Colt, it's easy to forget everything waiting for me back home.

We're still laughing as we wander past the dance floor, hand in hand, the music soft behind us. Colt's arm is warm against mine, and my body feels too light—like something in me got shaken loose during that dance and hasn't landed yet.

He glances down at me and gives my hand a squeeze. "Not bad for a girl with two left feet."

"A good partner makes a difference," I shoot back.

He leads me down a row of tents, where booths are selling candles, hand-stitched aprons, and homemade jams. Someone waves him over for a raffle ticket. Another woman hands him a flyer for the quilt auction on Monday.

"Oh my God, there you are," a voice calls from behind us.

We both turn as a blur of denim moves toward us. Fenix.

She skids to a stop in front of us, cheeks flushed, holding a clipboard like she's on a mission. Her anger from seeing Jace has faded.

"I've been looking for you everywhere." Her eyes lock on Colt.

He raises an eyebrow. "Why?"

"You, dear brother," she says with dramatic flair, "must've

forgotten you volunteered for the Valentine Rodeo Bachelor Auction."

"I have a girlfriend," Colt says immediately, already taking a step back. "Absolutely not."

"Oh, come on. You were a selling point. You're on the list," she says. "Backing out is a bitch move."

I meet his eyes. "She's right."

Colt scoffs. "You're serious? What if I meet the woman of my dreams?"

"Then it was meant to be," I tell him, hating that idea.

"It's one evening," she says. "Only a few hours of light flirting for charity. You're being auctioned off to help the animal shelter. It's harmless."

"Flirting for charity?" I repeat, trying not to laugh.

Fenix winks at me. "You know it."

Colt sighs and scrubs a hand over his face. "This is ridiculous."

"Community service," she corrects. "With a spotlight."

I enjoy their dynamic. It's cute. I can see how much he cares for her.

"She's forcing me, and you're allowing this," he says, playfully bumping into me.

"It's for a good cause," I remind him.

Fenix beams, holding up the clipboard. "You're up first, big bro."

"Of course I am."

She turns on her heel and disappears into the tent, shouting something about checking the microphone.

I turn to Colt, who is watching her go with defeated patience.

"You okay?" I ask, nudging him.

He looks down at me. "I'm getting auctioned off like a prize-winning steer. I'm hanging on by a thread."

I laugh. "You'll be fine."

He narrows his eyes playfully. "You'd better bid on me."

My heart skips. "Or what?"

"You gonna let someone else take me home?"

The question is teasing, but it lands deep.

"No," I say quietly, "I'm not."

I glance toward the stage, where a few men are lining up, all in button-ups, muscles, and fresh jeans.

"Guess I should get goin'," he says, leading me inside.

The auction tent is packed. People are gathered in rows of folding chairs, drinks in hand, buzzing with anticipation, like this is the main event—and apparently, it is. I had no idea fundraising for an animal shelter could come with so much eyeliner and competitive energy.

Colt's dragged off by Fenix, and the expression on his face as she shoves him behind the curtain is priceless.

Summer waves me over to a seat near the front, and I slide in beside her. Kinsley's already on my other side, fanning herself dramatically with a flyer that says *Bachelors & Bulldogs* across the top in curly font.

"This is my favorite part of the summer," Kinsley says, practically vibrating. "You never know who's going to bid on who —or who's going to throw a drink over it."

Kinsley leans over and hands me a flask. "Want a drink?"

"Sure," I tell her, downing a huge gulp of cinnamon booze. My nose scrunches. "Yuck."

I pass it to Summer.

"No thanks, I'm pregnant."

"Oh, wow! Congrats. I had no idea," I tell her.

For some reason, I hug her, and Summer leans in and hugs me back.

"Are you enjoying your time here?"

"Loving it," I say, glancing around the room. "Is this auction competitive?"

"Oh, yeah. One year, a woman drove here from Houston to bid on Harrison."

"Did she win?"

"Oh, she won," Summer says. "But he ghosted her the next day."

"Rough," I mutter.

Kinsley sips from her lemonade. "Cowboys are only loyal to their dogs."

"Except Colt," Summer adds, nudging me. "Colt's one of the good ones."

I try to smile like I'm unaffected, like I didn't feel something low in my stomach turn over at the sound of his name.

The emcee—a woman in a rhinestone-trimmed blazer and jeans—welcomes everyone to the show. She introduces the first few bachelors. They're all local ranch hands and volunteers from nearby towns. The bids are playful, mostly in the forty-to-sixty-dollar range. One guy gets one hundred dollars and a standing ovation. The crowd's having fun.

But when Colt's name is called, the mood in the room shifts.

There's an audible buzz, mixed with low, unhinged excitement. The lights fade, and he steps out onto the stage, wearing dark jeans, boots, and a black button-down. His hat is pushed up enough to show the sharp line of his jaw. He has the nerve to look both annoyed and amused at the same time.

A woman two rows behind me gasps.

"Oh, he's in trouble," Kinsley whispers, realizing the vultures are out.

Colt offers a tight smile and a mock salute. Fenix, who is now the emcee's assistant, grabs the mic and starts listing his "skills," which include house repairs and being good with his big, strong hands.

"Show them those abs," she says. "Go ahead. Unbutton the shirt."

Colt glares at her, and if looks could kill, she'd be over. He begrudgingly opens his shirt, and the women in the room go feral.

"Opening bid is twenty dollars!" the emcee calls.

Ten bidding paddles, shaped like the state of Texas, shoot up.

Summer leans toward me. "Okay, you should be nervous."

"Should I?" I ask.

"One hundred!" someone calls.

"One hundred fifty!"

"One seventy-five!"

A woman near the back raises her hand and purrs, "Two hundred fifty. Take it off!"

The tent erupts with laughter.

Colt shakes his head. "My mother is here somewhere!"

"He's gonna have to move out of town after this," Kinsley says, delighted.

"Three hundred. Do I hear three fifty?"

"Four hundred!"

"Five hundred!"

The number climbs, and I try to act like I'm entertained. But something shifts inside me, and it's undeniably possessive.

I don't want someone else to win him. I don't want this to be a joke anymore. I want it to be me.

The numbers keep climbing.

"Five fifty!"

"Six hundred!"

"Seven hundred!"

Women fill every corner of the tent—laughing, shouting, waving their bid cards with lust in their eyes. They all want that cowboy fantasy named Colt Valentine.

He stands on a plywood platform, visibly annoyed and slightly pink in the ears, resembling a model. I've met men in New York who wished they had this facial structure and physique. He shifts his weight, one boot slightly in front of the other, arms crossed over his chest like he's refusing to play along, but it drives the ladies wild.

His eyes scan the crowd, and he finds me.

"Help?" he whispers.

Beside me, Summer leans in. "Not gonna bid?"

"I'd rather let him sweat a little," I whisper.

"Seven hundred fifty!" a high-pitched voice calls.

Colt's brow lifts slightly.

"Eight hundred!"

Kinsley lets out a low whistle. "This is starting to get serious."

"I don't like this," I admit, even though I don't sound nearly as casual as I want to.

"Eight fifty!"

"Nine hundred!"

The emcee's smiling so wide now; I'm half worried her face might crack.

"Do I hear one thousand for Colt Valentine?"

A new voice cuts through the noise. "Two thousand."

It's not shouted. It doesn't have to be because the second we all hear it, the entire tent goes quiet.

Colt's head snaps toward the sound, and I already know who it is before I even turn.

Tessa.

There she is, standing at the edge of the crowd in a white tank top, skinny jeans, and heels that don't belong anywhere near hay. Her arms are crossed, her chin lifts enough to be condescending, and her eyes are fixed on Colt like she's claiming something from lost and found.

Whispers ripple around us, and Summer stiffens beside me. Kinsley mutters something under her breath that sounds an awful lot like a threat. Colt's jaw tightens.

The emcee clears her throat, suddenly flustered. "Uh, do I hear twenty-five hundred?"

Every eye in the tent turns to his ex, who's smirking like she's already won.

CHAPTER FOURTEEN

COLT

The emcee clears her throat, caught between surprise and panic. She's in shock; I think the whole damn tent is, including me.

"Well," she says, her voice pitched a little too high, "we've got a strong contender. I have two thousand on Colt Valentine. Do I hear twenty-five hundred?"

The silence stretches. No one moves. No one speaks.

Every eye in the tent has shifted toward Tessa, who's standing tall with her chin lifted and arms still folded across her chest. She's so sure of herself, so smug, like she played her winning card and is waiting for the applause.

Going on a date with her, even if it's for charity, would be a nightmare.

My hands curl into fists at my sides. But I stay standing on this damn stage, being treated like something for sale, while the one person I care about is sitting a few feet away, rigid as stone. Sunny's expression hasn't changed, but something in her eyes has. They're sharper now, like a firm decision has been made behind them. Hawks get the same focus right before they dive for a mouse.

The emcee tries again.

"Two thousand going once ..."

My chest tightens as I snap my shirt closed. I'm going to have a discussion with Fenix after this.

"Going twice ..."

Sunny lifts her paddle, her voice steady and clear, not loud, but commanding. "*Ten* thousand."

The words don't ripple through the tent; they crack it wide open.

The entire crowd gasps. Someone near the back drops a plastic cup. A few people stand from their seats to stare like they might've misheard.

The emcee freezes. For a moment, she acts like she's trying to process the number.

"I—sorry," she stammers. "Honey, did you say ... *ten* thousand? Ten?"

Sunny nods once, deliberately. "That's correct. But since it's for a good cause, let's make it twenty."

The emcee blinks and lets out a strangled laugh before she drops the mic. It hits the stage with a hard, echoing thud, and the tent erupts into whispers, others flat-out shocked into silence. I'm one of them.

My mouth falls open, and I stare at her, knowing she placed a twenty-thousand-dollar bid on me like it was the easiest decision she's ever made. She didn't hesitate. She didn't flinch. She raised her paddle and said I was hers in front of this whole damn town. That number ensures everyone knows it too. No way in hell I'll be able to pretend this doesn't mean something. The money is real.

The emcee clears her throat like she's trying to restart her brain, then picks up the mic with hands that are visibly trembling. Her eyes are as wide as saucers.

"Okay," she says, dragging the word out, buying time. "We have a bid for ... twenty thousand dollars. Going once ..."

The stunned silence continues to progress. Most are staring at

Sunny now, who's cool, composed, with a straight back, like she won a masterpiece at an art gallery. She blew the roof off this tent.

"Going twice ..."

No one answers. No one would pay a fortune to have me. Just her.

I stare at Sunny because it's so much more than the bid. It was the way she claimed me, like I was hers.

The emcee swallows hard and presses forward, voice shaky, but still doing her best to carry on. Not a damn person in the room even breathes. I'm not.

"All right then! Last chance to bid on Colt Valentine," she says.

I glance across the crowd. Fenix stands near the edge of the stage with her clipboard clutched to her chest, eyes wide, mouth hanging open like she witnessed something illegal. Kinsley is frozen beside Summer, hand clamped around Summer's forearm, who's whispering something I can't hear, but her eyes are locked on me. Off to the side, Vera has a hand over her mouth. Her other hand is gripping a half-eaten caramel apple like she forgot she was holding it. And in the back of the tent, I spot Remi standing next to Cash.

She looks at me, then at Sunny, then back at me, and mouths, *What the fuck?*

Sunny winks at me as she smirks, enjoying this. And at that moment, the rest of it—the crowd, the whispers, the chaos—all drops away. All I can see is her.

The emcee exhales, like she's finally convinced this is real.

She lifts the mic one last time. "Sold," she says, her voice cracking slightly, her tone still stunned as she brings the gavel down against the podium. "To the pretty lady in the front row for twenty thousand buckaroos."

There's a beat of silence before the tent erupts into laughter and applause. There are a few shocked gasps.

Someone whistles low from the far side of the stage, and I hear Emmett shout, "Get it, big bro!"

Seconds later, I'm off the stage and moving. I cross the distance between me and Sunny with one thought only—I've been hers since the second I saw her.

Reaching out, I grab her hand and pull her to her feet, eyes soft, mouth parted slightly, but I don't give her the chance to speak. I cup her face with both hands and slide my mouth across hers in front of the entire town. Her lips meet mine with urgency, soft but unshy. It's the kind of kiss that doesn't ask for permission, one that already knows the answer. She tastes like lemonade and heat. Her lips open, and I take the invitation without thinking, allowing our tongues to twist together.

My hand slips down to the curve of her waist, fitting perfectly around her like this was always supposed to happen. She exhales against my mouth like she's been holding her breath for days. Her fingers curl into my shirt, pulling me closer, anchoring herself to me, like she's finally allowing herself to fall.

The crowd around us fades away. The noise, the lights, the people watching—all of it blurs until there's nothing but the wild, electric heartbeats between us. Her other hand lifts, brushing along my jaw, and I swear to God, I almost lose it right there. Because this isn't a performance. This isn't for show. This is her choosing me—not just in front of everyone, but with her whole damn body—and I'm choosing her back.

None of the chatter, whispers, hoots, and hollers breaks us from the moment. The kiss deepens, and her body molds against mine like she's always known exactly where she fits. Right here, with me.

"That's my brother!"

I recognize that voice. It's Harrison.

I pull away, breath caught somewhere between her mouth and mine, and I keep my hands on her face for a second longer than necessary to memorize the feel of her skin, the way her lashes are still low, and how her cheeks are flushed from more than the heat. She looks at me like the ground shifted beneath her feet. Hell, it did. At least I felt it.

The emcee laughs into the microphone. "If you don't marry that woman …"

The tent bursts into applause again. I pull away from Sunny, realizing we lost control.

I rest my forehead against hers for half a breath. "Let's get out of here."

She nods.

I wave at everyone, unable to tuck the smile back as I wrap my arm around her, leading her out of the tent with all eyes on us.

"See, you never know what kinda show you're gonna get at the rodeo!" The emcee recovers. "Next, we've got Emmett Valentine!"

There's a chorus of shrieks from the middle rows. I glance back toward the crowd in time to see my brother strut onto the stage, arms raised like he's already won something.

He grins at the crowd. "Any woman out there wants to drop twenty grand on me? I'll give you the time of your damn life!"

The tent roars with laughter.

Emmett winks, reaches for the hem of his shirt, and yanks it off in one motion, tossing it into the crowd like he's a damn rodeo-themed Chippendale. The single women lose their minds.

Sunny presses her face into my shoulder, laughing so hard that I feel it in my chest. "Oh my God. This is a fever dream."

"Nope," I say, resting my hand at the small of her back. "This is Valentine."

She doesn't let me go, and I'm not letting go of her either.

The bidding for Emmett is absolute chaos.

Someone shouts, "Two hundred." Then, "Three." Then a woman near the back yells, "Four fifty," and throws her hand in the air like she's claiming a prize-winning pig at the county fair.

When it gets up to a thousand, Emmett beams, shirtless and soaking it up like the crowd's roaring for him, which they are.

The emcee pounds her gavel and shouts, "Sold to the lovely lady in the fringe tank top for one grand!"

Emmett blows a kiss and flexes like he's leaving with a trophy.

"Last year, Emmett auctioned himself twice to raise more money."

"Seriously?" she questions as we step outside.

I lead her away from everyone until we're in the shadows behind the tent. All I can think is that I kissed the woman I can't stop thinking about ... and she let me. Actually, she *met* me in it, matched it, and claimed me as I opened my mouth. We stand there for a minute longer, letting the energy of the tent swirl around us. People are still laughing, shouting out names, and clapping like this is the best entertainment they've had all month.

Our eyes meet.

"Wanna get out of here?"

"When do I need to pay?" she asks.

"Later," I explain. "They know where to find ya."

She nods, still grinning, cheeks pink, eyes bright. "Lead the way."

We cut through the crowd, still holding hands, still wrapped in that buzzing afterglow.

Every few steps, someone stops us to clap me on the shoulder or say something like, "Way to reel her in, cowboy."

I've never seen Sunny more alive. She's radiant. Free. And she's mine.

We make it to the truck, beyond the edge of the lights, tucked in the soft dark, where the country music fades. I open the door for her, but she doesn't get in right away.

Instead, she leans against the cool metal, arms crossed, eyes on me. "Is this when the curse sets in?"

"Yeah, sorry about it," I say, heart hammering in my chest. "Twenty thousand dollars is a lot of money," I say.

"I'd have paid double." She shrugs, easy but not careless, as she hooks her fingers in my belt loops and tugs me closer. "You belong to me, cowboy."

The words knock the air out of my lungs.

I don't move at first. I stare at her mouth, her eyes, and the storm still swirling behind them. I study the girl who walked into my life as if she owned it—because maybe she always did.

Fuck this.

I press her back against the truck and kiss her again, harder this time, with all the tension that's been sitting under my skin since the moment I first saw her. I pour every emotion I haven't known how to say out loud into it. She kisses me back like she means it, like she's not going anywhere, but I know that's not the truth. Her hands fist into my shirt, pulling me as close as possible. I press my palm against the truck beside her head, steadying us there, both of us breathing heavy and wrecked in the best damn way.

I pull back enough to see her.

She's breathless. Eyes wide. Lips swollen. The night dancing in the lines of her face.

"You're like a dream," I whisper.

"I'd say the same about you, cowboy," she admits.

I lean forward, capturing her lip into my mouth and sucking on it.

"Love to hear it," I whisper, knowing the lines are already too blurred. "Now let's go home."

I say the word like it's ours, and, fuck, it sure does feel like it is.

CHAPTER FIFTEEN

SUNNY

By the time we get back to the house, my blood is boiling, and my skin feels like it's carrying leftover electricity from the way he kissed me.

Colt kills the headlights but doesn't move to get out right away. The truck clicks and settles beneath us, the air warm and quiet in the cab. The only light comes from the porch, glowing across the ground, like it waited up for us.

We sit there for a second, both breathing a little harder than normal, not talking yet. I don't know what to say. I kissed him in front of the entire town. Correction: he kissed *me*, but I kissed him right back like it wasn't the most reckless thing I'd done since driving halfway across the country with a designer wedding dress stuffed in my trunk.

He glances over, and his grin is lazy.

"Are we gonna survive that?" he asks.

"I hope so," I say, even though I'm not entirely sure, not with the invisible clock ticking down.

My heart hasn't settled since I heard the emcee say "twenty thousand buckaroos."

"How do you have that much money?" he asks. "You threw it away on me."

"No, I didn't. I have more money than I know what to do with," I explain.

He shifts his body toward me. "Who are you?"

"I'm just a girl who's trying to figure out her life," I tell him, hoping that answer is enough, not wanting to scare him away.

"Okay," he says, not pushing me—because he never does. His smile returns. "Leave a place for me in it."

Before I can respond, Colt climbs out and comes around to open my door, offering his hand like we haven't been dancing around this moment since the second we met.

His fingers are warm and steady in a way I'm not. I step down, and he doesn't let go of me.

The crickets are loud tonight, and the stars are clearer than I remember them ever being. My boots thud across the porch as we step inside.

He sets his keys on the hook by the door, then leads me to the kitchen. Without asking, he pulls down two glasses, then reaches for an unopened bottle of whiskey beside the coffeepot and the unopened pasta.

"No offense," he says, glancing back at me, "but I think I need a drink."

My mouth lifts. "I could use one myself."

He pours two fingers into each glass and hands me mine. I follow him to the living room, where we both drop onto the couch, shoulder to shoulder, legs stretched out in front of us. It resembles déjà vu, and I wonder if maybe we've done this before, in a different life. Maybe that's why the pull between us is so strong.

This man belongs to a place that's so far removed from everything I left behind.

We drink, and the whiskey burns, but it's a welcome kind of heat that grounds me enough to stay in the moment.

Colt leans his head back against the couch cushion, eyes half closed, smile still tugging at his mouth.

"I don't know where we go from here," he says after a moment.

My heart thuds once—hard.

I don't answer right away. I sip again, watching the way the porch light casts shadows across his jaw.

"I don't either," I finally say, knowing I felt something awaken in me that I thought would never exist again.

He turns his head to face me, and the space between us shrinks.

"I liked watching you lose it a little," I add, grinning.

He huffs a laugh. "I was panicking. I thought you were gonna let Tessa win me."

"Please," I say. "No one else gets to walk away with you but me."

His eyes flicker toward me. Neither of us laughs this time.

I take another sip, and he leans in enough for his knee to brush against mine.

The whiskey is warm in my blood now. His presence heats everywhere else.

I don't know where this night is going, but I don't want it to end when it feels like something real is happening between us.

Colt breaks the tension, walks down the hallway to grab the bottle of whiskey, then returns. He fills our glasses fuller this time, and I shoot it back instead of savoring it.

The second glass hits me in a way the first didn't. It settles low in my belly, softening everything that's still spinning inside me. My head is floaty, but my heart is anchored to him, to this couch, to this house.

Colt shifts beside me, resting one arm along the back of the couch. His fingers are only a few inches from my shoulder, and I wonder if he knows how badly I want him to touch me.

"How does this end for us?" I ask, turning toward him.

His mouth tilts into something slow and dangerous. "I don't know. You keep me guessing."

"An honest answer I can appreciate," I say, but my voice sounds too soft. "I don't know either."

He doesn't say anything else, only watches me, eyes tracing the lines of my face like he's memorizing the moment.

I set my glass on the coffee table and shift onto my knees, the cushions sinking beneath me as I crawl into his lap without thinking, without planning it, because I need to be closer. Because all night, I've wanted his hands on my skin and his mouth on mine, and now I don't have any more excuses.

His breath hitches when I straddle him.

His hands move to my thighs like he's making sure I'm real.

I'm in his lap, remembering exactly what it's like to want someone so damn bad that it almost hurts. It's been years.

I slide my hands up his chest and over his shoulders, letting my fingers curl into the back of his hair as I lower my mouth to his.

The kiss is immediate, deep, and aching. There's no warm-up. Just heat and breath and the sound of my name somewhere in his throat. He's hard beneath me, and I rock once, gently. His grip tightens on my hips like he's barely holding on. His mouth opens wider beneath mine, and our bodies fall into rhythm, breath syncing, heat rising. With strong hands, he roams higher, one slipping under the hem of my shirt to rest at the small of my back.

My heart is thudding so loud that I can't hear the crickets anymore.

I can't hear anything but his ragged breathing and the sounds of my whimpers. But even as my body pushes closer, something in me pulls back. It's not out of fear, not because I don't want this. I want him. But I can't hurt him.

I break the kiss and press my forehead to his, breathing hard, trying to steady the crash inside me.

"I want you," I whisper, my voice shaking slightly. "God, Colt, I do, but ..."

"This is enough." His hands stay on my waist, grounding me. He doesn't move or pull away. His lips brush against my jaw as he exhales, and then I feel him smile. "But don't make rules with me, darlin'. I already warned ya once. I'll purposely make you break them."

I close my eyes, swallowing against the ache in my throat. He slides his hand up to my face, brushing a piece of hair behind my ear with a kind of gentleness that undoes me more than anything else tonight.

"You're so damn pretty," he says. "You're the one in control of us."

I open my eyes, and he's watching me like I'm the only thing in the room worth waiting for. And just like that, I melt into the safety of him. Of knowing that he respects me so much that he doesn't push. He holds me like I'm enough, even if I don't believe I am.

Not wanting to move, I stay on top of him for a while longer, tangled up in something that's too important to break. I'm still straddling him, and he holds me in his arms. His thumb traces mindless circles along the curve of my hip. Neither of us talks. We breathe in the quiet and let the weight of everything that's happened settle between us.

I move from him, but I am still close enough that we're still touching. Colt leans forward and reaches for the whiskey bottle.

"More?" he asks, pouring more into our glasses without waiting for an answer.

"I suppose," I say, drinking this one slower.

We've both made it through some invisible test neither of us knew we were taking.

The room is dim, lit only by a lamp in the corner. Outside, I hear the crickets again, and they sing like they're trying to fill in the spaces between our words.

Colt leans his head back against the cushion and exhales. "You ever have one of those nights where everything seems like it might work out?"

"You mean like tonight?"

"Exactly," he says.

We drink in easy sips, and after a few minutes, I shift to face him. My knees draw up, my elbows resting against them, and I study the side of his face—his scruffy jaw, his perfect mouth, the way his lashes curl.

"I didn't know what to expect when I escaped to Texas. Meeting you wasn't on my agenda," I admit.

He lets out a chuckle. "Starting this conversation strong. Truth be told, you weren't on mine either. But we were both in the right place at the right time. I don't know what happened that made you want to escape, but I'm real damn glad it did."

I memorize the blue specks in his eyes, knowing it's time to be honest with him.

"I walked out on my wedding," I admit, my voice softer now. I can't look at him this time, so instead, I down the rest of the whiskey in my glass and grab the bottle. "I saw my fiancé with his hands in my sister's panties forty-five minutes before the ceremony."

Colt doesn't say anything. The silence is filled with understanding and anger that only shows up when a person hurts someone you care about.

I risk a glance at him. His jaw is tight, but not with judgment.

"I was ready, wearing the designer dress that had been made for me," I say. The words come out too fast, but I don't stop. "Hair and makeup were done. The bridal room was too loud, so I stepped out for a breather. I saw them laughing, kissing, and fooling around."

He finally speaks. "Fuck him. Fuck your sister too."

The air conditioner clicks on, and the hum fills the space. I grab the bottle and take a long drink, finally telling someone the truths I've kept buried for weeks. I've only written about them in the journal Colt gave me.

"I didn't cry—and I still haven't," I admit. "I didn't cause a scene or call them out. I left. I didn't even tell anyone. I took his cherished car that we were supposed to drive to the airport for our honeymoon, stopped at a gas station, changed in the restroom, and kept going until I made it here."

Colt sets his glass down carefully on the coffee table, then shifts to face me. His firm hand rests on my thigh.

"I hate that this happened to you, but I'm glad you didn't marry that cheating prick," he says.

"Me too." I nod. "I ran, which is something I never do. For the first time in my life, I needed to disappear."

His voice softens. "And here you are, in my house."

"Sleeping in your bed," I whisper before I can stop myself.

His eyes never leave mine as he reaches for my hand. "I'm really fucking sorry."

The words hang between us.

My other hand is still curled around the whiskey bottle, but I'm not drinking anymore. I sit with my shame and my truth and a man who somehow makes me believe it's okay to put it out in the open.

"My name isn't Sunny."

He doesn't react, doesn't pull back, or question me. He watches me with that steady calm he always carries, the kind that tells me my world's not ending, but somehow beginning.

His thumb brushes circles over mine, and it's more comforting than any words I've ever been offered.

A few seconds pass. I keep my gaze forward.

Then he speaks. "Will you tell me your real name?"

It's not demanding, not invasive, just a simple invitation.

He asks because he wants to know me, because I know he cares.

I take a breath, and for the first time since I left everything behind, I let it out without fear tightening around it.

"Stormy," I whisper.

He doesn't repeat it, only chuckles. "That suits you really fuckin' well."

The corner of my mouth lifts. "What's that supposed to mean?"

"You're more of a tornado than sunshine, darlin'," he says.

"I'm sorry I lied. People are searching for me, and I don't want to be found. Please don't be upset with me."

"Fuck, I'm not," he says, and I can hear the grin in his voice now. "Thank you for telling me. *Stormy.* Mmm. Sexy. I think I always knew, but I figured you'd tell me when you were ready."

Right now, I'm not sure whether I need space or closeness, but he somehow gives me both. I keep my breathing steady.

"You made me realize not all men are trash," I admit. "When I left New York, I didn't think I'd ever be happy again. I didn't believe anything good could ever come after being betrayed by two people I loved. Then I met you, and it turned my world upside down."

"Well, that's the best damn compliment I think I've ever received."

I squeeze his hand and lean into him. He wraps his arm around me and holds me tight as he lightly draws circles on my arm. We stay there—two people on the old couch with whiskey and my heartbreak and whatever this is blooming between us.

"Will you still call me Sunny around your friends and family?" I ask.

"I'll call you whatever you want, darlin'. Your secret's safe with me."

I yawn, and he notices.

"Come on. Let's go to bed. It's been a long night."

Colt stands, and so do I. The whiskey hits me, and the world sways. He hooks his pinkie with mine and leads me to the bedroom.

As I fall asleep in his arms, I ask myself what I did to deserve finding him. I should send Donovan and Skye a thank-you note.

CHAPTER SIXTEEN

COLT

Before I open my eyes, the first thing I notice is the weight of her leg draped across mine. The second thing is the smell of her citrus shampoo. Sunlight filters in through the curtains, casting long beams across the bed and cutting through the quiet like a gentle reminder that morning has arrived.

I shift slightly, not wanting to wake her and not wanting this moment to end. There's something sacred about the way she fits against me, like she's always belonged in my arms. When I finally blink my eyes open to steal a glance of her, she's already watching me.

She smiles, and I return it. Her cheek rests against my arm, and her dark hair fans out across the pillow she didn't use. Her eyes are soft with sleep, but there's something else there too.

"Mornin'," I say, my voice rough from sleep.

Her green eyes sparkle. "You're a dream."

The way she says it, unguarded and slightly breathless, makes my chest tighten in the best way.

I stretch, then shift to hold her tighter. The sheet slips lower across my waist, but I don't bother adjusting it. Her gaze drops for half a second, and her cheeks turn pink.

I let the moment hang before speaking. "Did we share a twenty-thousand-dollar kiss last night, or did I imagine it?"

She laughs and buries her face in my chest for a second. "It happened. I'm sure the local rumors have exploded."

"Still waiting for the wedding rumors," I reply.

I reach out and lightly brush her shoulder, where my T-shirt has slipped, exposing the smooth skin there. I let my thumb trace the edge of the fabric.

"Can I kiss you?" I mutter.

My politeness stuns her.

"You don't have to ask." Her voice is quiet. "If you ever want to kiss me, I want you to."

It's the permission I need. I lean in, one hand rising to cradle the side of her face. My fingers slide into her hair, and I watch her eyes flutter shut before our mouths meet. It's gentle at first, tender in a way that feels like we have a future. Her lips move against mine with a familiarity that stuns me. There's nothing unsure about the way she responds. She shifts closer, her hand pressing flat against my chest. Her palm is warm and steady, her breath brushing my cheek.

The kiss deepens naturally and says more than either of us has been willing to put into words. I lose myself in her mouth, in the heat of her body so close to mine, in the quiet vulnerability that fills the space between us.

When we finally break apart, I rest my forehead against hers. Her eyes are still closed, and her mouth is curved into the sleepiest smile.

"I'm gonna need more mornings like this," I whisper.

She lets out a breath and nods. "Yeah. Me too."

We stay in bed for a while after that kiss, wrapped in quiet smiles and skin-warmed sheets. I don't think either of us wants to move, not when something real is taking shape between us. But eventually, the sound of birds outside pulls us out of the cocoon we made.

She stretches like a cat before slipping out of bed, wearing one of my old T-shirts, and heading down the hallway barefoot. I pull on some jeans and run a hand across my face that still smells like her hair.

The kiss still lingers on my lips, and I can't stop smiling.

By the time I get to the kitchen, the air smells like freshly brewed coffee, toasted bread, and something else I can't quite name yet. She sits on the counter, legs swinging. Her hair is a mess, toast in one hand, coffee mug balanced in the other, like she's claimed this kitchen for herself.

"You're making yourself at home," I say, pouring a mug and moving closer to her.

She shrugs and doesn't even try to hide her smirk. "I earned it."

"Twenty thousand dollars does buy a certain level of comfort."

She rolls her eyes but can't stop grinning. "You kissed me and put on a show for everyone."

"You kissed me back." I take a long sip of my coffee, fighting a grin.

"I wanted to." She huffs a laugh and pushes her shoulder into mine when I step closer. "I couldn't deny myself."

I move closer and brush a kiss along her jaw, like it's something I do every morning.

Her breath catches.

"You keep doing that," she says, "and I might not leave."

"Counting on it." I watch the smile curve at the edges of her mouth.

She sips her coffee but watches me over the rim of the mug.

Whatever this is, whatever we are now, it's intense and full of possibility.

"We need to run into town," I say, still watching her. "We should make the donation official."

"Perfect. I have the cash in my car."

"Cash? Please tell me you didn't drive across the country with twenty thousand bones in your car."

"Uh, actually, it was fifty thousand, stuffed in a leather bag in my trunk." She says it like it's normal. Like keeping that much money on hand is another Tuesday.

My mouth falls open. "You sound like a mobster."

She lifts one shoulder. "Maybe I am."

I stare at her ... stunned. Not because she has money. I figured that out by her clothes, her attitude, and how she carries herself in every situation. It's formal training that a person doesn't learn on a ranch.

"You know, normal people carry debit cards, right?" I ask, still trying to piece together what I know about her.

She grins. "There's nothing normal about me, Colt."

"You're living a full-on outlaw fantasy. Guess you stayed at roadside motels that took hundreds under the table?"

"Yep. But I like your bed better than any of them," she says, lifting her mug for another sip.

That one lands harder than she probably meant it to.

She knows exactly what she's doing to me.

"You want to take your getaway cash to the shelter after I feed the horses?" I ask.

"Sounds good. I need to change clothes." She hops down from the counter and brushes past me. "If anyone asks about the money, I won it in a poker game."

"I'm not sure that'll help the rumors that are undoubtedly floating around."

She glances back at me, eyes sparkling. "You didn't seem too worried about that when you slid your tongue in my mouth last night."

I smirk and lean against the counter again, watching her move through my kitchen like she owns it. "Keep it up, and I'll do it again."

I take a moment to drink in her long legs, messy hair, and the way she wears my T-shirt like it was made for her. If I'm not careful, I'm going to fall madly in love with this woman. I currently am.

She exits the kitchen, and I finish my coffee. I tug on my boots and head out to the barn. Cheerio and Froot Loops lazily walk into their stalls, knowing it's time to eat.

I move into the feed room and scoop grain into the buckets, the rhythmic sound grounding me while my thoughts run wild.

Stormy.

I roll her name around in my head like I'm still getting used to it. Sunny does fit her: bright smile, sudden warmth, along with the ability to light up a room by walking into it. But Stormy? Now that I've seen what's under the surface … yeah. That fits too.

I grab the buckets, pour one into Cheerio's trough, and scratch the spot behind his ears. He pushes into my hand like he misses me.

"We're gonna go on a ride soon, I promise," I say.

He snorts and goes back to eating. It's been a while since I've gone riding because I've been so focused on the house, but it's my favorite hobby. I move into Froot Loops's stall and feed her, giving quality pets before putting up the empty buckets.

I stare at the back pasture that seems to go on forever.

Last night, I kissed her. When we came home, she climbed into my lap and made the first move. That kiss wasn't sweet. It was scorching. Messy. Real.

And now?

Now I'm standing in a barn, body buzzing with thoughts of her, and I still don't know her last name.

Stormy probably has staff and stock portfolios and God knows what else tucked behind that perfect smile. I'm just a country guy with dirt under his nails and a house I'm rebuilding piece by piece.

I lean against the post and drag a hand down my jaw.

Does knowing these details about her change anything?

No. I don't give a damn what her last name is, where her money comes from, or what kind of world she walked away from. But I'd be lying if I said I wasn't reeling a little. Not because I'm intimidated, but because I've never wanted something this bad and still felt like it wasn't mine to have.

I glance back at the half-painted house. The windows reflect the morning light. She's probably moving around in there, pulling on jeans, brushing her hair, not even knowing how she's already sunk her claws so deep into me that I can't breathe without thinking of her.

I lock the feed room and take a moment to watch the sky shift. It's pale blue this morning with no signs of storm clouds.

After ten minutes, I move back inside and grab a baseball cap. She's wearing exactly what I imagined, along with a smile that's reserved for me. Before we head to the shelter, she leads me to her Camaro, and knowing it's her ex's makes me want to set it on fire. The sun is higher now, baking the gravel beneath our boots, and the breeze has all but disappeared.

She pops the trunk. The lid lifts with a soft groan, and for a second, I think I'm only going to see a duffel bag or some spare clothes. But what's there makes me go still.

The wedding dress is balled up and shoved deep in the corner. It's wrinkled, but still unmistakably expensive. White lace, silk, a flash of satin that probably cost more than every rental property I own. One diamond-studded heel is lying on its side, the other wedged beneath the bag. It looks like something she meant to throw away but couldn't.

I glance at her, but she doesn't say anything. She stares into the trunk like it's something she's been avoiding for too long.

Without hesitation, I place my hand on her shoulder. My palm rests there gently, firm enough to say I see it, soft enough to say she doesn't owe me an explanation.

"We should burn it," I say.

"What?" she asks, startled. She's unzipping the duffel bag now, stacks of cash spilling into view like it's nothing more than old clothes. She grabs several stacks of cash.

"The car. The dress. All of it."

She stops moving. Her hand lingers on the zipper, eyes flicking toward mine.

"I can't tell if you're joking." She stares at the crumpled gown, and then she laughs. "At one point, I thought about putting it in neutral and pushing it off a cliff, but I didn't want anyone to believe I was dead. That would cause too much commotion."

"Wait right here," I tell her.

I head inside without a word and walk straight to the closet in my bedroom. I reach for a small duffel and the aluminum bat that's leaning in the corner. It's old, scratched, and dented from years of backyard use, but it's reliable.

I carry it back out to the front yard, where she's standing, staring down at the black Camaro like it insulted her.

"What's that for?" she asks. "The bat, not the bag."

Quickly, she puts the cash inside.

Then I hold the aluminum bat out to her, grip first. "It's his car, right?"

She stares at it like it's a snake.

"Yeah. He loved it more than he ever loved me." Her tone is bitter, but there's something beneath it, like pain.

"Well," I say, nodding toward the Camaro, "seems only fair you give it a proper goodbye."

She hesitates. "You're serious?"

"As a heart attack," I say. "He wrecked you. What's the difference?"

She takes the bat, like it might burn her palms, and holds it for a second. The first swing is hesitant, but it's enough to knock the driver's side mirror clean off. She jerks from the sound, but something shifts in her eyes. She steps forward again, and this time, she doesn't hold back.

The driver's window explodes with the next hit, glass falling in sheets across the leather. She rounds the car like she's got a checklist. Every window. Every mirror. A dent down the passenger door.

She's not crying, but the power behind every swing says enough.

I cross my arms, watching her destroy what it represents. The betrayal. The lies. The hollow future she almost walked into, wearing white. She's not only leaving dents and breaking glass, but she's also breaking out of the hold her ex had on her.

When she finally stops, the bat clatters to the ground. Her shoulders rise and fall, hands trembling, chest heaving like she's outrunning every version of herself that was still holding on.

I move closer, and she turns to me, cheeks flushed, hair falling from its tie.

"I feel better," she says, breathless, pleased by her havoc.

"Love to hear it," I tell her.

She lets out a laugh that's halfway to a sob. "Payback is a bitch."

I reach for her hand and kiss her knuckles. "He doesn't get to have any power over you anymore," I say. "Not here. Not now."

She nods. "Thank you."

I brush a strand of hair from her face. "You sure you're good?"

She glances over her shoulder at the wreckage. "I am now."

"Great. Let's get the fuck outta here," I tell her.

I open the passenger door to my truck, and she slides in, chest rising and falling, but there is a lightness to her. I slide into the driver's seat and start the engine. The old truck rumbles to life, and we ease down the gravel driveway, the tires crunching over sunbaked stone as the house disappears behind us.

The windows are down. The air smells like fresh grass and hay. She leans into the door, one elbow resting on the window frame, her other hand clutching her phone, like she's trying not to look at it. Not able to resist, she unlocks the screen, taps, and scrolls. Her posture shifts almost immediately. It's small, a tightening of her shoulders, and it's like she's trying to brace against something.

She doesn't make a sound, but the energy in the cab changes fast. It goes from soft and easy to something dangerous.

I keep one hand on the wheel, and the other reaches for hers.

"You good?" I ask as our fingers interlock together.

She doesn't answer right away. Instead, she swallows and locks her phone, placing it face down on her lap.

"I searched myself," she says. "I shouldn't have."

I glance over at her with furrowed brows. "Do you want to talk about it?"

"New articles about me were posted. They're lying about me and saying I'm having a mental breakdown, that I've been unstable for weeks." She pauses. "I'm *pissed*." Her jaw tightens, and she blinks hard, like she's trying to push the sting back where it came from. "They're rewriting what really happened. They're rewriting the whole damn story because I'm easy to villainize."

My grip on the steering wheel tightens. I don't know what I dislike more—that people are lying about her or that she's been carrying this alone since she walked out on what should've been the happiest day of her life.

"Fuck 'em," I say. "The truth always comes out. You'll make it through this triumphantly. Promise." I pull into the parking lot outside the shelter. "And if not, I'll happily kick someone's ass," I offer.

"Not needed," she says, chuckling, then finally turns her head to meet my gaze. "Thank you for everything. For accepting me and my mess."

"I'm not here to fix you, darlin'. I want to be the man who stands beside you while you figure it out."

"You're not real," she mutters, shaking her head.

"Ah, well, I can guarantee I'm not a figment of your imagination," I say, and her smile is enough for now.

CHAPTER SEVENTEEN

STORMY

The gravel crunches beneath our boots as we walk across the parking lot to the front of the shelter. I swing the bag of money in my hand like it's laundry and not twenty grand. It's just money, and I genuinely love giving it away, especially to a good cause.

The building is small but clean, with flowerpots lining the windowsills. A bulletin board is near the entrance, covered in laminated flyers of lost pets and photos of animals available for adoption. A handwritten sign taped to the glass door reads in big red letters: *The first weekend of the rodeo auction broke all records!*

Colt holds the door open for me, and the blast of cool air makes me realize how hot it is outside. I might be getting used to this heat. Inside smells like dog shampoo, floor cleaner, and something warm and comforting, like sugar cookies. A candle flickers on the countertop. The receptionist's head pops up from behind the desk, her smile wide and immediate.

"Well, lookie who the dog dragged in," she says in a thick Southern accent. She's older, very cheerful, with a bright smile, and bleached-blond hair. Her name tag says Jenny. "It's Mr. Valentine and the woman who nearly gave the entire town a heart attack last night. Everyone's still talkin' 'bout that—and may be until the end of time. Honey, I hope he gives you the date of your life."

I chuckle.

"Oh, I'll make it worth every damn penny. That's a Valentine guarantee." Colt rests his hand on the small of my back, and the simple touch has me buzzing.

"Thought I'd stop by and fulfill my obligation," I explain, lifting the bag onto the counter.

Jenny raises both of her penciled-on eyebrows. "Sweetie, you don't have a money order or a check? This is a lot for me to be carryin' to the bank."

"No, ma'am," Colt replies, fighting a smile. "Never heard anyone complain about cold, hard cash. What's this world comin' to?"

He's being playful, and I love it.

Another woman, who's taller and younger, wearing a Valentine Animal Shelter T-shirt, emerges from the back room. Her eyes widen at the stacks of money. When she sees me, she smiles wide, like I'm an old friend.

Jenny fans herself with a manila folder. "Ember, come help me, please. I think I'm having a hot flash."

As they count the donation, Ember chats freely. "You have no idea how much this will help us. It's very generous of ya. Everyone 'round here is sayin' you're some sorta heiress or something. Maybe a princess."

I freeze for half a second, then nervously laugh. Colt notices my unease, even though I believed I was a professional at hiding it. The subtle shift of his thumb brushing once over my back is enough to let me know he's still right here.

"No comment," I say lightly, trying to be playful. "But if I were a princess, I probably wouldn't stay in an unfinished house with questionable central air."

Jenny laughs. "Well, regardless of what you are or aren't, we're thrilled you're here either way. Now, do y'all want to take a picture for our monthly newsletter? It's optional, but I warn you, if we don't get one, Mavis *will* track you down. She takes her manager job very seriously."

"We'll take our chances." Colt leans against the counter, adjusting his baseball hat, like he's done this a thousand times. "Mrs. Mavis will have to get over it. Don't want to distract from the real stars in this place—the animals."

"She'll call your mama," Jenny warns.

"Call her," Colt says back.

"Oh, while you're here," Ember says to Colt, rushing down the hallway.

The door in the back opens, and before I can say anything, something soft and wet brushes against the back of my calf. I turn around and see a Border collie mix with oversized paws and caramel eyes, wagging his tail like we've been friends forever.

"Boots," Colt says with a grin, crouching to scratch behind the dog's ears. "How ya been, buddy?"

The pup leans into the affection, his little nub of a tail wagging, happy as can be.

I kneel beside them and rub under his chin as he tries to lick me. "You're so cute."

"Agreed," Colt says.

When I glance at him, he's not talking about Boots; he's focused on me.

"I'd adopt him, but I promised myself no more animals until the house was finished," Colt explains. "The horses are enough to handle for now."

Boots licks my face.

"Guess we'd better get to work before this guy gets adopted?"

"Guess we'd better," he tells me, then hugs Boots. "If it's meant to be, you'll still be here when I'm ready."

Jenny and Ember watch us, and after we sign a few pieces of paper for tax purposes, we're sent on our way with hugs from both. I'm happy with my decision to donate twenty thousand dollars. Hell, I might give them the rest of the cash I have in my trunk.

"Coffee?" Colt asks as we pull out onto Main Street.

He cranks the air conditioner since it's much hotter outside than earlier, and I lean into the vent. Wisps of my hair blow in the breeze.

"That would be amazing, but I prefer it cold, not hot," I say. "I need something sweet to balance out the emotional whiplash of today."

From waking up in Colt's arms, to destroying that Camaro with every bit of strength I had, to doing a good deed, it's a lot to process.

He smirks. "Your wish is my command."

We pull into the small drive-through coffee stand on the edge of town—a converted feed shack with faded wood siding and a hand-painted menu hanging under the eaves. There's a planter near the window with a cactus and a tip jar that reads: *Be nice or leave.*

"This place is kinda new, but it's great. It's called The Coffee Shack, and it opened a few weeks ago."

We pull up to the handwritten drink menu, screwed to the side of the building. I lean closer, my body nearly on his, so I can read it.

"Hmm. I think I'd like a large blended white mocha with whipped cream and chocolate drizzle."

"Fancy drink for a fancy lady," Colt says, and his eyes trail down to my lips.

A car pulls up behind us, so he moves forward.

The window of the shack slides open, and he repeats my order. "And an iced caramel coffee for me."

Not long after, his card is swiped, and our coffee masterpieces are being handed over.

My eyes widen at the size. "Everything really is bigger in Texas."

Laughter falls from him as we drive away. "I want to taste it."

I raise an eyebrow, sipping through the straw. "Dunno if you can handle this sweetness."

"Mmm, I can handle more than you think, darlin'," he says with a low laugh.

He parks a block away in a spot that overlooks the town square.

"Tell me about Valentine and your last name. How is your family connected?"

"Ah. It's a fun story. My great-great-great-great-great"—he takes a deep breath—"grandfather laid the groundwork and founded the town. Settled here because of the railroad, started the three-thousand-acre cattle trading ranch my parents currently live on, and the rest is history. The bank building was the first structure constructed in Valentine, followed by the general store and post office. Lots of history here."

"It's charming," I say.

"A Valentine trait." Colt winks.

I smile and offer him my sugary drink. He waggles his brow as I remove the lid so he can taste the whipped cream drizzled with chocolate. Some is on the corner of his lips, and I reach over without thinking and wipe it away. I place my thumb in my mouth, tasting it.

"Should've licked it off, straight from the source."

"Contemplated it," I admit.

We drink and steal glances at each other. Colt eventually gets out of the truck, and I follow him to a weathered park bench that's shaded by an overgrown tree. The sun filters through the leaves. Next to it is a painted sign that says, *Thank you for shopping local.*

Colt stretches out beside me, one ankle hooked over his knee, his mouth around the straw of his iced coffee, like it's the best thing he's tasted all week. He wraps his other arm around me, and I scoot in close to him as we people-watch. This shouldn't feel romantic, but somehow, it does.

"Back at the shelter ..." I say. "You read me well. That's not easy to do."

He glances at me, a small, knowing smile pulling at his kissable lips. "I disagree. But it is easier to tell when you're nervous. Or holding something back."

"Really?" I tilt my head, skeptical. "What's my tell then? Since you seem to have me all figured out."

He chuckles under his breath.

"Don't laugh," he warns, brushing his fingers lightly along my arm. "But I can feel it. It's like a shift in the air. You carry your tension in the way you hold still. And your eyes? They give away everything you don't say."

I stare at him, stunned silent.

His gaze softens. "Like right now, you're wondering how that's even possible."

My heart stutters. "You shouldn't be able to read me like that."

He shrugs, and it's easy. "Guess these days, I can predict storms."

My breath catches at the way he says it. Not just the word, but the way it carries meaning.

"You never cease to amaze me," I tell him.

And then he leans in, his hand grazing my jaw as his mouth brushes mine.

It's not demanding. Not rushed. Just a soft, certain press of lips that's more like a promise than a question. Like he already knew I'd meet him there. And I do.

There's no need to hide the way I feel. Not here. Not with him.

His lips move against mine with confidence, not demanding more than I'm ready to give, but offering everything if I want it.

I tilt my chin, opening my mouth wider to taste his tongue, deepening the kiss. His hand slides from my jaw to the back of my neck, fingers threading gently through my hair. There's nothing rushed. It's a slow burn that starts in my chest and melts outward.

I taste him, the sweetness of the coffee, and something unmistakably him. A low sound escapes from the back of his throat, and I feel it vibrate against my skin. I shift closer until my fingers find the edge of his shirt and grip the fabric like I might float away if I don't hold on to something.

When we finally pull apart, I'm breathless, not only from the kiss, but from everything behind it.

He rests his forehead against mine, his thumb still brushing lightly at the base of my neck.

"You have no idea what you do to me." His voice is barely more than a whisper.

A smile ghosts across his lips as he kisses me again, quick and soft this time, like a punctuation mark at the end of a sentence that already said everything. The edges of my old life fade. This version of me—the one in cutoff shorts, having cowboy coffee dates—might be the one I want to keep.

We finish our drinks and toss the empty cups in the trash bin. He grabs my hand as we return to the truck, stealing glances. Being with him is uncomplicated, and I appreciate that more than he'll ever know. He expects nothing, and that makes me want to give him everything.

The sun casts long golden streaks across the road as we drive home. It beats down so brutally that it makes the air above the highway shimmer. I rest my head back, eyes half-lidded, my stomach full, and my heart doing this weird fluttering thing I don't know how to control. Outside the window, the trees blur past in soft green streaks, and the sky stretches wide and open above us.

"You free tomorrow?" he asks casually as he turns down the long gravel road.

The house sits at the back of the property, half-painted.

"Hmm," I say playfully. "Let me check my schedule. Seems I'm free."

"Perfect," he says, flashing a grin. "Would you like to go on a date with me?"

"No," I say, giving a brief pause, followed by a short laugh. "I'd *love* to."

"Great. I have the perfect place."

I shift in my seat, and the butterflies in my chest turn into something a little more dangerous, like a swarm of bees.

"What should I wear?"

He grins. "Whatever you'd like."

My pulse races.

His smile tugs a little deeper. "Why are you nervous?"

"Well," I reply, stretching my legs out in front of me, knowing I can't deny it because he sees straight through me, "I'm waiting for the bottom to fall out of this."

"That's not happening, Stormy. Unless you decide I'm too young and there's no space for you and me in your life." He parks in front of the house but doesn't immediately kill the engine.

"I'm giving us a chance," I admit for the first time, and it doesn't scare me.

Colt doesn't answer right away. He stares at me, and a pull starts low in my stomach. The way his eyes soften, how his fingers tighten slightly around the steering wheel, like he's remembering this very moment.

He shifts in his seat, turns toward me, and kills the engine.

"I'm glad," he says. "Because I've already made up my mind about you."

My breath catches.

He leans in, elbows resting casually on the middle console, but his eyes never leave mine. "I knew the second you walked into my sister's house, looking like trouble, wrapped in heartbreak, that you were fixin' to be mine."

I laugh, stunned and a little breathless. "You really said that to yourself?"

"Swear on my boots."

I shake my head, grinning now despite the hum running beneath my skin. "You don't know what you're getting into."

He tilts his head, that cocky little smile tugging at the edge of his mouth. "No, darlin', maybe I don't. But I still want in."

That swarm in my chest settles into something steadier.

I reach for the door handle and glance back at him one more time. "Come on, cowboy. We have a house to finish and a dog to adopt."

He's already getting out of the truck with a grin that says I'm his.

And maybe, just maybe, I am.

Colt walks beside me, his hands relaxed at his sides as we take the porch steps. He unlocks the door and stops in the entryway, kicking off his boots. "You seriously up for working on the house today?"

I arch an eyebrow as I step inside behind him. "Can I use power tools this time?"

"You get a paintbrush, a roll of tape, and a motivational speech," he says.

I laugh, already heading toward the front room, where the supplies are stored. "Great. But I get to control the music today."

"That's fair," he says, trailing after me. "As long as it's not depressing."

"Oh, so no sad love songs?"

"Exactly. No heartbreak on a loop."

I shoot him a glance over my shoulder, but I'm still smiling as I walk into the huge room to grab brushes, paint trays, tape, and caulk. The air in the house still smells faintly of wood and joint compound, but it's cooler in here now; the air conditioner is keeping up enough to make it bearable. It doesn't stop him from turning on every box fan he has available.

"Ready?" he asks. "I think we can finish the rest of the baseboards throughout the house by dark since everything is already cut."

"Let's do it," I tell him.

We share a high five, then fall into a rhythm almost immediately.

The sounds of light footsteps, the tearing of tape, and the sliding of boards against the floor fill the quiet without overwhelming it. In the background, '90s rock plays, and Colt sings along with some of the songs. There's no pressure, no awkwardness in the space between us, only the comfort of shared tasks and building something better together.

At one point, I glance over and catch him watching me, and we exchange smiles.

Hours pass, and he finishes hanging the baseboards in other rooms as I wrap up painting the hallway. It already seems like a completely different house. I'm amazed by how much we've accomplished together in such a short amount of time.

The two of us move into the kitchen to clean the paintbrushes and rollers when Colt leans his hip against the counter and glances over at me. His shirt is speckled with paint, and there's a smudge near his jaw that he hasn't noticed yet. The light coming through the kitchen window catches in his dark hair, and for a moment, I allow myself to admire him.

He clears his throat like he's been debating whether to say something.

"Kinsley texted me," he says. "She and Summer were wondering if you'd want to hang out with them tomorrow. Said they'd love to help you get ready for your date, but only if you're up for it."

The offer takes me off guard, not because I'm surprised they'd be kind, but because it seems normal. Like something women in small towns do for each other when someone's got a big night. It's not something I'm accustomed to.

"You want me to hang out with your older sister and her bestie alone?" I ask, drying my hands for too long, to give myself something to do.

He shrugs, but I can see the smile tugging at the corner of his mouth. "Only if you want to. There's no pressure. They're fun, and you might enjoy hanging out with someone other than me."

I nod, my chest tightening around something. "Okay. Sure. I'd love to."

His grin spreads wider. "They'll be happy. Said they loved chatting with you at the rodeo. Be careful though. If they fall in love with you, they'll never let you leave town."

"I like them a lot. I don't have many friends back in New York," I tell him.

"You already have more than enough here."

CHAPTER EIGHTEEN

COLT

I never thought picking out a damn shirt would be so hard. The bed is covered in options, most of which are the same —a handful of button-downs in various shades of blue or black, three clean white ones, and several pearl snaps.

The full-length mirror beside my dresser catches my reflection as I stand there, barefoot in jeans, one hand dragging through my hair. I've got a dull ache in my lower back from crouching over baseboards yesterday, but none of that's what has my chest feeling tight.

It's *her*.

This isn't some casual dinner. It's not a fake dating situation or a favor. Tonight is real for me, and I want to get it right.

I settle on a crisp white shirt—no pattern, no distractions— and roll the sleeves. I run a clean cloth over my boots and check the time out of habit, even though I already know there is no rush. There's a knock at the open door, followed by the unmistakable clatter of bracelets. Remi leans against the frame, arms crossed, eyebrows already raised.

"Wow," she says, dragging the word out like she's impressed and smug about it. "You even shaved."

I glance at her in the mirror's reflection. "I want to do this right."

"You will," she says, walking into the room and flopping onto the end of the bed. "But I know you. You only do the full routine when you're either going to a wedding or falling for someone."

I pause, one hand hovering over the cologne bottle.

"She's not like anyone I've ever known," I admit.

Remi smiles, and it's kind. "I'm concerned you're going to get hurt."

"True love is worth the risk," I explain, feeling the weight of what this is. Tonight is a bridge between what Stormy and I have been and what we could be. "Our connection isn't like anything I've experienced with another woman. I can't ignore that, even if heartbreak is part of it."

Remi stands, smoothing the edge of the comforter, before stepping over to me. She squeezes my shoulder once. "I want you to be happy."

I turn around and hug my sister. She's been beside me through everything, even birth.

"Just look at her the way you always do. Flowers and the picnic basket are in the living room on the coffee table. Now, gotta head to work."

"Thanks, sis. Love ya," I say.

"Love you too," she says, then moves toward the door. "Still convinced you met your wife?"

"Without a doubt," I tell her with a laugh.

"Love that for you!" she says as she leaves.

A minute later, I hear the front door creak open, then click closed.

When I'm alone again, I sit on the edge of the bed and slide on my boots.

Whatever happens tonight, I won't play it cool. I'm going to show Stormy exactly what it means to be chosen.

The truck is clean. I even vacuumed the floorboards and

wiped down the dash with one of the lemon-scented wipes Remi left in the glove box months ago. I take the long way to Kinsley's house because I need the time to stretch a little, to give myself space to think.

When I pull into Kinsley's driveway, her house is the same as it's always been. It's small, a one-bedroom cabin that she's lived in since she was eighteen. Now she and Hayden live there together. Eventually, they'll upgrade because it's barely big enough for the two of them, but they make it work. The front windows are open enough to let the sound of music drift out, and it's followed by laughter.

I grab the flowers from the passenger seat and head up the front steps. Before I can knock, the door swings open, and Summer appears, grinning like she already knows this is the beginning of forever.

"She's almost ready," Summer says, stepping outside onto the porch. "You're lookin' real nice. *Wow.*"

"Thanks," I tell her.

"Don't worry; we didn't overdo it or get too personal," she explains. "But that woman likes you ... *a lot.*"

The smile that touches my lips might be permanent. "Reckon you're right about that."

"It's funny because I can see how compatible you are. I'mma need you to go ahead and marry her so that the three of us can be The Three Musketeers. Oh, Kinsley did a tarot card pull. True love, apparently."

Laughter spills out of me. "Okay, but when has she done one and it hasn't said that?"

Summer nods. "You might be onto something there."

Before I can respond, I hear footsteps coming down the hallway, and then she appears.

Stormy.

Every damn thought in my head disappears.

She's wearing a soft rose-colored dress that hits above the

knee. It's simple, but it fits her like it was made for this exact moment. Dark hair falls in loose waves around her shoulders, and there are small gold hoops in each ear that catch the late afternoon light. Her bright green eyes find mine as she walks toward me, and something in her expression slightly falters.

Summer and Kinsley move inside, giving me waves, and then we're left alone.

"Gorgeous," I mutter. "Wow."

"Not too bad yourself, cowboy," she says as I offer her the flowers.

"For you," I say, my voice lower than I intended.

She takes the bouquet, her fingers brushing mine. There's a pause that allows the weight of this to settle between us.

"Ready?" I ask, offering my arm.

"Absolutely," she says, taking it.

I help her into the truck, careful with the bouquet as she climbs in. She settles into the seat, and it hits me again how much I want tonight to matter. It's the start of a new beginning, not another page in her story.

As I circle the front of the truck and climb in beside her, I glance over and catch her watching me.

"You're makin' me nervous," I tell her, adjusting the key in the ignition.

She bursts into laughter, and I love the sound. "No, you're making me nervous."

"Then let's stop with that," I say.

She reaches across the console and takes my hand. I kiss her knuckles and interlock my fingers with hers. The drive out to Bar V, my family's ranch, is quiet in a peaceful way. The kind of quiet that settles when two people don't need to fill every second with words. When she gets in her head, I let her stay there without interrupting her. I know she's still working through everything that happened with her ex and sister. She's handling it better than I ever could.

The sun has started to lower behind the ridge, stretching the shadows long across the fields as we pass the front gates. The cattle guard rumbles under the tires. She's watching the landscape as it opens—wide and golden and still—and I wonder if she knows how much of this I've wanted to show her.

We pull around the main barn and follow the dirt road past the fence line until the trees thicken again. There's a side-by-side parked near the tool shed, exactly where I asked Emmett to park it for me. The second she sees it, her head tilts in that curious way she does when she's trying to figure out what I'm up to.

"Is this part of the date?" she asks.

"Every bit of it," I say, putting the truck in park and grabbing the picnic basket full of goodies from behind the seat. "Come on."

The late sun hits her perfectly, glinting off her earrings, catching in her dark hair, and I have to take a breath to remind myself to stay focused.

I place the picnic basket in the back and strap it in.

"Can I drive?" she asks.

"Um, sure," I tell her, climbing into the passenger seat. "Do you know how?"

She gives her signature Stormy expression with one brow slightly raised and her mouth quirked, like she's two seconds away from making me eat my words.

"I've driven faster things than this with more horsepower and worse steering," she says, sliding into the driver's seat with way too much confidence for someone who's never taken a side-by-side down a Texas trail.

I buckle in and brace my arm on the frame. "All right, hotshot, try not to flip us."

She grins like that's a dare.

The second she turns the key and hits the gas, we lurch forward with a jolt that throws my hand instinctively to the grab bar. Dust kicks up behind us in a thick trail, the engine roaring louder than I expected.

She laughs—a wild, free sound—and glances over at me, her hair whipping in the wind.

"This thing's got more bite than I thought," she shouts over the rumble.

"Maybe slow down before we find ourselves off-road."

"Oh, come on," she calls out, swerving us down a narrow path that cuts through the trees. "Where's your sense of adventure?"

"Back there with the picnic basket I strapped in with a seat belt," I mutter, though I'm grinning too.

She takes the turns sharper than I would, but she's not reckless, just fearless. Her hands grip the wheel like she's in complete control, even if her laughter says otherwise. Every bounce sends her giggling and adjusting in her seat like she's trying to prove she belongs in the dirt as much as she ever did in stilettos.

She catches a bump, and we lift off the ground for half a second. When we land, her hair flies around her face, and her mouth opens in a squeal that turns into a breathless, unfiltered laugh.

"Okay," she gasps, taking her foot from the gas as we round the final curve. "We were airborne."

I pretend to clutch the dashboard. "Glad you're enjoying yourself, darlin'. Can't feel my spine anymore, but go on."

She nudges me with her elbow and eases the side-by-side to a stop near the overlook. Dust settles around us in a golden cloud.

With a flick of her wrist, she kills the engine, then yanks the parking brake. "You survived."

"Barely." I reach out, brushing a windblown strand of hair behind her ear. "Will I survive you?"

"That's still to be determined," she says, then leans in and kisses me like she knows exactly what she wants.

"Come on, cowboy," she says, climbing out. "The night is ours."

And like that, I'm following her again. Like I always will.

The firepit is stacked and ready, with a box of matches tucked into a coffee tin beside it. I'll have to thank Emmett for helping me with this. A thick blanket is already spread out near the water, close enough to see the reflections ripple across the surface. There's a light breeze coming off the pond, and the whole place smells like pine and earth and fading sunlight.

She takes it all in.

"Colt," she says, barely above a whisper. "This is stunning."

I grab the basket and follow her. She glances back at me, her face softer now, eyes wide with something I can't quite name.

"You did all this?"

"I did," I admit. "I want tonight to be special, quiet, just us and the big, open sky."

She kneels on the blanket and opens the basket. I settle beside her as she removes the wine bottle from inside, turning it between her palms.

"I've never had anyone do anything like this for me."

"I'm not anyone, darlin'," I admit.

"That's true." She smiles, and it touches something in me I didn't know was still aching.

As I uncork the bottle and pour each of us a plastic glass full, the sun dips low enough to paint everything in gold and shadow. The breeze rustles the trees, and a pair of dragonflies skates across the surface of the water.

This is what I wanted for her. Nothing fancy and full of flattery, but space to breathe and live free. Money can't buy this experience.

We sit back on the blanket, legs stretched out, shoulders almost touching.

She takes a sip, eyes still on the pond. "It's so quiet."

"Yeah," I say. "It's one of the reasons I love living here."

Stormy turns toward me then, tucking one leg beneath her. Her face is still pink from the ride, hair a little tangled from the wind, but I don't think I've seen her look more alive.

I nod toward the pond. "I used to come out here when I

needed to think. Back when everything felt like a plan I hadn't quite earned yet. But now? I'm not thinking about what's next. I'm here, living in the moment with you, drinking wine out of a plastic cup like we're fancy."

That earns me a laugh, and she tips her head back as it spills out.

"You knew exactly what I needed," she says, scooting closer.

I reach out and rest a hand on her knee. "You don't notice it, but your whole face changes when you're with me. You just … are."

"For a long time, I didn't know what it felt like to sit still. In my world, life moves fast, and there's so much to prove. I worked nonstop and hadn't taken a vacation in five years. These past two weeks have …" She swallows hard. "Being here, being with you, has changed my outlook on life, and I realize I was stuck in the rat race."

Stormy leans her head on my shoulder, and I feel her breath slip out.

"You've changed me too. And that's fucking scary because what happens next?"

"I don't know," she admits. "Taking it one day at a time."

Stormy's stomach growls, and I laugh.

"Hungry?"

"Starving," she says, pulling away.

I open the basket and pull out napkins, a container of Mama's fried chicken, macaroni, and a tub of still-warm peach cobbler. There's cornbread, too, wrapped in foil.

Stormy watches me unpack it like I'm going to do a magic trick.

"You made this?" she asks.

"Mom made it with a knowing smile and too many questions about you."

"Like what?"

I hand her a plastic plate. "Mostly how serious we were. And whether she should set another plate for you at dinner next month."

She laughs, but I don't miss the way her smile lingers afterward.

Stormy picks up a piece of cornbread and breaks off a bite-sized corner. "What did you say?"

"I hope so," I admit.

"Me too," she tells me.

"When you return to the city, you think you'll forget about this?" I ask.

"Not possible." It's a simple truth, one I hang on to.

For a few minutes, we eat without talking much. The pond ripples with the breeze. A pair of birds chases each other between branches overhead. She chews like she's savoring more than the food. I study her out of the corner of my eye, watching the way the gold light touches the slope of her shoulder, how her ankle rocks back and forth slightly when she's thinking.

She's present with me, and that's enough.

"This is really good," she says, pointing her fork at the cobbler. "Like, dangerously good."

"I'll let Mom know you enjoyed it."

"Please do," she says with a grin.

Her expression softens, and she shifts slightly, her knees brushing mine.

"You do this often?" she asks. "Bring women out here with home-cooked meals and perfectly timed sunsets?"

"Just you," I say without hesitation. "It's a special place. Each of my brothers has brought dates out here, and I thought, *Why the hell not? Worked out for Beckett.*"

Her gaze holds mine, steady now. "He brought Summer here?"

"He did and proposed not long after."

"She's very nice. So is your sister. Everyone is so kind and welcoming."

She doesn't look away. She doesn't smile this time either.

Instead, she sets her empty plate and fork inside the basket and leans a little closer.

"This is where I usually deflect," she says.

"You don't have to," I tell her.

"I know, and that's what's terrifying."

The air between us changes, tension wrapping tightly around us. I place my plate inside the picnic basket as well and refill our wine. The light is fading now, the sky turning shades of rose and indigo, and the first stars are beginning to appear. I reach out and tuck a piece of hair behind her ear. My fingers brush the shell of it, and she doesn't pull away, but her breath catches enough to make my own shallow.

"This is terrifying," I say. "You're the person I've been waiting to meet."

She blinks, and I can see the way that hits her.

"I'm scared of how much I want this," she admits.

I press my palm over hers. "Then let me be the one thing you don't have to be scared of."

Stormy doesn't speak right away.

Her hand stays pressed against my chest, fingers resting over the beat of my heart, like she's listening with more than her ears. She doesn't look down. Her eyes stay locked on mine, like she's waiting for one last sign.

I lift my hand, giving her every chance to stop me, and gently cradle her jaw. My thumb traces the edge of her cheekbone, the warmth of her skin grounding me in the reality of this moment.

When she leans in, it's not rushed or uncertain.

It's her saying yes.

And when I kiss her, it isn't careful. Everything I've been holding back is poured into it. Her lips part beneath mine, and my heart comes unstitched. She tastes like wine and sugar, but there's more beneath that, like I'm wrecking and rebuilding her world at the same time.

She exhales sharply, and I feel it against my mouth.

Stormy grips my shirt, pulling me closer, like maybe she needs something solid to hang on to, and I want to be that for her. I want to be the thing she can count on when everything else starts to blur.

Her kiss deepens, and I meet it with everything I've got. My hand slides into her hair, fingers threading through the soft strands at the nape of her neck. She tilts her head, letting me in further. She's not kissing me like someone who's leaving. She's kissing me like a woman who's finally found home. And I kiss her back like a man who's been waiting his whole damn life to find her.

The world narrows down to the pressure of her mouth, the sound of her breath, and her body leaning into mine. The pond in front of us, the fading sun, the breeze in the trees—it disappears, leaving only us.

Eventually, I ease back, giving enough space to breathe. Her lips are parted, her eyes still closed, like she wants to stay suspended in this moment a little longer. I do too.

When her eyes finally open, she looks at me like I'm the man who sees her, and I do.

"It's never felt like that with anyone else," I say quietly, my voice rough around the edges.

A smile curves her mouth, small but completely unguarded.

"For me either," she whispers. "Even if I don't want to admit that."

I rest my forehead against hers, letting the air settle between us. My hand is still in her hair. Hers is still fisted in my shirt, and we don't rush. We just fall.

CHAPTER NINETEEN

STORMY

Colt and I lie on our backs and stare up at the stars above us. There are so many that it seems unreal, like someone punched holes in the sky to let sparkling magic leak through. The fire that he built crackles a few feet away. I tilt my body toward his. He hasn't said a word since our confession, but he doesn't have to. His silence isn't uncertain. It's confident, like he knows what passed between us was more than a kiss. It was a shift, a surrender, a confession neither of us can walk away from, even if we wanted. This has been building since the moment we met, and tonight, it might finally spill over.

I keep staring at his mouth, still parted, tasting like wine and cobbler.

Colt reaches out and brushes a piece of hair from my cheek. The back of his hand drags down the line of my jaw before dropping away again, like he doesn't trust himself to linger.

"You good?" he asks, his voice so low that it sounds like a secret.

I shake my head, and the motion feels heavier than it should. "I'm drowning in you."

His eyes don't waver. "That's allowed."

"I know," I say, curling my fingers into his shirt as he props his head up on his hand.

"You don't have to have all the answers right now. Just hold space for the way you feel."

"I don't trust myself and my decisions after ..." I can't finish, but I also don't need to.

He gives me his lazy grin. "You think I'm a rebound?"

"I don't want you to be."

"Then, darlin', I'm not."

The night air wraps around us, warm from the fire but cool at the edges. Somewhere behind us, a cricket chirps. I focus on the sound, on the way Colt is watching me like I'm not fragile, but something he's willing to protect and fight for. I turn toward him fully, my body shifting closer to his. Our knees brush, then our thighs. Heat radiates off his skin, and it grounds me in a way that has nothing to do with desire and everything to do with living in the moment.

Right now, I'm not hiding my feelings or pretending I don't want him. And neither is he. This man makes me remember what it's like to be chosen in return. Mutual attraction, want, and need aren't something I'm used to.

I shift forward, capturing his lips, making the first move this time. I kiss him like he's erasing every man that came before him.

My breath catches, and so does his. His hands find my face, fingers gently touch my cheek, as though he's afraid I might vanish if he's not careful. My pulse is everywhere at once as his tongue traces my lower lip, coaxing me open, and I let him see what I am like when I'm hungry, desperate, and no longer fighting myself.

"I need you," I confess.

"Are you sure?" he asks, voice gravelly. He searches my face as if he needs to memorize the answer.

"I'm so damn sure; it hurts," I say, swallowing hard.

Colt's groan rumbles from deep in his chest. He sits up, taking me with him. Suddenly, I'm straddling him, my line of sight now level with his. His hands are steady on my hips, as if he's claiming me, and I bite back a nervous laugh because I'm clinging to his shirt, breathing like I ran here from New York.

His kiss grows rougher, less a question, more of a claim. My hands run through his messy hair, and Colt shivers beneath my fingers.

I barely notice my dress hitching up until the heat from the fire meets the skin of my lower back. His hands move under the fabric so that my entire body aches for more.

With him rock hard underneath me, I carefully unbutton the buttons on my dress until it's more like a robe. I remove it, offering my body to him.

Every touch is amplified, as if someone dialed my senses to a fever pitch.

One of his hands slips beneath the band of my bra, fingers hesitant. I want to laugh and cry and moan at once, but my body chooses moan, and it vibrates straight through both of us. My nails dig into his scalp, and he bites my neck, not hard, just enough to claim a ravenous part of me that wants him.

I rock my hips, feeling how hard he is beneath me, and the whole world fades away. The trees, the moon, the pond basically vanish. When Colt lays me down on the blanket, his hands gentle but greedy, I realize I don't want him to stop, not now, not ever. And maybe that's what undoes me the most. That I could picture forever with him.

His mouth finds its way down my neck, across my collarbone, mapping every freckle and scar. I arch beneath him, helpless and happy. He kisses the skin above my belly button and then lower, leaving a heat trail I'll never forget. Goose bumps cover me as he reaches my panties.

"We can stop. We don't have to go any further," he whispers, not just so I can hear, but so the stars can too. "We can wait."

"Claim me, cowboy," I say. "*Please.*"

My heart thuds against my rib cage like it's trying to be heard through my skin.

Colt doesn't devour me immediately; instead, he continues his worship. Slow, like we have all the time in the world, kissing his way back up until his mouth finds mine again, honey sweet and urgent. There's nothing rushed about our undoing, and the way he cherishes me makes me crumble. Somewhere between his laughter and my contented sigh, Colt slides his hand up my thigh and touches between my legs, careful as a prayer. His hands warm every inch of me as he takes his time. My panties are soaked through and have been since we kissed. This man turns me on in unexplainable ways, even from a simple glance.

"You're trembling," he says, his fingers brushing across my panties.

"So are you," I mutter, and then we both laugh.

It's a big step, a line we can't uncross. I find our nervousness adorable.

"If you want to stop ..."

"Are you kidding?" Colt kisses his way down to where my thighs meet, pressing his lips flat, teasing with stubble. "I want you as much as you want me," he confesses. "More, if I'm honest."

I think about the girl I was at the beginning of this year, the one who would have shied away from the pleasure. If I could go back in time, I'd shake her by the shoulders, tell her that she needed to leave, and to find a man who knew her worth, who cherished and worshipped her. He exists, and his name is Colt Valentine.

Carefully, he hooks his fingers in the seam of my panties and slides them down, revealing all of me.

A choked gasp releases from me when his fingers brush along my pussy, discovering every want I've tried to hide.

"Fuck," he mutters. "You're so wet."

"You do that to me." I'm naked and exposed, and I'm risking it all for him. Emotionally and physically. Fuck, mentally too. Regardless, I give myself to him, hoping this isn't reckless.

By the time his mouth closes over my clit, I'm pure electricity, and every nerve is wired for him. He's learning me, tongue and lips, and careful questions. Every time I shake or shudder, he says my name in that deep, ruined way, like I'm a language he's teaching himself to speak.

"Mmm, Stormy. Your pussy is perfect."

"It's yours," I gasp out, my fingers grabbing the blanket beneath me.

"Yeah? Tell me who it belongs to."

"My pussy belongs to you," I whimper when his large fingers slip inside and curl upward. The pleasure is so intense; I fist his hair so hard that I almost apologize.

He groans between my legs, and I see sparks behind my eyelids. I'm not quiet, but it's not like anyone could hear me out here, screaming his name in this secluded oasis. Let the entire goddamn state know I'm alive beneath this man, painted in starlight, and greedy for more of his mouth and fingers.

His face is buried between my thighs like he's starving, and I'm the last meal on earth. His breath is hot and wet against my pussy. The tip of his tongue teases my clit, flicking it with precision, causing my back to arch off the blanket. My tits bounce as I gasp, my fingers tangling in his hair, pulling him closer, deeper.

"Colt," I moan, my voice trembling, "don't stop. Don't you fucking stop."

He doesn't.

"Love it when you moan my name like that." His tongue is relentless, sliding down to my slit, lapping at my juices like he's fucking addicted to the taste of me.

I can hear the obscene, wet sounds of his mouth working me over, and it drives me wild. His hands grip my thighs, spreading me wider, and I feel so fucking vulnerable with him, but I don't care. I trust him. And I want him to devour me, to ruin me, to claim me like no man ever has before.

When his tongue plunges inside me again and he fucks me so damn good with it, I cry out. My hips buck against his face, creating more friction, and he groans. The vibration sends shock waves through my cunt. His tongue darts in and out, curling and twisting, hitting every sensitive spot until I'm a wet, writhing, moaning mess.

"Colt," I whimper, my voice breaking, "you're the first man to ever do that and ..."

He pulls back for a moment, his lips glistening with my arousal, and he looks up at me with those hungry blue eyes.

"I love being your first, darlin'," he growls.

Then he's back on me, his tongue circling my clit, sucking it into his mouth, and I scream.

My legs are shaking, my whole body trembling as he works me closer and closer to the edge. I'm losing control.

His fingers rejoin the party, sliding inside me, curling and stroking that sweet spot that makes me see a kaleidoscope of colors. I'm panting, my tits heaving, my nipples hard and aching for attention. I grab them, pinching, allowing the pleasure to soar through me. The pressure's building, twisting tight in my belly.

"I'm gonna come." I gasp, my voice barely a whisper. "I'm so close. Colt ..."

He doesn't let up, his fingers pumping faster and deeper. His tongue flicking harder. I scream out, the orgasm pulling me under, and I fall off the edge. My body convulses, my cunt clenching around his fingers as I scream his name. Pleasure rips through me, but he doesn't stop. He keeps going, milking every last drop from me until I'm a trembling heap on the blanket.

He finally pulls away, his face slick with my juices, and he grins up at me like the fucking devil.

"You're so fucking beautiful when you come," he says, and I can't help but laugh, even as I'm still trying to catch my breath.

"You made me come," I pant, but I'm already pulling him up to kiss me, tasting myself on his lips. "Only I've ever been able to do that."

"Mmm. Something we share."

By the look in his deep blue eyes, I know this is only the beginning. He's not done with me yet. Not even close.

"I need more of you."

"I'm not prepared," he says, his breath brushing across my cheek. "I didn't bring a condom. I wasn't planning to go there."

"That's cute. But we did." I study him. "And I'm on birth control."

His eyes search mine, like he's making sure he understands. His hand moves to the nape of my neck, fingers slipping into my hair.

"Are you sure?" he asks, voice low and hoarse.

"I seriously love that you're so damn polite, but please fuck me." I breathe harder now.

The stars above us are sharper and brighter, no longer floating in the background. They're witnesses as he unbuttons and unzips his jeans. I prop myself up on my elbows, breasts still rising and falling, watching as he reveals himself to me. My mouth falls open when I catch a glimpse of his large cock.

"Okay, now I'm scared."

Laughter roars out of him as he moves closer to me. "We'll go slow."

When his body settles against mine, there's a long pause. He doesn't rush but waits. As I watch him, seeing how careful he is with me, I've never been surer of anything in my life.

I stop overthinking. I stop trying to predict what this might mean tomorrow. I stop bracing myself for loss before it ever touches me. I let the feeling in my chest stretch into trust that whatever this is will work out between us.

He's backlit by the fire, eyes deep blue and steady, shirt hanging open, chest rising and falling in measured breaths. When he enters me, it's careful. I widen my thighs, adjusting to his length, and appreciate how he's so damn patient.

My breath catches, and his forehead presses to mine again, like he's right there with me, every inch of the way. Eventually, there's no space between us. No room for fear. Only him. Only this. Only us.

"Are you okay?" he asks.

"Yes, it feels like you're ripping me in half," I whisper breathlessly. "It's good."

"You'll know exactly where I was tomorrow," he says.

His strong hands grip my hips. Carefully, he guides himself out and then back in again.

"So fucking tight," he mutters as I wrap my legs around his waist.

Our bodies fall into a rhythm. Every time he thrusts deeper, I meet him there. Every kiss, every sigh, every moan—I give freely. I take too.

The shift pulls us closer—skin to skin, breath to breath—and everything else around us disappears. There's only the press of his body into mine, the ache of being filled too tight, and the relief of it too. Our rhythm builds with certainty, like we're following something older than time. Older than restraint. Something that's bigger than either of us could have ever imagined.

I drag my hands down his back, nails leaving reckless little scratches over muscle, and he responds by angling deeper. My toes go numb.

He leans in, mouth at my ear, his breath hot. "I don't remember what life was like before you." He rasps out his wild confession.

I don't even remember what it felt like to want anything but him.

There's no room left for our little differences, only for need and how my whole body's singing, begging for more. Every cell is tuned to the same frequency as his, and I'm already addicted.

Every time he thrusts deeper, it pulls a sound from me I've never heard myself make. It's an overwhelming release of finally being *wanted* in a way that doesn't ask me to be anyone else. He holds me through it, his breath catching in his throat each time I move to meet him. It's instinct now. Muscle memory. A conversation written in touch and exhale.

"I've got the Valentine curse, don't I?"

"Yes," he says with a laugh.

Our mouths find each other again and again, open and needy, lips swollen, tongues sliding in communion. His kiss is messy, almost like he's apologizing and replacing every man before him who touched me like I was temporary. This feels like forever. Like I never want it to end.

Every sigh that leaves his chest, I feel against my ribs. Every moan I give him, he takes with gratitude and answers with more.

There is no part of me hidden under the stars. No mask. No angle for the media. I'm cut wide open for him, in my rawest form, and that's the woman he wants.

My hands are in his hair. My spine arches into the next pump and the next, and he groans like he's the one unraveling, not me.

"You feel so damn good," he says in a hushed tone.

He slows his pace like he wants me to understand I'm falling apart for someone who won't use me. I clutch at his shoulders and drop my guard, too gone to remember when I ever thought I wasn't worthy of this. Of him. Of the way he whispers my name like it's something worth keeping.

The thought takes hold, and I go rigid around him, inner muscles clenching in a way I can't hide or control. He groans like he's ruined and gives himself over to it too. Colt grinds deeper and harder, spilling and pumping into me. Every part of him is locked to me until we're both shaking.

We stay that way, breathless, for as long as it takes for our hearts to stop tripping over themselves, and then he helps me clean up.

He shifts and pulls my naked body closer, arm beneath my shoulders, hand tracing my spine, like he's counting vertebrae. I bury my face against his throat and laugh. I'm giddy and maybe a little unhinged as I float on cloud nine with him. He laughs, too, then kisses the top of my head. For a long while, neither of us says anything. There's only the sound of our heartbeats and ragged breaths and laughter.

We crossed a line that can never be uncrossed. And tonight, I gave him parts of myself no one has ever had.

Eventually, he props up on one elbow and looks at me like he's searching for something specific. Whatever it is, he finds it because his mouth goes soft at the edges, his gaze unguarded. His thumb brushes over my cheek, following the damp trail beneath my eye. It's overwhelming to experience this with a man I barely know, a man who seems to understand me better than anyone in my life. It's the first time I've cried in years, but it's from pure happiness.

"Stormy?" he asks, like he'd burn the world down for me.

I kiss his pulse on his neck, feeling his heartbeat beneath my lips. "I've never—" I'm not sure how to finish. He waits patiently. "This is all very new for me."

A smile tugs at his mouth before he steals a sweet kiss. "Love to hear it, darlin'. Hope you have the time of your life with me."

"You'll catch me if I fall too hard?"

"Every damn time," he confesses.

His fingers are in my hair as my thumb brushes across his cheek.

By the sparkle in his eyes, I know this wasn't sex, and this isn't an escape for me. This is trust and a sacred kind of knowing that we have found what we were searching for in one another. And the thought of that scares me shitless.

CHAPTER TWENTY

COLT

The night wraps around us like it's trying to eavesdrop, the stars out in full above the pond. There's something holy about being with her like this. It's like the world paused long enough for us to carve out a piece of forever.

We get dressed and watch the fire with her comfortably on my lap. Stormy sighs with content, like she finally stopped fighting herself.

What we shared was a huge decision we made together, and there is no going back.

I've got one hand resting on her thigh, the other holding her steady, not because she's about to fall, but because I'm not ready to let her go yet. I watch the way her fingers move over the inside of my forearm, tracing the veins. I'm not sure she even realizes she's doing it. I hold her a little tighter, kissing her hair, and notice her breathing has evened out.

Her walls aren't down; they're gone.

For a minute, we don't talk. We just sit and watch the fire fading in front of us. The night carries on like nothing has changed, but I have. All of me has. I didn't know I was missing anything until she gave it to me. This feeling. This closeness. This reckless hope that maybe life can be more than plans and repairs and staying one step ahead of being left behind.

I press a soft kiss on her shoulder, where her dress has slightly fallen. She shifts closer, and that small movement undoes something in me that I didn't realize was still wound tight. I've been with women before. I've touched skin and heard my name on someone's breath. But I've never felt like this. Not once. Nothing even comes close. It scares me, but also excites me.

Stormy chose me.

Not as a hiding place, not as a distraction, but as her safety net.

And now that I know what it's like to be needed by her, I don't think I can go back to pretending I ever want anything less than *forever*. The word cements in my chest as we watch the flames die until it's mostly ash and memory. The last few embers glow hot, but they're fading fast.

I should put it out, and we should leave. But I stay like this for another minute, holding her, not wanting the night to end. I run my hand down her spine, committing it all to memory. This night. Her laugh. The way her body curls into mine, like she's been waiting her whole life for someone to cherish her as she is. Stormy isn't just in my arms; she's in every plan I make. And, damn, that puts a smile on my face.

Even after everything we've experienced, in the back of my mind, I know she's still leaving.

Her thumb rests on my wrist, and I wonder if she notices how erratic she makes my pulse.

"Is this real?" she whispers, like she's woken from a dream and the world is waiting to snap her back to where she was before us.

I don't answer right away, not with words. I lift her hand to my mouth and press it there.

"Seems real to me," I say, voice heavy with everything I'm trying not to say too soon. The last thing I want to do is scare the shit out of her.

She shifts on my lap and turns to face me. I never want to

forget how she's swimming in my eyes. Tonight, she's allowed me to see every vulnerable part of her. Right now is no different.

"I didn't want to like you," she says, half a smile tugging at her lips.

"I got the memo with that whole *you're too young for me* bullshit," I say.

"And yet," she says, drawing out the words, "here we are."

"Here we fucking are." I grin. "Regrets?"

She shakes her head, chewing on her bottom lip. "I'm asking myself when we can do that again."

"Yeah?" I lift a brow, grinning.

"Yeah," she whispers.

I push a strand of hair away from her temple, tucking it behind her ear.

"I don't know how I'm going to leave," Stormy admits. "My life away from here is so messy."

"Trust it'll work out how it should." I realize I'm sounding woo-woo, like my sister Kinsley. "But I wouldn't be able to walk away from me either."

Laughter escapes her, and damn if it isn't the best sound I've ever heard.

She leans her forehead against mine. "You're getting cocky, Valentine."

I tilt my head just enough to brush her nose with mine. "I've earned it."

She hums, thoughtful. "You did just ruin me out here. Twice."

I chuckle. "Darlin', I'd ruin you everywhere, if you let me."

Her eyes flick to mine—wide, amused, maybe a little scandalized. "You're serious."

"I have a few places I'd like to be adventurous." I waggle my brows.

"Yeah?" she asks. "Like where?"

"Back of the truck. My old bedroom. Tree house behind my

parents'. Every single room at the farmhouse, upstairs included. A bar in town. In the church bell tower."

Her mouth falls open. "You *sinner.*"

I chuckle. "You asked."

She playfully nudges my chest with her fingertips. "Is this your way of asking if I'm in?"

"I mean, it does take two to tango, but now that you've brought it up, I'd love for you to be my partner in crime ..."

Stormy rolls her eyes, but there's color rising in her cheeks that tells me she's not as unaffected as she pretends to be.

"Let's not get carried away," she says, already starting to shift off my lap.

I pull her back down. "Too late. You're sittin' on the lap of a man planning his entire life around your desperate moans."

She gasps, "Colt!"

"What?" I grin. "You said you wanted to do it again. I'm just being supportive and suggestin' locations."

She laughs again, but this time, she hides her face in my neck. Her lips are against my skin as she mutters, "You are absolutely going to be the death of me."

"Nah," I whisper, turning my mouth to her temple. "I'm gonna be the life of ya."

That stills her. Just for a second. Her fingers curl into the collar of my shirt, like maybe the weight of that line settles somewhere inside her. And maybe it settles in me too.

We sit for another beat; the fire is a whisper. The stars have shifted overhead, and the night air has cooled enough to raise chill bumps across her skin. I kiss her shoulder one more time before she slides out of my arms and stands.

I grab the metal bucket we use to put fires out and dip it into the edge of the pond. The surface is calm, reflecting starlight in the ripples. I fill it, then carry it back to the firepit, pouring it over the glowing remains. The pit hisses, and smoke curls up in a spiral before it vanishes.

Stormy watches me with wild hair and kiss-swollen lips. She's a dream I only dared to have.

"You ready to go?" she asks.

"Not even a little."

She laughs. "Come on, cowboy. We have to drive that thing back before someone thinks we eloped."

"Not the worst idea you've ever had," I say, offering her my hand.

She takes it, fingers lacing with mine. I grab the picnic basket and blanket.

"I don't know if I'm bride material," she says.

"You are, darlin'. Just haven't found the right man yet."

"Maybe I have."

By the time we make it to the side-by-side, Stormy pauses before climbing in, glancing back at where we just were.

"I'm going to remember this forever," she says.

I place a hand on the small of her back and guide her up into the seat. "Good. But know that I plan on givin' you a hell of a lot more nights worth remembering."

And with her hand back in mine and the stars stretched out above us, I know we've only just begun.

"So, was it worth twenty grand?" I ask.

"Cowboy, I'd have paid a million."

We ride back in the side-by-side, the engine loud in the stillness, and I keep all four wheels on the ground. She leans into me, her hand resting on my thigh. I reach down and cover it with mine.

I park it where I found it, and then we walk to the truck, giddy and full of smiles.

"What have you two been up to?" I hear from the shadows, seeing Emmett sitting on a lawn chair with a bottle of Hot Damn in his hand.

"Fuck!" I yell at him. "You scared the shit out of me."

"*Us*," Stormy says.

His laughter echoes into the night. "Y'all look guilty."

"Bitch, so do you," I tell him, and we continue.

"I get to be the best man! I'm claiming it first!" Emmett hollers with a chuckle.

"Remi is my best man," I say over my shoulder. "Her balls are bigger than yours."

He howls with laughter as I lead Stormy to the truck. I give her a soft kiss before I close the door.

Once I'm inside and crank the engine, she turns to me. "You think he heard my moans?"

"Possible." I chuckle. "But I dunno how long he's been there."

By the time we pull into the driveway, it's late. The house is dark, except for the porch light I left on earlier. I run around and open her door, and instead of letting her walk, I lift her into my arms and carry her. I kick the truck door shut.

"This is princess treatment." She wraps her arms around my neck, kissing right under my ear. "You're too romantic," she says, squeezing her thighs together.

"Nah, just Southern." I set her down on the porch and steal another kiss.

We head inside without turning on the lights. I catch her watching me in the glow of the living room lamp.

She looks tired in the way that comes after incredible sex, not exhaustion. Her body is loose, eyes soft, lips parted just slightly, like she hasn't quite caught up to what the night gave her.

"Want to take a shower with me?" I ask.

She raises an eyebrow. "Right now?"

"Yes," I say. "While I wouldn't mind getting you naked again, I'm sweaty, I smell like campfire, and I want to rinse off. The invitation is open. Always."

She studies me for a moment, then nods. "Sure. I'd like that."

I reach for her hand and lead her down the hall.

When we walk into the bathroom, I flick on the light, and she removes her dress, leaving it in a heap by the door. The mirror throws our reflection back at us, and we're equal parts wild and spent.

I turn on the shower, giving the pipes a second to shudder awake as I undress. Her arms slide around my waist, fingers splayed across my stomach, and her cheek settles between my shoulder blades. We stand, quiet, listening to the water gather force.

Steam fogs the edges of the mirror first. When the shower's hot, I guide her in, watching her hair darken and stick to her skin. She doesn't shiver; she just tilts her head back, lets the water fall on her face, and stays like that, breathing, the corners of her mouth softening.

I grab a bar of soap and work up a lather, hands slick and careful, trailing over her arms, down her back, mapping every hard-earned line. She leans into my touch, and her throat releases a sound that's half purr, half prayer.

"You ever get tired of taking care of everything?" she asks, voice muffled by the hiss of the shower.

"Sometimes," I admit, rinsing her shoulders. "But it makes me feel useful, I guess. Like I'm doing something that matters to someone besides myself."

She turns to face me, eyes searching mine. "It does matter."

I wash her hair, fingers digging gently at her scalp. She closes her eyes and lets her head fall forward, surrendering to it, and I hold her up with an arm around her rib cage. We don't talk for a while. Just the rhythm of water, the regularity of our breathing, the comfort of each other's bodies.

I don't know what is written on her skin or how many times someone else has used or hurt her, but that ends now. Stormy is mine.

When we're clean, we towel off together, and I give her another one of my T-shirts, loving to see them on her. I don't bother with anything but boxers. We collapse onto the mattress, limbs tangled.

The only light left in the house is the lamp by my bed, and I reach over and turn it off. She curls into me, fingertips tracing the family brand tattooed on my chest.

Her breathing slows. "Thank you for the best date of my life."

I smile. "Backatcha."

She lifts her head and meets my eyes. "I still have to leave—you know that, right?"

"Yes. When that time comes, I won't ask you to stay even if I want you to," I confess. "You have to make that decision on your own, darlin'."

"I know." She settles again, arm hugging my chest in a way that manages to restrain me and comfort me at the same time. She's warmer now, almost feverish, and I can feel her breathing even. She's already drifting, but she holds on for one last alert minute—maybe panicked, maybe greedy—her words crowding out in a rush. "I don't want to hurt you."

I consider her words, exhaling, as she melts into my side.

"I think you saved me," I say finally, letting it hang there.

She's asleep by the time I've spoken out loud.

I lie awake after, listening to the settling of pipes and the ancient creaks of the old house. Our skin sticks where we're pressed together. I try to memorize this moment with her because I don't know what our future holds.

Even now, under the weight of her sleep, I can feel the ripple of some inevitable goodbye traveling through me. She's going to leave, but the reality is she's always been leaving. Every day that passes is one less day I'll have with her, and that thought nearly destroys me. I hold her a little tighter because I already miss her. But no matter what happens between what we were and what we're becoming, I have hope, and I hang on to that.

CHAPTER TWENTY-ONE

STORMY

I'm still barefoot and flipping through paint swatches in the hallway when Colt finds me.

"Are you sure you want me to pick the color?" I ask. Leaving my imprint on his walls seems like a big deal to me, and I can't decide.

"Positive," he tells me as he leans against the doorway, arms crossed, wearing that lazy smirk that drives me wild. "Could use your touch."

He's shirtless again, and he still smells like soap from the shower he just took. Colt looks annoyingly good without even trying. Today, we woke up at sunrise and have worked nonstop, taking only food and water breaks. However, every wall is up and painted with a base coat now. We're a good team.

"You doin' anything tonight?" he asks casually.

I raise an eyebrow. "Well, I was gonna spend some quality time with paint samples, maybe light a candle, whisper sweet nothings to eggshell whites."

He chuckles. "Cancel your plans. Let's go out."

I pause, the paint swatch in my hand already forgotten. "Like … out, *out*?"

"Yeah. Out on the town," he says. "A change of scenery would be nice."

I stare at him for a beat, trying to gauge how serious he is. But he's watching me with that steady look he gives me right before he rearranges my rules. Right now, I want him to rearrange my guts, but I keep that to myself.

"Can I ask where we're going?"

"There's a bar downtown called Boot Scooting. It's one of the local country music bars that has a nice dance floor and pool tables in the back. London's band is playing, and I'd love to support them. Plus, the drinks are cold."

"Sounds like fun, but I dunno if my two left feet can handle any more dancing," I tease.

He steps into my space, and I look up at him.

His voice drops. "Oh, come on. Need to teach ya how to two-step."

My stomach dips, heat flaring under my skin. "Uh ..."

He moves forward, grabbing my body. He guides me gently, his hand firm against the small of my back, the other holding mine in a loose, confident grip. "It's easy. One step, then two, just like this. One," he murmurs, stepping back. "Two. Step together."

I follow, a little clumsy at first, but his body doesn't waver. He's patient, and he moves in an easy rhythm, his bare feet sliding across the old hardwood like he was born, knowing how to do this.

"I suck at this," I mutter.

He grins, eyes locked on mine. "You're doin' fine. It's not about perfect steps. It's about how it feels."

"How does it feel?" I ask, breathing a little shorter now.

I'm overly aware of every inch of him—his chest brushing mine, the scent of soap clinging to his skin, the way he holds me close.

"Like it's meant to be," he says and spins me suddenly, pulling me right back into him before I can even squeal.

I crash into his chest, laughing as I grip his shoulders. "Okay, that wasn't a beginner move."

"That was a cowboy move," he says, smirking. "Had to make sure you were paying attention."

"I'm paying attention," I say, heart thudding, smile wide.

We sway in place for a few more beats, no music playing except the rhythm of our feet and the quiet thrum of something sweet and wild between us.

He dips his head, brushing his nose against my cheek, and his voice comes low. "Not sure if you realize this yet, but you're a damn good partner."

"Only when you're leading," I whisper, then laugh against his chest when I step on his toes.

"That's true. But I think you're ready," he says, spinning me around again. "It'll be fun."

"I trust you," I say, grinning wide. "Do I have time for a shower?"

"Yep, sure do."

"Will you pick out my clothes?" I ask.

"Fuck yeah," he tells me.

I flash him a grin, disappear into the bathroom, and quickly shower.

By the time I walk into the bedroom, Colt is dressed in Wranglers and a nice button-up, smelling like temptation on legs. Several outfits are laid out on his bed, and he's sitting next to them.

"Dealer's choice," he tells me, ankles crossed, looking so damn relaxed.

I drop the towel, and his eyes stay focused on mine.

"Tempting," he says.

I smirk, moving forward, thankful that Kinsley and Summer gave me so many clothes. I slide on a blue jean skirt and a tank top, then move to the mirror in the corner. I swipe on a bit of mascara and lip gloss, then run my fingers through my hair to shake out the waves. No need to overdo it—he's already seen me at my worst, and somehow, he still looks at me like I'm the only woman in the world.

Behind me, I hear the soft creak of the mattress as he stands.

"You look incredible," he says, voice full of that easy warmth that makes my knees weak. "And you smell so damn good."

I turn to him. "Thank you. I'm almost ready. Just need my boots."

"I'll get 'em."

He walks into the closet and emerges with them in his hand. He places them in front of me like they're something sacred. Then, without saying a word, Colt drops to one knee. I look down at him as he bows before me. He just smirks up at me, all relaxed confidence as he picks up the first boot. His hands slide up my bare calf, steady as he slips the boot on. Then the other. When he's done, he smooths his palm over my shin and looks up at me with that unrushed stare that makes me unravel.

"There," he says, standing, his blue eyes never leaving mine. "Now you're ready to drive every man in that bar to drink."

I step in closer, wrapping my arms around his neck. "Good thing I only care about one man's attention."

He leans in, brushing his lips over mine. "You've had mine since the day you walked into my life like a damn storm."

He kisses me again before pulling back with that devilish grin. "Let's go raise a little hell, darlin'."

And just like that, I follow him out the door, boots on my feet, his name on my heart, and every intention of dancing like I finally belong. Because he makes me believe I do.

Twenty minutes later, we arrive at Boot Scooting.

I can tell I'm going to love it by the neon sign in the window and the haphazard line of dollar bills stapled to the ceiling of the entryway. Inside, it's all rough pine walls and old metal signs for motor oil and chewing tobacco, and it's crowded for a weeknight, but I guess it is still summer. The stage lights are on, and guitars are on stands, along with the drum kit. On the front of the bass drum, it says, *The Heartbreakers*.

The bar is already half full by the time we get there. Locals are scattered between high-tops and booths. The jukebox is humming something familiar under the low rumble of voices and laughter as everyone waits for the show. There's a partition to the side that's full of pool tables, a dartboard, and a line of stools at the bar, which is so used that the wood is worn with wear.

Colt's hand doesn't leave the small of my back from the second we walk in. It's not subtle. Not a friendly guide-through-the-door kind of touch. It's possessive. Intentional. And every time his fingers flex, I feel it like a spark under my skin.

People turn and glance at us. It's not in a dramatic way, but I know we've been talked about.

London approaches us, gives me a tight hug, and then swings her arms around Colt. "You came!"

"Of course I did. I'm your biggest fan," he tells her. "Wouldn't miss it for the world, little sis."

She beams wide. "I'm so lucky to have you."

I feel the same sentiment.

"Happy you're here too," London says to me, then glances at the time on her phone. "Oops. I gotta go!"

"Break a leg," Colt tells her.

London disappears toward the stage with a final wink, and the overhead lights dim just slightly as the band starts to warm up. The crowd's energy shifts, and it becomes more excited. Someone whistles from the back, and Colt chuckles beside me.

"She's got herself a fan club," he says, looking at the crowded room.

"It's a Valentine trait," I tease, leaning into him as he wraps his arm around me.

London steps up to the mic, the strap of her guitar sliding over her shoulder. She tucks her dark, curled hair behind her ear and flashes the crowd a smile that's all cheekbones and shine.

"Hi, y'all! My name is London, and we're The Heartbreakers! This first one's kinda new, a song I wrote for my big brother," she says, her voice clear and confident. "He's my biggest fan, and he recently inspired me to write this love song. It's called 'Right One, Right Time.'"

I glance up at Colt, but he's already looking at me. His jaw's tight, but his eyes are warm. Wrecked really.

"Guess that's about us," I say.

"Seems like it," he says, lips grazing the side of my temple.

The first notes of the song roll through the bar, honey sweet, full of slide guitar and yearning. The melody of the guitar doesn't need lyrics to pull a person's heart in. It's free and light, a twinkle of a song that's followed by her twang.

Colt holds out his hand. "Dance with me."

I hesitate for half a second, but he's already pulling me toward the open space near the stage where other people are dancing. A few other couples follow behind us. Some are older, swaying like they've been dancing together since Reagan was president; many are younger, around London's age.

When Colt pulls me into his arms, the room falls away.

His palm finds the center of my back, his other hand clasping mine just right. We move barely more than a sway. His eyes stay locked on mine, and all my worries disappear. At this moment, I'm his, and that's all that matters.

"You good?" he asks, dipping his head to whisper against my ear.

"Better than good," I say.

"Love to hear it." He pulls me closer.

The song builds gently around us—London's voice strong and sweet, wrapping around the words like she wrote them just for this moment. I rest my head on Colt's chest, breathing in his scent, the low vibration of his hum under my cheek.

When the last note hits, he tilts my chin up, kissing me, like he's sealing something permanent between us.

When we part, there's a small burst of applause around the room, but I hardly hear it.

Colt smiles, brushing a thumb across my cheek. "Perfect partner."

I look up into his eyes and almost believe it.

The next song is upbeat, and several people flood the stage so they can sing along with London, who works the crowd like she's in a huge stadium.

"You know, your sister has talent."

"I know," he says with a laugh. "She's gonna be huge."

I cross my arms in front of me. "You do see the best in everything."

"Yes, ma'am, I sure do," he says.

We slide onto a couple of stools near the corner, and we're half shadowed, half visible.

He leans forward, getting the bartender's attention. "'Scuse me, sir."

A guy comes over—a cute bartender, wearing a cowboy hat. "Sunny, this is my friend Boone Tucker. His parents own this place."

Boone takes my hand and kisses my knuckles.

Colt's jaw clenches. "I will fuck you up."

I laugh. "Nice to meet you."

"If it doesn't work out with Colty, lemme know," he says. "Whatcha drinkin'? You look like a dry martini type of woman. Or you like drinkin' your whiskey neat."

My mouth falls open. "How did you do that?"

"I'm good at readin' people, especially those boss-babe women from the city. It's the vibe."

My brow lifts. "I'll take the martini. Extra dirty. Make sure the glass is clean," I tell him matter-of-factly.

"The regular?" he asks Colt, who gives him a quick head nod in return.

Colt smirks and turns back to me. "I love it when you turn that part of you on. It's like a light switch."

A few minutes later, Boone returns with our drinks.

"Y'all need anything, holler. Nice meetin' you, miss. Treat my bestie right. He's a good guy."

"Aw, stop. She's going to think I told you to say that," he says with a laugh, lifting his glass.

We twist on the stools, so we can look at one another more easily.

"Is he related to Jace?"

"You're good at paying attention, aren't you?"

"You have no idea," I say.

"They're brothers," he explains. "Jace is three years younger than us. More of an asshole, if that's possible."

I commit that fact to memory, then focus back on him. "When I return to New York, I'd like to speak to someone about London."

His eyebrows rise. "What do you mean?"

I lean in and whisper in his ear, "I have contacts who could help her."

His fingers thread through my hair. "Seriously?"

"I have contacts in every area of the entertainment industry. She could be the next Taylor."

Colt just stares at me for a second, his whiskey halfway to his lips. "You're serious."

"As a heart attack," I say, taking a sip of my martini. "That girl has talent. Real talent. And she deserves more than playing covers in dusty bars and hoping the right person stumbles through the door."

He looks toward the stage, where London's setting up with her band, adjusting her mic, and laughing with the drummer. "But you literally stumbled through the door of a dusty bar. You're the right person, apparently."

I tilt my head at him and laugh. "I guess you're right."

I stir my drink once, keeping my tone casual. "I can't

guarantee anything, only an introduction or a conversation with someone at a label I know. The rest would be on her. She has the talent; it will be an auto yes."

He drags a hand over his mouth like he doesn't know what to do with that. "I'm shocked."

"Colt," I say, setting my glass down and reaching for his hand, "she's gonna be huge. Take some video of her on your phone right now, playing in this bar. Trust me."

His eyes soften, but there's something fierce flickering in them too—pride maybe. "Right now?"

I laugh. "Yes. Go make her a music video with your cell phone. Walk through the crowd. But bring your focus back to her singing and playing with her band." I grab his arm. "Go!"

Colt cuts through the crowd like he owns the place—camera up, grin wide, energy buzzing off him in waves. People laugh and cheer as he spins, recording the bartenders pouring drinks, couples two-stepping, and the band in full swing. But every few seconds, he brings the lens right back to London. She catches on somewhere in the second verse, brows lifting as her smile shifts from confused to thrilled. Her voice doesn't falter—if anything, it soars. She's feeding off the moment now, playing like she's standing in front of a stadium instead of on a hardwood stage in a Texas dive bar.

And Colt? He's still filming, hollering her name between whoops like he's her entire PR team and fan base, rolled into one man with a cowboy hat and a camera phone. It's perfect.

I drain the last sip of my martini and wave Boone over for another, my gaze locked on Colt as he hops onto the edge of the dance floor and spins in a full circle for dramatic effect. He stays out there for the entire four minutes, making sure he's got as much footage as possible.

London laughs into the microphone. "My brother Colt, everyone."

He turns around and waves with a smile before heading back toward me, cheeks flushed, eyes bright blue.

He drops onto the stool beside me, slightly out of breath. "Like that?"

"Exactly," I say, tapping the screen. "Don't ever delete it. The first music video she has, use that. Any footage you have like that is gold and a documentation of the very beginning. It's to be cherished, but also, she'll be able to share it with her fan base."

With his hand on my thigh, he leans in. "Who are you?"

I grab his phone and google my name, then hand it to him. His eyes slide down the countless articles, and he shrugs like he doesn't give a damn.

"That's your reaction?" I'm shocked.

"What? That's supposed to impress me?" He shakes his head with a laugh. "It doesn't, darlin'."

I stare at him like he just handed me the whole damn world. "I've never felt so *normal.*"

He shakes his phone. "This woman doesn't matter. I don't know her. Just the one who's sitting in front of me."

I blink at him, caught somewhere between undone and completely floored.

His arm is still casually draped across my leg, eyes steady on mine.

I blink fast, trying not to cry in the middle of a bar that smells like whiskey and barbecue sauce. "You're gonna ruin me."

He chuckles. "Payback's a bitch, ain't it?"

I laugh into his shoulder and wrap my arm around him, breathing in the scent of cedar and skin.

London starts another song, slower this time.

He pulls me close, his hands steady on my hips, and leans in and kisses me. London's voice swells as she hits the chorus again, and the whole crowd sings with her now.

When we pull away, he whispers, "I'm happy."

"And I'm the reason?"

"Sweetheart," he says as I take a sip of my martini, "you've been the reason for a while now."

The gin goes hot in my throat, and it buzzes through my bloodstream, settling somewhere in my belly.

We talk for a little while—about nothing, about everything. I catch him watching me instead of listening. When I lift my glass again, his eyes follow the movement like it's the most interesting thing in the world.

"You're staring," I say.

"Can't help it," he replies. "You're mesmerizing."

We don't make it through the second drink before I'm ready for him to throw me over his shoulder and take me home.

I shift slightly, and his thumb drags a circle across my skin.

"Colt," I whisper, more warning than protest.

His gaze flicks to mine. "I need you to stop looking at me like that."

I lift a brow. "Like what?"

"Like you want me to lose my damn mind in this bar."

I take a sip, not smiling. Not denying it either.

Then I lean in and whisper, just loud enough for him to hear, "Then maybe stop looking at me like you already have."

That's all it takes.

He stands, reaches for my hand, and pulls me away from the bar without saying a damn word.

CHAPTER TWENTY-TWO

STORMY

My heart hammers against my ribs, but I follow him past the pool tables, past the dartboard, down a dim hallway lined with scuffed walls and posters for events that already happened.

He doesn't ask. He doesn't have to. We slip into the single-occupancy restroom at the end of the hall, and the door slams shut behind us. The lock clicks into place with a finality that sends a shiver down my spine.

"Oh, was this on your list?"

"Yes," he says. His hands are already on me, rough and desperate, as he pushes me against the countertop.

All I can smell is his cologne, his need, his fucking hunger. My ass presses into the edge, but I don't care.

I want this. I want him. I want to help him cross things off his sex list, including that damn church bell.

Our kisses aren't sweet or the kind that asks for permission because it's already been given. The lines between us have been erased, and there are no more boundaries. There is no reversing last night.

His hands find my waist, then slide lower, gripping just tight enough to make me gasp against his lips. I fist the collar of his shirt, dragging him closer, until there's nowhere left to go but into me.

"I want you so bad," he whispers against my mouth, even as his hand is already slipping under the hem of my skirt.

I nod, breathless. "What a coincidence ..."

"Isn't it?"

The restroom is small—too small for how fast we're moving—but neither of us cares.

His mouth crashes into mine, all teeth and tongue, and I moan into him, my hands clawing at his shirt, yanking it up to touch the heat of his skin. He's already hard, his thick cock straining against his jeans, and I can't wait to get my hands on it. I fumble with his belt, my fingers trembling with anticipation, and he lets out a guttural growl that echoes off the wall as I finally free him.

"Fuck," he groans, his hand tangling in my hair, pulling my head back to expose my throat.

His lips are on me in an instant, sucking and biting, leaving marks that I'll feel for days. I don't care if anyone sees them. Let them know. Let them all know what he's done to me.

His other hand is under my skirt, fingers sliding under the edge of my panties, and I gasp as he finds me wet and ready.

"Already soaked," he mutters, his voice full of lust. He doesn't waste time, pushing my panties aside and sliding two fingers inside me, curling them just right to make me cry out.

"More," I beg, my hips rocking against his hand, desperate for more friction, more pressure, more of him.

He listens, adding a third finger, stretching me open, and I can't help but moan his name, the sound echoing off the restroom walls.

He pulls his fingers out, placing them in his mouth, sucking them before spinning me around and removing my panties completely. I bend over the counter, my hands gripping the edge for support. I hear the rustle of his jeans, and then he's there, his cock pressing against my entrance, hot and hard and so fucking ready. He doesn't enter me immediately, and my body nearly quivers for him.

"You want this?" he growls, his voice demanding.

"Yes," I gasp, my voice trembling with need. "I need you."

He doesn't make me wait, just slams into me in one brutal thrust, filling me completely. I scream, the sound muffled by my own hand as I bite down on my fingers to keep from being too loud. But, fuck, it's impossible to stay quiet. He grabs my hips, pulling me back onto him with every stroke, his cock hitting that spot inside me that makes me see stars. He stretches me in ways I didn't think possible. Shock waves of pleasure flood through my body.

The bathroom is a fucking steam chamber. The mirror's fogged up, but I don't need to see myself to know how I look—hair a tangled mess, lips swollen from his kisses, my tits bouncing with every brutal thrust he drives deeper into me. I'm bent over the sink, my hands gripping the edge so hard that my knuckles are white, my ass in the air, and his cock buried to the hilt in my dripping cunt.

I'm so close already, my body trembling with the desperate need to come, and he knows what I need. He reaches around, his fingers finding my clit, rubbing it in tight, circles that push me over the edge.

"That's it, darlin'. Come for me," he says into my ear, nibbling the shell. "You're so fucking close."

I gasp out, the orgasm ripping through me. I lose my balance, and he holds me up as I squeeze his cock so fucking tight. My body convulses around him, and he groans, his thrusts becoming erratic as he chases his own release.

"Fuck, you feel so good." His voice is strained.

He's not gentle, not anymore. Not after I came the first time, screaming his name like a fucking banshee.

Now it's raw, primal. The hard fucking that leaves bruises and marks. It's the kind that makes me feel alive and reckless in the most depraved way possible. His hands are on my hips, fingers digging into my flesh as he slams into me, each thrust sending me to outer space. Every thick inch of him stretches me open, filling me in ways that make my toes curl and my pussy clench around him like a vise.

His soft pants send shivers down my spine. I moan, loud and shameless. I love the way he fucks me like he owns me but cherishes every minute. My pussy's already throbbing, another orgasm building deep inside me, and I know he can feel it, too, the way my walls are tightening around him, trying to milk every drop of cum from his cock.

"Yes," I gasp, my voice trembling. "Yes. Harder."

He doesn't need to be told twice. His pace quickens, his hips slamming into mine with a force that makes the sink rattle and my tits bounce even more. I can hear the wet sound of his balls slapping against my clit. Every thrust drives me wild. My clit's swollen, aching for attention, and he reaches back down, like he can read my mind. His magic fingers work me again as he fucks me senseless.

"Lose control with me," he says.

"Too late," I pant out.

"Mmm. I'm going to fill your tight little pussy full."

I'm close—so fucking close. I'm clenching around him, my body trembling as the pleasure rebuilds, and then it slams through me. I scream his name as I come, my cunt spasming around his cock, my juices gushing out of me as he fucks me through it, his thrusts never slowing down.

"Fuck yes. Three is the minimum tonight," he mutters, his grip on my hips tightening. "That's it. Take it. Take every fucking inch."

He pulls out of me, his cock still hard. Creamy cum drips out of me, running down my thighs. He spins me around, and with his hands on my ass, he lifts me up and sets me on the edge of the sink. His mouth crashes into mine, his tongue forcing its way into my mouth as he kisses me hungrily, his hands roaming over my body.

"You're not done," he growls against my lips. "I'm not done with you yet."

Younger men and their stamina.

And then he's on his knees in front of me, his hands spreading my legs wide as he buries his face in my soaked pussy. His tongue is everywhere—licking, sucking, fucking me with it—and I'm already coming again, my hands tangled in his hair as I ride his face like a fucking animal.

His tongue is a fucking weapon, and he's wielding it like a sword.

"Fuck," I whisper as he swings my thigh over his shoulder. The pleasure is almost too much.

My pussy glistens, and his face is buried between my legs like he's mining for gold. His mouth is hot, wet, and relentless, lapping at my clit like it's dessert. His tongue flicks, swirls, and plunges into me, over and over, driving me to the edge of sanity.

"Colt," I moan, my voice trembling as my hips buck against his face.

He's holding me upright, his fingers digging into my flesh hard enough to leave marks.

I've already come twice—three fucking times—and my body is shaking, greedy for another. His tongue is fucking me deep, curling inside me.

"You taste so good." His voice is muffled against my pussy. He pulls back just long enough to glance up at me, his lips slick with my juices, his blue eyes hungry. "I could eat you all fucking night."

And then he's back at it, his tongue diving into me like he's trying to fucking drown in me. I can feel every flick, every goddamn movement as he works me over. My clit is throbbing, swollen, and sensitive, and every time his tongue brushes against it, I feel like I'm going to explode.

"Oh God, oh God," I whimper, one hand thrusts in his hair. "I'm gonna come again." I gasp, my voice breaking as the pressure rebuilds inside me.

He doesn't stop. He doesn't let up. His tongue is a fucking piston, driving me closer and closer to the edge.

And then it hits me—a wave of pleasure so intense that it feels like my soul is being ripped out of my body.

I scream his name as I come, and he laughs between my legs as my hips jerk uncontrollably. He keeps fucking me with his tongue, drawing out my orgasm until I'm nearly sobbing.

"Fuck, fuck, fuck," I chant, my voice hoarse as the pleasure washes over me in waves.

He finally pulls back with a smug smile on his lips. "Good girl," he purrs, his voice dripping with satisfaction, just as a knock taps on the door.

I'm breathless, and his cock is hard, dripping with cum. I bend over as I lower my skirt and lick the tip. His eyes watch me.

"We should go," he whispers.

"And what about you?" I ask breathlessly.

"I got what I wanted."

He kisses my temple like he didn't just ruin me in a public restroom. But it's not an answer I can accept. Instead, I drop to my knees in front of him, begging with my eyes.

The pounding continues.

"Sorry! It's going to be a while. Go to the men's!" I say.

He's hard and hot in my hand. I lift my brows.

The cold tile bites into my skin, but I don't give a fuck because his beautiful cock is inches from my face, throbbing and glistening with the slick evidence of what he just did to me. I can smell myself on him—that primal scent of my own arousal, mixed with the raw, masculine heat of his body.

My lips part, and I don't hesitate to take him into my mouth— all of him. My tongue flattens against the underside of his shaft as I swallow him down to the base.

The sound of his moan vibrates through me. His big hand fists into my hair, pulling me closer, encouraging me to take him even deeper. I revel in the way his cock stretches my throat, the way it pulses against my tongue like it's alive, like it's fucking me from the inside out. I can taste myself on him, that salty flavor that makes my pussy clench in memory of how he made me come, over and over, until I was a trembling, dripping mess beneath him.

I pull back, my lips dragging along his length, sucking hard as I go, and then I plunge down again, taking him even deeper this time. His hips buck, and he lets out a curse, his voice rough, like sandpaper.

"Fuck, your mouth," he whispers as his cock twitches against my tongue.

His balls tighten, and he's already so close to the edge. I don't let up—I can't—because I want this. I want him to lose control, to explode in my mouth, so I can taste every sweet drop of him.

I swirl my tongue around the head, teasing the slit, and then I take him deep again, my throat opening wider, like it was made for him. His grip on my hair tightens, and I can feel his thighs trembling as he fights it, but I don't let him.

"I'm in control," I tell him, pulling away, lifting a brow.

He smirks and bites that lip as I move back to him, sucking harder and slower until it's agonizing for him. My lips seal tight, and then his mouth falls open. I feel the first hot spurt of his cum hitting the back of my throat. I swallow it down greedily, my tongue working him through every pulse, every shuddering release, until he's spent and panting above me.

I don't immediately pull away. I keep him in my mouth, my tongue lapping at the sensitive head of his cock, savoring the last drops of his cum as they spill onto my tongue. He's still hard, still throbbing.

I smile up at him, my hands on his thighs. "Guess you can mark it off your list now."

"Hell yeah," he says, pulling me to my feet. "You're fucking amazing," he whispers against my lips.

"You're not so bad yourself," I say. "You've given me more orgasms in twenty-four hours than my ex gave me in four years."

He gives me that cocky grin that always makes my heart race, and I know this isn't over. Not by a long shot.

"What a piece of shit."

"Yep," I say, lips swollen, pussy still throbbing.

The knock returns.

Colt interlocks his fingers with mine. "Don't meet their eye, whoever it is."

When we step back into the hallway, hand in hand, his youngest brother, Sterling, is standing there with his arms crossed, leaning up against the wall. He pulls his phone out and takes a picture of us.

"What the fuck?" Colt asks.

"Hey, Beckett and Harrison bet me a hundred dollars each that you weren't the two banging in the restroom. I needed proof," he says.

Colt takes the phone from his hand.

"Delete it, and I'll give you one thousand in cash," I say, grabbing Sterling's cell phone from Colt and handing it back to him.

"Seriously? That's not how bets work," he says, confused.

"So? You take an ego hit and earn eight hundred dollars," I explain.

Sterling holds out his hand, and we shake on it. Then he deletes the photo. "Smart woman. Welp, guess I didn't see you. Have a good night, lovebirds."

"Just wait until you start dating seriously. I'm gonna embarrass the hell outta you," Colt tells him, leading me back to the bar, and no one gives us a second glance.

I spot Harrison and Beckett by the bar and point them out to Colt. He takes my hand, darting us away from them as London finishes her last song. We stand at the edge of the room and watch the crowd scream and chant for her at the end. When they head offstage, Colt waves goodbye to her, then leads me out the door.

By the time we make it back to the truck, my skirt is wrinkled and my hair's a wreck, and Colt looks just as shameless—shirt untucked, collar crooked, lips a little too swollen to be subtle.

He climbs behind the wheel.

I smooth the hem of my skirt, but it doesn't matter.

Colt glances at me, the corner of his mouth pulling upward. "I don't know what to say."

"I don't either." I shrug. "I'd do it again though."

He laughs, full-bodied and totally unrepentant. "Fuck, me too."

I chew on my lip. "Want to stop by the church on the way home?"

"Now who's the sinner?" he asks, resting a hand on my thigh.

"I'm just enabling." I slide my fingers over his knuckles.

"It's locked. We'll have to sneak in on a Sunday afternoon."

I lift my brows. "You've done recon on this?"

"Nah, darlin', just paid attention to details when everyone else wasn't."

The ride home is full of stolen glances and smirks. My legs are tingling, and I don't bother pretending I'm not replaying the last thirty minutes in my head. From the look on Colt's face, he is too.

When we pull into the driveway, the house glows like it was waiting for us.

Inside, it's cool and dark and familiar. The moment the door clicks shut behind us, I let out a long breath.

Colt watches me for a beat, then steps forward and cups my face in his hands. "That," he whispers, brushing his thumb over my cheek, "was the best weeknight I've ever had."

I laugh, curling my fingers into the front of his shirt. "I think we'll keep our talk-of-the-town crown."

"I don't care." He kisses me. It's soft and deep, all desperate aftermath that's full of promise.

We end the night tangled together in bed, a blanket draped across us like an afterthought.

My body's sore in the best way. My heart's too full. And as he holds me against him, I let myself imagine a life where I don't leave.

Is it even possible?

CHAPTER TWENTY-THREE

COLT

The smell of paint hits me before I even step inside. It's a familiar scent of something becoming new again.

Stormy's in the living room, bent over the tray, reloading her roller with a light yellow that reminds me of her. She's barefoot, wearing soft gray shorts and a black tank top that clings to her curves. Her hair's up, but barely. Messy strands fall against her cheek, and every time she pushes one behind her ear, I lose my thoughts.

The color is turning out better than I expected. I'm glad she chose it because I might have kept every wall white. She's quick, efficient, and focused. While she works, she hums the melody of the song London wrote for us. She turns and catches me staring.

"Focus, cowboy," she says, stretching up on her tiptoes, painting as high as she can up the wall.

"I am. On you."

She glances back at me, one brow raised. "You have a dog to adopt, remember?"

"Yes, ma'am. But I gotta enjoy the view while I can."

I move forward, grabbing my roller and dipping it into her

tray. With a long swipe, I stroke up the wall where she can't reach. I have six inches on her, so she takes the bottom, and I take the top.

"You flatter me," she says, stepping closer.

"It's the truth, darlin'."

"So"—she lingers for a second—"how do you like this color so far?"

"It's perfect. Happy. *Sunny*." She grins. "I love yellow. Reminds me of the countryside. Summer. Sunshine. Happy thoughts. These walls deserve that."

"You do too," I tell her. "I was almost scared you'd choose millennial gray."

"Is that your way of calling me old? Aren't you a millennial?" Her brows lift.

I scoff. "No. I'm Gen Z, baby."

"Fuck," she whispers and laughs.

I set the paint roller against the wall and pull her into my arms.

"Does this make me a cougar?" she asks.

"Does it make me your cub?" I quickly snap back.

"Shut the hell up," she tells me, and I lean in and kiss her as I laugh against her mouth. "You should be glad I like you."

"Glad? Nah. I'm fuckin' thrilled," I say, picking up my roller so we can finish painting the color on the walls.

The midday sun creeps in through the windows, and the only sound is the soft glide of paint and the occasional creak of the ladder.

"We won't finish before I leave, will we?" she asks after a while.

I pause, roller hovering halfway up the wall. "Probably not."

She nods like she already knew but needed to hear it out loud.

"But it's getting there. It's much closer than it was when I was working alone."

She keeps rolling. "That's true. Progress is progress."

"Yes, it is."

We keep working, side by side, the walls around us turning from bare to complete, like everything else between us.

I finish the wall and lower my roller, wiping the back of my arm across my forehead. Stormy's across the room, cleaning up, her tank top clinging to her back, shoulders flushed from the heat.

"Come on. I want to show you something," I tell her.

She follows me through the house, barefoot and curious, a light bounce in her step despite the hours we've been working.

I take her hand, leading her to the stairwell off the main entrance of the house. It's unfinished, and it still needs a handrail, but the steps are solid even if they creak. At the top, the temperature shifts slightly, and the light changes too. There's no door or drywall, just framed outlines and exposed beams. The floors are still in their original worn state, and all that stands is its potential.

"Careful," I say, steadying her as we step onto the landing. "It's rough."

She looks around, taking it all in. "I didn't expect it to be this big."

I gesture to the right. "That'll be the main bathroom for the largest bedroom. Back there ..." I motion toward the deeper end of the hall. "A game room or an office. A Jack and Jill bathroom goes here. And these two rooms ... one day, they'll be my kids' rooms."

I pause at the last door, my hand braced on the frame.

Stormy doesn't say anything, but she shifts beside me.

"I drew the layout before I purchased the place," I admit. "Had it in my head that if I started on the remodel, the right person would show up."

She walks to the nearest doorway and leans against it. Still, she smiles like she can see it.

"Have you ever imagined them?" she asks. "Your kids?"

I nod. "Not their faces or anything. The noises of kids. Little feet running down the hall. Laughter bouncing off the walls." I exhale. "It's quiet here. Always has been. But I never meant for it to stay that way."

She doesn't turn around and stares into the framed rooms with thoughtful eyes.

"I've never let myself picture it," she says. "Not really. A house. A life. The noise."

"You should," I say, smiling. "Kinsley calls it manifesting."

I don't say anything else. I let her stand in the space that will one day be something I only imagined, just like her.

Stormy steps deeper into one of the unfinished rooms. Her fingers graze the edge of a stud where the drywall hasn't been installed yet, tracing the grain of the wood.

I lean against the doorframe and watch her.

"This one. I always figured it'd be a nursery first," I explain.

She turns slightly, not speaking, but her hand pauses against the beam.

"Crib near the window," I add, quieter now. "Rocking chair in the corner. Maybe a bookshelf and a nice lamp."

Stormy swallows. "You have it all planned out?"

"Only in my mind." I run a hand along the back of my neck. "Didn't know who I was building it for. But I knew I wanted to be ready when she showed up."

"Colt," she says, almost like a warning.

"I'm not saying this is a pitch," I explain. "I won't ask you to stay. I want you to know—this house, this life—I built it to be shared with someone like you. Whether it's now or five years from now ... I'll wait for you."

She crosses the room to me, barefoot on the plywood, moving until she's standing right in front of me. Her gaze searches mine. "I don't want you to stop your life because of me."

"Stop my life? You jump-started it."

She leans forward and presses her forehead to my chest. I wrap my arms around her and hold her there, breathing in the scent of paint, sun-warmed skin, and something that feels dangerously close to hope.

We don't speak for a while.

"I hope your dreams come true," she finally says.

"They will."

We head back downstairs, the air much cooler on the first floor. Stormy's quiet beside me, not withdrawn, just deep in thought. When she gets like this, I like to leave her alone to work through her thoughts.

"I think we were cleaning up," she says, voice casual, but not light.

I nod, grabbing the roller I left leaning against the wall. "Perfect. Looks incredible in here. Thank you."

I slide my lips across hers, and she grabs my T-shirt, holding me tight.

We've barely pulled apart when the knock comes on the front door.

It's a quick two pounds, then a turning of a knob. I make my way to the hallway, wondering who has the fucking balls to let themselves into my house. Whoever it is doesn't believe in asking for permission.

The door creaks open, and a familiar voice calls out, "Please tell me you're decent."

I step into the hallway, and Remi's standing in the entryway, her hair in a low bun, sunglasses on her head. She's holding a gallon of lemonade.

Stormy follows me into the entryway, her cheeks a little pink, arms speckled with yellow paint.

Remi takes one glance at the two of us and smirks like she already knows more than she should.

"Wow," she says. "I didn't expect HGTV and foreplay, but I love a good renovation love story."

Stormy lets out a surprised laugh.

I rub the back of my neck. "It's not like that."

"Uh-huh." Remi hands me the lemonade. "This place is coming together."

"We're trying," I say.

Remi walks through every room on the bottom floor, and I follow her.

"Wow. I'm shocked you were able to turn this dump into a mansion."

"Still a long way to go." I breathe out.

My sister grins at Stormy. "You've inspired him."

"Maybe a little," Stormy says, brushing her hands on her shorts.

Remi grins. "Mama told me to bring you that lemonade, and I'd like to invite you to dinner on Friday. Cash and I are grilling. It's nothing big. Burgers and beer, and I invited Fenix. I'm worried about her."

I cross my arms over my chest. "Why?"

"I dunno. Ever since the rodeo has been in town, she's been standoffish."

My Spidey-Senses go off again, and I instantly think of Jace. I glance at Stormy, who lifts one brow like she already knows what's on my mind.

"We'll be there," I say, wanting to know what's going on with Fenix.

"Good. Don't tell anyone else, please. I don't want it to be a big deal," Remi nearly begs.

When all our siblings are there, it's a lot of work.

"Okay," I say with a nod.

"Well, I'll let y'all get back to whatever domestic moment I interrupted. Gotta go to the B and B for my shift," Remi tells us, giving us hugs, then leaves.

Stormy glances at me. "Do you think Fenix is acting like this because Jace is here?"

My jaw locks tight, and I breathe out, "My gut says yes."

She swallows hard. "What will you do?"

"Fuck him up."

With a shake of her head, she moves close. "You can't do that. Maybe you should talk to Fenix. Ask her?"

"I have," I explain. "She deflects and denies. No way she'd ever admit it to me. Maybe you should talk to her?"

Stormy studies me. "I'll try."

After we finish cleaning up our mess, I step outside onto the back porch, watching the horses graze in the pasture.

The sky starts to shift, and it's beginning to get darker sooner, the way it does in the late summer. I lower myself onto the bench, speckled with dry paint.

I rub the back of my neck, my muscles still tight from manual labor, but that's not what has me wound up. It's everything else.

Remi's visit shouldn't have affected me like it did, but I know Fenix is hurting.

The screen door creaks, then clicks shut behind me. I don't turn around, but I hear her footsteps. She doesn't say anything at first. Just walks across the porch and lowers herself beside me with two cups in her hand. It's the lemonade Remi brought.

I take a big sip, and my eyes go wide as I gulp it down. "You spiked it."

She giggles. "Oh, guess I should've warned you first. I poured vodka in it because why the hell not?"

Stormy leans back on the bench, her thigh rests against mine as she takes a big gulp.

"Fenix isn't like my other sisters," I say after a beat, eyes still locked on the horses in the distance. "She keeps things to herself, and she doesn't have many friends other than London and Vera, but they don't know either. London would tell me."

Stormy tilts her head thoughtfully. "Maybe she needs more time."

I glance over at her, taking in the paint streak on her jaw, the way her hair is starting to slip loose from its knot. "Maybe you're right."

She laughs under her breath. "I know how it feels to walk around, pretending everything's fine while drowning. It's easier not to talk about it. She's lucky to have you."

I take her hand, my thumb brushing across her knuckles. "So are you."

Her eyes lift to mine. "Oh, I'm aware. I don't take you for granted."

The breeze picks up, rustling the tall grass in waves. Somewhere off to the east, an engine rumbles in the distance.

Then Stormy shifts. "Colt …"

"Mm-hmm?"

"Thank you."

"For what?"

"For everything." She turns and presses a soft kiss to my jaw. "For letting me in so easily."

I tip my head, meeting her lips fully this time. "You're welcome. I'm lucky to be a part of your world."

Her eyes soften, and I stare out at the pasture, at the soft light casting long shadows, and I swear, for a moment, I can hear the future echoing back to us.

Little feet. Laughter. A life loud enough to fill every inch of this house we've made into a home.

The weight of the day slips off my shoulders.

We sit there until the sky turns purple, then fades to night.

And even then, I don't want to move.

"Hungry?" she asks.

"Could eat a horse," I tell her, and her brows furrow.

"Wait, you eat horses?"

Laughter rolls from me. "It's an expression. It means I'm

starving. Come on. Let me make you dinner, and then I want you for dessert."

"Love the sound of that," she says, standing and pulling me to my feet.

When she looks at me with adoration in her eyes, I think maybe we're doing something right. Maybe love doesn't have to be perfect. Maybe it's supposed to be a little messy with unknowns.

CHAPTER TWENTY-FOUR

STORMY

We wake up, have breakfast, then immediately get to work. The day I leave is coming fast, and I want the bottom floor finished before I go. Two and a half more days. That's all I have before I fly back to New York to face everything I ran from. Tomorrow is dinner at Remi's. Saturday is my packing day. Sunday, I'll leave. I've already scheduled a private jet, and I know my father was notified. I don't care anymore.

We spend the better half of the morning mounting face plates for the outlets and doing final touch-ups on the walls. It doesn't resemble the same house.

By the time I make it to the kitchen for lunch, Colt's already pulled the lids off the leftovers and warmed them. The house smells like fresh tortillas, fajita chicken, and cilantro.

He's tucked napkins under two paper plates on the worn table we've sat at a handful of times. A fan hums lazily in the corner, stirring the humid air as soft afternoon light spills through the windows. He glances up when I walk in, eyes sweeping from my hair to the bare skin beneath the hem of my tank top.

"You can make anything look good," he says.

"Even you," I tell him.

"Damn, ain't that right?" His mouth curves into a lazy grin as he pats the spot beside him. "Come eat before I lose my manners and hand-feed you."

I drop into the seat in front of him with a soft sigh and fold a leg beneath me. "Smells amazing."

"You do too," he says.

There's heat behind his voice. His words warm my skin like I've stepped into sunlight.

I don't realize I'm staring until Colt nudges my leg with his knee.

"You okay?" he asks.

I shrug. "Sorry, was thinking."

"About?" he asks.

"The future," I explain. "And how I suck at this."

His eyes crinkle as he scoops up another bite. "You mean the philosophical future or tomorrow? And you suck at what?"

"Tomorrow. Forever. I suck at this. At being ... well, not to put titles on this, but I don't think I'm girlfriend material." I take a bite of a taco and avoid his gaze, not ready to see how he's taking this.

"You're not," he confirms. "You're wife material."

"Always stealing my breath," I mutter. "I'm used to the idea that everything is temporary. That if I get comfortable, something or someone will come along to kick the legs out from under me. I'm waiting for the floor to drop out below me."

Colt's quiet for a beat, fork hovering in the air like he's weighing my words against something heavier. "It doesn't have to be like that," he finally says. "You deserve stability and safety. I'll give that to you."

His voice isn't a promise. It's a conviction, like he already decided I'm worth the risk.

"I want that. I want you," I confess, "but I never get what I want. That's the pattern. Want something too much, and life takes it away."

"That's bullshit," Colt says. "I won't accept that."

A drop of sour cream clings to his lip, and he swipes it away. I wonder what it'd be like if this all really belonged to us—the afternoons, the tacos, the silence, and the future. I've never been allowed to want these things. Donovan used to treat me like I was a winning trophy. Colt cherishes me like I'm his future.

Right now, I'm thankful I didn't say *I do*.

While we eat, I allow myself to admire his messy hair under his baseball cap and bright blue eyes. He's too handsome and tempting.

There's something about the way he sits—shoulders relaxed, forearm resting on the table—that makes me feel like I could have this. Colt makes me want to say *fuck it* to all my responsibilities and stay here with him forever. That's a fantasy though. And fantasies have expiration dates, even if they feel like home when you're in the middle of one.

My plate's almost empty now. Colt's still chewing like this is any other day.

My chest tightens with every beat that ticks us closer to goodbye. I know he feels that strange stretch in the air that's followed by the hush of our time winding down because I can't escape it.

Today, his shoulders aren't quite as relaxed, and we both know we're nearing the end of this.

"I keep waiting for this to feel fake," I say suddenly, before I can second-guess myself.

"What?"

"This. Us. The house. All of it. But it never does."

He watches me for a beat. "It's 'cause it's not."

I try to push past the ache that's building in my chest. "I don't want to ruin it."

"You're not," he says. "Even if you go, I'll be so damn grateful to have met you and for showing me the spark is still alive. I didn't think I'd ever feel this way again. You proved me wrong in the best way possible." He doesn't smile when he says it. It's not a line. It's his truth.

I swallow hard, understanding it more than he knows. I've been so worried about hurting him, but I'm not sure I'll survive leaving either.

He's not only become my lover but also my confidant and friend. Colt doesn't ask for anything in return, only my company. He continues showing up every day, reminding me that I deserve better than I believe and that he's here. And each time I hear my name on his lips, it's like I belong to him.

I clear my throat and set my plate in the sink. "Why'd you help me? That first day, when you didn't even know me?"

He doesn't answer straightaway, only gazes out the large bay window toward the barn. His jaw shifts like he's searching for the right words and trying not to overthink them.

"Some things you feel in your gut," he says finally. "You were one of 'em."

I want to believe there's such a thing as gut feelings and good moments that aren't a setup for heartbreak. I want to believe Colt and I are the exception, and we'll never have to experience that.

This place is still a work in progress, like us.

I take a deep breath, exhale, and sit on his lap now that he's finished eating. "Can we stay here for a little while?"

He shifts, wrapping his arms around me and inhaling my skin. "We can stay as long as you want."

The truth is, I must go to New York to confront my fears, but I don't know how to leave anymore.

Twenty minutes pass, and I know it's time to get moving. Colt washes our dishes, and I sit in my thoughts, letting the weight of them press down in the quiet.

I agreed to stay for a week and a half after we met so there would be no complications. And yet here I am.

I move to the bathroom and wash my hands. After I dry them, I notice there's one of his shirts folded beside the sink, like he left it there without thinking. I pick it up and press it to my nose, inhaling the smell of his soap and skin.

It smells like early mornings and safety.

When I glance in the mirror, I don't see the woman who ran away. I see someone who found herself.

For a second, the realization stings. How long had I been a shell of myself? *Years.*

I rest my hand on the edge of the counter and watch my reflection settle, but I know this is the calm before the storm. I've officially been gone for over two weeks since I took my time driving across the country to Valentine. My absence is a headline, and it's snowballing out of control. I must end the lies.

Friday night, before I leave, I'll check what people are saying about me. I can't handle it right now. I want to hide a little while longer and need time to mentally prepare myself. It will be overwhelming, and I'm already anticipating as much.

After ten minutes, I find Colt in the front room, where all his building supplies have been stored. His shirt's half tucked, half twisted, and I can tell he's deep in thought.

He treats me like I belong to him.

The softest smile pulls at the edge of his mouth when he sees me. "You okay?"

"Yeah," I say, sliding past him in the hall and giving his shoulder a careful bump. "Thinking a lot."

He cocks his head. "About getting me naked?"

"Actually, yes. That thought is on repeat," I admit, noticing how his shirt clings to his body. I force my gaze away and allow my eyes to trail around the space. "I can't believe what we've accomplished."

"It's finally starting to feel like a house," he says.

"More than that," I say before I can stop myself. "Feels like a home."

He wipes his hands on a nearby rag and nods once, almost to himself.

I press my back to the wall, needing something solid to lean on. "I'm leaving on Sunday."

He studies me quietly, as if I stunned him. "Forever?"

Colt's asking me if I'm about to walk out of his life after he opened every door for me.

I glance down at the hardwood floor, then back up. "I don't know."

There's a pause, brief, but it's so loud that I could scream.

"You can always come back to me," Colt says. It's a truth, not a plea. "You have a choice."

I want to stay in this unfinished house with this man who kisses me like I'm the only thing he's ever believed in. I can't move forward until I face everything I ran from first.

"Would you ever consider moving to New York?" I ask.

Colt shakes his head. "No. My life and family are here."

I walk toward him until I'm standing close enough to feel the heat coming off his skin. I place my palm flat on his chest, over his heart.

"I'm sorry," I whisper.

"Don't apologize," he says, grabbing my hand. "I just don't want this to be goodbye."

"You once told me you don't believe in goodbyes," I say.

"I don't," he tells me, tucking some wayward hair behind my ear. "I refuse to believe this is the end, but I can't leave, and I don't want you making sacrifices for me."

Something heavier than lust and quieter than love passes between us.

It feels like a future. One we haven't committed to yet, but somehow already have.

And just like this house, we still need work, but we're building this relationship piece by piece until it's complete.

CHAPTER TWENTY-FIVE

COLT

The afternoon settles quietly around us. Warm light filters through the windows, catching on floating dust and finished walls. Now that the walls are completed, we decided to do a deep cleaning of the first floor. Stormy works silently a few feet away, washing windows as if they had wronged her. I've got a shop vac, and I'm trying to get the sawdust from between the slats of the hardwood floor.

Stormy hasn't said much since lunch. Not that we're ever chatty when we're both focused, but today feels different. It feels heavier, like whatever's weighing on her has roots.

I glance over, pretending to look at the edges of the room, but really, I'm watching her shoulders. They're drawn tight, like she's holding something in. Stormy's the kind of woman who'll speak when she's ready and not a second before. So, I wait for her.

The silence stretches between us, comfortable and not. She steps back from the window, eyes trailing the streaks, but then she focuses outside.

Then, like she's trying the words on her tongue, she says, "No one's ever truly wanted me before."

I stop moving. Her voice is calm, like she's explaining the weather, but it cracks at the edges, just enough to gut me.

"Not for who I am deep inside," she adds, staring straight ahead. "No one has ever wanted this raw version of me."

I straighten, turn off the vacuum, but I don't speak.

"I've been loved for how I look. For my family name. For the image of me that fits into someone else's life. But never … never just because I exist."

Her hand falls to her side, the rag dangling uselessly.

"I've always known every relationship I've ever been in was for business expansion," she says. "I just didn't say it out loud before."

I cross the space between us.

She doesn't look at me until I take the soapy rag from her hand and set it in the bucket.

And even then, it's a plea, maybe.

I lift my hand and touch her cheek, just barely.

"Until now," I say, like a vow.

She blinks, and her bottom lip catches between her teeth like she doesn't trust it.

I let my body speak where words won't reach. My hand slides to her jaw, my thumb brushing the edge of her mouth, and then I kiss her. It's not rushed or hungry, just full of emotion, like I'm trying to kiss every piece of her that's ever been made to feel replaceable. Her hands grip my shirt, and she melts against me with a whimper.

"Until you," she whispers.

I hold her there, and the silence of the house wraps around us.

"I want you for the woman you are. The woman who's standing in front of me right now. Nothing else," I confess. "I wouldn't care if you were penniless or homeless. None of that shit matters to me."

I don't let her go, not when I can still hear the quiet break in her voice, like admitting the truth cost her something she can't take back. She's still close, standing there like she doesn't know what to do with herself now that the words are out. So, I reach for her hand and give it a gentle tug.

"Come with me," I say.

She nods with no hesitation or questions, only trust.

We step into my bedroom, and it's quiet in a way that feels holy. She stops just inside the doorway, her arms wrapped loosely across her stomach, like she's holding herself together. I turn to face her and take a step closer to her.

I don't touch her yet. I just study how fucking beautiful she is and let the silence settle between us. It's filled with everything we haven't said.

"You told me no one's ever truly wanted you," I say. "You need to know what it feels like to be worshipped."

Her breath catches, but she doesn't look away. Her eyes hold mine, and there's something behind them. Hope maybe. Admiration. Longing.

The room is dim in the late afternoon light. I move her until she's standing in front of the full-length mirror, her back to me, her body trembling with anticipation. In the reflection, those green eyes are wide, lips parted, breath hitching. I don't waste time. I grab her hips, my fingers digging into the soft flesh, and pull her back against me. She gasps, her ass pressing into my erection, and I groan.

"Look at how fucking beautiful you are," I softly say into her ear. "Do you feel what you do to me?"

I gently tug her hair, tilting her head back, and she meets my eyes in the mirror. Her lips part wider with a whimper, and I can see the flush spreading across her chest. Her nipples harden and beg for attention. My hand slides up her body, over the curve of her waist, and I cup her breast, squeezing. She gasps, her hips grinding against me, as my hand goes lower down her body. I dip inside the tiny shorts and can feel the heat of her pussy, even through the fabric of her panties.

"You're fucking soaked," I mutter, my fingers slipping beneath the lace, finding her clit already swollen and throbbing.

She cries out, her body arching into my touch, and I smirk, watching her face in the mirror as I tease her.

"Do you have any idea how much I want you? How much I've always wanted you?"

"Colt," she breathes, her voice trembling.

I don't make her wait. I spin her around, moving her to the bed. I push her shorts and panties down to her knees. I remove her shirt and bra until she's naked in front of me.

"On the bed on all fours," I instruct.

She does what I said as I move behind her, rubbing my hand firmly against her perfect ass. I can't resist giving it a sharp slap. She yelps, but I can see the way her body instantly responds.

I grab her hips from behind. "Watch us. Don't let your eyes leave this mirror. Do you understand?"

"Yes," she whispers.

The sun bleeds across the sky, painting the room in hues of amber and gold, but all I see is her. Her perfect fucking ass is arched over the edge of my bed for me, her thighs trembling slightly as she braces herself, her hands gripping the sheets like they're the only thing keeping her from falling into the abyss of pleasure I'm about to unleash.

I want her to watch every filthy second of this, and she obeys like a good girl.

Her reflection is fucking hypnotic—her lips parted, her chest rising and falling with shallow breaths, her hair cascading down her back like a dark waterfall. She's a goddess, and I'm about to worship her like one.

I drop to my knees behind her, the hardwood floor digging into me, but I don't give a fuck.

My hands slide up the backs of her thighs, feeling heat radiating from her skin. I spread her cheeks apart, and there it is —her pussy, glistening and swollen, begging for my mouth. Her asshole winks at me, tight and tempting, but I'll get to that later. Right now, I'm here for her sweet cunt.

I lean in, my breath hot against her folds, and she shudders, a soft whimper escaping her lips. I don't dive in just yet. No, I tease her first. I drag my tongue along her slit, from the base of her pussy up to her clit again, and she gasps, her hips bucking back toward me.

"Fuck," she moans.

I grin against her, placing soft, teasing kisses. This is just the beginning.

"See how fucking beautiful you are with my tongue inside you?" I ask, popping my head up to make sure she's still obeying.

I circle her clit with the tip of my tongue, savoring the way she squirms. Her juices are already dripping down her thighs, and I lap them up like a man dying of thirst. She tastes fucking divine— sweet and salty, with a hint of something primal that drives me wild. I bury my face deeper, my tongue plunging into her pussy, fucking her with it. She cries out, her hands clawing at the sheets, and I can see her reflection in the mirror—her eyes wide, her mouth open as desperate pants escape her.

I pull back for a moment, just to see her writhe, to see the desperation in her eyes as she looks at me in the mirror.

"Please," she begs.

"Please, what?" I ask, my voice rough. "Tell me what you want, darlin'."

She hesitates for a second, then whispers, "I want your mouth on me. I want your fingers inside me."

That's all the permission I need.

I dive back in, this time with a vengeance. I suck her clit into my mouth, flicking it with my tongue as my fingers slide into her pussy, curling to find that sweet spot inside her. I work her over, my tongue and fingers moving in perfect harmony. I'm lost in her, in the taste of her, in the way she's falling apart for me.

I pull my fingers out and bring them to her asshole, pressing against the tight ring of muscle. She gasps, but she doesn't pull away; instead, she pushes back against me, begging for more. I pull a tiny bottle of lube from my bedside drawer, wanting her to be comfortable, before I slide a finger inside her ass. She screams out as my tongue continues to devour her pussy as I add more pressure to her tight hole.

My tongue is working her slit like it's my goddamn job, lapping up every drop of her. She's moaning, and I can feel her body shaking. I force her pussy harder against my mouth. My tongue flicks her clit, faster and more relentless, and she lets out a whimper that's half pleasure, half desperation. I'm not ashamed to admit I'm fucking addicted to her, and I'm not stopping until she's a wet, quivering, sobbing mess.

I slide two fingers inside her, curling them just right, and she gasps, her walls tightening around me like a fucking vise. I whisper to her the whole time, telling her how beautiful she is, how good she tastes, how much I want her just as she is.

She grinds her hips against my face. She's panting now, her breath coming in short, ragged gasps, and I know she's close. I focus on her clit again, sucking it into my mouth and flicking it with the tip of my tongue. As she comes, her pussy pulses like it's trying to milk my fingers dry.

"Keep watching, darlin'," I say as I continue, not giving her a second to recover.

Her hands are gripping the sheets so tightly that her knuckles are white. Her legs are shaking so much that she can barely keep herself upright. I'm not done with her yet—not even close. We're not stopping until she knows how much she means to me.

Her body shatters with the force of her first orgasm. Her cries of pleasure echo through the room.

I stand up, wiping my mouth with the back of my hand, and look at her in the mirror. She's a fucking mess—her hair tangled, her skin flushed, her pussy dripping wet.

She looks at me with half-lidded eyes, a lazy smile spreading across her face.

"You make me feel so good," she whispers.

"Keep your focus," I tell her as I unzip my jeans, freeing my cock. I'm hard and too fucking desperate for her as I line myself up with her dripping entrance.

I slam into her in one brutal thrust. Her body jerks forward, and I hold her still, my hand wrapping around her throat as I start to fuck her hard and deep.

"Look at you, being so perfect for me," I mutter, tightening my grip on her neck just enough to make her gasp. "Look at how fucking wrecked I am for you."

Her eyes are wild in the mirror, her lips swollen from biting them, her tits bouncing with every thrust. I can feel the way her pussy grips me, tight and wet, and it drives me fucking insane. I pound into her harder, my balls slapping against her the sound ricochets off the walls of this quiet room. She's moaning nonstop now, little whimpers and cries that only make me fuck her harder.

"You're mine, Stormy," I growl, my voice rough with possession. "I don't give a fuck if you leave here. Every fucking inch of you belongs to me, no matter how far away you are."

Her hand reaches back, clawing at my thigh, and I know she's close again. I can feel her pussy clenching around me. I lean over her, my chest pressing against her back, and I bite down on her shoulder as I fuck her even harder. Her body shaking as she explodes again, and I can't hold back anymore.

I bury myself deep inside her, my cock pulsing as I fill her up.

We stay like that for a moment, both of us panting, our bodies slick with sweat.

I pull out, watching my cum drip out of her perfect little pussy, and I can't help but smirk.

She collapses against the bed, and I know she's mine in every way that matters.

I crawl up beside her and wrap my arms around her, pulling

her close, letting her come down in my arms. She breathes against my chest, fully relaxed. There's a new peace in her now, one I haven't seen before. And I think maybe, just maybe, she's starting to believe the things I say to her.

"You don't have to be anything else," I say, holding her. "Not for me. You're already more than enough."

She's still curled into my chest when I realize the light has changed again. Faded blue slips in around the edges of the windows, turning everything still. Stormy's fingers are tracing circles on my stomach. She hasn't said anything since I pulled her into my arms, and I haven't needed her to, but I feel something change in her breath. It's a new kind of tension, and I patiently wait.

She lifts her head so she can look at me. Her eyes are steady now, like whatever she's about to say is already decided.

"I have to go back to New York," she says.

There's no drama in her voice, no hesitation. Just truth.

I nod once. "I know."

She watches me carefully.

"I'm not running away from you," she says, like she needs me to understand. "There are things ... people I have to face. Loose ends I need to tie up. Family I need to look in the eye."

I don't look away from her.

She exhales like she's been holding that breath for days. Her forehead drops to my shoulder, and I feel the tension bleed out of her.

We lie like that for a while, breathing in sync. The fan hums gently above us.

She moves in my arms, her cheek brushing against my chest like she's working up the nerve to speak again.

"I want you to come with me," she says.

I blink because that's not what I expected her to say.

For a second, I think maybe I misheard her, but then she lifts her head and looks at me. There's nothing casual about the way she said it.

"You want me to ..." I trail off, trying to catch up. "To New York?"

She nods once. "I know it's a lot, but I don't want to go without you."

I sit up a little, leaning on my elbow so I can see her better.

It hits me all at once. She's asking for me to join her, not just here in this bed or this house, but wherever she's going next. It feels big. It is big.

"Stormy," I say, brushing her hair behind her ear, "you could ask me to follow you to the edge of hell, and I'd pack my bag before you finished the sentence."

She exhales, and her whole body relaxes against me.

"I don't know what I'm walking into," she says, voice barely above a whisper. "But I know what I'm walking away from."

"I understand," I say, watching her. "And what happens afterward? Will you return here with me?"

"Only if that's what you want," she says.

"What do you want, darlin'?"

"This," she stresses. "You. Us. A half-finished house and a dog that needs adopting."

I hold her tight, laughter and happiness spilling out of me. I press kisses wherever I can. "You're choosing me?"

"You chose me first," she says, smiling, happy, tears streaming down her cheeks. "I don't want this to end. I don't care about anything else."

We lie there like that for a while, and it feels like a decision is being made in the silence.

Eventually, I glance toward the clock and slide my hand across her lower back.

"What time will we leave?"

"Around eight in the morning on Sunday," she says against my chest, kissing my tattoo. "I'd say now, but I'm looking forward to dinner with Remi and Cash tomorrow night. And I have a lot of mental preparation to do."

I grin into her hair. "I'm here with you."

She laughs. "Should I tell them we're leaving?"

I shake my head. "Only if you want to answer five million questions. You can explain when we return, if you're comfortable."

"Okay." She's silent for a beat. "I'm glad I found you."

Her voice is certain, like she's not just saying it; she believes it.

My chest tightens. I pull her closer. "Fuck, me too, darlin'."

She exhales against my skin, and I can feel her settle, like something inside her has changed.

We lie there like that with our limbs tangled and hearts steady until the room fades to night. And in the stillness, I realize that she's not just choosing me. She's choosing *us*—this life, this future, this messy, half-built dream we're still putting together. And I'll follow her anywhere.

She's worth crossing the country for, especially if she's coming home with me afterward.

CHAPTER TWENTY-SIX

STORMY

When I realize Colt remodeled this place himself, I'm honestly stunned. It's gorgeous with its white picket fence, perfectly hung shutters, and manicured lawn.

A porch swing creaks gently in the breeze, wind chimes clink somewhere to the left, and that familiar smell of mesquite on a flame drifts from the backyard.

Remi opens the door before we knock. She grins and pulls me in without a word, hugging me like she's known me for years instead of weeks.

"Wow, you both have that love look on your faces," she announces. "Come in. Cash is in the back, barbequing."

As soon as his name is said, he appears behind her, barefoot and relaxed. He pops two beers from the fridge and hands them to us.

"Y'all want cheese on your burgers?"

"Always," I say.

"Right answer," Cash says. "Anyone who doesn't eat cheese on their burgers is—"

"A monster," Colt tells him.

"Lactose intolerant," Remi interrupts with a laugh.

Colt's hand brushes the small of my back as we walk through the living room toward the back door.

The space is tidy but casual. Blankets are draped over the couch, and a preseason football game is on mute in the background.

When we walk outside, the air is filled with mesquite smoke, laughter, and something sweeter I can't quite place.

String lights crisscross the backyard, strung from the trees to the roofline. They sway gently with the breeze, casting a soft golden glow over everything. There's a long wooden table set beneath them, mismatched chairs tucked around it, and Cash stands over the grill like a man who knows he's about to feed an army even if there are only five of us.

Fenix is already out here, seated at the far end of the table, half twisting her long hair around one finger as she scrolls her phone with the other. She's got that same quiet tension I've noticed the past few times I've seen her—like she's trying to be anywhere but here without actually leaving.

She looks up, gives a half smile, then returns to her screen.

Remi's behind us, setting a bowl of chips on the table. "Hope y'all are hungry. We made enough for a football team."

Cash calls over, flipping burgers, "Don't worry, babe. Colt eats like one."

Colt grins and tips his bottle in Cash's direction, then pulls out a chair for me. I settle in, but my eyes drift back to Fenix. Her shoulders are tense, and she hasn't said a word.

The conversation picks up around me—Cash asking Colt something about fence repair, Remi making a joke about her mother's group texts. But Fenix just quietly rises from her seat, phone still in hand, and slips inside without a word.

I count to ten before I follow.

The house is quiet again when I step through the back door. I don't call her name, just move through the living room until I catch sight of her near the hallway, standing half in shadow by the bookshelf. Her arms are crossed, phone pressed to her chest now like she's changed her mind about whatever she was going to text.

She hears me approach, doesn't turn. She gives me a small smile, one that doesn't quite reach her eyes. She's wearing jeans and a black tee with a faded band logo on the front.

"I'm fine," she says. "Just needed air."

"You left the backyard to come inside," I reply, keeping my tone even. "That's not air."

A beat of silence passes between us.

Fenix finally speaks again. "Have you ever felt like the version of you everyone sees is a total lie? Like they love this mask so much that they'd never survive seeing what's underneath?"

My breath catches. "Yes."

That one word seems to unravel her.

She blinks down at the floor, jaw tight, trying to hold something in. Then she laughs, but it's bitter and quiet. "A while ago, I … met someone. It was supposed to be fun. Just something that didn't matter. But it got serious fast. Too fast. He made me feel like the real me was actually *enough* until the second I started believing it."

I don't speak. I know she needs the space to express everything.

"We went our separate ways." She presses her thumb hard against her temple. "It wasn't just a breakup. It wrecked me. I dropped out of school. I told everyone I was bored, that it wasn't the right fit. But really, I couldn't stay there and pretend I wasn't falling apart."

The ache in her voice, the way she's standing, like she's still trying to hold herself together—I know that feeling. I've lived it.

"And I hate that I still feel everything. I don't want to. I want to be over it. I want to not care. It's been almost two years."

I move closer, not touching her, just being there.

"You don't have to explain anything to me," I whisper. "I get it."

She finally lifts her eyes to meet mine. There's something raw there. And for the first time since I met her, I see her without any armor.

"I know who you are," she says quietly. "I figured it out the second day I met you."

My pulse spikes, but I don't move. Don't flinch.

"I haven't told anyone. I won't," she says. "I just thought you should know that you're not alone. People think they know everything. But they don't. Sometimes, it's the ones who stay quiet that understand the most."

I nod, and the pressure in my chest loosens just enough to breathe. "Thank you."

She doesn't smile, but her expression softens. "Your secret's safe."

"So is yours," I tell her.

She slips past me, and I stand there for a second, staring at the space where she just was, knowing full well she didn't name him.

Some heartbreaks don't need names to leave scars.

If Colt finds out, Jace Tucker is a dead man.

I move to the bathroom and wash my hands, needing something to do. I look in the mirror, seeing my lips are swollen and cheeks pink, probably from the incredible sex Colt and I had before we arrived. After a deep breath, I return outside.

"Great! Everyone is back. Let's eat!" Remi tells me, and I move to the chair next to Colt.

We exchange a look, and he's curious, but I give him a smile, interlocking my fingers with his.

We pass around paper plates and napkins as Cash begins sliding burgers onto buns, stacking them high with sharp cheddar and grilled onions. The conversation lifts again—light, easy, filled with laughter and teasing.

Colt hands me a plate like it's second nature. His fingers brush mine for a beat too long, his thumb dragging gently across my skin before he pulls away. It's subtle, but it steadies me. He's watching me. He knows something isn't okay. He won't push, but he knows.

Fenix stays quiet. She returns to the table and takes her spot beside Remi, picking at her food more than eating it, but no one presses her either. We fall into that familiar rhythm that comes with small-town dinners—stories retold, inside jokes traded like currency, another round of beers passed around before anyone finishes the first.

I'm halfway through my burger when Remi stands and disappears into the house. A minute later, she returns, waving a folded-up newspaper in the air.

"Y'all seen this yet?" she says, half laughing as she fans herself dramatically. "Colt, you're famous again. You and Sunny made the front page."

My stomach knots.

She unfolds the paper and lays it down in the center of the table like she's just tossed a royal flush. It takes me a second to understand what I'm looking at. A full-color photo—me and Colt, mid-kiss at the bachelor auction. My face is angled slightly, but not enough to stay hidden. Colt's smiling like he's already won. I'm mid-step, caught between motion and surrender, hand in his.

VALENTINE GAZETTE

Record-Breaking Bachelor Auction Raises Over $30,000 for Shelter

THE TABLE ERUPTS into light teasing. Cash whistles low. Fenix's brow twitches. Colt glances down at the photo with a proud sort of smirk—until he looks at me.

I don't say anything. I don't move. I don't breathe.

He watches the way I go still and how my smile drops a fraction of a second too soon.

Colt's jaw tightens. Not with embarrassment, but recognition. He's starting to understand what this means.

"Sunny?" Remi asks. "You okay?"

I force a laugh, folding the paper in half like it's nothing. "Yeah. Just ... wow. Didn't expect that photo on the front page."

Colt doesn't speak, but he's still watching me. He's piecing it together.

Remi shrugs. "Small town. That kiss and the fundraiser—it's all anyone is talking about in town. Every single conversation is about Sunny and Colt."

"Of course," I say, trying to keep my voice light. "It was one hell of a kiss."

That earns a few whoops from around the table, but I can feel Colt's hand slide to my thigh beneath the table. His fingers squeeze gently, grounding me.

I keep my smile on like armor and eat my chips one by one. I nod and sip my drink, and pretend everything is perfect.

But Colt knows. He knows something's wrong. And later, when the laughter fades and the food's cleared, he'll ask.

I squeeze his hand back, and he leans into me just slightly, as if to tell me I'm still here, but the storm's getting closer.

And my location has been revealed.

The dread is already settling in the back of my throat, and I'm relieved to be going back to New York in two days.

I can't allow this to ruin the night, so I push the thoughts away.

The conversation softens, and our stomachs are full. The night is winding down, and Colt yawns.

"Dinner was incredible. Thank you so much for inviting us," he offers.

"We'll have to do it again." Remi meets my eyes. "I'm so happy you're still here."

"Me too," I say. "Thanks for hosting."

Fenix stands and helps clean up the table. She walks inside, leaving the four of us alone.

Cash and Colt shake hands, and Cash pulls me into a side hug that smells like smoke and bourbon.

"Thanks for joinin' us," he says.

After we say our goodbyes several times, we walk through the house and leave.

The truck is quiet as we pull away from his sisters.

Colt drives one-handed, his arm stretched across the window frame. The cool night air slips in and tugs at my hair. He doesn't say anything right away. We've gotten good at silence—comfortable with it even. But tonight, it sits heavier than usual.

"You've gone quiet," Colt says finally. He glances over, not panicked.

"Being on the front page is bad," I say.

He raises his brows. "That's what's got you twisted up?"

"It's not just that it's a photo of us. It's the article. The headline. The money." I pause. "People are already looking for me. This feels like a target."

His smile fades.

I continue, "All it takes is one person finding this image of me online. Valentine might be small and safe, but the internet doesn't work like that. That picture of us ..." I shake my head, not sure how to finish, knowing more lies will be made up about me.

Colt keeps his eyes on the road.

"We'll handle it," he says. "Whatever comes next."

I nod, but the anxiety streaming through me doesn't loosen. "We have to leave Sunday morning, no matter what. Maybe we can get ahead of this."

The farmhouse comes into view, porch light glowing warm and familiar. The gravel crunches under the tires as Colt eases the truck to a stop. Neither of us moves to get out right away.

I turn toward him. "I don't know what will happen in New York. I don't know what to expect."

He studies me. "I'll be right beside you through it all. We'll ride out the storm together."

That settles something inside me.

We step out into the dark and climb the porch together. Colt unlocks the door, and I follow him inside, my thoughts already spiraling.

I don't know how close the past is, but it seems like it's closing in on me.

Part of me wants to go online and search, but it's best if I wait, as it might lead me down a spiral. It will do me no good tonight, and I need a clear mind tomorrow so I can come up with a plan.

I follow Colt down the hallway, the sound of our footsteps soft against the old wood floors. I break away from him and wash my hands in the bathroom, staring at my reflection.

I dry my hands, bracing myself. Then I step out of the bathroom.

Colt's waiting in the hallway, barefoot, backlit by the light leaking from our bedroom. He holds out his hand without a word. I take it. And this time, I don't let go.

Tomorrow, we'll pack, and then we'll leave early on Sunday.

Whatever's waiting for me on the other side of that city skyline, I'll face it head-on. But tonight, I let myself rest. Not because everything's okay or that my problems are fixed. But because, for once, I don't have to face it alone.

CHAPTER TWENTY-SEVEN

COLT

S tormy sits cross-legged on the floor, folding clothes that I didn't even realize she owned.

There's a duffel bag open beside her, half packed, the zipper yawning, like it already knows this isn't a vacation.

I'm on the bed, leaning back on my elbows, watching her steal glances at me every few minutes, like she's trying to memorize my face before we get on that plane.

"Have you ever visited New York?" she asks, holding one of her rolled-up tank tops in both hands.

"Nope. Never had a desire," I say. "It'll be an adventure for sure. Cowboy in the city."

That earns me a soft laugh. She drops the shirt into the bag and sits back on her hands, hair slipping over her shoulder. She's not wearing makeup. Her toenail polish is chipped. And she's never looked more like herself than she does right now.

"I'm growing nervous," she says after a beat. "It's not something I'm used to."

"It will be over before you know it." I sit up fully, crossing to where she's sitting. "I'm proud of you for wanting to confront the past. It's not easy."

Her eyes are steady. "You don't think I'm crazy?"

"I think you're brave."

That makes her smile.

I stand, then dip down and kiss her when I hear tires on gravel and an engine.

Stormy goes still. "Expecting someone?"

"Nope." I freeze, listening for a familiar engine rumble, and she rises to her feet to join me.

Out the front window from the living room, I see a slick black car I don't recognize, idling next to the Camaro. It's shiny and out of place. A suit-and-tie kind of vehicle with the AC humming loud enough to hear from inside.

The driver's door opens, and a dark-haired man steps out. Stormy gasps.

"My fucking car!" he screams as he walks around the Camaro. "What the fuck?!"

I hold back a laugh, watching him lose his shit.

Stormy's half tucked against my shoulder like she's bracing for impact.

Her ex circles the Camaro like it personally betrayed him. His hands are flailing, his voice rising with every step. "Are you kidding me?" he shouts, crouching to inspect the dent in the passenger door. "My baby! The side mirrors are gone. Fucking gone! Destroyed."

He kicks one of the front tires, then yelps when his foot bounces off it the wrong way. He staggers back, holding his foot like the car bit him.

Stormy snorts next to me, then quickly claps a hand over her mouth.

"This can't be happening," he says to himself, to the car, to the universe. "Scratches? Dents? Who the fuck does this?"

I open the door. The sound of gravel shifts under his shoes as he turns and glares at me.

He's already halfway to the porch, walking toward me like he's got the right to be here. His suit is sharp, tailored for Manhattan, not Texas. The air-conditioning in the car is still running behind him, loud enough to break the quiet. He doesn't glance around, doesn't take in the house or the land or anything else that might remind him he's out of his element. His focus is locked on me.

"Excuse me. I'm searching for someone," he states. "Stormy Langford."

It's the first time I've heard anyone use her entire name.

Stormy steps up behind me. She doesn't touch me, but she's close enough to hear the way my breathing changes.

He sees her, but his expression doesn't soften. There's no emotion in it at all, just expectation.

"There you are," he says, like he's greeting someone late for lunch.

His eyes shift to me, and I stay standing between him and whatever part of her he thought he could reclaim.

I cross my arms over my chest, and his posture stiffens when I stand straighter. He's sizing me up, trying to figure out who I am and how much of a problem I'll be. He gives me a once-over that's meant to read as casual, but it's too pointed to be anything but a warning.

"You've got to be kidding me," he sneers, turning to Stormy. "You've been fucking him. What about us?"

Stormy doesn't flinch. She takes a step out of the house with the baseball bat tight in her grip. I remember leaving it by the door.

Her expression is scrubbed clean, like she doesn't have the energy to play a part for him anymore.

"What about *us*?" she repeats, then scoffs, her brows furrowing. "There hasn't been an *us* in years."

"Don't do that," he says, taking a step forward, reaching out his hand to grab her.

She lifts the bat and points it at him. "Don't come any closer."

I keep my feet planted.

"Don't pretend like I was the problem," Donovan says. "I knew that's what you'd do, leaving me crying and heartbroken at the altar."

"Choose your next words wisely," Stormy warns. Her tone is as sharp as broken glass.

He lets out an unpleasant laugh. "Real cute, baby. Come on. It's time to go."

"I'm not going anywhere with you."

He glares at me. "What? You're choosing this *child*? This boy could never give you what you need and require."

The dumb fuck is trying to provoke me, which is something he doesn't want. However, I see through it and don't take the bait.

I stare back at him because I don't owe him a damn thing.

"It's time to come home," he says to her, waving her toward him. "We have a wedding to reschedule."

"It's time for you to go," I tell him, knowing I could snap him like a twig.

I step out onto the first plank and put my arm around her possessively. My touch is solid. She wraps her arm around me and then smirks. It's enough to break the calm on his face, giving me the same expression as Tessa did. He sees what Stormy and I share; everyone does. It's electric.

His jaw tightens as he squares his shoulders. "You're not thinking straight, Storm. You must be having one of your episodes. I'll call Dr. Jacobson; we can talk this out—"

She barks out a sarcastic laugh. "Are you really name-dropping my therapist right now? You're a piece of shit."

He flicks toward the bat that she pushes into his shoulder.

Donovan takes a step back. "Please. I love you. I've always loved you. Neither of us has been perfect in our relationship, and I know we can work through this. Stormy, get in the car with me," he says, voice all command. "You've upset your entire family. If you want to embarrass yourself, fine. But don't drag us into your reputation meltdown and—"

"Don't you dare," she cuts in.

She's trembling with volcanic rage, and I'm scared she might kill this man with the bat she has tightly gripped in her hand.

"Stormy," I mutter, bringing her back to reality, "don't fuck him up."

I let out a laugh, and Donovan takes a step back like he's scared she might.

"I'm not going anywhere with you," Stormy says.

His gaze hardens. "Your parents and sister are worried. Get in the car now." His voice tightens, and he tries to command her like she's an animal. "You've already caused enough drama and damage. Now you're living in this dump with someone so young. Talk about robbing the fucking cradle. Are you okay? Did you have a mental breakdown?"

"That's enough," I say, moving toward Stormy and grabbing the bat in my hand. Now I'm getting pissed. "Say what you gotta say, but if you keep disrespecting her, I'll make sure you disappear. We don't like people from out of town 'round here," I warn. "You have no idea where the fuck you are."

Stormy stares at him, and his face is unreadable, but I see the pulse in his neck kick up a few notches.

"I get it," he goes on, watching Stormy. "You've made your point. This circus? It's over. We both know where you belong. Your clients are furious. Your father is disappointed. We already have a story scripted to erase it all." His words are picking up speed now, the smooth performance starting to fray at the edges. "But whatever this is, between you two, it's over. You made a mistake, and you've had your moment. You have the attention you've always craved. Now it's time we get back to what matters the most. Us, our family." He holds out his hand to her, pleading with his eyes. "This? All of this? It's temporary. You're not meant for this kind of life, and we both know it. Come with me, baby."

He says it like he's the only one here with a functioning brain cell.

By the way he carries himself, I know he's used to everyone shutting up and following his orders.

Stormy steps forward, putting her arm around me, and I hold her tight.

"No," she says. "I'm done pretending, and I'm done letting you talk to me like you own me. You fucking don't."

"Stormy"—he gives her a tilt of his head like she's being a stubborn kid—"this has always been your problem. No one will ever be enough for you. You burn down everything around you."

Her eyes widen, and then she bursts into laughter. It's cruel, but I find it delicious, considering this man deserves all her wrath for what he did.

"I don't believe anything that comes from your mouth anymore. Look at you. You're pathetic."

He flinches. It's the tiniest tic, but it's enough for me to see she's landed a hit where it hurts.

"Does he even know you, Stormy? Does he know who you really are and that you—"

"Yep," Stormy interrupts, her voice clipped. "He knows me better than you ever did, which is so fucking sad. You had me, Donovan, and you lost me. That will be your biggest regret."

"Damn," I whisper, not because I'm shocked, but because I've never seen someone burn a man to the ground with nothing but the truth.

I watch her—shoulders steady, chin lifted, every word precise. She's not breaking; she's choosing herself this time. And, God, I've never been prouder to stand beside someone in my life.

Donovan's nostrils flare, and he swallows hard like he knows she's right. His fists clench at his sides, fingernails digging hard into both palms. "You can change your mind. I'll forgive you. Plant a story about you and him and erase it. Call it a PR stunt. We can work through this."

"Absolutely not," she says. Her words hook hard.

The silence stretches long enough to make him uncomfortable, which might be the first time that's ever happened.

I don't say a word either. I'm not here to save her, only to stand beside her.

Stormy steps forward. My arm drops naturally, and I let her go. She walks down one step, then another, stopping a few feet from him.

"Want to know the best part, Donnie? When the truth is revealed, I won't be the one trying to rescue my reputation. It will be you." Her smile is sad as she stares at the man she once loved.

"Please," he nearly begs her. His voice lowers. "I flew here because I love you. I drove all this way because I miss you," he says.

Lightning breaks over the world and settles in her throat.

"You're here," she says, "because you're saving face. Because you realized that you needed me for your public image. When I reveal the truth, you will sink. I'm not sorry for the karma that's coming for you."

He tilts his head at her. "What are you talking about?"

I can see satisfaction already ticking in her jaw. "How long have you been messing around with my sister?"

He stays frozen in place, staring at her.

"Oh, you didn't think I knew. That explains this ridiculous performance," she says. "You're ruined."

The air changes, and the cicadas hush.

Donovan's mouth falls open a full second before he recovers. In it, I see every decision he's ever made, rushing like a floodwater through a single doomed grin.

"What are you talking about?" he asks. "That's ridiculous. With Skye?"

"I knew you'd lie," Stormy says, voice rising. "I saw you myself at the venue with your hands down my sister's panties in the back room forty-five minutes before you were supposed to marry me." Her nostrils flare, and she glares at him. "Now deny it."

He flushes a deep, spectacular shade of crimson. She caught him off guard, and I love this for him.

"How many people knew? Who of our friends did you force to keep this secret from me?" Her voice is calm, cold, and final. "The truth shall set you free, baby."

He opens his mouth like he might protest, but she doesn't give him the chance.

"I've already contacted LuxLeaks for an exclusive tell-all interview. It will publish"—Stormy pulls her phone from her pocket—"actually, right now. What a coincidence that you're here when that article is dropping in New York." She pauses, cupping her hand to her ear. "You hear that? That's your reputation circling the drain. You won't recover. Not from me. Not from this. Next time, choose someone dumber. Oh, wait. You did. My little sister. Did you see the surveillance video?" she asks coldly.

A flicker of panic flashes beneath that polished confidence.

"Everyone will know you lied and tried to fool the public with bullshit stories about my mental health. That's what they call *bottom of the barrel* around here. The world will finally see you for the cheater you are. But I do owe you a thank-you. Thank you so much for showing me exactly who you are. You saved me from future heartbreak. Because of you, I found something that's worth *everything*. Donnie, you never could've made me happy. You were the best thing that didn't happen."

He tries to speak, but she keeps going.

"You came here, thinking I'd run back to you. In the beginning, I might have let you wrap your lie in a tailored apology, and I'd stupidly thank you for it. But the blindfold has been removed. You don't have control anymore. Neither does my family. Or the company. Or anyone. I'm in control again." There's no rise in her voice, no flare of emotion.

Donovan stares at her like he already misses her. There's a pulse in his jaw now. "See, now that's the woman I fell for."

"That's the woman you destroyed," she states. "And if you ever come near me again … if you speak my name publicly or whisper it to a tabloid or try to leverage your fuckup in any way, I will make it even worse for you. And you know I'm capable."

He's scared shitless.

"I will ruin every alliance you've ever built. I will bury your entire family name. I will make every publication you've ever used to manipulate a narrative turn on you so fast that you won't be able to see your reflection without thinking about me. And now you're here, acting like you own me, like you can tell me what to do?" Her eyes narrow. "You lost me the second you touched her."

Donovan doesn't speak. He can't.

Stormy steps back. "Now get in your car. And fuck straight off."

"Listen. Wait, Stormy, please," he says. "You have it all wrong. It wasn't anything like that. It was a onetime thing, a mistake, and it meant nothing. She threw herself at me—"

"I saw you laughing together. Heard the two of you. Stop lying for once." Stormy's voice cracks through the air. She exhales.

I take a step forward, knowing this is enough. "If you don't get in your car and leave now, you won't be walking away. At this point, you're trespassing," I threaten.

Donovan stares at her for a minute, almost as if he doesn't recognize the woman before him. He doesn't say another word, just turns like someone yanked his strings, jaw tight, steps clipped as he walks back to the car.

"Oh, hey. Get someone to come pick up this junk from our yard, or I'll have it towed away. And remember what I said," Stormy continues. "You won't be the only one in crisis mode if you fuck with me."

Stormy doesn't move until the car reverses out of the

driveway, tires crunching over gravel. We both watch it go until the taillights fade away. I slide my arm around her waist. She leans into it without a word, like she's been waiting to fall into something steady. And I'm here for her. I'll always be.

She exhales the bullshit and grabs my hand, pulling me up the porch steps with her. Her eyes are sharp, glassy, but dry as we walk inside. There's color in her cheeks, and right now, she's not wrecked; she's radiant. Unshaken. Fierce.

"The audacity," she says. "To think I almost married him. What was wrong with me? Why would I choose that?"

I nod. "Glad you woke up 'cause ew."

She laughs, and I pull her into my arms.

"That's one confrontation already knocked off my list. After that, are you still sure about going with me tomorrow?"

I don't hesitate. "There's no place on the fuckin' planet I'd rather be than by your side. Now, tell me, how do you feel, getting that off your chest?"

"Great," she says. "I'm in control of my life again. I got stuck in a loop of trying to make everyone else happy but myself. I realize that, and it's so sad."

I cup her cheeks, then kiss her, enjoying the way she tastes. I pull away, meeting her eyes. "What about now, darlin'? Are you happy?"

"Yes. The happiest I've ever been," she whispers against my mouth, then dives back in for more.

Our tongues twist together as I push her up against the door.

Her arms wrap around my neck as she moans against me.

"You're a little terrifying," I mutter against her ear, teeth grazing her skin.

She holds me like I'm the safest thing she's ever known and the only man she's ever wanted.

"Guess you'd better take me to bed, cowboy. Don't want to give you my wrath."

"Mmm, give it to me. I love your sassy wrath. It's lightning," I say, scooping her up and carrying her down the hallway as she presses soft kisses against my neck.

I set her down on the bed as she removes her shirt and pulls me toward her. As I lay her back and slip her panties off, I know she's not running anymore. She's walking toward me. And, God help me, I'm ready to drop down on one knee and enjoy the calm after the storm—with her.

CHAPTER TWENTY-EIGHT

STORMY

The sun hasn't risen yet. But it will.

The black SUV slows to a stop just past the security gate, and the driver nods at me through the rearview mirror. Beyond the windshield, the private jet is already waiting —sleek and silver, its sharp nose pointed toward the runway, like it's impatiently waiting to leave.

I glance at Colt, who hasn't said a word since we turned onto the access road. He's leaning forward slightly, forearms resting on his thighs, eyes locked on the plane, like he's still trying to decide if it's real.

"Ready?" I ask, trying to ease the silence.

He looks over at me, then back at the jet. "You own this?"

"Yes. Several." I smile, but I don't miss the way he gives me a second glance as he gets out. Not tense, but aware that this is my world.

The tarmac is cold beneath our feet as we cross toward the open stairs. A flight attendant in navy slacks and a crisp blouse greets us with a polite smile, but her eyes flick to Colt with brief curiosity. She doesn't ask questions because she wouldn't dare.

Once we're on board, the cabin door seals behind us with a

soft hiss. The air inside is cooler than I expected. The plane is exactly how I remember it—with white leather seats, wood trim, and soft lighting. Colt takes it in with a turn of his head, not speaking yet as he processes it.

"Wow," he says, running a hand through his hair.

Colt lowers himself into the seat beside me, his eyes still moving over the space, like he's trying to memorize the layout.

"You okay?" I ask, watching him.

"I'm shocked," he says, then glances at me with the smallest smile. "You're a princess, for real."

This makes me laugh. "No. Trust me. Princesses are a lot more spoiled. I know a few."

The captain's voice crackles through the speaker, announcing a several-hour flight time and smooth conditions. The jet begins to taxi down the runway, and Colt's hand finds mine on the armrest. I don't think he even realizes he reached for me.

I glance down at our hands and grin. He's leaving everything he knows behind to come with me without hesitation.

Before we left this morning, he asked Fenix if she'd feed the horses. She said yes and promised she wouldn't tell anyone where we were going. I'm building her trust , giving her space, but I do want to help her the best I can.

Outside the window, the horizon tips and lifts as we rise. The light shifts, and big, fluffy clouds float across the sky.

For a while, there's nothing but the soft pulse of the ascent, the drone of the engines, and the rhythm of our breathing melting into a cabin hush.

Colt's thumb strokes the space between my knuckles as he stares out the window. His fingers trace lazy patterns—a silent reminder he's still with me. I don't speak, just watch how his brows draw inward. I love the faint stubble along his chiseled jawline. This man is gorgeous.

I lean over and press a kiss to his shoulder, and he glances at me curiously.

I give his hand a gentle tug and stand, leading him into the private cabin in the back of the jet. Inside is a softly lit bedroom with a low bed and smooth paneling. I close the door behind us and let the silence settle between our bodies.

Colt stands in the middle of the room, his hands at his sides, his chest rising and falling in measured breaths. I step closer, reaching for the hem of his T-shirt. He lets me lift it over his head, his arms rising automatically, like we've done this a hundred times. But this time is different.

I smooth my hands over his chest, trailing down the line of his carved abs. His skin is warm under my palms, his muscles like stone. I sink to my knees in front of him, not because I want to tease him, but because I want him to feel what it's like to be worshipped.

Words catch in his throat, but I shake my head, quieting him.

I look up at him—so quiet, so still, like he's waiting to be told he's enough. He doesn't ask for much, this man. But I want to give him everything.

"I want to make you feel good," I whisper.

The hum of the jet's engines is low, and it vibrates through the floor and into my knees. We're not even touching yet, but he's already hard, straining against the fabric of his jeans, and I can't help but lick my lips at the sight of his bulge.

I'm going to make him forget every other blow job he's ever had. This will be the one he jerks off to for the rest of his life.

I reach up, my fingers trembling with anticipation, and undo his belt. The sound of the buckle clinking is like music to my ears. I yank his pants down just enough to free him, and, fuck, it's perfect. Thick, veiny, and already leaking pre-cum, like he's been thinking about this as much as I have.

I wrap my hand around the base, feeling the heat of him and how he pulses in my palm. I lean in, my breath hot against the tip, and flick my tongue out to taste him. Salty, musky, and so damn good. I moan against him; the sound vibrating against his skin, and he groans, his hips jerking forward.

I guide him into my mouth and savor every thick inch. My lips stretch around his girth, and I hollow my cheeks, sucking him deep. I can feel him twitch against my tongue, and I swirl it around the head, teasing the slit before taking him down my throat. I don't gag, and I don't stop. I want to taste every inch of him.

My nose brushes against the coarse hair at the base of him, and I breathe him in, his scent filling my lungs. I pull back, dragging my lips along his shaft, and then plunge down again, faster this time. My hand works with my mouth, stroking what I can't keep inside me unless I don't want to breathe.

He's panting now, his hands tangled in my hair, guiding me but without being forceful. I love that he lets me take control, allows me to worship him the way he's always deserved. I bob my head faster, my lips tight around him, my tongue working overtime. I can feel his balls tightening against my chin. I reach down with my free hand and cup them, rolling them gently in my palm. He lets out a strangled moan, his hips bucking uncontrollably.

"Fuck," he growls. His voice is desperate and raw with need.

I don't stop. I force him deeper, my throat opening more. I take my time, feeling his muscles tense, and then he grabs my hair with a tight fist. When he finally explodes, it's with a guttural cry that sends shivers down my spine. His hot cum floods my mouth, and I swallow it down, not wasting a single drop. I keep sucking until he's spent, until he's trembling and gently pushing me away with a shaky hand.

I look up at him, my lips swollen, my chin glistening with spit.

"Welcome to the Mile-High Club, cowboy," I whisper, my voice hoarse from taking his length so deep.

He looks down at me, completely wrecked, and I can't help but smile.

Mission accomplished.

My tongue flicks over my lips to savor the salty tang of him. My chest heaves with every ragged breath, the lace of my bra barely containing my tits. He stands over me, tip glistening and twitching like it's begging for round two. But his hungry eyes say he has other plans.

"My turn," he growls, his voice gravelly and so damn sexy.

Before I can even think, he's on me, lifting me to my feet. His hands grip my thighs, spreading them wide, like he's claiming his territory. My skirt's already hiked up around my waist, and my soaked panties cling to my pussy like a second skin. He doesn't bother with foreplay; he rips them off with one swift tug, the fabric tearing like it's nothing. Colt lays me down on the bed, and I gasp, but it's drowned out by the sound of his growl as he buries his face between my legs.

His tongue is relentless. It's like he's trying to devour me whole, lapping at my slit with a hunger that makes my toes curl. He starts by teasing my clit with the tip of his tongue, circling it in tight little spirals that make me whimper. But then he gets serious, his mouth clamping down on me, sucking my clit like it's the last thing he'll ever taste. I arch my back, my hands clawing at the sheets, my moans echoing through the cabin.

"Fuck yes," I pant, my voice trembling. "Just like that. Don't stop."

He doesn't. His tongue dives deeper, plunging into my pussy with quick, shallow thrusts. I can feel his stubble scraping against my inner thighs, the rough sensation only adding to the fire burning between my legs. He's relentless, his mouth working me over, like he's trying to wring every last drop of pleasure from my body.

And then he slips a finger inside me, curling it just right to hit that sweet spot. I'm trembling now, my legs shaking as he adds a second finger, stretching me open, fucking me with his hand while his tongue continues its assault on my clit. It's too much and not enough, all at once. My vision blurs white.

"I'm gonna—" I whimper, my voice breaking.

He doesn't let up. If anything, he drives harder, tighter, like he's chasing something only I can give him. His fingers piston in and out of me, his tongue flicking my clit faster and faster. I can feel the orgasm building, and my control is ready to snap. With that thought, it does.

I come with a scream, my body convulsing as wave after wave of pleasure rushes through me. He takes every sliver of ecstasy from me until I'm a trembling, whimpering mess.

When he finally pulls away, his face is glistening with my juices, his lips swollen and wet. He looks up at me with a smirk, his eyes sparkling with satisfaction that he can bring me to the edge so easily.

"Damn, darlin'. That might be a record," he purrs, his voice dripping with confidence.

The air is thick with a heady cocktail of sweat, musk, and us. His cock is a monument, veins thick, like they're about to burst. I'm sprawled on the silk sheets of the bed, my legs spread open, waiting.

"Give me what I want."

"Just admiring you," he murmurs. His voice is like gravel being dragged over my skin.

"My pretty little storm. You're mine."

I whimper, nodding, my body trembling with need. "Yours."

He doesn't make me wait any longer. In one brutal motion, he slams into me, stretching me to the limit. I scream, my back arching off the bed, my nails digging into his shoulders. He's so big; it feels like he's branding me from the inside out.

"Every fucking inch of me belongs to you," he whispers, his hands gripping my hips so tight that I know I'll bruise.

"Yes, I want all of you," I confess.

He fucks me like he's mine, his hips bucking into me with a

rhythm that's relentless and unforgiving. The sound of skin slapping against skin fills the room, mingling with my moans and his grunts. My pussy is wet and aching for him, and every thrust sends shocks through my body.

"So damn perfect. You were made for this, weren't you? Made to take me."

"Technically," I gasp, my head thrashing against the pillows, "you were made for me."

Colt leans down, his lips brushing against my ear, his breath hot and ragged. "You gonna squirt for me, darlin'?" he asks.

He shifts his angle, hitting that spot deep inside me that makes my entire body convulse. He keeps driving into me, deeper, harder, until I can't catch my breath.

"That's it, darlin'," he encourages. "Let it go, sweetheart. Give it all to me."

I explode, my pussy spasming around him as I squirt all over his cock, the sheets, everything. The sensation is so intense that it feels like I'm being ripped apart and put back together at the same time. He doesn't stop, doesn't give me a moment to recover. He keeps pounding into me, driving deep with a force that leaves me trembling.

"You're mine to fuck, mine to claim. Say it."

"Yours," I sob, my body still shaking with the aftershocks of my orgasm. "All yours."

He growls, an almost-animalistic sound, and then he's coming, too, his length pulsing inside me as he fills me with his cum. Every hot drop spills into me. He collapses on top of me, his body heavy and sweaty, his breath ragged against my neck. We stay like that for what feels like forever ...

He's still inside me, warmth spilling between us, like even our bodies don't want to let go. I'm a mess, my body limp and spent, but I've never felt more alive.

"You're so pretty," he says, brushing hair from my face.

"So are you."

Colt slides out of me with agonizing slowness, as if drawing out every second he can keep us tangled. For a long moment, he watches me with rawness in his eyes. I'm still reeling. Even after he fucked me like he tried to break me, the way he studies my face is gentle.

"I love you," he whispers.

My breath catches. My pulse skips. He just said it—out loud, without fear, without condition.

I try to remember how to breathe.

"You don't have to say it back. I know it's a lot, but I can't go another minute without telling you. I knew I'd love you the moment you said my name. And you deserve to know that."

"I love you too," I whisper.

He gently moves back to me, sliding his mouth across mine. I kiss him back, tasting myself on his tongue. We breathe each other in and out, and when he pulls back, he brings a thumb up and wipes the tear from my cheek.

"You're crying," he says.

I sit up, feeling the wetness on my cheeks, knowing I haven't cried in over a decade. Not over Donovan or my sister. "I'm so happy."

"You deserve to be," he says, voice like velvet.

"You do too."

His breath is ragged, his hair an absolute disaster, and he's stunning in that wild, ruined way I can't look away from.

He studies me. "I'm gonna marry you one day."

"I hope you do, cowboy," I say, but I already know I'm his, body and soul.

Every storm led me right here. And I wouldn't have it any other way.

CHAPTER TWENTY-NINE

COLT

The city rises around us like it's made of steel and glass and unfinished business. I've seen pictures of New York and watched plenty of movies featuring it, but nothing has prepared me for how small I feel, being here.

Stormy sits beside me in the back seat of the SUV that picked us up at the private airport. Her expression is calm but focused, and she hasn't said much since we landed. I haven't pushed her to speak either. My girl has a lot on her mind, and she'll talk when she's ready.

The SUV stops in front of a high-rise with a private entrance, paparazzi waiting out front, and a doorman who probably makes more in a week than I did working on my parents' ranch for a month.

Stormy grabs my hand and turns to me when the vehicle stops.

"Are they here for you?" I ask, not completely understanding the gravity of this situation.

"Yes. Ignore them. Ignore what they say. Keep your eyes forward, okay?"

I give her a nod, and she squeezes my hand. Seconds later,

Stormy's door opens. The moment her heels hit the curb, her name is shouted from different directions. The flashes nearly blind me.

"Stormy! Is it true you called off the wedding at the altar?"

"Stormy, who's the new guy? Is this your replacement for Donovan?"

"Are the rumors about your mental breakdown true?"

She keeps moving forward, and I stay beside her as she pretends this is the most natural thing in the world.

It's intense, and I don't know how anyone lives their everyday life this way.

One guy steps too close for comfort, and I slam my shoulder into him. "Back the fuck up, bud."

My voice isn't loud, but it doesn't need to be. Based on my expression, he knows I'm not asking. I don't care what kind of photo they're trying to get of her or us. He lifts his camera to angle past me, and I shift my body to block him. Stormy reaches for my hand, and I take it without question. Her small frame dragging me at six two must be a scene.

"Stormy! Give us something!"

"She's not answering questions," I say over my shoulder. "Respect her space."

They keep their distance but continue screaming her name.

My hand stays in hers as she guides me closer to the building. *Park Towers* sparkles in golden letters above the entrance.

The guard nods as we approach, and the doors slide open. When we slip inside, the noise cuts off, as if someone flipped a switch. I immediately feel out of place.

She exhales, but her stiff posture doesn't change. She's not rattled, but I can see the difference in her here versus in Texas. She's tense, calculative, and wearing armor I haven't seen.

The elevator opens, and she presses her thumb against the pad. We zip upward, and she leans against the mirrored wall, lost in her thoughts.

"Do you deal with that all the time?" I ask.

She nods. "Since I was a young child."

I squeeze her hand. "How?"

She glances over at me. "I didn't have a choice. I was trained for this life from birth."

"You walked through it like you were bulletproof," I mutter, impressed.

She stares at me for a long moment, like she can't believe I'm here. I pull her closer, and she wraps her arms around my waist.

Leaning forward, I press my lips against her forehead. "You're safe."

"I'm so happy you're here," she says, squeezing me a little tighter as the elevator doors open.

We step into a private foyer, and then she unlocks the door and allows me inside first.

Two walls are made of glass with crisp lines, offering a view that stretches across the city. I can see the river and Central Park.

"This is your home?" I take a glance around.

Everything is beautiful and expensive, but it doesn't feel lived in.

Stormy sets her bag down on a marble counter. "It never felt like one."

"Yeah, I get that vibe. Doesn't feel like you." I notice how the air smells like lemons and money, and every wall is millennial gray.

This makes me chuckle.

"What?"

I shake my head. "The color on the wall."

A pretty smile touches her lips, and it's the first one I've seen since we deboarded the plane.

"I need to grab a few phone numbers from my office upstairs. Please make yourself comfortable. I'll be right back."

"I'll be right here, waiting."

She disappears up the stairs. There's something about the way she walks away with her shoulders squared and jaw tight. I hope she takes a quiet moment for herself while she's up there.

I move to the windows and stare outside. Buildings stack on top of each other, and it's beautiful, in a way. Nothing like Valentine, where the sky's so big that it's easy to forget your name.

I hear her voice before I see her.

"No. First thing tomorrow. Not a call, in person. Just make it happen." She's direct. Upset. I can hear it in her voice.

I turn toward the stairway as she steps back into view, phone still in hand. She looks executive, like someone who knows how to walk through fires.

When she notices me watching, she lowers the phone to her side.

"I have a meeting with my father tomorrow," she says.

There's a beat before I respond because I'm still catching up to the pace of her world.

"Great. Can't wait to meet him," I say.

Stormy walks past me toward the kitchen without missing a beat. She opens the fridge, pulls out a bottle of water, and takes a long drink before answering. "It won't be a happy get-together. I'm quitting," she says, setting the cap back on.

I tilt my head at her.

"I was groomed to take over the family business since I was old enough to speak. I'm the best at what I do, but it was never my dream. I was never given a choice."

She's not unraveling. She's organizing. Planning her next move with the kind of focus that comes from knowing exactly what she wants in life.

"What is your dream?" I ask.

She pauses, bottle still in her hand. Her eyes lift to mine, and there's no scripted answer behind them, only a flicker of something unfinished.

"I don't know," she says and pauses. "But I know what's not. I don't want to spend the rest of my life spinning lies and truths into something marketable. I no longer want to protect men like Donovan because they cut the biggest checks. And it sure as hell isn't pretending I'm proud of being a part of a family that never felt like one."

I move to her, wrapping my arms around her. "I support any decision you make."

She holds me tight. "I used to think power was having a seat at the table. The real power is knowing when to walk away."

I let that sit between us for a second because there's something sacred in how she said it. Something that sounds a lot like freedom.

"I'm proud of you," I tell her, because I can't imagine how hard this will be. But I know the ache of letting go of something you built.

"I met you, and my entire outlook on life changed. I felt alive, something I wasn't used to. In Texas, I learned how to breathe without being worried about who was watching or snapping photos."

My hand finds the edge of her hip.

"What about your sister?" I ask. "She's still on your list, isn't she?"

Stormy doesn't answer right away. Her eyes shift toward the window, then back to mine, her jaw working through whatever she's not saying yet. But when she speaks, her voice is clear. Certain.

"Yes. But I won't have to chase her. She will come to me after I confront my father," she says with confidence. "I know her better than anyone. Or at least, I thought I did. Her secretly being with Donovan shocked me."

I don't speak as I tuck loose strands of hair behind her ear and listen.

"She doesn't get to rewrite what she did. I've let them control the version of me they liked best. That stops now. I'll look her in the eye, and I will not let her forget that she was one of the reasons I had to rebuild my life from ash."

Every word she says lands with weight.

"I'll do whatever I can," I tell her. "Whatever you need."

She nods, and the tension in her shoulders ease. "I don't want you to fight my battles."

"I'm not," I say. "I'm standing beside you while you win them."

Her lips twitch, and it's something between a smile and a breath of relief.

We don't move for a while. I hold her and hold on to the space between who she was and who she's choosing to be.

Since we landed, I realize she was never returning to New York to walk back into her past, but to confront it so she can leave it behind.

Stormy leans in and presses her mouth against mine. I kiss her back, one hand brushing her jaw. There's no need to say anything else; it's already been said.

When we pull apart, her forehead rests against mine. Her eyes stay closed.

"Thank you," she whispers.

"You don't have to thank me," I tell her. "I'm exactly where I want to be."

I mean it, and she knows I do.

After a while, she steps back from me and lets her fingers trail down the front of my shirt. "I'm hungry. We should get some food."

I nod once. "Lead the way, darlin'."

She glances back at me, one brow slightly raised. "You sure you're up for this? We might get followed."

I steal another kiss, and she melts into me.

"I flew across the country to be by your side. I think I can handle a walk through the city. Should I change clothes?"

Her lips quirk up like she's trying not to smile. "Only if you want. I don't care what you wear."

"I know. But like you wanted to be a cowboy princess at the rodeo, I want to fit in your world too. It would make me feel more comfortable with so many pictures being taken. Worse than my damn grandma."

"We'll stop at one of my favorite boutiques before we eat."

We escape from the building by taking a back entrance. Her hand is tucked in mine, and a smile plays at the corners of her mouth.

She leads me down a quiet block lined with boutiques that only those from a particular social class shop at. The storefront she leads me into looks like a museum. It has no name, no hours, and zero price tags. A man in a sleek gray suit greets her like she's royalty returning from exile.

"Ms. Langford," he says with a gracious nod. "It's been a while."

"Hi, Dominic," she says, as if they've done this dance before. "I'd like to get a few things for my boyfriend."

Boyfriend. I love how she unapologetically claimed me.

"Boyfriend? Let me guess. You're a model." Dominic's eyes slide over me.

"Hell no," I tell him.

"You should be," he says and gestures us toward a back room.

We're led into a private lounge that's more like a hangout than a dressing area. There's leather furniture, a wall of mirrors, a bar cart stocked with whiskey, and an empty rack, waiting to be filled with clothes.

Stormy turns to me with a grin. "All right, cowboy. Ready to play dress-up?"

The gentleman returns and measures my shoulders, length of my legs, chest, arms, basically everything. Five minutes pass, and he hangs clothes on the rack. I eye the different colors of button-up shirts, slacks, and dress shoes, and then he leaves us alone.

Stormy's fingers graze over the fabrics. "This is a little different from your usual denim and charm."

I smirk. "Good. Make sure I can pull off being a real househusband of Manhattan. Dress me."

"Really?" she asks, her eyes lighting up as she moves to the rack and starts pulling things like she's been waiting for this exact moment. "You're giving me total creative control?"

"Yes, ma'am."

Stormy pulls what she likes, then hooks the hangers on my finger.

"I only draw the line at bow ties," I say.

"I agree." Her lips twitch like she's trying to hold back laughter. "But I make no promises about tight pants."

I shoot her a glance as I turn toward the fitting room.

"Would be a whole lot better if you were in here with me," I mutter as I change into the first outfit.

It's a crisp white button-up and charcoal slacks. I glance in the mirror, rolling the sleeves to my forearms. I'm not used to clothes that fit like they're made for me.

I return to the lounge, tugging at the collar a little. "Well?"

Stormy's sitting on the arm of the leather couch, sipping sparkling water like she belongs in a magazine spread.

Her eyes slide from my mouth, down my body, then back up to my eyes. "Damn. Took my breath away."

"That good?"

"Wow. So happy you're mine. You look like a man who closes deals and breaks hearts before lunch," she tells me.

I shake my head, smiling as I turn back to the mirror. "I feel like I need to call my lawyer."

She laughs and stands to circle me. Her fingers brush the line of my shoulder as she straightens the collar, and then she smooths a hand down the front of my shirt.

"This is a keeper," she says.

"You're a keeper," I say, touching her elbow.

Her lips slide across mine. "You are too."

I admire her for a second longer. "All right, what's next? Do I get a glass of scotch and a lesson in hedge fund lingo?"

"You get to try on the gray suit. And a tie." She slaps my ass. "Go on, cowboy."

Back in the fitting room, I swap into the charcoal gray suit, slim fit, just structured enough that I feel important. When I come out, Stormy's already holding a pair of polished shoes and waiting for me like we're preparing for a red-carpet moment and she's my publicist.

"These," she says, handing them to me.

I sit down to change, glancing up at her from the bench.

Her eyes on me the whole time. "You look so fucking good."

"So do you, darlin'."

She waggles her brows at me, and I'm tempted to lay her down on the leather couch.

Dominic enters. "Suggestions?"

"No, we'll take it all. Add it to my account. Deliver everything to my penthouse at the Park," Stormy tells him. "He's wearing this out."

Dominic doesn't even blink. He just nods once and grabs the rest of the clothes like it's routine for Stormy to waltz in, transform a man, and buy out the rack on her way out.

Stormy watches him go, then turns to me. "I love you."

I brush my thumb against her cheek, stealing a kiss. "I love you, my little storm cloud."

Her smile stretches across her face. "Don't be surprised if people track you down to put you on the cover of a magazine."

"Honey, hush."

"I'm serious," she tells me. "You have the sex appeal, and because you're with me, agents will call."

I chuckle. "Thanks for the confidence boost, but I know this life isn't for me."

"It's not for me either," she admits. "Not anymore."

I take her hand and interlock my fingers with hers. We walk

out into the street, the wind sweeping past us in a sudden gust that lifts her hair. She's the main character in a movie, and I'm walking beside her like I'm a part of her world.

"So," I say, wrapping my arm around her, "what's next? Gallery opening? Dinner with royalty?"

Stormy laughs under her breath. "How about a big, fat, juicy burger and fries? Then maybe a glass of wine somewhere quiet so we don't get bombarded by paparazzi."

I smirk. "Speakin' my language, darlin'."

We cross the street, her stride steady and self-assured, and her smile doesn't falter.

And me?

I'm right where I want to be, at her side, like I belong.

CHAPTER THIRTY

STORMY

The light comes in soft, filtering through the floor-to-ceiling windows that oversee the edge of Central Park. The sky is pale and cloudless, the city still wrapped in that early hush before the traffic begins to hum.

I lie still for a while, watching the way the sunlight moves across the marble floor in my penthouse bedroom. It catches on the edges of my bookshelf, warms the foot of my bed, and then settles over Colt's bare shoulder, where the blanket's slipped down.

He's on his stomach, arm stretched across the bed, like he was reaching for me in his sleep. One leg hooked over the edge of the sheet, his hair a mess, his beautiful face relaxed while he sleeps.

I don't move.

I admire this version of him. My body aches in that familiar, simmering way as I remember how thoroughly he made love to me last night.

There's a softness in the air that has never existed in my penthouse before, and it clings to me when I exhale.

He stirs when I shift to my side to get a better view. His eyes stay closed, but his hand finds my hip beneath the sheet and rests there like it never left.

"You watchin' me again?" he mutters, voice full of rasp.

"I can't help it. You're a cowboy dream."

A lazy smile pulls at his mouth, scooting close. "I love waking up next to you."

"Me too," I admit. "I think it was always supposed to be like this. You and me."

His blue eyes sparkle as he opens them. "You and me."

My confession wakes him a little more. His fingers tighten at my hip, and he pulls me even closer, guiding me into the curve of his body without saying a word.

His mouth finds my collarbone first, then my neck, then the corner of my jaw. Each kiss is like he's relearning me all over again.

We don't rush.

We're nothing but breath and skin and want.

His hand slips under the sheet, trailing down my thigh. Our mouths meet, and everything fades away. New York, the meeting I'll have with my father, the headlines about me and Donovan that were posted last night. None of it matters right now. Just this.

I cherish how his touch says *you're safe*. The way his voice says *you're mine*. How his body fits against me like he was built to hold and keep me.

We make love until we're both a mess, breathless, lips swollen.

When we finish, we stay tangled in the sheets, breathing hard, foreheads pressed together. I don't open my eyes right away. I want to memorize this—his weight over mine, the way he whispers my name like it's not borrowed or broken.

Eventually, he shifts onto his back, pulling me with him until I'm sprawled across his chest.

"You ready for today?" he asks, fingers combing gently through my hair.

"I am now," I whisper.

His arms wrap tighter around me. "That's my girl. You got this."

The quiet doesn't last.

It never does here.

Colt eventually rolls out of bed to shower. I hear the water turn on and the soft thud of his footsteps across the tile. I stay in bed a little longer, watching the sunlight stretch higher across the skyline. My fingers trail across the crease in the sheets where his body was.

The clock ticks closer toward eight, and my reality returns.

There's a version of me that wants to stay in bed with him all day, hiding beneath these soft sheets with his naked body. However, that version can't exist until I finish what I came here to do. In an hour, I will relinquish my responsibilities and start living my life on my terms. That thought gives me the energy to get out of bed.

I swing my legs over the edge of the mattress and stand, pulling on a robe from the hook by the closet.

Colt steps out of the bathroom a minute later, towel around his waist, hair damp and tousled. He crosses the space without hesitation.

"You planning a coup?" he asks, voice teasing enough to pull me out of my head.

I let out a breath I didn't know I had been holding. "That's one word for it."

He reaches for my hand, lacing our fingers together. "You don't have to burn the whole city down in one day."

"Only the part that has its hold on me."

He studies me for a long beat, then nods once. "You're a firecracker, darlin'."

"You know it," I tell him, moving inside my closet. "This is almost over."

The lights come on automatically, spilling warm white across rows of silk, cashmere, structured wool, and shoes lined up like soldiers. It's massive. Every inch of space is curated for the season. Neutrals up front. Color-coded accents. Clutches arranged by designer. The whole room smells faintly of my favorite perfume.

I stand there for a second, taking it in.

There was a time when I would walk into this space and transform into someone powerful. Untouchable. Like I could become whatever the room demanded by picking the right pair of heels.

Now?

It's a costume department. My wedding dress should be hung here to complete the show.

I run my fingers along the hem of a blazer I once wore to a board meeting in Dubai. It's flawless. Tailored to the inch. And completely irrelevant to the woman I've become.

I move past it. Past the towering heels and the pristine whites. My fingers brush across the silk dresses that hug my body and reveal all my secrets. None of them are right.

Then I see it—tucked between a few older pieces. A tailored black suit with slim-cut pants and a fitted jacket. Clean. Sleek. With an edge. I pull it out and grab a dark charcoal tank to go underneath. There are no frills for this career funeral.

When I step out of the closet, Colt is waiting by the window, already dressed, adjusting the cuffs of his new shirt. He turns when he hears me, and his eyes drag over me.

"That'll do, babe," he says, voice proud. "Damn. Now I know why you drink your coffee black."

I smirk, grabbing a pair of dark sunglasses off the console and sliding them onto my head. "I guess it's go time."

We take the elevator down and slip out through the private exit, where a car is waiting for us. Colt stays close, his presence behind me. When we step onto the main sidewalk, the noise finds us immediately.

Cameras click in quick succession. Voices rise in a chorus of speculation. Someone must've spotted my car and told the paps where I'd be.

"Stormy, are you back for good?"

"Are you here to take over the firm?"

"Do you have a comment about the wedding?"

I don't respond. I keep walking, eyes forward. Colt moves with me, and he's close enough that I feel him with me every step. The driver pulls the door open as we approach.

"I'm sorry," he says. "I don't know how they knew."

I slide in first, and Colt follows. The door closes behind us, muting the chaos to a dull throb.

I watch the street through the tinted window as we drive away. People blur together. Glass towers rise. Somewhere between Park Towers and the office, I let go of whatever part of me wanted to disappear.

Today is not about disappearing. It's about finally being seen.

When we arrive, I get out, and Colt follows. The wind pushes at my coat. I straighten the collar and glance up at the tall building.

Langford Media is in tall silver letters above the entryway. I used to be proud to enter this building, but now I'm disgusted.

The bottom-floor receptionist stiffens when she sees me, then quietly reaches for the phone.

"Ms. Stormy Langford has arrived. She's heading there now."

Security glances at us as we step into the elevator. They let us go through.

"Is he expecting you?" Colt asks when the doors slide closed.

"He refused to see me today, and I'm not waiting. He'll see me now," I explain. "I'm ready to have this conversation regardless of his schedule."

The rest of the elevator ride is silent. Colt stands beside me, one hand resting lightly against the small of my back. The gesture is quiet, and it steadies something inside me.

When the doors open, his executive assistant is already waiting.

"He wants to reschedule for tomorrow," she says. Her eyes flick between me and Colt, but she doesn't ask questions.

I grab his hand and pull him past her and into my father's office, where he's on the phone.

"I have to let you go," he says, ending the call.

The space is clean, deliberate, and cold. My father stands and crosses his arms over his chest.

"Stormy," he says, as if I'm stopping by for lunch, "I thought my secretary—"

"I'm not here for pleasantries. You're not busy. And you will listen to what I have to say right now before I torch this company's reputation too."

His gaze moves to Colt, and something shifts behind his expression. "You brought company."

"This is the man I'm going to marry one day. Colt Valentine."

Colt is polite and nods, but my father is rude. He motions to the chairs across from his desk, eyes and jaw set.

I don't sit.

"I'm resigning," I say. "Effective immediately. My legal team will send over the documents by the end of the day."

He watches me like I'm a boardroom problem he didn't anticipate. "Stormy, you don't need to do this. There's a path forward. We can manage the fallout."

"There's no fallout," I say. "There's truth. And I'm done letting you decide how much of it gets to exist. I'm done with the cover-up stories. Did you know Skye was sleeping with Donovan behind my back? What has been said about me online makes me seem like the villain, and I will not tolerate the smear campaign against my name. I will not be made out to be some *jealous woman who had cold feet*. I've already begun destroying that narrative, which I'm sure you're aware of."

My father doesn't react right away.

He leans back in his chair, folding his hands in front of him like this is another negotiation, like we're haggling over a line item instead of the truth that wrecked my life.

"I assumed that you'd come here to speak calmly. Strategically. With real solutions."

"Leaving is my solution," I snap.

He doesn't flinch. Of course, he doesn't. He's been in too many rooms like this, too many crisis meetings, where the goal was never truth; it was silence.

"I was the one being lied to," I continue. "You made me seem unhinged with those headlines. Do you know what it's like to lose everything and still have to sit back and let your own family feed the narrative that you're unstable, dramatic, and difficult?"

He says nothing. He's watching me now, not as a daughter, but as a threat. I know too much. I'm dangerous.

"I'm not asking for your blessing," I explain. "I'm giving you a warning. The next time I see my name associated with cold feet or a breakdown, I will take it personally. And I will not protect this firm. I will not protect *you*."

"That's not necessary—"

"No," I cut him off. "It's well overdue. So, fix what you broke."

I step closer to the desk, placing my palms flat against the surface. "Skye betrayed me. Donovan humiliated me. And you—this firm—allowed the world to think I'd unraveled. They laughed at me. I was picked apart for sport in the media."

"I didn't know about them," he finally confesses.

The words land quieter than I expected, and it almost stuns me.

He leans back slightly in his chair, and since I walked in, he's not acting like a man in control. He's acting like my dad.

"You didn't know? How is that possible?" I ask, my voice sharp.

"I didn't. I wouldn't have allowed that." His brow tightens. "I'm not a monster. The smear campaigns didn't come from here."

I breathe a little. "I don't want to be in the city anymore. I'm moving. I'm done. While I'm gone, I hope I can find it in my heart to forgive what Skye and Donovan did to me. And I'll rest easier, knowing you weren't trying to smear my name."

"I'm sorry," he says.

I have no response to that because I didn't expect an apology, and it almost makes me crack. My dad moves toward me and pulls me into his arms for a hug. He pulls back slightly and looks at me—not as the future CEO, not as a father trying to regain control, but as my dad.

"I'm okay with you quitting if it will make you happy."

The words settle something in me.

I nod once. "It will. It's the first time I've ever felt free."

He exhales, and I can tell he means it when he says, "Then go be happy."

I don't expect the tight hug that follows or the way my chest tightens when I let myself lean into it. He holds me like a father who regrets not doing better. I don't forgive everything, not yet. But I forgive enough to let this moment exist.

When we pull apart, Colt is already moving toward the door, giving us space.

When we're alone, my dad clears his throat. "Were you serious about marrying him?"

"Yes," I say with a smile. "When you know, you know."

"He seems like a good man."

"He is," I tell him, and then I leave.

Colt waits for me outside the door, and I take his hand into mine. The elevator ride is quiet, but not full of regret. It feels like coming up for air after being underwater too long. I lean into Colt's side, and he wraps his arm around me.

"Love that wrath," he says with a laugh.

Outside, the city hums like it always does, but I feel like I'm visiting, and I know where home is.

"You did it," Colt says with a boyish grin.

"I did." I breathe. "And I didn't break."

He looks at me like I've rewritten the ending to my story. "No, you didn't. Now you're stronger than ever."

I tip my head against his shoulder and close my eyes as we climb inside the car. Once we're buckled, it pulls away from the curb.

I'm not proving anything or escaping everything. I'm free.

"How do you feel?"

"Like the elephant is finally moving off my chest. This is almost over."

He leans over, brushing his lips across mine, and we nearly lose control in the back seat.

When the SUV glides to a stop in front of Park Towers, we're still kissing and laughing.

I step out in front of the paparazzi with swollen lips and messy hair, and stand taller with him beside me.

Colt takes my hand, holding me close, and I glance over at him. He shoots me a wink, like we've always belonged side by side, even here.

I chose the right man—and he chose me right back.

CHAPTER THIRTY-ONE

STORMY

By the time we're back in the penthouse, the adrenaline is wearing off. The door clicks shut behind us, and the silence settles over everything.

I kick off my heels without thinking. They land beside the front door in a way that feels final, like they've walked their last boardroom hallway. My feet sink into the cool hardwood. I walk to the kitchen and pour two glasses of wine. I hand him one, and then we plop down on the couch.

"Thanks," he says. "Are we celebrating at ten in the morning?"

I nod. "Yep! Two down. One to go."

He takes a sip, and I drink half mine in one go. "She'll be here. I need to decide what I'm going to say to her and change clothes," I say, already moving toward the bedroom. "Order us something to eat. Delivery. Make sure it's greasy. I've missed being a trash panda while in Valentine."

"Greasy coming right up," he says with a laugh.

I peel off the suit the second I'm behind the door, hanging it neatly on the back of the chair before slipping into a soft pair of leggings and one of his T-shirts. It still smells like cedar, cotton, and home. I move into the bathroom and pull my hair into a messy knot, wanting it off the back of my neck.

When I return to the living room, Colt's on the couch, one leg stretched out, his phone in hand. Bare feet are propped on the edge of the coffee table like he's a part of the furniture.

"Food's on the way," he says. "Lo mein with a double order of egg rolls."

I cross the room and drop onto the couch beside him, curling one leg under me. "You figured right."

His eyes sweep over my face. "You okay?" he asks.

"I think I am."

The smell hits before the knock. Colt jumps up, barefoot, looking like sex appeal on legs, and answers the door. Seconds later, he's returning with the bag of Chinese food like it's sacred. We don't bother plating it. He opens the containers one by one, and steam rises, filling the air with garlic, ginger, and heaven.

"Egg rolls," he announces, holding one up like a trophy.

I grab it from his hand before he can finish the sentence. "Gimme."

It's hot, and I toss it between my fingers, blowing on it.

He laughs and sits beside me, opening a carton of lo mein. "You sure you don't want a plate?"

"This *is* the plate," I say, holding out my hand, already grabbing a second egg roll.

I lean back on the cushion, watching him. It's weird, how he fits here like this place is adjusting around him. Or maybe it's me who can't imagine him not in my life, wherever that is.

For a while, we eat without saying much. There's music playing in the background—some chill acoustic playlist Colt must've cued up. Sunlight from the late morning sun glows against the surrounding glass windows in the distance and reflects gold.

"You know," he says, wiping his hands on a napkin, "you

should keep this place, and we'll come visit when you miss the city."

"You think I'll miss it?"

He nods. "Eventually. With time, people tend to grow nostalgic. I know you're still very pissed, which is understandable. But you won't always be so hurt, and maybe one day, you can return here with a smile."

"How do you always know the right thing to say?"

"Mama only raised emotionally intelligent men." He pauses and smirks. "Never mind. Forgot about Emmett."

We fall into a fit of laughter, and I reach for an eggroll, but he beats me to it. Colt dips it in soy sauce and offers it to me with a kind grin.

"You're sexy when you feed me," I mutter, taking a bite.

Colt wags his brows. "I've got something to feed you."

"You are so bad," I tell him with a laugh, noticing how free and happy I am.

We finish eating, and Colt cleans up our mess, then returns to me.

"You're really good at this," I tell him, scooting closer, inhaling him.

"At what?" he asks, wrapping his arm around me.

"Making me happy."

Before he can say anything, there's a knock at the door.

Three soft raps. Not urgent. Not hesitant. There.

I tilt my head at him. "Told you so."

"Do you want me to get it?" he asks, shifting so he can stand.

"No." I shake my head. "It's her. I know it is."

I walk to the door. The hardwood is cold on my bare feet. I stop with my hand on the handle and open it.

As I predicted, it's Skye. She's standing there with perfect posture in a designer dress without a hair out of place. Her lipstick is the same shade she wore on my wedding day. I wonder if she suggested that color, so when Donovan kissed me after saying *I do*, he would think of her.

For a second, we stare at each other. My pulse quickens, and then I notice the shift in her expression. It's relief, hesitation, guilt, and anger twisted behind her perfectly smooth face.

She opens her mouth like she might speak, but I don't let her control the conversation.

"I should slam the door in your face."

Skye flinches, but she doesn't step back. She stands there with her hands folded neatly in front of her, like she's here to apologize for being five minutes late to brunch, not for helping detonate my entire life.

"I needed to see you," she says.

"You don't get to want things from me anymore."

She saw my kindness as weakness, and I will no longer tolerate her disrespect.

Her mouth opens, closes, and I've never seen her stunned and silent. For a woman who's always had a performance ready, she's finally out of rehearsed lines.

"Can I at least come in?" she asks.

I want Colt to see the person who betrayed me, so I happily stand aside, ready to bring this conversation to a place where there is a witness so she can't twist my words or hers. She walks in like she has a thousand times before. Her heels click against the floor.

His brows pinch together, but he doesn't say anything.

Skye turns to face me, hands clenched now, her knuckles white. "Who is he?"

The question lands like a scratch in the middle of a record.

"He's mine," I state. "Not taking that one from me too."

She glances toward Colt, and he watches me like she doesn't matter.

"So, that's it? He made you like this?" There's an accusatory tone in her voice.

"No," I say. "You can thank yourself for that."

She blinks at me, like she wants to protest, but nothing comes out.

I stare at her. "How long were you sleeping with Donovan?"

"I don't know what you're talking about," she says.

The heat rises in my chest again because she still doesn't get it.

"Now you're going to deflect?" I ask, my voice colder now. "I saw you two together. You have no idea what that did to me. Not because I lost Donovan, but because I lost you."

Skye staggers back a half step, and her face crumples, but I don't soften. I can't. Not now.

"I could never have imagined you would do something to me like that. I trusted you, Skye."

Tears slide down her cheeks now, but I don't care.

"I would've burned the world down for you," I say, quieter now, but no less fierce. "I protected you from everything—our parents, the press, your own messes. And when I needed you most, you were stabbing me in the back. Had I not found you two, I'd have gone through with that and then been a third wheel in my marriage. That's not okay."

"I didn't know how to stop it," she confesses.

"No, you just didn't want to. You've always been selfish."

She glances down at the floor like it might give her a place to disappear. "I can't change what happened," she says.

"I agree."

The truth hangs in the air.

She wipes away her tears. "Dad fired me—because of you."

I shake my head. "When you're ready to grow up and take responsibility and apologize, call me. Until then, I cannot do this. You and Donovan were made for one another."

I put my hand on her shoulder, leading her to the door.

She opens her mouth, as if she's ready to apologize.

"Save it," I say.

She swallows hard. "I'm pregnant."

I blink at her. The room tilts a little, like the floor beneath me isn't quite solid.

Pregnant.

The word echoes in my head, but I barely comprehend it. Donovan didn't want to have kids with me and was very clear about it. It was something I accepted and made peace with.

She's blindsided me.

I stop walking and cross my arms. The ache behind my ribs pounds.

"You knew he didn't want kids," I say quietly. "You trapped him. *Wow.* Determined."

Her throat works around something she doesn't know how to say.

I hold her gaze for a long time. "I don't know you."

"I'm so sorry." A tear slides down her cheek. She doesn't wipe it away. "Will you ever be able to forgive me?"

"You've got bigger issues to concern yourself with." I walk to the door and open it. "I hope you got what you wanted."

She walks away, and I shut the door, leaning my forehead against it.

My heart feels like it's beating in a different rhythm now.

Colt appears beside me, his hand at the small of my back. "You okay?"

"No," I say, turning to him. "But I will be."

I let myself cry—not for my sister, not for Donovan, not for my career, but for the version of myself that stayed quiet for too long. She's gone now.

Instead of this being the end of something, it feels more like the beginning of my new life.

CHAPTER THIRTY-TWO

COLT

She doesn't say anything after I pull her into my arms.

She stays pressed against me, her body finally softening after hours of holding herself together. I feel the moment she shifts—not a collapse, but like she's giving herself permission to feel the things she's buried since leaving the city behind.

I let my presence speak louder than anything I could offer.

She cries, and I keep my arms around her.

Eventually, she steps back. Her eyes are red, her face streaked with emotion, but her shoulders are still squared. She looks like a woman who walked through fire and knows exactly what kind of burn she can survive.

"I think I need a shower," she says hoarsely.

I nod. "Take your time."

She disappears down the hall without another word. The sound of the door closing is soft. A few seconds later, the water turns on.

I stand in the stillness she left behind and glance around.

I've been in this space for two days now, and the weight of who she is finally settles around me.

The penthouse is too curated. The furniture is expensive leather. The art on the walls is original and bold. A grand piano sits in the corner of the room, untouched but cared for. On the marble counter is a stack of unopened mail, a few envelopes embossed with logos I recognize from magazine covers and corporate towers.

Stormy isn't successful or connected. She's known. Her name doesn't echo through rooms like mine does in Valentine; it shapes them before she steps through the door. Stormy left behind a family name, a corporate legacy, headlines, and expectations.

Somehow, she found me in the chaos. If that's not meant to be, I'm not sure what is.

I stay by the window, my hand resting lightly on the glass, staring out at the city spread beneath us. It's so different than what I'm used to.

I move to the mantel where there are photos of her and her friends. My eyes scan over them, and that's when I see a face I never expected—someone from home. I pick up the frame, still half convinced I'm imagining things. But there's no mistaking her —Lexi Matthews. Well, now it's Calloway, after she married the love of her life, Easton. In the photo, her arm is slung around Stormy's shoulders, like they've known each other a long time. And maybe they have.

The world always seems so damn big. But right now, it feels small enough to fit in the palm of my hand.

Behind me, I hear her footsteps. She comes up quietly, still towel-drying her hair, barefoot in a fresh pair of leggings and one of my T-shirts.

I smile at her. "You know Lexi?"

Stormy steps beside me, a small grin tugging at the corner of her mouth. "Yeah. She's married to Easton—one of my close friends. She's the one who told me about Valentine. Said it was the perfect place to get lost. Peaceful. Kind. Beautiful in the ways that mattered. I'd never have known about the town if it wasn't for Lexi."

I glance back at the photo and am so damn grateful. "Guess I owe her a thank-you."

"I do too." She pulls back slightly.

A question sits heavy in my chest. It's not new, but it's grown louder with every minute I've spent in this city, surrounded by proof of her past life.

I could keep it to myself. I could let the moment pass. But I don't want to move forward with even a shadow of a doubt between us.

"Do you believe I'm the man who can make you happy?" I ask.

Her expression doesn't shift. She holds my gaze like she's been waiting for the question.

"Absolutely," she says.

I study her face, every curve and line of it, every bit of strength and softness. "I don't think it's a weird question, but why?"

She doesn't hesitate. "Because you see me. Not the brand, not the version of me that fits in a press release. Just me."

I feel something in my chest pull tight, and I smile. "I do."

"Now that you know everything ... does it change anything for you?"

I shake my head once. "Not even a little. I don't care what the rest of the world sees when they look at you. I know the real you. The woman I fell in love with the moment our eyes met."

A tear slips down her cheek.

"I'm so lucky to have met you," I tell her.

She reaches for my hand, her fingers threading between mine. "I'm so lucky to get to love you."

The city hums quietly behind the glass, but neither of us gives it attention. We've seen enough today. Said enough. And yet I can feel there's still one more truth she's holding.

She lets go of my hand, only long enough to turn and sit on

the edge of the couch. Her elbows rest on her knees, her eyes fixed on the floor for a second, then up at me.

"I want to go home," she says. Her voice is soft, but there's no uncertainty in it.

Hearing her call our place home does something to me.

I sit beside her, close enough that our knees bump. "You're staying with me forever?"

"Yes. I can find a place if living together is too soon, but I'm done here. I've said what I needed to say. I've faced the people I needed to face. I don't want to wait. I want to leave now. Tonight, if we can."

"Darlin', my bed is your bed from now until the end of time," I tell her, swooping her in for a kiss, feeling like the happiest man on this planet. "You're sure?"

She nods again. "I've never been surer of anything. The only thing I want to take back with me is you."

I reach up and tuck a piece of hair behind her ear, watching her eyes stay locked on mine.

"Whatever makes you happy, darlin'," I say. "Let's go home."

"If we leave soon, maybe we can make it for sunset?"

"Lead the way."

She reaches for my hand, and we don't waste time.

Stormy makes one call, and the jet is ready in under an hour.

We don't talk much as we pack. We're all smiles and random kisses.

"I'll have everything shipped to the house," she says with one suitcase that I wheel outside.

The SUV pulls up to the private terminal in the afternoon. We won't make it home by sunset, but we'll definitely make it there for sunrise in the morning. The city is washed in orange and blue and steel, and when the private jet takes off, she doesn't glance back. Not once.

"You okay?" I ask, pressing my lips to the softness of her neck.

"I am now."

The cabin lights are low, and I lace my fingers with hers without a second thought.

She leans her head on my shoulder. "Want to get your Mile-High Club card stamped again?"

"Hell, yeah," I say, and she stands, leading me to the back of the jet.

CHAPTER THIRTY-THREE

STORMY

The wheels hit the tarmac with a low thud that travels through the floor and into my chest. I grip the armrest out of habit more than fear. There's nothing scary about landing in Texas. Not now. Not anymore.

Outside the window, the horizon stretches in a dusky blur. The last strips of sunset have already faded. From the plane, I watched the sky shifting from bruised orange to indigo to darkness. The airport is small—just a single lane of runway, tucked behind a chain-link fence and a row of mesquite trees. This part of the country is wide-open spaces and silence. My favorite.

Colt glances at me and smirks as the jet comes to a crawl.

We deboard and descend the stairs into a thick heat that wraps around my skin. It smells like dirt, cows, and sunbaked gravel. I let it fill my lungs.

The SUV I arranged waits off to the side. He opens the door for me, and I slide in.

The cab smells like leather and spearmint gum. The driver doesn't say anything as we take off toward Valentine. We don't talk much, both spent from rocking each other's world on the flight home. His thigh presses against mine, and his hand rests warm on my leg, thumb tracing lazy circles just above my knee. The hum of the road is the only sound between us. And it's enough.

"By the way, I called my friend about London while I was in the city."

His brows pinch together. "Really?"

"He's going to make it to one of her shows. The rest is up to her."

His mouth curves, but it's his eyes that catch me off guard. That pride, the kind only family brings out. I don't think he knows how easy it is to love him when he looks like that.

The rest of the drive slips by quietly.

We take the back roads; the driver swears they're faster. I rest my hand on his, and neither of us says anything until the turnoff to the house comes into view.

The gravel crunches under the tires as the SUV rolls to a stop. We get out, and Colt grabs our bags. Soon, we're left standing in front of the half-finished house beside a Camaro I destroyed with my bare hands.

"I missed this place," I tell him.

"We're back," Colt says, but it's quiet, like he's talking to himself more than me.

We pause at the top of the porch without meaning to. Just … stop. Standing side by side, our hands still joined.

The sky above is dark now, but the stars are out—clearer here than they ever are over Manhattan. I tilt my head and look up. For a second, I let myself just breathe it in.

This place. This life. This version of me.

Colt speaks beside me. "You ready to go in?"

"Yeah," I say, the smile already blooming. "Home sweet home."

When I cross that threshold, everything inside me exhales.

The door clicks shut, and I stand inside the entryway, taking it all in. I can't help but smile.

"You hungry?" he asks.

"A little. Not for anything big."

"Grilled cheese work?"

I smile. "Perfect."

He grabs my hand and leads me to the kitchen. I sit at the table, watching him work around the kitchen. He opens the fridge, reaches for butter, and flips the burner on without checking the dial.

"The only thing that would make this better is if you were shirtless," I tell him.

As if I snapped my fingers, he peels his shirt from his body. "For your watching pleasure."

I lean my elbows on the table, chin resting in my palm, watching the muscles in his back shift as he grabs a skillet. "You gonna make me a sandwich *and* give me a show?"

He glances over his shoulder. "Multitasking, darlin'. It's one of my many cowboy skills."

"Oh, yeah?" I smirk. "What else you got in your bag of tricks?"

He turns just enough to flash me a look over his bare shoulder. "Guess you'll have to stick around and find out."

A minute later, the smell shifts—less buttered toast, more singed edges.

"Colt ..." I warn.

"Shit." He flips the sandwich too late and winces. "Still edible."

"Let me guess. Another one of your cowboy skills?"

"Making things work, even when they're a little burned? Absolutely."

We eat in the kitchen for a bit, then relocate to the living room, plates still in hand. The two of us sit cross-legged on the couch, plates balanced in our laps, the sandwich cut diagonally, how I like. I take a bite, still warm in the center, and nod with approval.

"Best grilled cheese of my life," I say.

"You're biased."

"Only when it comes to you."

The bread is buttery. The cheese is hot enough to sting my tongue. Our knees bump, paper towels under our plates, no background music, no phones. I'm not watching the clock.

When we're done, he looks toward the porch and then back at me. "You want to sit outside for a bit?"

"Yeah. That would be nice."

We step out onto the porch and into the deep hush of a Texas night. The swing creaks as we sit, and I pull my knees up beside me, one leg tucked under the other. The breeze is warm, but it carries the edge of fall. Fireflies blink in the field beyond the fence line.

Colt settles in beside me, his fingers brushing my shoulder.

We let the swing rock beneath us in an easy rhythm.

The moon hangs low, casting a pale light over the yard. Somewhere out in the dark, a cricket chirps. A truck roars in the distance.

This is peace.

He presses a kiss to the top of my head.

Something in the way he touches me makes me feel safe and cared for.

I lead him inside and straight to the bedroom. He steps forward; his hands settle lightly on my hips. Mine slide up his chest, and his breath catches under my palms.

"I want you. Now and forever."

His eyes soften. "Good."

I rise onto my toes and kiss him. He kisses me back like we've been holding our breath since New York and we're finally letting go.

Clothes come off piece by piece in a feverish blur. Every look he gives me says, *I see you, I want you, I love you, and I'm always here.*

He lays me down gently, his body covering mine. His mouth trails over my collarbone, my shoulder, the inside of my wrist.

There are no words between us as he enters me. Just the quiet sound of breath, the creak of the bed frame, the weight of everything I've carried finally slipping away.

I wrap my arms around him and pull him closer. We move together, like we're trying to carve out a space that only belongs to us.

When I come undone, it's with a whimper.

He follows moments later, burying himself deep with a low groan that sounds like relief.

Afterward, he doesn't pull away. He stays wrapped around me, our legs tangled, my head tucked beneath his chin.

"Welcome home," he whispers into my hair. "This is where you belong."

And when I look into his bright blue eyes, I believe it.

CHAPTER THIRTY-FOUR

COLT

Stormy's still asleep when I wake up.

The light hasn't fully broken through the curtains yet, but the room is tinted in silvery blue that only shows up right before sunrise. I let the weight of her beside me sink in like something holy. Her hair is a dark, tangled mess across my chest, and one of her arms is wrapped around my ribs. Her breathing is even, and her pretty lips are parted just slightly.

I don't want to move, but I carefully slide out from under her arm and watch as she shifts, curling into the warm spot I left behind. She's here. In *our* bed. Stormy is no longer running.

Proof dreams do come true.

I move quietly through the house, barefoot on wood floors that creak in familiar places. The morning is cool.

In the kitchen, I grind the beans she likes and fill the pot. I know how she takes her coffee now—dark roast only. I pull our two mugs from the cabinet and smile at the chipped one.

The drip of the coffee maker and the rustle of birds starting up outside the window keep my attention. I crack the door open to let in some air and welcome the promise of another day ahead with my girl.

I lean against the counter and stare out the window. The pasture's quiet. Fence line still holding. No wind yet. I'll need to feed the horses soon.

The only thing that pulls me away is her soft, unhurried footsteps. I turn just as she walks into the kitchen. She's wearing my old T-shirt and nothing else. Her hair is still a mess from sleep.

She sees the mug waiting on the counter and gives me a look. "I can't believe you always wake up this early without an alarm."

"Some things are just ingrained in you." I chuckle. "But I'm always excited to start a new day with you."

She crosses the kitchen and steps up on her tiptoes to kiss me. "Good morning," she whispers.

We're not in a rush to be anything but here. Her hand brushes the side of my face before she pulls back.

"Good morning, my love."

I fill her mug full, and she grabs it, cradling it in both hands.

As she watches me pour mine, she blows lightly on the surface of her coffee. Her eyes sweep the kitchen like she's checking to make sure it's all still real.

Today is different. It's the first morning that feels like ours.

I glance at the clock, not because we have anywhere to be, but because my body's still used to measuring mornings by when she was leaving. Not anymore.

Stormy leans against the counter, one hip cocked, the hem of my old T-shirt grazing her bare thigh.

"I don't want to waste this," she says.

I raise an eyebrow. "Coffee?"

She gives me a small smile. "No. This feeling. This ... clarity."

She's quiet for a second. When she does speak again, her voice is more certain than I expected. I take a sip of coffee.

She looks up at me, and there's something vulnerable in her expression. "I want to build something that's mine here in Valentine. Lay some real roots."

"Love that idea. I support any of your dreams." I set my mug down and close the space between us. "What do you want to do?"

She tilts her head. "Paint."

"Really? Are you an artist?"

She laughs, and the sound settles something in me. "No. But maybe one day, I will be. Valentine could use an art gallery," she says, voice soft but sure.

"Yes, ma'am. Can always use some fine arts around here," I say. "Takes some logistics and cash."

"I have plenty of money."

"Don't want you for your dollars, darlin'. I've got plenty of money from my rental properties and from flipping houses through my twenties."

She tilts her head. "Like, how much money?"

"A couple million."

She looks surprised but also impressed.

"I invested some too," I explain, grabbing her hand. "So, we don't need your money."

"It's a cherry on top then," she says with a laugh. "I plan to give a lot away. Maybe start a nonprofit that restores homes for those who need extra help."

"You'd do that?" I ask.

She smiles. "I found myself surrounded by half-finished walls, Colt. I rebuilt my life here, and I have more than enough funds to make a huge difference. More than either of us could ever spend. *Billions.* We have the ability to positively change lives and living situations by remodeling homes, so why not?"

I place my hands on her cheeks and kiss her like tomorrow might never come. "You're incredible. I'm so damn lucky to have someone so generous and caring by my side."

"I'm the lucky one," she whispers.

I take her hand and lead her past the living room, down the short hallway, toward the front half of the house.

We stop at the door of what used to be the main storage room for extra wood and supplies. She raises an eyebrow, waiting. I push it open.

The space is brighter than it used to be. Inside is a hand-carved wooden desk, a nice chair, and a lamp. I had my brothers move the furniture in while we were gone. There is even a fluffy rug beneath our feet.

Stormy steps inside, her fingertips grazing the edge of the window trim. "You did this?"

I nod. "Figured you might need a place to plan your dreams. We could also make it a partial art studio. Set an easel by the window. If you were serious about learning to paint."

She turns back to face me, eyes wide, like she's still in shock. "You did this for me?"

I shrug, suddenly a little self-conscious. "Of course."

She throws her arms around my neck. I catch her instinctively, lifting her just enough off the ground that her toes skim the floor.

"This is perfect. Thank you," she whispers into my shoulder. "You have no idea how much this means to me."

I've never been thanked for anything that felt this simple. But her voice? It makes me want to build her a hundred more rooms.

This isn't just a space for her to call her own. It's the beginning.

We linger in the office for a few minutes after she pulls away, neither of us saying much. We stand in that sunlit room, knowing it will hold pieces of the life we're building.

Eventually, I nod toward the porch. "You want to sit out for a bit?"

She smiles. "Always."

We make our way to the front door, her hand tucked lightly in mine. The morning breeze is mellow. We step outside, and the boards creak beneath our feet.

She sinks into the swing first, and I drop beside her and

stretch one arm along the backrest. She leans into me automatically.

The air smells like fresh-cut grass, and in the distance, I can hear the horses.

I'm about to speak when my phone buzzes in my pocket.

Stormy looks up at me, eyebrows raised.

It's a text from my mom.

MOM

Heard you two are back in town. Dinner's at six. No excuses. You two are the talk of Valentine right now.

I exhale a laugh and hold the phone out so she can see.

She reads it and snorts. "They don't waste time, do they?"

"Nope. And if the whole town's already talking, it means someone spotted us within ten minutes of landing."

She shakes her head, amused. "Do they know what happened?"

"Hard to say." I pocket the phone again. "But you know how it goes around here. One whisper turns into a full sermon before breakfast."

Stormy's expression shifts. "Are you okay with it? Them knowing?"

I nod without hesitation. "Let 'em talk. The people who matter already know what kind of woman you are. And the rest? They'll figure it out when they see the way I look at you."

She nestles closer, her head resting lightly on my shoulder.

"I love moments with you on the porch," she says.

"Me too."

BY THE TIME we pull into my parents' driveway, the sun has dipped behind the hills, leaving just enough light to paint the sky in dusky gold and lavender. The front porch is glowing, strung with the same twinkle lights Mama hangs up every time she hosts something bigger than our monthly family dinner. Which means this is a welcome-home party.

I glance over at Stormy as I shift the truck into park. Her hands are folded in her lap, fingers interlaced, shoulders straight, but I can tell she's nervous.

"You don't have to say anything you don't want to," I tell her. "They'll ask, but they'll also understand if you're uncomfortable."

She grins. "I know. I'm not nervous about what they'll think about my past."

"No?"

She gives me a soft smile. "Just want them to like the real me."

"They love you. Trust me."

The front door swings open. Emmett comes bopping down the steps, grinning, as obnoxious as ever.

"Well, well, if it isn't Manhattan's finest," he says, opening Stormy's door before I can get there. "Back from taming the big city?"

Stormy steps out with a playful roll of her eyes. "Hardly."

I round the front of the truck and catch Emmett winking at her.

"Good to see ya came to your senses and came home. Family missed ya."

"'Scuse me." I clap a hand on his shoulder and move past him. "Come on, darlin'."

Stormy takes my hand as Emmett chats with her about New York.

"Maybe I should go sing in my underwear while wearing a cowboy hat. I'd be rich."

"You can't sing," I tell him as Stormy laughs.

"With what I'd be showin', no one would care. Who knows? Maybe London will teach me."

The second we hit the porch, Mama's there. She doesn't hesitate, just opens her arms and pulls Stormy into a hug like she's known her all her life.

"You look tired, honey," she says, brushing Stormy's hair back, like she used to do with Kinsley when she came home from college. "But good. Real good."

Stormy nods, lips parting like she might thank her, but Mama just waves it off before the words come.

"Now, all of you go in. Don't want the food to get cold."

Mama didn't want too much attention on the moment.

Inside, the kitchen smells like roasted chicken, biscuits, and something sweet. The house is loud—voices layered over music, silverware clinking, Harrison laughing too hard in the living room with Vera and Sterling.

"Come on, y'all," Dad says and lets out a whistle.

My brothers and sisters and their partners rush into the dining room.

Every seat's full, except for the ones waiting for us. Stormy sits first, and I move beside her. Our hands clasp under the table. I give her a smile, and goose bumps trail across my skin. I want to get lost with her.

"Stormy, baby, welcome home," Mama says, using her real name. Cheers and laughter follow, and everyone is just as happy as me that she's here. That she's staying. "You're a Valentine now."

Stormy smiles, but I don't miss the way she blinks a few extra times, like she's holding back something bigger than a thank-you. Gratitude. Relief. Maybe even peace.

Dinner's a blur of overlapping stories and half-finished jokes while being full of stolen glances. My older brothers argue about preseason football. My sisters trade gossip. Dad throws in the occasional one-liner that makes Mama swat him on the arm.

No one asks about New York. No one brings up headlines or drama. They talk to her like she's one of us because she is.

Vera leans over at one point and whispers, "When are you proposing?"

I give her a smile. "Soon."

After dessert, people drift into the living room or outside onto the porch. The house stays full, warm, and buzzing. But for a second, Stormy and I are alone in the kitchen, standing by the sink with dirty plates in soapy water.

"Sorry about the dishes," I say, nodding toward the sink. "You know the rule. Unfortunately, no passes."

She leans against the counter, facing me. I move forward, pressing my lips against hers, and we get lost in the moment.

"You taste good," I whisper. "Like ice cream and cherry pie."

She looks up at me, her voice just a breath above a whisper. "I didn't think I'd ever have this."

"But you do," I say. "And to think, we're just gettin' started, darlin'."

She steals another kiss, and it takes every ounce of strength I have to pull away.

"Let's hurry so we can get the fuck outta here. I want real dessert."

"God, yes," she says, biting her bottom lip.

I lean forward and pluck it into my mouth, slightly sucking on it. She sighs against me, and then we pick up our pace. I wash and Stormy rinses, then places the plates in the dishwasher.

Since she stormed into my life, I realize we're not figuring out if we belong to each other anymore.

We already do.

And, hell, we're building something damn near unbreakable.

CHAPTER THIRTY-FIVE

STORMY

TWO WEEKS LATER

The shelter looks like I remember—flowers in planters, a faded sign that reads *Valentine Animal Rescue*, and a corkboard full of animals who still need to be adopted. I park my Bronco out front and sit for a moment with my hands on the wheel, staring at the front door like it might shift into something else if I blink.

It doesn't.

Inside, the air is cooler than expected and smells exactly how I remember, like a vanilla candle and old kibble. Ember waves at me from behind the desk.

"You're here for Boots, aren't you?" She stands up and nearly cries. "Thank you! I was hoping I'd be here when he finally got adopted. This makes my whole year!"

I smile. "Today is the day."

Ember stands and grabs the paperwork. All it takes is a few signatures, and it's a done deal.

A minute later, Boots runs toward me with his nub of a tail wagging. I bend down and hug him.

"Boots," I say. "Time to go home, buddy."

"Your house and all that land is gonna be perfect for him. He loves to run," she says, coming around the counter to put a bow on his neck. She gives him a tight squeeze, then looks up at me.

"You think I need a leash?" I ask.

"No, he listens," she says. "Just open the door of your vehicle, and he'll hop in. He's a cattle dog. He knows his place."

Before I go, I pay my clinic fee along with a one-hundred-thousand-dollar donation. Ember looks at the check, and her brows furrow.

"Uh, Stormy, you made a mistake. It was one hundred dollars."

"I know," I say. "I'm making a donation."

Her mouth falls open, and she tries to call someone from the back to come up front as I walk out of the clinic, chuckling. I open the door to the Bronco, and Boots hops inside, like Ember said.

I pet his head. "Good dog."

I roll down the window for him on the ride home, and his tongue hangs out the entire time. He moves from the window, back to me for a few licks, then returns, barking at horses grazing.

When I pull down the long road leading to the farmhouse, the gravel crunches under the Bronco's tires. Boots shifts in the front seat like he knows we're home. He's already memorized the route —sat up straighter when we passed the feed store, perked his ears when we rounded the bend.

The porch comes into view, freshly painted and framed with the new railing Colt finished last week. The house looks different now—solid, finished in ways it hadn't been when I first showed up here with nothing but a trunk full of secrets and a duffel bag of clothes. The entire bottom floor is done. Floors sealed. Kitchen tiled. Trim installed. And at this pace, we'll have the second floor completed by Christmas.

I smile to myself, feeling the warmth of that word again. *We.*

Boots lets out a low, excited whine as I shift the Bronco into park.

"Shh. Don't ruin the surprise," I whisper, petting his head. "Let's do this the right way."

I step out and round the front as Colt comes out of the house, wiping his hands on a rag. He's shirtless, jeans low on his hips, hair slightly messy, blue eyes shining for me.

He spots me as I reach for the passenger seat.

"Stormy," he calls, walking down the steps toward me, "you didn't text me back. I was worried."

"Sorry, I was driving," I say, stepping aside and opening the passenger door. "Both hands on the wheel, ya know."

Boots leaps down like he's been waiting his whole life for this exact cue.

Colt freezes halfway across the yard.

"Is that—" he starts, but the words fall apart when Boots barrels toward him. His bottom wags so hard that I think he might grow another tail.

Colt crouches, and Boots launches himself straight into his arms like they've known each other forever. Colt rubs behind his ears, laughing in that stunned, chest-deep way I've only heard a handful of times.

"You really brought him home," he says, eyes shining in that way that always steals my breath.

"It was time," I confirm. I swallow past the lump in my throat. "You always said you'd adopt him when the house was ready. And the bottom floor's finished. Outside is painted. Upstairs is started. What's a few months?"

He doesn't say anything at first. Just stands and crosses the distance between us.

"Darlin'," he says. "This is me digging deep roots for a future with a porch swing and a dog at our feet."

"I figured you could use someone else following you around," I joke, trying to keep it light.

But he doesn't laugh. Not right away.

He reaches for my face and kisses me slow, then faster, like he can't help himself.

"Thank you. I love you," he whispers against my mouth.

"Love you so much," I say as Boots wiggles between us.

Colt bends and ruffles his ears again, his voice low. "Welcome to the family."

THE MORNING STARTS warm and lazy, like honey on toast. Boots is curled up in the corner of the porch, lifting his head every time I move. I'm barefoot in one of Colt's old shirts again, sipping my coffee as I watch the sun climb its way over the horizon.

Colt rounds the house a few minutes later, already in jeans and boots, a horse trailing behind him. It's Froot Loops, and he's saddled.

I raise a brow. "What's this?"

He grins. "Go get dressed. Thought we'd go for a morning ride, and we could check out the south ridge as the sun rises. Haven't been up there since spring."

I glance down at my mug, then back at him. "This is very cowboyish of you."

"Darlin', go get dressed before I swing you over my shoulder and show you the cowboy way."

I burst into laughter.

He smiles. "Go on now. Time's a-tickin'."

I rush inside, throwing on some jeans, my borrowed boots, and a T-shirt.

Ten minutes later, he helps me into the saddle and sits behind me, grabbing the reins. My back is pressed against his chest, and I don't know why, but sharing a horse is sexy as hell.

The soft creak of leather and the rhythmic thud of Froot Loops's hooves fill the quiet. I lean back into Colt's warmth, letting the breeze play with my hair as he trails kisses along my neck. The land is greener than I expected, but I see the early signs of fall. The trees are starting to yellow. The Texas sky overhead is big and open, which makes me feel small in the best way. Colt guides us along the fence line, past the dry creek, and up a trail I didn't realize existed.

The path curves uphill, winding through a patch of trees. Colt's quiet, but I can feel something buzzing beneath his silence —like he's building toward something. When we crest the ridge, I see why he brought me here. There's an overlook and a view that opens up like a held breath. Below us, the land rolls out in soft hills and golden fields, dotted with trees. The house is visible in the distance, its fresh white siding bright in the sun. From here, everything looks small and peaceful, like we're sitting on top of our own little world.

Colt dismounts first, then reaches for me. I slide off the saddle and land lightly in the dirt, brushing my hands on my thighs.

"It's beautiful," I say, turning in a circle.

He ties the reins to a nearby post. "You're beautiful."

I glance at him and smile. I love it when he tells me that because I know he means it.

Colt walks toward me. When he stops, we're face-to-face, and there's something different in his expression. There is a weight behind his eyes I haven't seen before.

"I've been thinking about this for a while," he says. "About what it means to build something with someone. Not just a house. A life."

I swallow, my pulse suddenly louder in my ears.

He reaches into the pocket of his jeans and pulls out a small box, then drops to one knee in the dirt.

"This isn't about what you walked away from. It's about what we're walking into together. I want it all with you, Stormy. Every sunrise. Every sunset. Every plan, mess, and morning coffee. Will you please make me the happiest cowboy alive and be my wife?"

The world stops like it's waiting for my answer.

I look down at the ring, with a gorgeous diamond nestled in the center. It's exactly what I've always wanted.

"Yes," I whisper. "You're the love of my life," I say, wrapping my arms around him and kissing him so sweetly.

He lets out a breath, and then he's pulling me into his arms, lifting me off the ground as I laugh into his neck.

Laughter falls from him, and he spins me around, my feet off the ground.

I kiss him until I can't feel the difference between his breath and mine.

When he finally slips the ring on my finger, the sun catches it at the perfect angle, like we're meant to be.

We stay at the lookout for a little longer, then head back when the sun gets too hot.

When we're back at the barn, he looks at me with that grin that makes my stomach flip—the one that says he loves me and that we're going to spend the rest of our days together.

Boots meets us at the door, tongue lolling like he's been waiting to congratulate us. He sniffs my hand, then noses it like he's inspecting the ring.

I scratch behind his ears. "You approve?"

He jumps up on me, and I laugh.

Inside, the house is cooler, and soft light filters through the kitchen window.

Colt heads straight to the sink, rinsing off his hands. I admire his windblown hair, sun-kissed cheeks, and how he steals kisses whenever he wants them.

"You hungry?" he asks.

"For you," I whisper.

He smiles. "Good. 'Cause I'm starving."

Colt lifts me into his arms, and I laugh as he carries me to the bedroom. He lays me back on the bed and smiles, like he's memorizing me.

He tips his head toward me. "When do you want to get married?"

I smirk. "As soon as the second floor is finished."

"Fuck, guess I'd better have it done by next week," he says, carefully unbuttoning my jeans and sliding the zipper down.

He falls to his knees, his eyes not leaving mine. "Stormy Valentine. Mmm. Sounds sexy."

His laugh is low, warm against the inside of my thigh. My heart skips, and it's not just the name; it's the way he says it, like his name belongs to me.

"I knew the moment I saw you, you were fixing to be mine," he confesses.

I smile, loving his Southern drawl. "I knew it too."

"Is this where I say I told you so?" he asks as he slides my panties down.

This moment feels like it could stretch out forever.

Everything feels like it's finally settled where it belongs.

"I'll take a million of them if it ends with us being together."

"And to think, we still have a lifetime more of this, darlin'," Colt says, burying his face between my legs.

"Love the sound of that, cowboy." I gasp out, the pleasure all-consuming, my heart so damn full.

The thought of forever doesn't scare me anymore. Not after this man taught me that some things don't need fixing, just someone who loves you right.

EPILOGUE

STORMY

The moment we pull into the gravel lot of the big barn at Horseshoe Creek Ranch, I can already tell Grace has been here since sunrise. She's a wedding planner, the best in the state, and I'm so happy that she's volunteered to help us with this.

Colt parks the Bronco in the back, kills the engine, and turns to me. He doesn't say anything before he reaches across the console and tucks a piece of hair behind my ear. His fingers linger on my cheek for a moment. Long enough to settle me.

"You ready, darlin'?" he asks.

I nod with a grin. "As I'll ever be."

This isn't only an engagement party. It's the first time we've been in a room full of people celebrating us. Not the PR version. Not the city version. Not the girl who ran away or the man who followed. Just us together.

Colt hops out and circles the front before I even get the door open. He offers his hand, as if I'm wearing heels, not the most comfortable pair of ankle boots I own. I will always take his hand.

The sun is dipping low behind the trees, casting everything in a golden wash. It makes everything look a little softer around the edges, like this is a dream. The breeze carries a whisper of excitement.

Inside, the barn is unrecognizable.

Twinkle lights are strung from every beam, flickering against the early evening sky. I catch glimpses of glowing candles, and small arrangements of fall flowers on every table—deep burgundy dahlias, rust-colored mums, and sprigs of eucalyptus, tucked into mismatched glass bottles that look freshly polished but still antique. The air smells like cinnamon, vanilla, and something savory.

They've cleared the barn and made it look like it was plucked from a country bridal magazine. London strums her acoustic guitar and sings into the microphone.

"Oh, there they are!" London says, and everyone's attention turns toward us. "I'm thrilled to announce Colt and Stormy have arrived!"

The barn bursts into cheers and applause. It feels like the whole town is here with drinks in hand, dresses swirling around boots and loafers alike.

I stand inside the doorway for a second, letting it all sink in.

Colt's hand rests lightly on the small of my back, grounding me.

"Not bad, huh?" he says near my ear.

"It's perfect," I whisper.

He leans in, lips brushing my temple. "Like you."

I glance around the room—at the people smiling, at the warmth in the lighting, at the way the space feels like it's already wrapped itself around me. I'm not an outsider or a guest. I'm in the place where I belong.

Colt gently tugs me forward, toward the noise, toward the people who are already turning with smiles and lifted glasses.

I don't brace for what's coming next; I walk into it with my head high.

Remi's the first to reach me. She appears from behind a table, carrying two glasses of champagne and a proud smile that tells me she's been waiting for this moment all evening.

"I was growing worried," she says, pressing the glasses into our hands before wrapping us in tight hugs. "What do you think of the barn?"

I laugh into her shoulder, and then we pull away. "Honestly? It's stunning. I'm blown away."

She waves her hand toward the candlelit tables and the carefully draped chiffon hanging from the rafters. "Grace insisted we keep it simple but elegant. 'West Texas romance meets understated chic,' I think were her exact words."

I glance across the room and spot Grace adjusting a floral arrangement near the dessert table, her sleek ponytail bobbing as she gives instructions to a young server. She catches my eye and gives me a cute wave. Harrison is beside her, stealing kisses, and she swats him away.

Colt slips off to talk to Beckett and Emmett for a few minutes, and I'm passed to each family member and family friend.

Everyone says the same thing. "We knew Colt was different when you came into town."

A few of them joke about the auction and that he won the best prize. I blush, laugh, and take it all in stride.

Eventually, I find myself near the dessert table, eyeing a tray of mini pecan pies, when a voice beside me says, "So, you're the reason my bestie has gone soft."

I turn and see Boone standing there, looking like he walked out of a Southern Gothic novel. Dark gray eyes, sharp cheekbones, a mouth like a dare. He's wearing a black T-shirt.

He holds out a hand. "Boone Tucker. You probably don't remember me."

"I remember you from the bar," I say, taking his hand. "How have you been?"

"Good." He smiles. "Busy working now that I'm home. Happy looks good on Colt. That's because of you."

I grin wide. "Thanks. You should join us for dinner one day."

"Actually, I'd like that." He picks up a glass of whiskey from the edge of the table and takes a sip.

Before I can say anything else, Colt appears beside me again and slides a hand around my waist. His presence shifts something between us—makes the air feel grounded again.

Boone raises his glass in a lazy salute. "Congratulations, both of you. Don't screw it up."

Colt laughs and gives his friend a hug. They chat for a little while longer before Boone is pulled away by his aunt.

I glance up at Colt. "I invited him to dinner."

He snorts. "Awesome. Thank you for that. I've been neglecting a lot of people."

"Because of me?"

He shakes his head. "Because of the house. When I'm in reno mode, everyone knows I focus. You were an added bonus."

Colt takes my hand and leads me outside, away from everyone. The noise of the party fades the moment we step away.

It's not loud to begin with—nothing like the city or even the rodeo—but inside the barn, there's a steady hum of voices, laughter, and the occasional burst of music. Out here, it's quieter.

Colt guides my back against the cold metal and slides his mouth against mine. I grab his shirt, losing control as our tongues twist together. When he pulls away, we're both breathless.

"What was that for?" I ask.

"I needed it," he tells me, pressing kisses on my neck. "Couldn't stop watching how pretty you are from across the room."

I can hear the muffled sound of Emmett laughing inside. Kinsley is retelling a story about how they wrestled in wet horse shit when they were kids. The tempo of the music picks up and it floats through the barn doors.

"This feels like a real beginning," I say quietly. "Not the next chapter, but the part where the whole story shifts."

Colt hums in agreement. "It does."

He reaches for my hand again, lacing our fingers together.

"I love you," he says, like a truth he's lived in for so long.

I tilt my head back to look at him. "I love you too."

Seconds later, we're interrupted. It's Fenix. "Y'all gonna stand out here and make out all night or enjoy your party?"

I burst into laughter, and so does Colt.

We return to the barn as someone's bringing out another tray of towering mini pies. Colt grabs one and hands it to me without a word, a little grin tugging at the corner of his mouth.

I bite into it and immediately recognize the flavor. "Is this ... maple pecan?"

He nods. "Mama's recipe."

"Wow," I say. "Do you know how to make these?"

He shakes his head. "Nope. But she might teach you."

"I'd love that."

I glance around the barn, taking it all in one more time. The lanterns. The people. The flowers wrapped in twine. My name is written next to Colt's on a little wooden sign that says *The Future Valentines.*

It's a lot, but it doesn't feel like too much. It never does with him. Right now, I'm the happiest I've ever been.

EPILOGUE

COLT

The room's buzzing with warmth and excitement. Glasses clink. Laughter spills over country music London is playing. Someone's passing around a bottle of whiskey.

Stormy's across the room, framed by a halo of soft light and surrounded by my sisters—Kinsley, Remi, Fenix, Vera, Summer, and Grace. They're talking over each other and laughing in a way only sisters and in-laws can. Their voices overlap like they're layered harmonies. She's relaxed, laughing easily, her hands flying with whatever story she's telling. She fits perfectly into my life.

I let the sight settle in my chest for a second, then shift my gaze toward my father, who's chatting with Beckett. He's got a drink in his hand.

I weave through the crowd toward them.

He sees me coming and offers a nod. Beckett leaves us to ourselves.

"Congrats, son."

I smile. "Thanks, Dad. How are you survivin' all these people?"

He chuckles low in his chest. "Crown helps."

I lean beside him, my eyes scanning over the crowd. From here, I can still see Stormy. My fiancée. My future.

"She's perfect for you," Dad says.

"Yeah, she is," I tell him proudly.

He lifts his glass a little, like a toast only meant for the two of us. "She's got fire and grace."

I nod. "Hell, yeah, she does."

For a moment, neither of us speaks. The noise of the party fades slightly.

"You've done good," he says finally. "Not just with her. With the house. With your own dreams. Maybe teach Emmett and Sterling a thing or two?"

My dad's not one to hand out compliments like candy.

"Oh, they're hopeless," I say. "Hopefully, in a few years, they'll grow up. But I dunno."

Dad chuckles. "You're damn right about that."

There's a beat of quiet between us, heavy but full of something good. He claps a hand on my shoulder, firm and warm.

"You ever need anything, let us know. Happy for ya both."

He pulls me into a tight hug, and I give him a thank-you.

Across the room, Stormy laughs at something Vera said, and the sound wraps around me, even in a crowded room.

I don't think I've ever seen her look more herself. There's a light in her eyes that's mesmerizing.

Someone passes a glass of whiskey into my hand before walking away—Beckett. I swirl the amber once, watching it catch the glow from the twinkle lights strung along the ceiling. Then I lift it to my lips and take a sip.

It's good. Warm. Familiar.

Fenix is chatting with London about something no one else is listening to. The whole damn place is buzzing and grounded, all at once. Stormy catches me watching her. She tilts her head slightly, eyes narrowing with that teasing look that still wrecks me. Like she knows exactly what I'm thinking and is already two steps ahead.

I lift my glass in her direction.

She raises her brows and mouths, *Happy?*

I nod. More than I ever knew I could be.

I drift toward the back wall, nursing the last of the whiskey in my glass. From here, I can see everything, but mostly, I see her. Laughing. Glowing. Her cheeks are pink from wine or joy or both. She tosses her head back and says something that makes them shriek like they're in high school again, and I can't help but notice how easily she fits in like a missing piece.

She's not just mine now. She's theirs too.

Stormy belonged to us before the ring. Before the first kiss. Hell, before I even knew her real name. But now? Now she's stitched into the fabric of this family like she's always been part of it. Not a guest. Not a visitor. Ours.

I take another sip, proud of the life I built. I didn't know I was chasing this until she walked into it like a storm with nowhere to land. And here she is—rooted, radiant, wrecking me in the best way.

From across the room, she catches me watching her, and then I notice how her eyes widen with alarm.

I turn to see someone wearing a cowboy hat standing at the threshold of the barn.

Tall. Lean. Boots worn and dusty.

He removes the hat and holds it in his hand like he knows how to make an entrance without even trying.

Jace Tucker.

It's been years since I've spoken with him, but he still has the same cocky stride, like he's half man, half rodeo legend. He looks around the room with a sun-creased grin and a look in his eye that says he's up to something—always has been.

He spots me, crosses the room, and reaches out with a firm grip.

"Well, I'll be damned," he says with a half-smile. "Guess the rumors were true. Congratulations."

I clasp his hand and give him a shake. "Didn't expect to see you back in town anytime soon."

"Didn't expect to come back," he says with a smirk. "But here I am."

Before I can ask why, I catch the shift in the air, a pause in energy. I follow his line of sight and see him looking at my sister.

Fenix.

She's standing near the dessert table, mid-sip from a wineglass. Her hand stalls halfway, frozen like someone hit pause on the whole scene.

Jace doesn't blink.

And Fenix? She downs the rest of the glass, and her jaw clenches tight.

Seconds later, she's storming toward us with her glass clasped tight in her hand.

"You weren't invited. Leave," she says, loud enough for only us to hear.

Jace tips his hat to her with a smirk. "Missed you too, Firecracker."

Her eyes narrow. "Don't fucking call me that."

"Come on," he says, still grinning. "Thought you liked that nickname."

"I liked a lot of things I shouldn't have," she snaps.

There's heat in her tone and a dash of hate mixed with something messier. Sharper. Like the edge of a broken glass.

"Do you want me to leave?" Jace turns to me, and I'm put in an awkward situation.

"I think we can all get along," I say to him and glance at Fenix, who's livid.

She lets out a huff.

Jace chuckles and focuses on my sister. "Guess I'll be seeing you around now."

"No, you won't," she fires back, quick as ever.

"I'm back in town for a little while at least. You *will*."

Her jaw tightens. I think I see her hold her breath before she explodes. "Fuck you, Jace Tucker."

She turns on her heel and walks away, chin high, spine stiff. Jace watches her go, his smirk slipping, before he recovers. He glances back at me and exhales. "If you want me to leave, I will."

"No, it's fine. Please behave," I tell him.

"Thanks, man," he tells me, giving me a nod before he finds his brother, who's entertaining my mom and grandmother.

Stormy comes to me, and I wrap my arms around her.

"What happened?"

"I don't know. Lots of anger from Fenix," I admit, spinning her around as we slow dance to a fast song. "I think things just got a hell of a lot more interesting around here. Jace is back."

"You're kidding," she says, glancing over her shoulder at him.

Then I watch her eyes scan the room for Fenix. She's nowhere to be found.

I kiss along her neck. "I was serious. If he's the reason Fenix quit riding, I'll hang his nuts off the back of my truck."

She howls with laughter, and I love to see that bright smile.

Stormy glances over her shoulder. The barn is still full of laughter and movement. Vera dances with Emmett. Mama's trying to force mini pies into unsuspecting hands.

"You ever think it would look like this?" Stormy asks.

"No," I admit. "But I hoped. And it's better than I imagined."

Her eyes shimmer, and she rises up on her toes to kiss me. I feel the weight and promise of everything we've built.

When we break apart, she tilts her head. "So … what now?"

"Now?" I grin. "Now we finish the second floor. Plan a wedding. Maybe adopt another dog. Change some lives. Have some kids. Whatever we want."

She grins. "I love the sound of that."

The night settles over the barn, like a worn quilt. Stars are tucked high in the sky. Most of the guests have filtered out, shoes in hand, coats draped over shoulders, voices happily hushed.

"Let's go home," I tell her, pressing my lips against her temple, then one to her jaw.

"That sounds amazing, cowboy," she tells me. "We have some celebrating to do."

"Mmm, if by celebrating, I hope you mean …" I waggle my brows.

"That's exactly what I mean. And thank you," she says, pulling back enough to meet my eyes.

"For what?"

"For making me the happiest woman alive."

"In one hour, I can guarantee you'll be a lot happier than what you are right now," I mutter, capturing her lips again.

"Don't keep me waiting."

She laughs, and I take her hand, pulling her with me.

As we walk away, the barn glows behind us. The music fades. Gravel crunches under our feet.

And in front of us? Well, that's what we call forever.

THE END

Want to find out what happens between Fenix and Jace?
HOLD YOUR HORSES
https://books2read.com/holdyourhorses

Need more of Colt & Stormy?
Download an exclusive bonus scene featuring them here:
https://bit.ly/fixingtobemine-bonus

WANT MORE OF LYRA?

The Billionaire Situation Series

The Wife Situation

The Friend Situation

The Boss Situation

The Bodyguard Situation

The Hookup Situation

The Hockey Situation

The Royal Situation

Fall I Want (connects with this world)

Valentine Texas Series

Bless Your Heart

Spill the Sweet Tea

Butter My Biscuit

Smooth as Whiskey

Fixing to be Mine

Hold Your Horses

Very Merry Series

A Very Merry Mistake

A Very Merry Nanny

A Very Merry Enemy

Every book can be read as a standalone, but for the full Lyra Parish experience, start with book 1 of the series, as they do interconnect.

KEEP IN TOUCH

Want to stay up to date with all things Lyra Parish? Join her newsletter! You'll get special access to cover reveals, teasers, and giveaways.

lyraparish.com/newsletter

Let's be friends on social media:
TikTok 🖤 Instagram 🖤 Facebook
@lyraparish everywhere

Searching for the Lyra Parish hangout?
Join Lyra Parish's Reader Lounge on Facebook:
https://bit.ly/lyrareadergroup

ACKNOWLEDGMENTS

I honestly don't know where to begin, so I'll start with a big fat thank you to you! Thank you for reading this book and supporting the Valentine series! I've said this a million times, but I do have the best readers in the world. So if you're reading this, thank you!

I'm so appreciative that so many of you continue to show up for me and the Valentines! Your excitement with this book completely blew me away. It was so unexpected, and I don't think I realized how many people enjoy this series. It just keeps getting better and better. That's always my goal!

A huge thank you to my advanced readers/influencer team for being so excited. Thanks to Bookinit! Designs (Talina & Anthony). Triple thank you to my lovely and incredible assistant, Erica Rogers. I'm so lucky to have you! A big thank you to Kate Kelly for creating the cutest things on the planet! Thank you to my editor, Jovana Shirley, and my proofreader, Marla Esposito. You make my words sparkle!

With every release, my team continues to show up and elevate me, and I am forever grateful for all the hard work each of you put into making me better. I couldn't do it without any of you. I don't take any of this for granted and never will.

As always, I'll end this with a big squishy thank you to my hubby, Will Young (@deepskydude). Thank you for listening to me ramble about bookish stuff and being the best cheerleader a girl could have. I love you so much! To the stars!

ABOUT LYRA PARISH

Lyra Parish is a hopeless romantic obsessed with writing spicy Hallmark-like romances. When she isn't immersed in fictional worlds, you can find her pretending to be a Vanlifer with her hubby and taking selfies with pumpkins. Lyra loves iced coffee, memes, authentic people, and living her best life. She is represented by Lesley Sabga at The Seymour Agency.

Made in the USA
Middletown, DE
04 July 2025

77728837R00208